ATTACK FROM THE RISING SUN

Something was wrong.

A glint of metallic reflection high above caught Hawk Hunter's eye. In an instant he pulled back hard on the stick of the 'XL and booted in his afterburner. A second later he was screaming straight up at full military power.

It took him just two seconds to appraise the situation. Right above him, at about 1,500 feet, was a pack of airborne unfriendlies diving toward him, guns blazing in his direction. Hunter was uncharacteristically stunned. He knew that aircraft like these hadn't seen combat since the days of World War Two. The enemy aircraft were Mitsubishi A6Ms, the airplane once called the "Zero."

He thought, *Maybe I'm in a dream* . . .

But now he had a more immediate concern. The flying museum pieces had initiated hostile action against him. He had to answer it in turn. With a flick of his finger he armed his nose cannons. An instant later, the climbing F-16's snout erupted in a fusillade of vicious fire.

This might be too easy, he told himself.

Seconds later, he knew he was right . . .

ACTION ADVENTURE: WINGMAN #1–#6
by Mack Maloney

WINGMAN (2015, $3.95)

From the radioactive ruins of a nuclear-devastated U.S. emerges a hero for the ages. A brilliant ace fighter pilot, he takes to the skies to help free his once-great homeland from the brutal heel of the evil Soviet warlords. He is the last hope of a ravaged land. He is Hawk Hunter . . . Wingman!

WINGMAN #2: THE CIRCLE WAR (2120, $3.95)

A second explosive showdown with the Russian overlords and their armies of destruction is in the wind. Only the deadly aerial ace Hawk Hunter can rally the forces of freedom and strike one last blow for a forgotten dream called "America"!

WINGMAN #3: THE LUCIFER CRUSADE (2232, $3.95)

Viktor, the depraved international terrorist who orchestrated the bloody war for America's West, has escaped. Ace pilot Hawk Hunter takes off for a deadly confrontation in the skies above the Middle East.

WINGMAN #4: THUNDER IN THE EAST (2453, $3.95)

The evil New Order is raising a huge mercenary force to reclaim America, and Hawk Hunter, the battered nation's most fearless top gun fighter pilot, takes to the air to prevent this catastrophe from occurring.

WINGMAN #5: THE TWISTED CROSS (2553, $3.95)

"The Twisted Cross," a power-hungry neo-Nazi organization, plans to destroy the Panama Canal with nuclear time bombs unless their war chests are filled with stolen Inca gold. The only route to saving the strategic waterway is from above—as Wingman takes to the air to rain death down upon the Cross' South American jungle stronghold.

WINGMAN #6: THE FINAL STORM (2655, $3.95)

Deep in the frozen Siberian wastes, last-ditch elements of the Evil Empire plan to annihilate the Free World in one final rain of nuclear death. Trading his sleek F-16 fighter jet for a larger, heavier B-1B supersonic swing-wing bomber, Hawk Hunter undertakes his most perilous mission.

WINGMAN
WAR OF THE SUN

MACK MALONEY

ZEBRA BOOKS
KENSINGTON PUBLISHING CORP.

ZEBRA BOOKS

are published by

Kensington Publishing Corp.
475 Park Avenue South
New York, NY 10016

First printing: June, 1992

Printed in the United States of America

Part One

Empty Souls

One

Nauset Heights, Cape Cod

The two Norse soldiers thought they were dreaming.

One moment they'd been dozing on guard duty; the next, they were faced with a vision from Hell itself.

It was the heat that woke them first. A searing, hot breath, at first mistaken for just another part of a lusty dream, suddenly turned absolutely scorching. Then the noise came. A hundred claps of thunder, a thousand bombs exploding, a million screams of fear— they could not equal the unearthly howling these men heard this night, their last.

The heat and the noise were joined by the brightest light either man had ever seen, so intense, it seared their eyeballs.

They both screamed. Surely this was the Raven of Death itself hovering over them. Watching them. Now diving down at them!

They ran, but with legs of weaker men. They stumbled, one into the other, and wound up in a heap on the ground. There was a bright flash. A tongue of flame sprouted from this giant metal bird, leveling part of the nearby forest like a fiery scythe.

"Thorgils!" one screamed hysterically. *"Where are you now?"*

The winged creature of fire and heat and noise roared again and then slammed down into the ground, obliterating the guards' campfire and kicking up a storm of sand, dust, and flaming ashes.

It was black, with a metal body, and a large teardrop of glass that served as its eye. There were flashing red beacons on its tail and under its nose. Weapons of unspeakable terror hung from its wings.

Paralyzed with fear, the guards watched openmouthed as the eye of the creature popped open. A man was emerging! In the light and the smoke and the exhaust, he looked like a creature, too. His armored skin was black, and he wore a strange helmet with lightning bolts painted in gold on its sides. In one hand he held a firearm; in the other, a long, gleaming sword. He turned and pointed the sword directly at them.

Trembling, crying, their teeth chattering so much their gums bled, the Norse guards drew their own swords. But not to do battle. To do so now would be against their religion. They had been bested by an enemy, and damn quickly at that. To die now on his sword would condemn their souls for eternity. Their only choice was to deliver the killing blow themselves.

With screams that equaled that of the banshee itself, the men plunged their long, razor-sharp swords into one another's stomachs, waiting momentarily, and then applying the essential gut-ripping twist.

They were both dead within a second.

As they fell for the last time, one man dropped his

field canteen, causing a thick, gooey substance to run from its mouth. The man stepped out of the airplane and onto its wing and then jumped to the scorched ground. He walked over the pair of still-quivering bodies, picked up the canteen, and took a tiny dot of the thick syrup with the tip of his finger.

He put the finger to his tongue. *"Myx . . ."* he whispered.

The dozen Norse soldiers charged with guarding the small farmhouse on the bluff had scattered a long time ago, frightened away by noise and flame they'd spotted on the beach below.

The house itself was somewhat battered, but the roof had held through the stormy weather, and the inside had done the same. The hayfield was overgrown, as were the vegetable garden and the strawberry vine. The barn and the small storage shed looked a little worse for wear.

The boot on the front door was not so powerful as to do a lot of damage. It would have to be fixed later, after all.

A thin red beam of laser light searched the darkened rooms. All the furniture was gone—remnants of the chairs and couches could be seen in the fireplace. Even some of the floorboards had been ripped up, used no doubt as kindling. The walls were covered with crude drawings. Battle scenes. Ravens. Sea serpents. Some were drawn in chalk, others in charcoal or with burnt sticks. Some of the pictures had strange writing beside them, others, simply one or two letters. In one corner, someone had apparently started to write the English word "victory," but never applied the last letter. Another wall was stained with what at first looked like blood, but on closer examination, turned out to be some kind of lager.

The pilot walked up the stairs without making a sound. At the end of the narrow hall was a closed door with a flickering light behind it. He pointed his firearm at the ceiling and squeezed off one round. The noise of the gun blast seemed to shake the whole house. The light in the room went off.

He walked down the hallway, not slow, not fast, but at an even gait. He heard the sounds of a window lock being hastily opened, and then the creak of a window being opened itself. He fired another bullet into the ceiling. The noises on the other side of the door became more frantic. Pushing. Shoving. A sharp, hushed argument. High-pitched whispered voices. A touch of panic.

He fired a third bullet and then kicked the door in, this time with such force it splintered on impact.

The only illumination in the room now was candlelight. There were probably a dozen of them in all, and half had blown out when the door broke in. The others were wavering in the breeze from the open window.

Two figures in black were halfway out the window, but were now frozen at the sight of the man in the opaque uniform and helmet with his gun raised at their throats. The breeze turned to a gust, blowing back the veils of these figures. They were women, one young, one old. Both unarmed.

The pilot raised the gun, but could not pull the trigger.

"Go!" he yelled at them. He was not in the business of shooting women.

They departed, leaving through the window as if they were witches, their feet never hitting the ground.

He turned and saw her on the bed. She looked peaceful, in a white gown, her hair braided and tied. Her head rested on a silk pillow. On the table beside her were a large plastic container and two glass beer mugs, their rims sticky with *myx*.

He was frozen on the spot. He hadn't seen her in so long — not since that horrible night in the spring when the world turned upside down. It was now early fall.

He lay down his gun and knelt beside her. He put his finger to her lips and felt a slight breath. They were also sticky with *myx*.

He'd become all too familiar with the effects of this mind-altering, coma-inducing hallucinogen. A little meant an orgasmic experience unrivaled by any drug ever known. A lot meant a coma so close to death, a person's metabolic rate was reduced to near-hibernation.

But the drug was not without its quirks. One of them involved the precise method for raising someone from its death glow.

He took a deep breath and removed the glove from his right hand. Then, with a firm pinch, he tweaked the woman's nose.

Her eyes opened instantly.

"Dominique . . ." Hunter breathed, stroking her hair. "I'm back, honey."

She smiled as if she was awaking from nothing more than a stolen nap.

"Hawk . . ." she said, putting her hand lightly to his face, "I was dreaming about you."

Two

One month later

A thick fog covered Vancouver Bay.

The harbor was nearly deserted. A Free Canadian minesweeper was performing routine patrol further out on the Strait of Georgia. Occasionally a helicopter gunship would sweep over the shipyard nestled into one corner of the recently-dredged bay. But other than that, there was no visible activity in the damp, fog-enshrouded bay. Yet in the gloom, hidden by both mist and shadow, was the enormous silhouette of an aircraft carrier.

There were no airplanes on her deck, no crew in evidence, not a light on her anywhere. To the eye, the huge hulk of a ship looked unoccupied, abandoned, forgotten.

But in this case, looks were very deceiving.

There were exactly one thousand, four hundred and ninety-two men aboard her, all of them well-trained, highly-professional citizen soldiers. All of them were also volunteers.

There were twelve airplanes inside its huge mid-deck hangar, a place big enough to hold eighty planes or more. At this moment, about five hundred men were working on or near these airplanes, several of which were in various stages of disassembly. The men—all of them air service technicians—were concentrating on the airplanes' bomb delivery systems—or the lack of them, in many cases.

Though the airplanes were all jet-powered, not one of them was a true bomber. The majority were actually jet fighters—high-tech dog fighters and interceptors—not designed to carry an ordnance load very well. Yet the mission they were being prepared for called for aircraft to carry bombs, and lots of them. So most of the airplanes had to be adapted to do so—and fast.

It was just past midnight when the trio of open-bay tractor-trailer trucks pulled up to the pier next to the darkened aircraft carrier. Each truck carried a large wooden crate, tied to its trailer and covered with black tarps. The trucks were met by a contingent of Free Canadian Naval Security Forces, all of them dressed in civilian clothes and waiting in the shadows on the dock. With little fanfare or conversation, these soldiers helped the truck drivers unlash the tarps covering the rear of each truck, and then, with the help of a small portable crane, began unloading the crates themselves, placing them on the moving cargo ramp that led up to the carrier's deck.

Within ninety minutes, the unloaded trucks had departed and the crates were sitting on the deck of the carrier. Two men were checking the list of serial numbers on the crates against a manifest one man had attached to his clipboard.

"Looks like they're all here, Captain," the man with the clipboard said, crossing out the last serial number. "Should I get the loading crew to bring them down to the hold?"

The other man shifted uneasily for a moment. He'd yet to get used to being called "Captain" again.

"Yes, let's get them below," he said finally. "And make sure there's no unnecessary noise or lights."

The man with the clipboard departed, leaving Stan Yastrewski all alone on the vast flight deck.

Yastrewski—"Yaz" to his friends—took in a deep breath of damp, foggy air and let it out slowly. He considered himself a simple man, yet in the past few years, he'd led anything but a simple life. He'd seen nightmarish combat. He'd been kidnapped by Norsemen. He'd been imprisoned by Nazis. He'd been kept as a sex slave by a woman who believed she'd one day be the undisputed "Queen of America."

And now, in the latest twist in his life, he was captain of the huge aircraft carrier.

It was the USS *Enterprise,* CVN-65, or least, it used to be. Its recent history had been as strange as Yaz's. On the day the Big War ended, the ship was reported sailing in the Indian Ocean, launching air strikes on positions deep within Kyrgyzstan. Its crew vanished, and the vessel was apparently seized by black marketeers. It was refurbished to a degree, and eventually sold to the Fourth Reich, the so-called "Super-Nazis" who had briefly conquered the eastern section of the American continent. Indeed, a sneak attack launched from the carrier by the Fourth Reich against the battered United American Armed Forces paved the way for the Super-Nazi invasion of the eastern seaboard. Not two months before, the Fourth Reich had surrendered in the titanic battle of *Fuhrerstadt,* more recently known as Football City and before that St. Louis, and their surviving armies had either been placed in POW camps or sent packing back to Europe.

It was shortly after the Nazi invasion had begun that the *Enterprise* was found drifting in the Caribbean, its fascist crew dead, victims of the vicious one-man campaign carried out by Hawk Hunter, the man known to many as the Wingman. Once the fighting against the Super-Nazis ended, the carrier was refurbished once again, and secretly sent to Vancouver to prepare for a very critical mission.

Yaz had overseen this voyage. Both a former commander in the U.S. Navy and a member of the informal group of military advisers that made up the leadership of the United American Armed Forces, he seemed like a natural choice. However, his U.S. Navy duty was on submarines, not aircraft carriers—could there be any two ships more different? Plus, while he'd been given no indication that his mission to get the carrier to Vancouver in one piece was the extent of his involvement in the overall operation, he never dreamed they wanted him to be its captain for the upcoming secret mission.

But here he was, skipper of a supercarrier, on orders from General David Jones, the top military man in United America himself.

But it was an unusual command, to say the least. He had but one-fifth the normal complement of crew. And until this night, only twelve airplanes.

But now that the crates had arrived, at least that had changed. Inside, they contained the components of a very special aircraft.

He considered this now as he looked out across the barren flight deck and into the foggy gloom of the bay.

"Thirteen airplanes," he whispered glumly. "My lucky number."

Three

Twenty-four hours later

The airplane swooped low over Vancouver Bay, banked to the left, and came around again.

There was a sudden thunderous noise, almost like a mechanical wind, as the plane stopped in mid-air. It hovered there for a moment, and then descended slowly, its pilot deftly bringing the VTOL airplane in for a textbook dead-of-night landing.

No sooner was the Harrier down on the deserted deck of the *Enterprise* when Hunter had his safety harnesses undone. He popped the canopy and crawled out of the cockpit over to the wing and then down to the deck of the carrier itself.

He took a long, silent, sober look around. For the first time since he'd single-handedly defeated its Super-Nazi crew, he was back aboard the USS *Enterprise*.

It was close to midnight. The message calling

17

him to Vancouver had reached him at his Cape Cod farm two days before. It had come from General Jones, and it "invited" Hunter to a top-secret meeting to discuss a matter "of extreme importance."

The request had served to effectively end what had been a fulfilling few weeks spent nursing Dominique back to health and getting his small coastal hay farm back into shape. Dominique was making a fine recovery, but his farm was a mess. Fixing the doors and the three bullet holes in the roof had been easy—the hard part was trying to undo the many months of neglect and abuse that the Norse soldiers had wreaked on the place.

But he loved it. With each day worked, he felt he was regaining a very important part of himself. Once again, the place called "Skyfire" had become safe haven from the wars and turmoil that had raged over the globe. More important, it was a place for him and Dominique to be together. They had been forced apart so often over the years that Hunter wanted nothing more than to be with her. And knowing that he could be called away any moment made their time together more precious.

So when it came, the message from Jones served to douse his brief idyllic respite like a bucket of ice water.

But he was a soldier. And obviously something big was up. After yet another painful good-bye with Dominique, Hunter was on his way in a few short hours.

Leaving her in the care of a friend who ran the highly-touted New Boston Militia, Hunter flew the Harrier up to Montreal, where he began a series of refueling stops which had him over Vancouver inside of six hours.

Now another adventure was about to begin.

He turned to see the slightly diminutive figure of Yaz walking across the deck toward him.

"Permission to come aboard, Captain?" Hunter asked his old friend, complete with a deadpan salute.

Yaz waved off the gesture. "You're not making this any easier, Hawk," he told him. "I'm the last guy that should have his hand on this rudder."

Hunter yanked his helmet off. "Look at it this way, Yazbo," he said. "When your old sub friends hear about it, it'll drive them nuts."

"Yeah," Yaz replied, in mock agreement, "nuts from laughter."

The conversation quickly turned serious as they walked across the flight deck and toward the carrier's massive superstructure, known as the Island.

"I thought we weren't supposed to meet for another month," Hunter asked Yaz.

Yaz just shook his head. "There been some new developments," he replied soberly. "This is a real emergency, I'm afraid."

They walked up to the carrier's nerve center, a place called the CIC, for Combat Information Center. The last time Hunter had seen it, the room was shot-up and very nearly destroyed. Now it was

19

up and operating at almost full capacity.

They moved through the CIC and toward a small adjacent conference room. Yaz opened the door and Hunter walked in. He was greeted with a round of semiserious applause.

"You didn't bring coffee?" one of the half dozen men sitting around the large table yelled out. "No doughnuts? No booze? *No nothing?*"

Hunter pretended to slap his forehead, as if he had truly forgotten something. This act was greeted with a chorus of fake booing.

Seated around the table were Hunter's brothers in war, the leadership of the United American Armed Forces. General Jones himself was at the head of the table. He quickly rose and came around the table to greet the Wingman.

"This looks just like the old days, General," Hunter told him, sweeping his hand around the room.

"You don't know the half of it," Jones replied.

Hunter went on to greet the rest of the men. He had fought beside them all at one time or another. Ben Wa and JT "Socket" Toomey, two of the best fighter pilots he'd ever known, had been with him since the very beginning. They had all flown together in the Air Force's Thunderbirds aerial demonstration team. They had also fought together in the same fighter squadron during the Big War.

The years since that nightmarish conflagration had been a constant struggle to free America from the various and varied tyrannies and dictatorships that arose from the ashes of the postwar United States. He had come to know the other men in the room during these conflicts.

Major Pietr Frost, the Free Canadian pilot who served as the military liaison officer between United American Armed Forces and the democratic Canadian government. Major "Catfish" Johnson, the African-American officer who was *de facto* commander of the United American ground forces. Bobby Crockett and Jesse Tyler, better known as the Cobra Brothers, the fierce two-man Texan attack helicopter team who were not really brothers, but brothers-in-law.

There was one particular face missing, though.

Mike Fitzgerald, a longtime member of this inner circle, was dead—heroically killed in the last minutes of the Battle of *Fuhrerstadt*. Hunter missed the crazy but dignified Irishman terribly. Of them all, Fitz might have been his best friend. Now he was gone.

Another part of the team was also not there, but for happier circumstances. Captain "Crunch" O'Malley, the F-4X Phantom jet jockey who at one time led a team of freelance fighter-bombers known as the Ace Wrecking Crew, was currently back on the East Coast, reorganizing what was left of the United American Air Force.

Finally the reunion was complete and Hunter took his seat next to Jones. The room got very quiet. Almost everyone around the big table had arrived just hours before Hunter, so they, too, were unaware of why the emergency conference had been called.

In fact, only Jones knew the full reason for the hastily-called meeting.

The general let a few moments of tense silence pass before he spoke.

"The reason we are here," he began starkly, yet matter-of-factly, "is that there's been a new development regarding the *Fire Bats* subs the Cult have operating in the Pacific."

The Cult. Just the words themselves were enough to make Hunter's fists ball up in anger. Known officially as the "Combined Greater East Asian Warrior Society," the quasireligious, completely-fanatical, more-aptly-nicknamed "Asian Mercenary Cult" was one half of the Second Axis, the notorious alliance which had invaded the American continent nearly a year before. And although the other half of the Second Axis, the Fourth Reich Super-Nazis, had been defeated by the United Americans at the pivotal battle of *Fuhrerstadt,* the Cult still held most of the American territory west of the Rockies.

Though smaller, the Asian Mercenary Cult was in many ways an adversary more dangerous than the defeated Super-Nazis. Not only did they have nearly fifty divisions occupying the American West Coast, the Cult also had nuclear missiles aboard two high-tech *Fire Bats* submarines which were sailing somewhere deep in the Pacific. Because of these missiles, a kind of enforced standoff had

22

come about. The United Americans couldn't readily attack the Cult forces as long as the Asian's "doomsday weapons" remained operational. If backed into a corner by the resurging Americans, the Cult would, no doubt, make good on their oft-made threat to immediately launch their nukes at the West Coast in a sort of ultimate kamikaze attack.

At the same time, the Cult was nowhere powerful enough to expand their ill-gotten occupied territory eastward. With the fascist European allies routed, they had no choice but to keep their forces in place and bide their time enslaving millions of Americans.

It was a tense situation, perhaps best compared to the "phony war" between Nazi Germany and France and England in early months of what would become World War Two.

It was also a very unpredictable situation for one large reason: the man in charge of the Cult.

His name was Hashi Pushi, and he was a very strange character indeed. Considered a "living god" to the Cult members, he was also widely rumored to be psychologically unstable in the extreme. Mysterious and elusive, Hashi Pushi was believed never in his life to have left Japan. Indeed, some intelligence reports said he never left his headquarters, which were located in the heart of Tokyo itself. Yet his far-flung mercenary armies had taken control of most of the Pacific rim, as well as the American West Coast.

By just about all reports, Hashi Pushi was quite literally insane. Reportedly a heavy drug user, he believed himself to be no less than a reincarnated samurai warrior. It was well known that he frequently issued bizarre orders based on "visions" which came to him almost daily. Some could be judged as pieces of sound military doctrine. Others were as crazy as their creator. One story had it that Hashi Pushi once commanded one hundred of his top military aides to commit ritual suicide simply because he supposedly had learned in a vision that they had entertained disloyal thoughts. An enormous and elaborate ceremony was arranged, and at its height, the hundred officers performed a mass *seppuku,* disemboweling themselves with their own swords. A huge dinner was then served, followed by a two-day orgy.

This was typical of the Cult's fanatical devotion to Hashi Pushi.

The American plan, up until now, had been to gradually rebuild the United American Army, while painstakingly trying to track the pair of Fire Bats subs. When the time was right, the UA would launch a massive air and land attack against the occupying Cult forces, at the same time ambushing both enemy subs at the precise moment. It was an operation that everyone knew would take time, patience, and extensive planning. It would also result in many, many casualties.

Now it appeared that that plan had gone awry.

"We've received information that the Cult is preparing to launch a first strike," Jones continued slowly and carefully, his tone grim.

Another somber silence descended on the room as the weight of Jones's words sank in.

"We know this because one of the POWs captured in *Fuhrerstadt* turned out to be a liaison officer with the Cult," Jones continued. "Under interrogation, he told us that just before the Reich was defeated, word had come from Tokyo that Hashi Pushi had ordered his occupying troops to prepare for a 'nuclear action,' as he put it. Specifically, the orders dealt with plans to have the target city looted before it was destroyed."

"What *is* the target?" Ben Wa asked.

"We don't know," Jones replied. "It could be any one of ten places, from San Diego up to Seattle. And that's the problem. Even the high Cult officers probably don't know. The real target will supposedly come in another of Pushi's visions."

"This is not good," Frost said with classic understatement. "He could secretly give the order at any time. It would take only a few hours for his whacked-out troops to strip the target city clean of anything of value. And then . . ."

"That's the problem in a nutshell," Jones said. "That's why we had to get together earlier than we anticipated."

The grim silence never left the room completely.

"Does this mean we have to take out those subs much sooner than we expected?" Toomey asked.

"Too risky," Jones replied, shaking his head.

"Those two subs are constantly on the move. They are always hundreds of miles from each other, sailing in completely random patterns. It would take us at least several days to pinpoint just one of them. And attempt a successful attack. And when we did, that would give the second one plenty of time to launch."

It was a well-studied catch-22.

"We simply can't take the chance of forcing their hand," Jones continued soberly. "With all the civilians on the coast in jeopardy, if we gamble and lose, they're the ones who'll go up in smoke."

Toomey gripped the table tightly, his voice rising. "But General, some of them are definitely gonna fry for sure if we *don't* take the chance."

Jones held up his hand and said, "There's another way."

All eyes were on him.

"We know that Hashi Pushi doesn't allow his officers any initiative or real authority," he went on. "He *is*, in effect, their entire command and control. His boys can't make a move without his okay, but they must think he is as unstable as we do.

"Now, if we were able to disrupt that situation, maybe his armies would be thrown into confusion. Maybe his officers would lose some of their willingness to jump on their swords at his every whim. Or launch a nuke."

Another silence enveloped the room.

"We also know that he never leaves his palace, never leaves Tokyo," Jones continued. "He's obviously well guarded, and our intelligence tells us the Japanese Home Islands themselves are heavily defended, with better equipment and men than they have running around half the world raping and pillaging.

"But Hashi Pushi is so well insulated from what is happening, it's like he has a big balloon around him. He's always drugged up, he's into everything from screwing little girls to ordering mass suicides. I'm sure he considers himself invulnerable."

Jones took another deep breath and let it out slowly.

"Now, if we were able to prick that balloon . . ." he said, his voice trailing off.

The comment was met with somewhat confused stares.

Toomey tried to say something, "Are you suggesting General, that we . . ."

Jones nodded. "I'm suggesting that we go after Hashi Pushi right where he lives."

Jones straightened in his chair slightly, and cleared his throat.

"I'm suggesting that we bring the battle right to him," he went on. "I'm suggesting we launch a surgical air strike on Japan itself."

Now a shocked murmur went around the room.

"But General, you're talking about committing our forces thousands of miles away," Jesse Tyler said in a thick Texas drawl. "I mean, we don't have the transport. We don't have the supply or the backup. And even if we did, we can't afford to dilute our strength here, on this continent."

Jones held up his hand and gently interrupted Tyler. "We have enough transport for a small force," he said. "And we've rounded up a small but capable unit of aircraft. *And,* we've organized a crew of volunteers to go on the mission."

The general stopped speaking for a moment, leaned back in his chair, and stared at the ceiling.

"But, as you may have noticed," he said soberly, "this operation is shaping up a little, well . . . differently."

Everyone around the table *had* noticed. In the past, whenever danger aroused to threaten America, this group of advisers was called together to plan the response. Now, for the first time, the plans were already done. But why? Only Jones knew.

"My thinking is that we run a kind of Jimmy Doolittle raid," he began again, slowly. "Remember? *Thirty Seconds Over Tokyo . . . ?*"

He was referring to the American bomber attack on Japan in the early days of World War Two. Led by Colonel James Doolittle, the raid launched a unit of B-25 medium bombers from the aircraft carrier USS *Hornet* and attacked Tokyo. Though not very militarily significant, the Doolittle raid sent a powerful psychological message to the Japanese, demonstrating to them that their Home Islands weren't invulnerable, and for Americans, it was a gigantic morale-booster.

At that point, Jones handed a thick envelope to each man. The packets were black with red tape running along the edge. Each was stamped "TOP SECRET."

Hunter and the others quickly scanned the four-page directive. They detailed a highly-ambitious mission calling for four ships—the *Enterprise,* two supply ships, and a "covering fire" vessel—to proceed to the east coast of Japan, where a small group of jet airplanes would launch, hit key targets, recover, and leave the area.

"I suggest we break up and study this and meet again in an hour," Jones said.

Immediately everyone stood, saluted and left—everyone except Hunter.

Without a word, Jones handed him another TOP SECRET document. Hunter opened it and quickly read it.

The one-page paper was titled "Special Targeting Mission." Hunter was not familiar with the term. But after he'd read just the first paragraph, the meaning became quite clear.

He felt a chill run through him.

Throughout all the years of war and violence, Hunter had always thought of himself simply as a soldier, a patriot, someone forced to become a warrior to defend his homeland. He'd led many major campaigns and planned many more.

Yet, the idea laid out in this paper was different. It did not inhabit the usual realm of war. Worse yet, the person slated to perform the mission was identified as Operative Blue One. That had been Hunter's code name in the past.

Jones sensed his misgivings right away.

"This kind of thing *is* a first for us," he said, his voice still stone-cold serious. "And, believe me, I regret having to come up with such a plan. It's caused me many a sleepless night already — and I expect many more. *That's* why I decided to keep the planning of this one under wraps until everything was in place."

There was a long tense silence between the two men.

"Let's face it, Hawk," Jones said to his old friend, "things are desperate. If we can pull this off *while* the bombing raid is going on, we'll go a long way to solving this very big problem. And maybe save millions of lives in the process.

"And you're the only one who can do it."

The meeting resumed one hour later.

Jones started off by explaining the "special targeting mission" to the rest of the group. Upon hearing the news, each man had the same reaction as Hunter: shock, followed by a grim realization that desperate times require desperate measures.

Jones smartly moved the discussion along to the specifics of the air-raid portion of the secret mission: sailing dates, tide levels, aircraft available, recon photos of the target, psy-ops, SigInt and air-strike particulars.

As far as the purely military end of the operation, Jones's plan was as innovative as it was daring. The stakes, however, were very high. The air strike on the selected Japanese targets would have to be hit-and-run; any delay could prove disastrous. Yet the targets were so heavily defended by the Cult, the American strike craft would have to perform all kinds of aerial tricks in order to get in on their targets, hit them, and get the hell out.

Still, the whole operation was so intensely dangerous, the casualty rate among the attacking pilots could be expected to be as high as fifty percent — or even higher.

There were other risks, and not just in human terms. It was obvious that it had taken a major concentrated effort to get the *Enterprise* operational again. It was once more a fairly formidable weapon. Though nowhere near the power projector it had been in its heyday, it was still not an entity that the general would put at risk lightly. Yet if something went disastrously wrong, the carrier could be sunk, or even worse, captured intact.

Over all, the most important element of the operation would be its timing. The four ships of the newly-created Task Force would have to sail to their attack coordinates very quickly and under the cover of absolute radio silence for secrecy. They would have to launch the airplanes with just the precise amount of fuel to carry a precise number of bombs. The air strikes would have to be pinpoint and accurate, yet done without much air cover. The strike craft would have to return to the carrier as soon as possible so the Task Force could exit the area just as quickly.

Getting the timing right also meant dealing with supplies. Since the mission wasn't an invasion or an attack in force, they could cut the risk factor down by taking only the minimum necessary. But this also meant there could be no room for error, waste, or delays.

Then there was the problem of Task Force security, specifically, the ship that Jones's directive identified as the "covering fire vessel."

As Yaz put it, "We're going to need something packing a lot of firepower. Who's it going to be?"

Hunter had been silent all during this second meeting, the words "Special Targeting Mission" still burning into his brain. But now, after hearing Yaz's question, he spoke up for the first time.

"I think we all have just the ship in mind," he said.

Four

The battleship USS *New Jersey* lay in the dark, still waters of the Panama Canal. Above it glowed a full moon.

It was nearly midnight. Inside the bridge of the ship's immense superstructure, its captain sat alone, brooding, as usual.

The enormous ship had been waiting to pass through the canal since noon that day. Repeated attempts to strike a deal with the people who controlled operation of the canal locks—they were ensconced in a gaudy, heavily-guarded 200-foot tower which looked out over the canal and the seedy city nearby—had proved frustrating. Some radio replies from shore claimed the main set of locks were not working. Others said the technicians needed to operate the locks were unavailable. Still others claimed the locks could operate only at unpredictable hours or by an ever-changing schedule.

The captain of the *New Jersey* knew this odd

behavior was actually a not-too-clever means of keeping him and his crew captive in the locks. One message, received shortly before sunset, said it all: *LET YOUR CREW COME ASHORE AND ENJOY THE PLEASURES OF OUR CITY WHILE WE SORT OUT THE TECHNICAL DIFFICULTIES WHICH DELAY YOUR PASSAGE.*

In other words, "Deliver your crew into the hands of the thugs and harlots of our city for one night, and then we will let you pass."

It was an offer the captain chose to refuse. Yet he was not a man of rash action or judgment. He knew that time itself could be a potent weapon. This is why he was waiting.

Ever since the sun had gone down, both sides of the canal had been ablaze with harsh neon signs. Bright reds, explosive greens, deep, throbbing blues—nearly all of them promised fulfillment of unimaginable sexual fantasies. Their garishness constituted a direct assault on the captain's dour sensibilities, not to mention his corneas. In fact, the bright lights hurt his eyes. He'd seen full-scale naval battles that looked less threatening.

Added to this visual pollution was a background strain of equally harsh sounds that drifted up into the night. Raucous music. Women laughing. Screams—of both delight and agony, mixed with occasional bursts of gunfire. Way off in the distance, a recording of a sultry voice, moaning in continuous orgasm, echoed through the hills.

These were well-orchestrated sirens, calls to entice men to leave their ships and sample the pleasures from the many bars, crack houses, bordellos, and sex palaces crowding the sleazy little town close to the canal's main locks.

The captain was determined to keep his crew aboard, however, and he had stationed several of the ship's burly security squads on deck to help enforce his order. These men patrolling the deck were a little older, more experienced than the rest of the crew. Years of sea duty had made them disciplined and, like the captain, they knew the dangers that lurked ashore.

Still, the captain knew his crew — and they were as professional as they were independent. He realized that some of the nearly 750 men aboard would inevitably get by the guards and swim to the place appropriately known as Sin City.

And indeed, he realized any sailor who made it stood a good chance of not returning.

In fact, he knew this firsthand.

The captain was known simply as Wolf. He wore a uniform which included a long black cape and a black mask which covered more than half his face. Who he had been before he assumed this identity was a mystery, to his crew and his various allies. He was, like most of the men on board, a direct descendant of the original Vikings. As such, he was a man given to dark moods, and his officers knew when to leave him alone with his thoughts.

This was one of those times.

It was a strange set of circumstances which had led to his being here in the Canal Zone. He was trying his best to get to the Pacific Ocean as quickly as possible—this at the request of a very special ally.

Wolf had first met Hawk Hunter a little more than a year ago. He had felt an immediate kinship with the legendary Wingman. They were, in fact, brothers of the same cosmos. Neither of them quite understood what it was that made them shoulder the burden they did as they struggled to liberate the world from the forces of oppression. Like Hunter, Wolf could have used his warrior skills and the high-tech weaponry under his command to be an outlaw or a pirate and enrich himself beyond imagination. Yet neither Wolf nor Hunter chose this way, nor did they choose to retire from the world's strife and live the quiet life of peace, security, and the love of a woman that surely their prior service had already earned them.

It was this kinship with Hunter and the cause he served that had brought Wolf to this godforsaken place—again. And, as terrible as this place was, even greater dangers no doubt lurked ahead. The conversation he'd had with Hunter over the COMSAT link had been brief. Hunter had asked that Wolf join the United American USS *Enterprise* and embark on a mission against the Japanese Home Islands and the Asian Mercenary Cult.

Upon receiving the message, Wolf had smiled to himself, not the sort of thing he did too often. The Americans had conjured up an insane, impossible plan—just the sort of thing that would bring him and the battleship *New Jersey* halfway around the globe to help.

It was now 0130 hours.

Wolf had spent the time staring out at the spectacle that was Sin City.

Though towns like this had sprung up all along the canal, Sin City was by far the worst. Although the canal itself was under protection of the United Americans, troubles up north had forced most of the troops to withdraw, leaving a vacuum which was quickly filled by various outlaws and other assorted lowlifes.

Yet as disturbing as Wolf viewed the place, it had, alas, an irresistible draw.

He knew this temptation well.

He had, in fact, secretly visited the place alone, not a year ago, shortly before the titanic battle against the Super-Nazis. Now the decadent, wicked memories of the clandestine trip filled his head with a mixture of unbearable guilt and indescribable pleasure.

37

Sin City could be best described as a real-life pornographic movie.

Soon after his arrival in the modern-day Gomorrah, he'd stumbled into a place called the Q Club. Here he saw a brutal reenactment of nothing less than an Aztec human sacrifice. A beautiful young Indian girl, nude and in a drug-induced trance, was led to a block of stone at center stage. As she was bound to the stone, a robed and masked figure entered the stage, attended by several more Indian girls. As the club's sound system blasted a deafening, rhythmic beating of drums, the robed figure danced and cavorted lewdly with his attendants. The beat of the drums increased in intensity. Smoke poured from some hidden source near the stage. As it had wafted out over the audience, Wolf had recognized the sickly-sweet aroma of opium.

He got up to leave but found his way out blocked by the crowd craning to get a better look at the stage. Their expressions feverish, their eyes glazed, the crowd pressed against him in the packed, suffocatingly hot room. A roar of approval went up around him, and he had involuntarily turned back toward the stage. There he saw that the robed figure had pulled a large dagger from under his cloak. He advanced toward the bound woman as his attendants rolled on the floor around him, their naked brown limbs twisted together in a variety of sex acts.

The drumbeats reached a crescendo and, horrified, the captain saw the robed figure raise his dagger high above the helpless girl's chest.

Wolf turned away and forced his way through the drooling, entranced crowds. He never did find out if the ceremony was real or not.

He found himself next on a dimly lit street, sweating, trembling from the bizarre experience. Almost immediately he was surrounded by an army of prostitutes, all of them beckoning to him, shouting out specialties and promises of low prices. Meanwhile, other hookers were servicing confirmed customers in the shadows. He saw one on her knees in front of a wizened old man. She turned slightly toward him and he saw that she was missing an eye. Her one good eye winked grotesquely at him as she gestured for him to take his place beside her customer.

He turned and staggered down the street, the night quickly turning into a garish blur. He wandered from scene to scene of incredible depravity, somehow compelled to witness the darkest and most ugly of human behavior. It was as if he needed to confirm what he knew to be true about man's ultimate nature.

But sometime during this nightmare of ecstasy, he was either slipped or secretly injected with a powerful drug, possibly even *myx*.

He woke up the next morning in a seedy hotel, lying atop a young girl dressed like a Dutch maid, right down to the wooden clogs.

She was still breathing when he fled.

He spent the whole night alone on the bridge, his conscience wracked by both horror and lust.

Finally the sun came up, and the neon explosion on shore began to fade away. At 0600 hours, his staff reported that thirty-three men had successfully jumped ship during the night, and seventeen of them were still missing.

Those that survived returned penniless, some missing their shoes, and even their pants. Several were victims of bad or tainted drugs. One of these had to be carried aboard by his exhausted shipmates. He was raving incoherently, caught in the violent grip of a drug-induced psychotic attack. Before he could be restrained in the ship's sick bay, the man broke loose and killed himself by dashing his head against a bulkhead.

Wolf ordered that a heavily-armed search party be dispatched to Sin City to turn up any trace of the AWOL crew members. They failed on all accounts, leaving Wolf no choice but to sail on without the missing men.

By 0830 hours, there was still no sign that the men inside the Canal Control tower would allow the *New Jersey* to pass.

Wolf ordered that radio contact be made once again with the extortionists. They had succeeded in getting the *New Jersey* for the night. Now that their cesspool had sucked in seventeen human beings, the messages from the Sin City authorities became more direct. At 0845 hours, Canal Control's rulers demanded that the *New Jersey* pay a bribe in addition to the exorbitant toll fee already paid. Only then would it be allowed to pass.

Wolf had had enough. For many reasons, he had patiently resisted using force to move through the canal. But now his patience had simply run out.

He ordered the crew to their battle stations. Then he opened a direct radio link between himself and the extortionists on shore.

"This is the captain of the battleship *New Jersey*," he told them in his heavily-accented English. "We have paid the required toll. We now demand that we be allowed to proceed immediately."

The radio's electronic distortion didn't hide the bizarre arrogance of the return message. The voice was so sing-songy it was hard to determine if it belonged to a man or a woman.

"This is Canal Control, Captain. May we remind you that you are in no position to make demands."

Wolf knew the arrogance on the other end of the radio line was well placed. Sin City's strong

41

hand was its control of this critical point in the canal. They felt they were invulnerable to attack because any use of firepower against them would risk damage to the canal and its locks. The perpetrator would thus be sentencing himself and his ship to be stranded in the canal, possibly forever.

Yet Wolf refused to countenance such behavior. Plus, he had some valuable intelligence on his side: he knew the lackeys controlling the canal locks were not actually in the tower, but hidden deep inside a bunker nearby. But he also knew these people would not make a move without orders from the tower itself.

"Canal Control," he called into the radio again. "Allow us to pass, or my guns shall be brought to bear."

There was no immediate response. After a few minutes, Wolf ordered the battleship's forward gun turrets brought to starboard. A shipboard alarm sounded as the two huge turrets, each bearing three massive sixteen-inch guns, swung into position, pointing in the general direction of Sin City.

Silence fell over the ship. The tension on the bridge was palpable.

Suddenly the radio crackled to life. "If you are bluffing, Captain Wolf, it is a pathetic attempt."

Wolf ignored the taunt. Instead he gave a few quick orders which resulted in the loading of shells into each of the forward guns. The shells, each the weight of a small automobile, had an explosive warhead containing enormous destructive capability.

"There are innocent people inside our city," the radio crackled again with the strange voice. "Even some of your own people. They have chosen to stay. Do you intend to kill them?"

"If they were foolish enough to be tempted by your lies," Wolf replied harshly, "then they are foolish enough to die."

There was a burst of static, followed by a hideous sexual laugh.

"You surprise us, Captain Wolf—you are so quick to judge us. You see, we know you yourself have partaken of us. Of our pleasures. We know this, sir, because we have your past visit in its entirety on videotape. This, too, can be had for a slightly higher adjustment in our toll fee, plus another . . ."

At that instant Wolf gave the order for the first turret to fire. The huge guns roared to life, expelling three shells at incredible velocity. But they did not hit the city itself. Instead, the salvo impacted directly on the 200-foot tower housing Canal Control. The top of the needlelike structure was instantaneously smashed to dust and fire. In a matter of two seconds, the rest of the tower collapsed, leaving nothing more than a gigantic rubble-filled smoking crater.

No sooner had the reverberation of the massive cannon shots dissipated when an alarm sounded from the control bunker on the far shore. Within seconds, the lock's great gates began to swing open.

Two minutes later, the *New Jersey* was once again on its way to the Pacific.

Five

Tokyo

The palace had three spires.

In each of these towers were three antiaircraft guns, each manned by a crew of three. Three flags flew atop each tower. Each flag contained the symbol of three red balls.

It was just midnight, yet the palace and its vast grounds were lit up almost as if it were daytime. There was a cacophony of sounds emanating from the flying-saucer-shaped main building. Loud music was blaring out of large speakers which seemed to be set up everywhere. Shrieks of laughter, drunkenness, and lust were falling in rhythm with the music's pounding beat. Multicolored fireworks were being set off overhead. Larger explosions could be heard in the distance.

Inside the main hall of the palace, the orgy was in full swing. The guests this evening were the top commanders of the Home Island's Air Defense units. There were nine of them in all, representing eighteen air squadrons. Each in turn had been allowed to bring two guests; most had invited their two top staff officers.

Each man now sat at the long low table which dominated the center of the great hall. Before him was a large jug of *sake,* a soupbowl full of cocaine, and a basket containing a pipe, some matches, and an ice-cube-sized piece of hashish. There were also dozens of small wooden barrels containing live fish, crabs, and squid.

Every guest also had access to three females, each one with long black hair cut to the exact same length. Many of these were girls still in their teens. They were all naked, and many were bound by the hands and feet with silk ropes. Each had been injected with a long-lasting barbiturate which would render her accessible, yet virtually defenseless.

The protocol of the party was lust fulfillment, the more decadent, the better. As all the guests had already ingested great quantities of liquor and drugs, they were trying to outdo one another as to who could come up with the most depraved act. Many of them had taken to eating their food off a girl's naked body, some while having sex with another girl. Others had forced two or three girls to have sex with each other, choosing only to sit back and watch. Still others were mercilessly whipping their procured partners, some to the point of death. While this was going on, just about all the men were eating squirming live fish from the small wooden barrels.

All in all, it was a typical night inside Hashi Pushi's three-tiered palace.

Yet the man who lay claim to all this madness was nowhere in sight. He was, in fact, in another part of the palace, in a grotto deep below the palace's inner wall.

Inside this place, it was cool and dark. The only light was a strange red glow emanating from the deep waters of the grotto's pool. This red light cast eerie shadows on the dark stone walls of the place. The scent of incense filled the damp air.

Hashi Pushi sat by the pool, staring into its bloodlike water. He was a grotesquely overweight man of undetermined middle age; his only garment was a long white robe. His fat face was partially covered with an unkempt, scraggly beard and a long, greasy mustache. His lips and nose were stained with the remains of his last few meals. His teeth were rotten, his ears perpetually infected. He hadn't bathed in weeks.

He was then, at that moment, a contented man.

Earlier in the evening he had commanded his personal physician to concoct one of the special mixtures of drugs which were the doctor's special talent. Using a blend of the bark of a tree and herbs and a certain part of the flesh of the poisonous puffer fish, the doctor had composed a paste which, he claimed, would enable the warlord to have visions of things to come. Actually, the physician had simply added some of the notorious *myx* to the *mélange,* which Hashi Pushi had drunk after it had been dissolved in a bottle of *sake.*

Now, as he stared into the red waters of the pool, he could feel the drugs begin to electrify his already-overloaded nervous system, so much so, his eyes were involuntarily closed tight.

Ten minutes went by with Hashi Pushi not moving, barely breathing. As the drug gradually altered his brain chemistry, he felt himself slowly entering a state of pure hallucination. Gradually he was able to open his eyes and stare into the blood pool. And in these red waters he thought he saw a vision.

He saw a giant tortoise lying on a tranquil sandy beach. Suddenly the sky darkened as a giant flock of birds flew in from the sea, blocking out the sun. Gulls, terns, ravens, crows, sparrows, and swallows descended on the tortoise and began tearing at its exposed flesh. The tortoise tried to hide in its shell, but the strong beaks of the smaller birds reached into the shell to peck and tear at his eyes. All the while a huge white eagle circled slowly overhead.

Slowly and in great agony the tortoise made its way across the beach, but all the while his attackers tore at him. The combined strength of the birds finally flipped the tortoise over on its back, exposing its softer underside to the skies. Helpless, its bloody limbs and head waving uselessly, the tortoise could only lie there as the eagle suddenly plummeted from the skies, its talons and razor-sharp beak poised to rip into the soft-shelled underbelly.

But an instant before the eagle would have torn the tortoise into pieces the vision ended, only to be replaced with the face of a dark, absolutely sinister bearded man. He was not quite Caucasian, but not Asian, either. His face seemed to be floating in a large bank of cumulus clouds. He was staring into Hashi Pushi's eyes and laughing, his cackle sounding like thunder. Then a shudder went through Hashi Pushi's huge, smelly body, and like some weird kind of cinematic special effect, this man's devilish face evolved into that of a young girl with unusually red hair.

That's when Hashi Pushi opened his eyes and discovered they were filled with tears.

"What could this mean?" he cried.

Six

One week later

Hunter stood on the flight deck of the *Enterprise* and watched the sun set over the Pacific Ocean.

Having left Vancouver under the cover of night and fog five days before, the giant aircraft carrier was now cruising at barely five knots in a circular pattern about ten miles off of Kittery Island, a small atoll located in the far western section of the Hawaiian chain, just east of the more famous Midway Islands.

This place had been chosen as the Task Force's rendezvous point for several reasons. Not the least of these was that although the Cult occupied all the major islands in the Hawaiian chain, there was no enemy present within 250 miles of Kittery. Kittery also supported an airstrip which had been hosting almost nightly visits from huge Free Canadian C-5 cargo planes, dropping off supplies for the Task Force. Finally, the island's harbor was sheltered on three sides and boasted several spots for deep mooring.

The preparations for the highly-secret mission had proceeded at a frenetic pace, twenty-four hours a day for the past six days. Typically, Hunter had slept but ten hours in that time, and had eaten next to nothing. There was just too much to do.

Much of the time had been spent going over the small, rather bizarre air unit General Jones had put together for the mission. It turned out that all the aircraft had come by way of Roy From Troy, the notorious used-airplane salesman who'd been instrumental in scrounging up aircraft to defeat the Fourth Reich several months before. Working a variety of leads from a variety of places, Roy and Jones had managed to secretly put together the patchwork air wing.

The twelve aircraft in the Task Force Squadron all had two things in common: they all were older, less advanced machines than the very best in the United American arsenal, and all were in some sense expendable. Hunter loathed thinking about the airplanes in this manner, never mind their crews. But he knew Jones was just being realistic when he assembled the dozen aircraft. Even though American air strength had almost doubled with the capture of many of the Fourth Reich's high-tech jet aircraft, few were designed for carrier use. Besides, what *was* on hand was needed at home, protecting the American continent. In fact, of the 120 or so workable warplanes in the United American arsenal, a hundred were on constant standby for action against the Cult armies occupying the West Coast.

On the other hand, the Task Force's mission was akin to the Hail Mary pass in football. Indeed, the official nickname for the mission was "Operation Long Bomb." In other words, while the chance for failure was high, desperation was running even higher. Under the circumstances, it would have been militarily foolish to risk what Jones called "the big everything" on such a long shot. Hunter and the others had to agree.

Of the dozen aircraft secured by the general, nine were of well-known, fairly-reliable, if older, designs. This A-list of sorts included two A-7J Corsair Strikefighters, two elderly GR, 1 single-seat British Tornados, two Swedish-built AJ37 Viggens, two German-built, single-seat Alpha-1 Jets, and a single ex-U.S. Naval Reserve A-4 Skyhawk. All these airplanes had seen service around the globe in the anything-goes days since the Big War, and their ilk could be had for premium prices on the burgeoning worldwide used-weapons black market.

On the flipside, the three remaining airplanes could have been pulled from an antique aircraft museum — and knowing Roy From Troy as Hunter did, they probably were. One was a prewar Italian

Air Force Fiat G.91, a so-called "tactical support" aircraft first built in the late 1950s. It bore a striking resemblance to the former-USAF's venerable F-86 Sabrejet, specifically the later so-called "Dog Fighter" version. The second oddball was a HAL HF-24 Mk 1 Marut, a poorly-designed interceptor built in the late sixties by the Indian Air Force. The third partner in this unlikely trio was the IAR-93 Orao, a cranky, clunking fighter built in the late seventies as a joint project between Yugoslavia and Romania, neither of which was known for its aerodynamic expertise. This airplane had already been rechristened the "Yugo" by the carrier's air service crews.

Still, Hunter had to give Roy From Troy some credit. Not only did the rascal procure the airplanes, he had delivered them already adapted for carrier use. This was truly an amazing feat simply because none of the aircraft had originally been designed for the rigors of carrier launch and recovery.

Giving each airplane some sealegs had not been an easy task: each jet's undercarriage had to be strengthened significantly to take the stress of gut-wrenching steam-catapult launching and slam-down arresting-wire recovery. Each also endured the addition of an arresting-hook system, a nose-tow assembly, and some over-water safety devices.

But once again, Roy had done it with mirrors. For just like everything else dedicated to the mission, the modifications for the odd mix of airplanes were intended to be temporary; with the exception of the A-7s (which were more adaptable to sea life than the others), the aircraft involved in the operation were guaranteed for one takeoff, one landing. Anything after that was "off warranty," as Roy put it, meaning anything could happen. Yet if everything went as planned, one takeoff and one landing were all the airplanes would have to do.

Just getting them on board the carrier had been an adventure in itself. Hunter learned that Roy had the aircraft modified secretly at an abandoned base in what used to be Key West, Florida, under the supervision of a mysterious local figure known only as "Big Seth." When all the planes were ready, they were ferried out to the *Enterprise,* which was anchored near the big key, in the same heavily-disguised Mississippi dredging barges which had played a pivotal role in the final battle against the Super-Nazis in *Fuhrerstadt.* At the same time, a group of experienced carrier pilots, half of them Americans, the other half Free Canadians, was spirited aboard. The mission ahead of them was daunting, to say the least: without the luxury of practice runs or test flights, they would be called on to take off from a carrier in an airplane which had never been sea-launched, carry out a high-risk bombing mission over heavily-defended targets, and then land back on the carrier, again using nonflight tested arrestor gear.

54

No surprise, then, that all the pilots were volunteers.

With the twelve airplanes carefully hidden away deep inside the ship, the carrier had then proceeded down the coast of South America, around Cape Horn, and then up to Vancouver, dodging the rather spotty Cult-allied naval and aerial patrols along the way. Once safe in port at Vancouver, work began in earnest to prepare the *Enterprise* for the mission.

Unbeknownst to Hunter, a thirteenth airplane had been secretly put aboard in Vancouver, this one coming disassembled and packed in three extremely large crates. It was Jones who, shortly before the *Enterprise* sailed, finally showed this plane-in-three-parts to Hunter.

Using the crowbar himself to open the largest crate, the general slowly detached one side of the wooden container. No sooner had the panel been lowered when Hunter felt like his eyes were going to pop out of his head.

Then they became misted.

Packed in the crate was the main airframe for his long-lost beloved F-16XL.

He hadn't seen it in what seemed like centuries. Actually, it had been barely two years since one of the country's neo-Nazi groups had stolen it and put it into the hands of the ultra-dangerous seriously-deranged Queen-of-America wannabe Elizabeth Sandlake. By the time the villainess's Alberta hideout was attacked by a joint American-Free Canadian force, the F-16XL had been trucked away. It was later chopped up and sold to some West Coast hoodlums. It was then won in a card game by a major Pacific drug dealer, and won again by an equally unscrupulous Hawaiian "businessman." It was the United American pilot named Elvis who found the airplane in Honolulu and arranged for its return to America shortly before the Fourth Reich's invasion. Sadly, Elvis was lost on a recon mission soon after that.

For most of the time that the east coast of America was occupied by the Super-Nazis, the F-16XL was hidden away on the top of a mountain in the eastern Rockies. Once the Fourth Reich's "instant occupation" regime fell, the airplane was repacked and brought overland to Vancouver.

Securing the famous 'XL was just another part of Jones's overall plan, and one he was certain would be important as far as Hunter's role in the upcoming operation was concerned. Jones knew that the Wingman was giving up a lot to take part in such an extremely dangerous operation, especially so soon after the titanic campaign against the Fourth Reich, and nearly a year after the famous pilot had announced his "retirement." By including the restorable F-16XL in the small air wing, Jones was offering Hunter some well-deserved payback. It also meant that Hunter would be operating the two airplanes that his talents were best suited for: the versatile Harrier jumpjet, and the futuristically-awesome F-16XL. With the inclusion of these two very high-tech aircraft, the Task Force's combat air capacity stood at fourteen airplanes.

For Hunter, it was a reunion that rivaled only his finding Dominique as the major event in his life. With the help of a dedicated crew of a hundred air service technicians, he had the F-16XL put back together in less than twenty-four hours, and ready for carrier-launches just twelve hours after that.

Now, as the sun finally disappeared over the distant horizon, the carrier was bathed in a dim purple light.

Plying alongside the *Enterprise* on a similar parallel course were the two supply ships that would accompany the Task Force. They were identical vessels of the mid-size cargo class; one was the USS *Tennyson,* the other, the USS *Cohen.* Both ships were crammed to the gills with ammunition, foodstuffs, fresh water, weapons, fuel, and the thousands of other necessities that would be required for what they had determined would be a six-day mission.

There was only one player yet to make an appearance — and Hunter knew that was about to change.

He turned his eyes to the east.

Airplanes were coming. He was certain of this, even though he could see nothing out on the darkening horizon. It was a sixth sense he had, this ability to detect the approach of aircraft even when they were many miles away. It was just one more thing about his extraordinary psyche, *the feeling* that came over him at crucial moments in his life. It gave him a wide edge in air-to-air combat and had saved his butt more than once. He trusted it completely.

Hunter was finally able to make out the distant sound of jet engines. Soon afterward he saw the two Strikefighters streaking toward the carrier. Ben Wa was piloting one, JT Toomey the other. Besides Hunter's two airplanes, the A-7s were the only aircraft on the *Enterprise* that they dared risk using more than once. They'd been scrambled to check out a report of an unidentified vessel somewhere over the southern horizon. When the long-range indication was first spotted by the *Enterprise*'s over-the-horizon radar, it was decided that a visual confirmation flight would be conducted to avoid breaking the strict radio silence each Task Force ship had been observing.

Hunter remained on the flight deck as the two Strikefighters marshaled in a holding pattern well behind the carrier. From there, Ben and JT would coordinate their approach with the landing signal officer before coming in for a "trap," or arrested landing, on the ship's angled deck.

Even in daylight, landing on a carrier was a tricky proposition. Yet within a minute, both jets had screeched in and recovered safely—Ben first, JT close behind. Hunter walked over to the elevator, where a blue-shirted crew was already preparing to move the A-7s down to the hangar deck. Even though they had had no chance to practice on most of the airplanes aboard the carrier, Hunter was still impressed with the efficiency of the *Enterprise*'s deck crew. The launching and recovery of modern jet aircraft from a moving ship was a complex operation which involved a precise coordination among the crewmen. From the air boss up in the primary flight control center to the blue shirts Hunter now watched moving the A-7s, everyone had to perform his or her specific duty as part of a precisely-choreographed team. With so little practice, it was amazing that men who had been working together only a few weeks were already functioning as smoothly as a well-drilled squad.

Toomey and Ben Wa climbed out of their airplanes and met Hunter near the ship's superstructure.

"It's the *New Jersey*, Hawk," Toomey reported. "Right on time, right on course. We spotted them about fifty-five miles out."

"It was hard to miss it," Ben said, pulling off

his helmet. "That's one big ship. They acknowledged our code okay. They'll be here in about two hours, two and a half at the most."

Hunter nodded purposely. The Task Force's "covering fire vessel" was here. Now that the final piece of the puzzle had moved into place, the Task Force could set sail immediately.

"Well," he said, "I guess this is where it starts to get interesting."

Deep inside the triple-turreted castle that was his headquarters, Hashi Pushi was sitting in the grotto, staring into the red waters of the Blood Pool.

He was lost in a dream of orgasmic ecstasy, brought on by his physician's concoction of drugs, whose secret ingredient was nothing less than the superhallucinogenic known as *myx*. In the pool, the grossly overweight madman saw thirteen maidens clad in only sheer nightgowns. They were gracefully floating down through the air, coming toward him, arms open. He could see that their thighs were damp with expectation.

The closer they came to Hashi Pushi, the more desirous they were of his flesh. Despite his bulk, Hashi Pushi felt his body responding in kind. His heart began to beat faster as the dull ache in his groin grew unbearable. As these delicious floating maidens came closer, he could smell their musky scents; they aroused him to the bursting point. He smiled and opened his arms wide to accept all of these ripe, tasty morsels.

That's when Hashi Pushi's ultimate wet dream turned into a nightmare.

Suddenly, he was in the dream itself, trying to run but finding his enormous bulk was making it impossible. Several of the maidens grabbed him, dug their fingernails deep into his flesh, and suddenly pinned his arms down. The rest of the maidens each drew heavy daggers from sheaths buried in the moist folds of their gowns. The knives were razor-sharp and gleamed in the rays of the early morning sun.

Hashi Pushi opened his mouth and tried to scream, but nothing came out. The maidens began to laugh at his helplessness. Their laughter then turned into deep-throated roars. Their beautiful faces transformed into hideous demon faces that oozed a bloody slime and smelled of rotting flesh.

Then Hashi Pushi saw them raise their daggers high above their heads. He tried to squirm free, but he was helpless. They brought the daggers down with all their might, and Hashi Pushi felt his chest cave in from the force and the chill of their cold steel blades as they penetrated his heart.

The bloodcurdling sound of Hashi Pushi's scream echoed throughout the cavernous dungeon and brought a squad of his Imperial Guards running toward the grotto. Smashing through the locked oaken door, three of his most loyal bodyguards threw themselves into the room, their AK47s at the ready, looking for a target.

All they found was their leader, bathed in sweat and gasping for breath.

Hashi Pushi could barely manage an angry croak. "Get out," he gasped, "or I'll have you gutted."

The men quickly left, confused at what they saw, but obedient to the words of their supreme master.

Alone again, Hashi Pushi rose and stumbled over to a full-length mirror. In the reflection, he saw thirteen huge black and blue bruises beginning to form on his chest, directly over his heart.

He nearly collapsed—this vision had been worse than the previous one. And unlike that nightmare, the meaning behind this vision was perfectly clear: he had just foreseen his own death.

How could this happen? he wondered, his ample body soaked through now with equal parts of reeking sweat and cold dread. After all, he *was* Hashi Pushi, Supreme Warlord of the Asian Mercenary Cult, a being more powerful than all the gods in the heavens combined.

Or was he?

He stared into the mirror again and was shocked to see not his own reflection, but that of a young girl with red hair, looking back at him.

He closed his eyes quickly and began crying again.

That's when a disembodied voice whispered in his ear, *"It is time to find a new soul. . . ."*

Several hours later

Hunter looked out from the bridge of the *Enterprise* at the silhouette of the massive battleship just three hundred yards away.

Even in the dimming moonlight, the *New Jersey* struck an ominous profile. Bristling with guns, the ship was a floating weapons platform capable of delivering an almost unimaginable rain of high-explosive destruction on anything that came within miles of it.

Launched in 1942, the *New Jersey* had seen action all over the globe for decades. It had been refitted on several occasions with the most advanced weaponry available. In addition to its nine massive 16 inch guns and its array of smaller 5-inch guns, it also boasted the Tomahawk cruise missile, a weapon capable of hitting land targets 700 miles away. The battleship currently had two such missiles on hand. The vessel was also outfit ted with the Harpoon antiship system, which could blast a ship out of the water at a distance of 60 nautical miles. It had three Harpoons on board. In the command of a capable captain such as Wolf, the battleship was a formidable weapon indeed. Hunter was glad it would be making the voyage with them.

As he studied the ship, a small motor launch appeared on its side and was slowly lowered into the water.

Aboard, Hunter knew, were Wolf and a party of his staff officers, ferrying over to the *Enterprise.* It would be the first face-to-face meeting since Hunter and Wolf had communicated over the NavStar satellite link.

It was a meeting Hunter had been anticipating for days.

Fifteen minutes later, the Wingman was shaking hands with Wolf.

"It is good to see you, my friend," the mysterious costumed figure told him. "Though it is always in times of crisis that we seem to meet."

"It might not always be that way," Hunter replied.

Wolf reintroduced his senior men, all of whom Hunter had met back when he'd first met the Norse captain. Then Hunter escorted the party up to the meeting room off the CIC, where Yaz, Ben, JT, and the captains of the *Tennyson* and the *Cohen* were waiting.

After the introductions, Yaz quickly outlined the specifics of "Operation Long Bomb" for the Norsemen. Then Ben and Toomey briefed the visitors on the carrier's odd collection of strike aircraft.

Using recon photos supplied to him by General Jones, Hunter pinpointed the targets the airplanes would hit. The pictures clearly showed that the proposed targets were well defended.

When the Wingman finished, Wolf was silent for a moment. His hand slowly fingering his Zorro-like mask, he seemed to be processing all the information, just as a computer might.

"This is indeed a very bold plan," he said finally. "But boldness is what we have come to expect from you. All of us here have been fighting for a long time, longer than any of us care to, I am sure. We have seen our friends, our family, our countrymen fall. If by this bold plan we can prevent others from having to fight, if we can ensure the safety of those whom we love and have left at home, then I say this is a good plan. You can count on my men and my ship."

Wolf's speech evoked a spontaneous round of applause. The Task Force was now complete. The men shook hands all around. A bottle of Scotch appeared, and a toast was proposed to the mission's success. There was a moment of silence as the men drank. Then Wolf proposed another.

"To absent friends," he said.

The men drank again, this time a little more somberly.

Once again the glasses were filled.

"To fallen comrades," Ben said.

At that point, Hunter produced a sealed envelope from his shirt pocket.

"Before the general left, he asked that we open this when the Task Force was finally assembled," he explained, handing the envelope to Yaz. "I guess this is as good a time as any."

The slight but rugged captain ripped open the seal and read the brief message inside. A wide smile spread across his usually concerned facial features.

"It's an official 'request' from Jones," he said. "He asks if there are any objections to renaming the carrier."

"To what?" JT asked.

Yaz passed him the letter, which he read. It caused him to grin, too. He then passed the note on to Ben.

"An aircraft carrier named after an Air Force guy?" he exclaimed. "I like it."

Hunter finally got to read the message, and he, too, had to smile for a second.

"I don't think anyone has any objections," he said.

From that moment on, the aircraft carrier was known as the USS *Mike Fitzgerald*.

The toasting and discussion continued for another hour. But Hunter wasn't there.

He'd slipped out of the conference room practically unnoticed and was now sitting out on the deserted bow of the carrier.

He was looking out over the ocean. As always, the questions had been flooding in. How much longer would he have to fight? Would he ever have the chance to enjoy the things he was fighting for? It was ironic, he thought, that all this time he was fighting for freedom, yet he didn't feel free at all. He felt imprisoned instead, chained to the responsibilities he had taken upon himself.

What the hell kind of life was that?

But the problems ran even deeper than that. Because with this mission, and his "special" part in it, he wondered for the first time whether he could continue as a soldier.

Just then he heard footsteps behind him. Hunter turned and saw Wolf approaching through the darkness, his cape snapping in the wind.

"The famous Wingman, all alone?" the Norse captain asked.

"Need time to think," Hunter replied.

"You think too much, my friend." Wolf said, sitting down next to him. "You would have made a good Dane."

"You're the first to accuse me of that," he replied.

"Perhaps not everyone understands the way I do," Wolf said. He gestured toward the carrier's island. "The men up there—good men, and brave warriors. But it is different for them. They do their duty. They go into battle, yes, and they fight valiantly, willing even to die for what they believe in. But rarely do they have to make the decisions that we have to. They do not know—nor can they know—the weight we carry on our shoulders.

"So why is it that we have to do these things? Why is this *our* special fate?"

Hunter remained silent. It was a question he'd been asking himself for years.

They sat there not speaking for a few minutes. Yet perhaps unintentionally, Wolf's words had touched at what was really bothering Hunter: the center of the plan—his special targeting mission.

"I know of this special mission," the Norse captain told him thoughtfully. "And I know how it troubles you. I also know that there is no choice in the matter. You could no more walk away from the things you feel you must do than I could. And, my friend, what you are about to do *is* the right thing—in the end. Of that I am very sure."

With that, the mysterious figure rose and walked away, leaving Hunter alone on the bow of the deck.

The newly-named USS *Fitzgerald,* the *New Jersey,* and the two supply ships set sail early the next morning.

Seven

Zobi, Japan

The bright orange glow of the rising sun flooded the small fishing village, bathing its tiny, neatly-kept shacks in the new morning warmth.

The day had dawned bright and cloudless, perfect weather for putting to sea and harvesting fish, seaweed, and pearls. Already the men of the village were heading down to the docks, their lunchpails and tins of tea clanging as they walked. Some of them were even singing to celebrate the occasion of the beautiful dawn.

Just waking up in her small home on the edge of this idyllic setting was a young girl of seventeen named Mizumi.

Mizumi was the most beautiful creature in the village of Zobi. Even as a child her delicate features and alabaster skin had made her enchanting. As she grew older, her body developed curves and her features matured, too. In the past year, she had turned into a gorgeous young woman.

But Mizumi's beauty was most unusual, too. For of the several hundred people in the village, only she had red hair.

Like everyone else in Zobi, her family made their living from the sea. Their boat was one of the largest of the small fleet and readily identifiable by its yellow gunwales and its orange mast. And though she did not go out on the brightly-painted boat like her father and her two older brothers, she worked with her mother on other essential tasks on shore.

Her favorite job was the mending of the fishing nets. Not only was it less messy than cleaning fish, it also provided her with a social life of sorts. On certain days she and her mother would take the nets to a beach near the town's docks. The other village women would bring their mending there, too, and gossip as they worked. Mizumi would listen to the other women's talk, and do her work conscientiously.

It was not an easy life, yet she'd been content there simply because she loved her family and her neighbors and the sea itself. She couldn't imagine wanting to live anywhere that didn't border the vast expanse of water.

She had awakened this morning happy and excited because it was net-mending day. Little did she know that this was the day her idyllic life in the village would end.

By full dawn she had seen her father and brothers

off to their boat, knowing if the fishing was good, they might not return for two days or more. She was helping her mother gather the nets that needed mending when her father suddenly burst back into the house.

He was out of breath, his features pale with alarm. There was a ghastly look of terror on his face.

Wild-eyed, he looked at Mizumi a moment, then ran to his wife's side.

"Soldiers are here!" he had told the mother in an anxious whisper. "They are looking for a girl to . . . to serve . . ."

"Serve *Hashi Pushi?*" her mother had answered, saying the words her father could not.

"They'll take Mizumi," her father had cried, no longer trying to mask his words in whispers. *"We must hide her!"*

From her room, Mizumi had heard everything— yet she was not even sure what her father was talking about. She had heard of this Hashi Pushi, but she had never thought of him as a real person. His name was spoken only in solemn murmurs, if at all, and more as a mythical character than anyone real. She had always imagined him to be a mighty godlike warlord, someone who lived in the clouds far away, his only connection to Earth the tribute the village paid on a monthly basis.

"We'll send her running up to the mountains," her mother said, fighting back panic. "My grandmother's sister-in-law's niece has relations there." As

71

she spoke she was already hastily gathering items to pack into a rucksack.

But at that moment three soldiers burst into the house. They were dressed in identical orange uniforms with garish black helmets. All three had their guns raised. Their eyes were full of desperation.

Mizumi's father bravely confronted them, but was immediately struck down with the butt of a rifle.

"We are on an errand for our lord, old man," one spat, leering down at the bloody face of her father, who now lay prone and dazed on the floor. "You were very foolish to interfere."

This soldier seemed to be the leader of the trio. With cold eyes, he shifted his attention from the father to the trembling mother and finally toward Mizumi. He studied her for a moment, taking in the classically beautiful face, her evolving figure. Then he saw her red hair.

The soldier smiled cruelly.

"We have found our treasure," he declared.

With that he gestured to the two other men. They rushed forward and grabbed Mizumi by the hands and feet. She struggled with them as they carried her out of the house and down the road toward their troop truck. She was screaming uncontrollably for her neighbors to save her, but it was no use. No one dared to challenge the soldiers.

Mizumi was now screaming desperately for her parents. But suddenly there was the sound of two rifle shots coming from within her house. At that moment, everything seemed to stand still. Mizumi was able to turn her head and see the soldier who'd struck her father come out of the door, his rifle still smoking.

That's when she fainted. Thus she was only dimly aware of being dumped into the back of the truck and driven away.

For Mizumi, nothing would ever be the same again.

Eight

Four days later

The USS *Fitzgerald* was coming apart at the seams. Or at least, that's what it felt like.

The massive carrier was shuddering, creaking, and groaning, all at the same time. It was caught in a cataclysmic pattern: giant waves would hit it broadside, allowing tons of water to crash down onto its huge flightdeck and knocking the vessel almost thirty degrees to port. Then, not a moment later, even larger waves would crash against its port side, serving to right the carrier again.

Alone in the hangar deck, Hawk Hunter was hanging onto the nearest stable piece of hardware, a fairly heavy support beam. Inside the cavernous deck, lit only by the soft red glow of the emergency lights, he could hear the sounds of unsecured gear clattering all around the decks.

Or were those really rivets popping?

They were sailing right through a full-scale tropical depression, a storm just one notch below an authentic typhoon. The winds were clocking at close to 70 mph, and the seas were running at fifty feet and more. The ship was being battered so badly that all but essential operations had been shut down, even to the point that no food could be served in the galleys. Not that anyone on board wanted to swallow anything more than antiseasickness tablets.

It was now 0300. The Task Force had first encountered the bad weather nearly twenty-four hours before, just as they'd passed the two-thirds mark on the way to the target area. And though the tempest was rough on the four ships and their crews, running smack into it actually turned out to be a beneficial twist of events: Nature's elements, though stomach-turning, had provided excellent cover for the Task Force to close in on their destination without detection.

Indeed, all indications were that the Task Force hadn't been spotted — yet . . .

Once the carrier finally stabilized, Hunter was able to let go of the support beam and resume his slow pacing. He'd been at it for nearly two hours now, walking, thinking, holding on, then walking and thinking again. He had much on his mind — too much — and he had sought the quiet peace of the hangar deck in an attempt to sort it all out.

So far, he'd been unsuccessful.

He was wrestling with the unorthodox mission that was before him, a mission that only he could undertake. For the dozenth time in two hours he took out the now-dog-eared sheet of paper that read "special targeting mission," and once again read the sealed

"FOR YOUR EYES ONLY" orders that Jones had given him shortly before the general had flown back to Washington from Vancouver.

The orders were brutally simple: while the Task Force air strikes were going on, Hunter was to land inside Tokyo, find Hashi Pushi, and execute him.

Once again those words burned their way into his overtaxed brain, this time even deeper. He was no stranger to the death and destruction of war. He had sent many enemies to their deaths in aerial combat and in hand-to-hand fighting. But there was a distinct difference here. Those men had been soldiers, too, fighting on a battlefield, with weapons on hand. As such, they at least knew what they could be in for once they stepped into that arena of combat, and they were prepared for it.

But this killing would be different—this killing, Hunter felt, might change him forever. For this was not going to be a typical combat situation.

This was to be an assassination.

He knew Jones was right when he had first explained the mission to him back in Vancouver. He knew that Wolf was right too; getting rid of Hashi Pushi would probably save countless lives on *both* sides. It would rid an already overly-troubled world of yet another set of catastrophic problems, akin to popping Hitler in 1933 or Saddam Hussein in 1991.

But was it right?

Bombing Hashi Pushi's palace might do the trick, but that wasn't the point. This was a case of making sure—*one hundred percent* sure—because there was no way they'd have the chance again.

So the motive was there.

The real question was: *Could* he do it?

He'd never shot anyone in cold blood before. Would he have time to look his target directly in the eye and squeeze the trigger? Would he keep squeezing until every breath of life had left his quarry? Would he have to pull that trigger one last time to administer the *coup de grâce?* Just to make sure?

He needed a plan — his own secret plan. Was there a way that he could accomplish the special targeting mission and still preserve his sanity and his honor?

Perhaps there was . . .

At that moment, the hair on the back of his neck bristled, instantly snapping him out of his gloomy meditation.

Deep inside him, his psyche had just received a very powerful message: *Something is wrong.*

He turned and began running. Across the hangar deck, through the fire door, and up the ladder to the next deck. Suddenly he heard the Phalanx Gatling gun on the port side of the flight deck open up with its distinctive, bone-rattling, mechanical burp.

Bolting up the next stairway and heading for the bridge, he literally ran right into JT, who was on his way down to the hangar deck to find him.

"We've got big trouble, Hawk," Toomey told him excitedly.

"I know," Hunter replied.

Yaz was going in five directions at once.

It seemed as if every light, bell, and buzzer was going off on the bridge simultaneously. All seventeen men in his bridge crew were at their stations, properly calling out information that somehow was pertinent to the sudden crisis.

But all Yaz could do was concentrate on the tiny colored light which was being tossed around on the rough seas about two miles off the port bow. His fire-control men said the light probably belonged to a Cult patrol boat, one which easily could radio back the discovery and position of the Task Force. If that happened, then the Task Force would lose its one and only advantage: that of complete surprise.

Yaz had given permission for his fire crews to open up on the wildly bobbing colored light in order to get a range on it, and now there were two lines of red-tipped 20mm cannon shells streaking out of the rotating six barrels of the *Fitzgerald's* Phalanx. At 600 rounds a second, their combined five-second barrage was simply awesome as it lit up the stormy darkness.

"They've got the range on him, Skipper," his fire control officer reported. "Next burst will nail him. Shall I give the order, sir?"

Yaz bit his lip for a moment. This was his first authentic combat decision since being crowned captain of the aircraft carrier. He had to make sure it was the right one.

"Are the *Tennyson, Cohen,* and *New Jersey* clear of the target area?" he called to his fire control officer.

"Yes, sir," came the immediate reply. "All three are running off our stern."

"And are we certain that's an enemy *military* vessel out there?" Yaz asked his radar men.

There was the briefest of pauses before the target-ID man replied, "I'm almost ninety-percent sure, Captain."

"Either way, it probably has a radio, Skipper," his fire control officer said.

Yaz put the NightScope glasses back up to his eyes. He could clearly see the small boat now, its engine pumping furiously, as it fought the windswept sea in an effort to get away. It seemed to be painted in odd colors. Its gunwales were yellow, while its mast was bright orange.

Yaz gritted his teeth. He couldn't wait much longer. Still, he knew that with his next order, he was sealing the death warrant for whoever was on the boat.

"Okay," he said finally. "Open fire . . ."

The Phalanx Gatlings immediately roared to life again and sent thousands of rounds of 20mm cannon shells ripping through the thin-skinned deck of the small boat, instantly exploding it into thousands of tiny splinters.

Yaz was startled by how quick it took. In less than three seconds, the small boat had been obliterated, leaving behind barely a wisp of smoke which was quickly taken away by the screaming high winds.

Yaz searched the waters for any sign of survivors — or bodies — but could spot nothing.

He finally lowered the glasses and slumped back into the captain's chair.

"What the hell is anyone doing way out here in the first place?" he whispered to himself.

The activity on the bridge did not cease with the destruction of the small boat. On the contrary, it increased twofold.

Yaz was informed by the radio room that no last signals of warning had been sent out by the doomed boat. Radar and sonar was reporting absolutely no contact with any other ships in the immediate area. Technically, it appeared that they had not been discovered. But Yaz knew from experience that there might be other enemy boats somewhere out there, and their luck might be better than the one whose pieces were now scattered across the surface of the water.

He also knew that the carrier was much farther out of range than what the plan had been designed for.

As captain he had to make another decision—this one much bigger than the first. Their "time and supply" strategy, when you came right down to it, was a simple math equation with no room for error. The trick was to keep the equation the same, even while changing the numbers. If the strike planes left early, they would use more fuel on their approach to target. But he would be able to increase the carrier's speed and get closer to the Japanese mainland, allowing the jets a shorter trip back to recovery.

The only thing that would change would be the odds for success.

They would be worse.

Then there was the question of the weather. It was also clear that the storm was starting to die down. It was still two hours before dawn, yet the dark sky had just become a shade brighter. They were losing the cover of the bad weather. If he gave the "go" now, the pilots would be over their targets in broad daylight, and not dusk, as was called for in the original plan.

He turned to find Hunter and JT were standing behind him.

"Can we go eighteen hours ahead of the plan?" he asked them.

"We've got no choice," JT said. "If those ja-mokes on that boat dropped a dime on us, they'll be waiting for us with open arms in eighteen hours."

Yaz looked at Hunter, who was nodding in solemn agreement.

"It's what Jones would do," Hunter told him. "It's what Fitz would do."

Yaz finally nodded himself.

"Then it's going to be what we do," Yaz said. "Let's alert the crew. We'll shoot for launch in ninety minutes."

Nine

Within an hour of sinking the small boat, the USS *Fitzgerald's* flight deck was abuzz with activity.

It was now 0530 hours. The storm had completely dissipated by this time, and though the seas were still very high, with the coming of dawn, the dark sky was brightening by the minute and the thick clouds were finally breaking. For the first time in a long time, sunlight was touching the carrier's deck.

But this was not the best of circumstances. The original plan had the TF Squadron arriving over the targets just after dusk; now they would be going in just after dawn. In bright, clear skies.

Right out of the rising sun.

It would be one of the Viggens going first. The *Fitz's* flight deck crew had already directed the Swedish fighter to the number one catapult and hooked it up. Beneath the launch channel the steam pressure was building. When it reached proper launch mode, the flight deck officer held his hand high over his head. This was the standby signal and it seemed that with his action, everything on the carrier deck did stand still for a moment. Once the first plane was launched, there would be no turning back.

Nearly all of the crew not working on the deck was crammed onto the carrier's side walkways or huddled along the side of the island, watching and waiting. The same collective thought was running through everybody's mind: Are we really ready?

It was not by chance that the delta-winged Viggen was selected to be the first airplane in the air. It was, in fact, the guinea pig of the group. With its 26,000-pound thrust turbofan engine, it was a powerful, dangerous fighter. It could achieve a maximum speed of 1,320 mph and normally was capable of carrying up to 13,200 pounds of bombs.

But because of the nature of Jones's plan, it was necessary for the TF Squadron to carry as many bombs to their targets as possible. To this end, the undercarriages of all strike craft had been heavily modified by the *Fitzgerald*'s air service crews to rack up many more pounds of armament weight than normal.

Viggen One was a good example. It was now loaded with nearly 17,000 pounds of ordnance, a combination of Mk82 GP 500-pound bombs and Mk82 Snakeye retarded bombs. Viggen Two was similarly overloaded. In fact, after the *Fitz*'s air crews got through with them, the ordnance weight of every plane in the TF Squadron had far exceeded "manufacturer's recommendations," some beyond dangerous proportions.

The intentional overloading was a risk everyone in the Task Force planning operation had to take. If they had put the question to a roomful of aerodynamic experts, they would have probably found it technically impossible for any of the TF Squadron airplanes even to be able to lift off, catapult assisted or not, and stay in the air long enough to reach their targets.

But Hunter and the others weren't too interested in labcoat theories at the moment. Instead, they were going by the old "bumblebee theory," to wit: if one studied a bumblebee's weight and aerodynamic shape, the conclusion would have to be that it is theoretically impossible for the bumblebee to fly. But it did — somehow.

And so would the TF Squadron.

It was Yaz who gave the final go-ahead. Ensconced on the bridge, practically ripping the sides of his captain's chair with tension, he looked down at the flight deck officer's raised hand and took a deep breath.

Then he spoke three words into his microphone, "Commence launching operations."

Not a second later, Viggen One was rocketing down the flight deck, its wings literally sagging from its bomb weight. It reached the end of the ship in 1.2 seconds and was suddenly flung out into space. For one tense instant it just seemed to hang in the air, its full-blast engine fighting for altitude against the strong winds and the weight under its wings. Then, with a great burst of power, the fighter began to climb, slowly at first, then gradually picking up velocity and altitude. When it banked away and leveled off, everyone on board heaved a great sigh of relief.

The launch of Viggen Two was equally flawless. It joined its brother not ten seconds later, and the two planes went into a long orbit around the carrier.

The two Tornados went up next. With no less than eight Mk84 2,000-pound GP bombs locked under each plane, the British warplanes were lugging nearly half again as much as they would normally be called on to carry.

Behind the Tornados came a tired, old friend, the Douglas A-4 Skyhawk. A relic left over from the old ZAP days, it was still one hell of a tough airplane. Usually capable of handling 8,200 pounds of bombs, this Skyhawk was loaded with more than 12,000 pounds of heavy ordnance; this in addition to its pair of 20mm cannons. With its extra fuel tanks, the little plane was so overloaded, it looked like it could barely roll into position, never mind actually get off the deck.

But it catapulted successfully, making room for the two A-7 Strikefighters which launched next. Though these subsonic workhorses were capable of a top speed of less than 700 mph, their internal fuel capacity, coupled with two 300-gallon pylons on each wing, translated into a flying range of more than 1,500 miles. This meant that out of all the other strike craft, the Corsairs had the fuel to spare to engage in any dogfights that arose on the way in. Thus each was outfitted with two AIM-9 Sidewinders, and two AIM-120 Advanced medium-range missiles bolted under their wings.

Next to go were the two Alpha-1 Jets. Essentially an advance trainer/light attack plane and armed with only a single 30mm cannon, one of these Alphas was now carrying six bulging BLU-27 napalm bombs, the other six, cluster bombs. Of all the attacking airplanes, it was the Alphas whose targets had to be hit with the most precision and at exactly the right time. If not, then the entire American effort would quite literally go up in smoke.

Next to launch in quick succession were the three weak sisters: the IAR-93 Orao, now the "Yugo"; the Indian Air Force Marut, and the *Italiano* Fiat G.91. Just like their more sophisticated counterparts, these airplanes had been modified to carry an extra heavy load of bombs. But because of their relatively substandard construction, their modifications had taken longer and were far more Mickey Mouse than the other strike craft. (Indeed, some of the extra ordnance was hanging from nothing more than steel cord and duct tape.) It was for this reason that the air service crew was most concerned about the fate of the trio of somehow endearing aerial oddballs.

Hunter's jumpjet was the last to go.

Unlike the other strike craft, the amount of ordnance assembled under the wings of the Harrier was not mind-boggling.

In fact, all he was lugging on the jumpjet was a 30mm cannon pod. Inside the cockpit, he was carrying his trusty M-16, plus a smaller pistol, which he considered the most important weapon of the mission.

There was no need to hook up the Harrier to the carrier's catapult system; the jumpjet lifted off after a short roll down the *Fitz*'s flight deck, and after ascending to 4000 feet, it joined the rest of the circling TF Air Squadron.

Once the 13 airplanes formed up, they turned as

one and headed west.

Yaz watched them quickly disappear over the ever-brightening horizon, and then told his communication officer to send a coded message to Jones back in Washington.

It read simply: "We're in the air."

Ten

Tokyo

Deep within his flying-saucer-shaped castle, Hashi Pushi, the Supreme Warlord of the Asian Mercenary Cult, was crying.

It was now close to dawn. Usually at this time of day, the whim to indulge in yet another orgy would hit him. On these occasions, he would order a dozen or more "pleasure girls" from the Teishintai Corps. These were young women snatched from each village and hamlet that his ruthless troops continued to capture and occupy throughout the Asian hemisphere. The most beautiful and desirous ones were, of course, immediately transported to his headquarters, where he would use them for his sole enjoyment. The castoffs were left for his top commanders to do with as they pleased. It was perhaps the most well-organized sex slavery operation that had ever existed, and neither he nor his bloodthirsty troops ever wanted for any kind of carnal pleasure.

It also did wonders for morale.

But there would be no orgy this early morning. Indeed, Hashi Pushi was convinced that there would be no more orgies at all. At least, not the kind he was used to.

So instead of ordering his adjutant officer to choose an assortment of young girls for his master, Hashi Pushi told the man to summon what was known as the Hi-Si String Orchestra. Famous throughout Asia as the most talented collection of Asian classical musicians ever assembled, they and their families were captured when the Cult overran the main island of Nippon. Hashi Pushi had them imprisoned in his palace, and whenever he felt the desire for music, they were brought before him to play.

Not a minute after Hashi Pushi had so commanded, the twenty-four men and women members of the Hi-Si were led into his combination ballroom/bedroom under the watchful eyes of a dozen armed guards. They quickly began to set up, ready as always to play the Warlord's requests, though it was obvious that the supreme leader was suffering much emotional discomfort.

But instead of requesting the usual show tune or score from some obscure *kabuki* play, Hashi Pushi had a different kind of song in mind this day.

"When one achieves the status of power and respect that great ones have achieved, as I have," he began, his voice fighting back the tears, "there are those that wish him dead. They do this for only selfish reasons, usually so that they themselves can step onto the pedestal of absolute power."

Hashi Pushi paused, wiped the tears from his eyes with his greasy hands, and then continued, "I have recently ordered every one of your family members arrested. They are now all in chains, right here in the palace."

The members of the orchestra began to stir uneasily.

"They will all be butchered," Hashi Pushi told them, his voice still quivering, yet unnervingly calm, "unless you fulfill the order that I am about to give you."

Hashi Pushi then carefully looked each of the musicians directly in the eye.

"When I command you to begin to play, you will stop only when I say so," he went on, his voice now rising, going shrill with madness. "And though you may one day be told that my mortal being has been destroyed, that will not be enough for you to stop. You will play forever, just as my soul shall live forever. If you cease to play, your families will cease to exist, as will their families, and their families after that."

It was deadly quiet in the room now. The musicians were absolutely terrified.

Hashi Pushi was literally clawing his face now, as if scratching his dirty skin alone would stop the seemingly endless flow of tears.

"Now!" he suddenly bellowed. "Now, *begin to play!"*

The musicians paused and looked to each other, confused over what they had been ordered to do.

"But, Master," the orchestra leader dared to ask. "What song shall we play?"

Hashi Pushi stared at the man for a moment. Even through his bloodshot eyes, his murderous glare was apparent. But then, strangely, a slight, benign smile washed across his bloated face.

"Play my favorite," he said, his voice seeming to climb an octave or two. "You know the one . . ."

Some of the Hi-Si giggled nervously; others fought back their own tears. Within a minute, they had tuned up and had launched into the opening strains of a shaky version of "The Firebird Suite."

Eleven

Seventy-two-year-old Sukisan Krotchoki was hauling in the first catch of the early morning.

He was trawling about thirty-five miles east of Tokyo Harbor. The tide was beginning to run out, and the fish were going with it. So it was time to head back into port, dump the load, and then go out again.

It had already been a good day. The hold below was two-thirds full of tuna and dolphin, just the kind of catch that would bring top payment for Krotchoki and his grandson, who helped him crew the boat. But it was not the three dozen or so fish in the hold which had Krotchoki in such good spirits this early morning. Rather it was the small crab that had got snagged in their net during the last haul.

It was called a warrior crab. The name was eerily apt, for the crab's shell was formed unmistakably in the face of a fierce *samurai* warrior. It was said that the crabs were actually the reincarnated souls of soldiers who had defended the Homeland centuries before, and it was the custom for anyone finding such a crab to throw it back, thereby preserving the hero's soul.

But such creatures were also very valuable to anyone who risked breaking the tradition. Krotchoki knew a certain Cult general who would pay him handsomely for the warrior crab. He would therefore risk the curse of bad luck which supposedly fell upon the family of anyone using the crab for personal gain. After seventy-two years, Krotchoki felt he was a little too old to believe in such superstitions.

The money he would receive from selling the rare creature was more important.

It was Krotchoki's grandson who spotted the three jets.

They were way off in the distance, hugging the waves, probably fifteen miles off their bow to the east.

He called out excitedly to his grandfather, who saw them at once. He knew the airplanes did not belong to the Cult air force—they were missing the distinctive three-red-balls emblem worn by all Cult aircraft. These strange airplanes carried no markings on their wings or fuselage. Plus, it appeared that they were three different types of airplanes, and not the standard sweptback jets flown by the Cult Defense air forces.

They watched as the three jets roared past them, not more than a mile and a half off their starboard side. No sooner had they disappeared over the western horizon than Krotchoki spotted three more mystery planes rocketing in from the same direction.

"It is an attack!" the old man cried. *"We must get word to the military. . . ."*

Krotchoki's grandson had already climbed up the mast and attached the long-range UHF antenna—it was important that they radio back to the Cult coastal patrol station that unidentified airplanes had been spotted. Krotchoki's shaking hands worked the radio dials, trying to raise the Cult naval base while at the same time keeping an eye on the second trio of airplanes as they flashed by. If this was in fact an enemy attack, he would be rewarded heavily for spotting the airplanes.

"More!" his grandson was screaming from the mast. "Three more! And three more!"

Krotchoki's fingers could barely turn the radio's tuner now. It usually took a minute or so to raise the naval base; he prayed that someone would answer sooner this time.

"Grandfather! *Quick!*"

Krotchoki looked up from the radio to see an expression of absolute horror spread across his grandson's face. He was pointing right off their bow. Three more of the strange airplanes were no more than a mile away, not twenty feet off the surface of the water—and heading right for them.

It was at that instant that Krotchoki finally got a reply from the nearest Cult naval base. But it was too late now. The jets were suddenly right on them.

The first one went directly overhead, the roar from its engine bursting his grandson's left eardrum. The second one was right on its tail. Krotchoki felt the skin on his face almost melt as this plane's jet exhaust bathed the fishing boat with searing hot smoke.

But it was the third airplane which struck the most fear into Krotchoki's suddenly feeble heart. This strange airplane actually seemed to slow down as it approached their boat. How could that be? he wondered, even as his grandson lay on the deck, his ear bleeding profusely, screams of pain coming from his dried, burned lips.

Just as the third airplane seemed to come to a complete halt, it started up again, and was now bearing down on the small fishing boat at an extremely high speed. Krotchoki could no longer hear his grandson's screams, his ears were filled with the roar of pure mechanical horror. He was certain the airplane was going to crash right into the boat. He immediately dived for the cover of a nearby net spool.

Then, just like that, the strange airplane streaked overhead, neatly clipping the top of the boat's mast and destroying the UHF antenna.

Then it was gone.

Krotchoki looked up and found the sky empty. His grandson was an arm's length away, still screaming from the pain in his ear. This was the only sound Krotchoki could hear—that, and the gentle lapping of water against the sides of the boat.

Krotchoki crawled along the deck on his hands and knees, his head shaking involuntarily. Reaching into a chum bucket near the hold lock, he took out the warrior crab and with all his strength threw it overboard.

His grandson stopped screaming soon afterward.

* * *

The pilots of the Tornados were both volunteers from the Texas Air Force. As such, their radio call signs were Texas One and Texas Two.

They were streaking along at barely a hundred feet off the ground, approximately sixty miles west of the coastal city of Nagashima. With their wings completely overloaded with Mk84 2,000-pound GP bombs, the airplanes were straining to maintain an altitude high enough to search for their assigned target.

They were looking for a narrow and deep valley hidden in a series of shallow hills that ringed the outskirts of a place called Hakkan San. The target was referred to as "Kimono Valley" in Jones's intelligence reports. It earned its nickname because a tremendous camouflage net had been stretched across it from the surrounding hills. Over three miles wide, the net made the valley appear as little more than a long, wide gully, a contour perfectly natural to the surrounding landscape.

Yet hidden somewhere in that valley was the entire satellite up-and-down link system that fed every Cult installation worldwide. In other words, Kimono Valley served as the long-distance communication service for the Cult's far-flung armies.

But because of its expert disguise, no one on the United American side knew exactly where it was.

Initially, this wasn't going to be a problem. Had the Tornados been launched for a night mission, as was originally planned, they would have relied on their superior infrared NightVision targeting systems to pinpoint the satellite station's location. In early morning daylight, however, the pilots of Texas One and Two would have to rely on their own hunting instincts.

One quick pass over the general area had the Tornado pilots eyeballing the terrain below, looking for any clue, any sign, that would distinguish Kimono Valley from the rest of the rolling terrain. Yet even from the low altitude, nothing looked out of place at all.

A dangerous game had begun. The pilots knew that the Cult air defense gunners had to be tracking them. But for the enemy to open up on them with antiaircraft fire would reveal the huge, heavily-concealed position. So would painting them with search radars from their SAM batteries.

But just how long this cat-and-mouse game could continue was impossible to say.

The Tornados banked around and crisscrossed the area again. Their valuable fuel was quickly burning up as they plowed through the sluggish air close to the ground. By the time they came around for the third time, each pilot knew they had enough fuel to loiter for about another minute. Then they would both have to make a very critical decision: abort the mission and return to the carrier with the bombs still attached. Or . . .

Suddenly the pilot of Texas One spotted something that wasn't quite right. A small patch of brown in the sea of green jungle below them looked slightly out of place. He signaled his wingman and then roared in for a closer look.

To the pilot of Texas One, the brown patch looked like dead foliage. Yet it was on the sunny side of a small hill and looked like it would get the same amount of groundwater as the rest of the growth.

Then why was it a different color?

Texas One had to think quick. Could it have been because the brown patch was foliage cut a while ago and not replaced with fresh foliage in the net in a while?

He had to take the chance that it was.

He streaked to the far end of the valley, rolled over, and dived right at the "ground," opening up with his two 27mm cannons. Instantly he saw his HE shells start to rip open the great net that was indeed stretched across the valley. He'd found it.

Now came the hard part.

Gulping two quick breaths of oxygen, he dived through the hole he had just made, disappearing from view of the higher flying second Tornado.

Texas One couldn't believe his eyes. Not only was there plenty of flying room underneath the net, but lining the flow of the valley below were row upon row of satellite dishes.

He also saw dozens of SAM batteries and Triple-A guns.

And they were all pointing at him.

Almost immediately, these antiaircraft batteries opened up with everything they had. Hundreds of tracer rounds from 23mm cannons, fired from the scores of ex-Soviet ZSU-23-4-Shilka mobile self-propelled anti aircraft guns systems, flashed all around the Tornado, searching for their marks.

But the Tornado pilot had little time to do anything else but line up his plane with a series of dishes, drop a couple of Mk84s, then try to get the hell out of there. But it wasn't as simple as that. The enemy cannon fire was starting to find him. He suddenly took a couple of direct hits right behind the cockpit, destroying his entire IFF and UHF data link, and his low/mid/high receiver systems. A second burst went through his right wing.

Releasing the two Mk84s, he booted in his afterburner and raced toward the far end of the valley. As he pulled back on the stick, he opened up once again with his 27mm cannons and sliced himself an exit hole. Zooming through into the open air once again, he just cleared the net when the pair of the delayed-fused 2,000-pound bombs detonated.

The pilot of Texas Two saw the gigantic net rise like an inflated balloon from the twin explosions and then settle back again. The concussion hit him a split second later. He tried to raise Texas One on the radio but got no response. But as the first Tornado got closer to him, he saw why: his partner's entire communications system had been shot away.

But Texas Two didn't have to talk. It was now his turn.

Aiming for the exit hole that his partner had just made, Texas Two dropped in and began his run up the valley. But this time, the Cult gunners threw up an additional wall of AA fire. Hundreds of D-30 howitzers, entrenched high up on the inner sides of the two ridges that made up the wide valley, were at the ready. They opened up on the Tornado as it entered their killing zone. Round after round of 122mm HE fragmentation shells outfitted with near-proximity fuses blasted down at him as he quickly tried to find a suitable target through the smoke and dust of the last explosions. A small concrete bunker, situated amid three satellite dishes, got his attention on his targeting screen. His thumb eased over to his weapon's release button.

Suddenly a tremendous explosion rocked his airplane. Smoke instantly filled his cockpit. He knew immediately that he'd been hit and hit bad. The 122mm shell had exploded just behind him, nearly blowing off his entire tail assembly. He barely had control of his jet, but somehow he kept his laser bomb sight steady on the concrete bunker.

"Just a little more, honey," he whispered to himself. "Just a little more . . ."

Suddenly, he was there. Releasing a pair of 84s, he took the Tornado straight up, not attempting to go for the hole at the end of the valley that Texas One had made. But his 27mm cannons didn't have time to open the net wide enough. Ripping through the steel cables supporting the net, he sheared off part of his left wing, a piece of his tail, his pilot tube, and his flight refueling probe.

But somehow he made it through and was still flying. His pair of GPs exploded a second later, but by then, he'd punched the Tornado to full military power and was safely away.

He formed up with Texas One and streaked across the hidden valley again. They both knew they had taken out a number of the dishes and communication bunkers—but there were plenty more still to go. And if just one remained, the mission would not be successful. So it was clear what they had to do: they would both have to go in again.

This time, there was only one way to do it.

Breaking off, each pilot headed to the opposite end of the valley, and, at the same time, dived in through the gaping holes in the net. Dropping deep down and as close to the floor of the valley as possible, the two crazy Texans streaked directly at each other, lining up to drop their remaining general purpose bombs.

Confused, the enemy gunners nevertheless threw up everything they had at them. The entire valley was filled with rounds of 122mm HE and 23mm cannon shells, as well as any Stinger, Blowpipe, or SA-7 Grail shoulder-launched SAMs the ground crews could muster. Added in were thousands of 7.62mm tracer rounds fired from hundreds of AK-47's belonging to the Cult ground troops stationed in the valley.

But the incredible fusillade didn't stop the Tornados. Ignoring the pings and clunks striking their jets, they continued on their high-speed collision course.

Releasing their payloads at the same time, the two Tornados appeared to just about plow head-on into each other, when they suddenly turned on their sides and passed each other belly to belly: it was a maneuver known as the Texas Rose. Continuing to opposite ends of the valley, they once again cleared the net a split second before their heavy ordnance erupted in one tremendous roar.

But they didn't turn for home yet.

Straddling the sides of Kimono Valley, the two Tornados raked the edges of the net with what was left of their 27mm cannon rounds, severing most of the camouflage covering's support cables and wires from their moorings. As they roared back overhead, the two pilots saw the entire net tremble, then collapse into the burning valley beneath it.

Out of fuel, bombs, and bullets, they formed up and immediately climbed up to safer altitudes. They knew they'd been successful in knocking out the target — what they hadn't destroyed outright had certainly been damaged by the collapse of the heavy, burning net.

But at what cost? They pulled up close to one another and each pilot surveyed the other's damage. They were both horrified. Large pieces of fuselage, wings, and tail sections were falling off both planes. Each Tornado was also perforated with dozens of holes of all sizes, most of which were smoking heavily. Both were also spewing long trails of ugly black smoke.

The pilots immediately turned east, toward the carrier, hoping against hope that there was enough left of their airplanes to make it back.

At just under 600 miles per hour, the IAR-93 Orao (AKA the "Yugo") and the Indian Air Force Marut twisted and turned through the desolate river canyons leading to their destination.

They had gone in the hard way — up the rolling, twisting Fusaki River, their tails sometimes no higher than twenty-five feet off the top of the dirty yellow water.

They'd been over enemy territory for twenty minutes now and had not been spotted. But the two pilots—both Free Canadians—knew all hell was going to break loose soon. For directly ahead of them now they could for the first time see their target: the snow-capped outline of Mount Nanzenji.

There was no need for any communication between the two pilots. They both were well versed in their roles for Operation Long Bomb and knew what had to be done.

All that was left was for them to figure out just how to do it.

Because of all the targets, this one had the least pre-strike intelligence simply because of its remoteness. In fact, the only thing known about the target was that it was heavily defended with SAM batteries that ran right up the side of the mountain, all the way to the peak.

So the plan all along was for these two oddballs to reach the target, recon it quickly, come up with a strike plan of their own, carry it out, and try to escape.

And do it all in less than fifteen seconds.

They took the last turn of the river and then popped up to 500 feet.

At that moment, a clock started ticking.

Fifteen seconds to go. Each armed his 30mm cannons, activated his missiles.

Fourteen seconds. Both pilots yanked back hard on their joysticks and punched in their afterburners.

Thirteen seconds. With an ear-splitting roar, the two jets seemed to shoot straight up out of the ground, sending the outer perimeter SAM crews diving for cover.

The Orao and the Marut kept going up hard and fast, trying to gain as much altitude as possible before the rest of the air defense system operators figured out what the hell was going on.

It wouldn't take them long.

Ten seconds. Each jet's warning system panel lights were blinking like it was the Fourth of July. They'd been locked onto by at least one SAM battery, and probably many more. It was now time for some serious evasive action.

Eight seconds. A half-dozen SA-13 Gopher SAMs had been launched and were closing in on their tails. Each of these SAMs was loaded with an 8.8lb contact-and-proximity-fused HE fragmentation warhead. Just one of these exploding in the right spot could bring both planes down.

Seven seconds. Both pilots waited for the last possible instant before the enemy antiaircraft missiles achieved contact/detonation range, and then banked hard away from each other, hoping to confuse them. It worked. The maneuver freaked the SAMs' gyrosystems, sending them tumbling out of control, and impacting to the ground below.

Six seconds. *KABOOOOOOOOMMM!!!!*

The pilot of the Marut was thrown hard against the side of his cockpit—a Gopher had exploded just off his nose. His jet pitched steeply to the left, his cockpit warning panels lighting up even brighter than before.

Five seconds. *KABOOOOOOOOOMMM!!!!* A second Gopher detonated just twenty feet from the Yugo's tail, out of killing range, but close enough to knock the airplane briefly out of control.

The Yugo pilot looked up and saw the Marut wobble but attempt to get steady. He also saw black smoke begin to pour from his wingmate's fuselage. And he saw yet another SAM zeroing in.

Snapping into a quick dive, the Yugo crossed the Marut's tail, hoping that the SAM would follow. It did. Now the Yugo pilot headed straight for the ground as fast as his jet would go.

Four seconds. The Yugo pilot yanked the stick back with both hands, pulling his machine up, while straining against tremendous G-forces. The SA-l3 kept going straight down and slammed into the earth.

Three seconds. The resulting explosion sent up thousands of red-hot pieces of shrapnel, many of which peppered the underbelly of the still-staggering smoking Marut.

Two seconds. Ignoring the loss of pressure in his hydraulic and fuel lines, the pilot of the Marut saw a SAM heading right for the now top-flying Yugo. Without thinking, he squeezed his cannon trigger and put a burst into the missile. A sudden red-orange burst obliterated the Gopher and set off a second missile directly behind it.

One second to go. It was too late to turn away. The Marut had to fly right through this explosion, the force shattering his windscreen and popping most of the rivets that held on his right wing's leading edge flaps.

Zero . . .

At last they saw the goal: the giant antenna farm covering the snow-covered dome of Mount Nanzenji.

The place was a major target. The two rows of

twenty antennas, each 300-feet high, first boosted and then sent off the signals that carried thousands of low-level radio orders from the high command to the lower echelon commands in all the countries now occupied by the Cult. Where the satellite stations inside in Kimono Valley served as a communication link between the high-profile commanders (and therefore carried the big orders to the big brains), the antennas atop Nanzenji provided the radio network for the heart, mouth, feet, and stomach of the Cult's legions.

To cut these down would be to slice the vocal cords of this great octopus whose tentacles were slowly strangling Asia and reaching out to the rest of the world.

Dropping down to 100 feet, almost to the height of the concrete bases of the antennas, the two jets entered between the rows of these steel towers and began dropping bombs.

The AS.37 Matras and AGM-78 ARM modified antiradar missiles went first. Then the AGM Walleye ASM and the AGM-88A Harms shot out from under the pair of oddballs as they twisted through this maze at close to the speed of sound. The bombs expertly blasted away at the bases that supported the great steel towers. These blasts caused the antennas to shudder and sway, and some began to twist and collapse under their own weight. The pilots were sowing so much destruction, the screech of the bending and stretching steel support beams could be heard even inside their cockpits.

At least thirty of the fifty towers were hit, but the pilots quickly realized that what they had done was not enough to bring down all these great steel superstructures. But suddenly, there was a tremendous explosion, followed by another and another and another. The four quick explosions caused the jet fighters to lurch forward and be tossed around, almost out of control. Looking back, the pilots discovered that what they had failed to do was being done by the enemy themselves.

Trying to stay locked on to the two jinking jets, a quartet of SAMs had bored through the standing towers that the jets couldn't topple, and the warheads began to explode as they struck the support beams in their paths. Each explosion toppled a tower into the path of another SAM, and it too exploded, furthering a domino effect.

As the two planes screamed to a higher altitude, the pilots looked behind them and saw what was left of the great antenna farm — a twisted and contorted pile of steel girders, occasionally rocked by secondary explosions, and now melting from the several fires.

And they had done it with not a second to spare.

Their victory, however, was quickly forgotten as the two pilots realized how heavily damaged their airplanes were. The Yugo was smoking and trailing oil from several large holes in its fuselage and wings. The Marut was in even worse shape: its left wing and tailplane was mangled, and worse, it was losing fuel.

Without a word between them, the pilots turned their severely wounded planes around and began the attempt to make it back to the *Fitz*.

Twelve

The commander of the Sakachita military base was worried.

His communication officer had just handed him a strange report. An SOS of sorts had been received by the Cult naval base twenty miles up the coast. Apparently sent from a fishing boat somewhere off the coast, the emergency call was garbled at best. In fact, no message ever came through from the civilian boat, and that was the problem. Civilian fishermen were under strict orders not to use military band radio unless they were reporting unusual activity, such as a spy plane or ship. Failure to adhere to this rule resulted in death by firing squad. Why then would a fisherman make an attempt to contact the military authorities, and then not follow through?

The commander checked his watch. It was 0615, just the beginning of his long day as the highest-ranking officer of the sprawling Sakachita installation. This was an unusual place: not only did it serve as an air station for a squadron of Cult interceptors, it was also the site for the central air defense radio network which linked all of the Cult air bases around the Home Islands. Responsibility for such a major Cult installation had been given to him by Hashi Pushi himself.

He looked out from his control tower window over the three rows of super-modified Dassault Etendard IV-Ms, the state-of-the-art aircraft of the Cult air defense forces. Usually when he gazed at these fabulous airplanes, he experienced a tinge of pride. But now a gut feeling told him that something was wrong. Suddenly the airplanes looked like sitting ducks.

He picked up his telephone and screamed a short order into it. Within 30 seconds he could see six pilots running to their Etendards, scrambled by him under the guise of a typical drill. He took a stopwatch from his pocket and started it ticking. He would be pleased if all six jets were in the air in less than four-point-five minutes.

The Viggens attacked two minutes later.

They had come in so low that the commander himself was the first to spot them. His air traffic officers were too busy getting the first three interceptors into the air to see the pair of blue dots streaking in from the eastern horizon.

But the commander saw them. They were flying faster and lower than he thought aerodynamically possible. Indeed, they were so low, their jet exhausts were actually leaving a trail of steam on the surface of the ocean as they roared in over it.

They looked *so* unusual, the commander had to take a few seconds just to make sure he wasn't seeing things. When the two airplanes finally made landfall, he knew it wasn't an illusion.

Who could they be? he wondered, just an instant before he let out a scream.

But his cry of alarm came about two seconds too late.

The first Mk 500-pound GP bomb off of Viggen One slammed into the Sakachita control tower, obliterating it and everyone inside, including the base commander.

Viggen Two came in right behind, pouncing on the three rows of parked Etendards, blasting away with its four 20mm cannons. The high-explosive cannon rounds shredded the planes, rapidly tearing apart their fuselages, engines, and cockpits, and igniting their fuel tanks.

Meanwhile, Viggen One swung back around and took out the taxiing and runway strips with a matched set of Durandel antirunway bombs. Each bomb exploded on impact, tearing up large craters and wildly spewing the runway with concrete and flaming debris. The coverted Swedish fighter then turned and made a second pass to do the same thing all over again. Three enemy airplanes had taken off just as he and his partner had roared in; he wanted to make sure that it would be a long time before any plane left this airfield again.

By that time, the pilot of Viggen Two had banked hard left, and was making his turn to come back and tear up more Etendards. Suddenly his airplane began shuddering. He looked over his shoulder and saw two of the scrambled Etendards bearing down on him from his six o'clock, their nose cannons ablaze. With his bomb racks still overloaded, the Viggen pilot quickly lit his afterburner and banked hard right. The

Etendards followed the maneuver and were soon back on the Swedish fighter's tail. The Viggen pilot then screeched hard left, bringing him back out over the sea. The Etendards mimicked this maneuver too, all the while closing in for the kill on the slower, overloaded airplane.

The Viggen suddenly pulled back and went straight up, its overworked engine straining for altitude. The Cult fighter pilots couldn't believe their good fortune. Their airplanes could climb much faster than an ordinary Viggen, never mind one so loaded down with bombs. Though the Cult pilots had no idea who the attacking pilot was, they were sure he was about to pay with his life for daring to attack their Homeland.

And that's where they were wrong.

For when the Viggen suddenly turned over at about 4000 feet, the Cult pilots found themselves looking up at a pair of A-7 Strikefighters coming out of the clouds and right down at them.

The Etendard pilots tried to break off and get away from the ferocious Strikefighters, but it was much too late for that. Each A-7 unleashed a wicked barrage of 20mm cannon shells. Each fusillade quickly found its mark. Within seconds, the pair of Etendards were falling into the sea, almost side-by-side, aflame and in pieces.

Meanwhile the pilot of Viggen Two was weaving his way through scattered anti-aircraft fire, intent on bombing his main target, the massive radio communication network complex located on the edge of the huge airfield.

Orbiting overhead, however, the pilot of the third and last of the Cult Etendards saw the Swedish fighter

111

begin its bombing run and quickly dived toward it.

As soon as the slower Viggen crossed his sight lines, the Cult pilot opened up with a long burst from his dual 20mm cannons. The shells danced along the thin outer edges of the Viggen's wings, causing the pilot to quickly break off his bombing run and roll hard off to the east. The speedier Etendard shot up past him but then twisted around, staying right on the tail of the slower Swedish airplane.

Undeterred, the pilot of Viggen Two snapped hard left and began a bombing run on the communications complex from the opposite direction. He knew he had to unload his ordnance if he was going to try to get out from under this pesky Cult fighter, yet he had at least to try to hit the main target.

The Etendard, now right on the Viggen's tail, opened up with his 20mm cannon again, this time chopping off good-sized chunks of fuselage, but the Viggen was able to jink and jag just enough to dodge most of the deadly fire. Then, for the next two and a half seconds, the Viggen stayed straight and true, aiming right at the communications complex. The Etendard pilot faithfully hung on the Viggen tail and increased his speed, trying to line up his sights for yet another burst that he hoped would finally put this infernal flying machine down once and for all.

Just as he was about to release a burst, the Etendard pilot saw the Viggen drop everything he had, the Beluga Cluster Dispensers, the Mk82 Snakeye retared bombs, and the Mk 500-lb GP bombs, right into the radio complex. With the sudden loss of all that ordnance, the Viggen virtually disappeared from in front of the Etendard, and the enemy pilot found himself heading straight into the resulting massive explosion. At that instant, his radar warning buzzed loudly, alerting him to the fact that a heat-seeking AIM-9 Sidewinder, fired from a tracking Strikefighter, was just about to fly up his exhaust. Caught between a rock and a hard place, the Cult pilot streaked into the rising ball of flame from the destroyed radio complex just as the Sidewinder slammed into his tail.

He never knew which one killed him.

The Strikefighters formed up and turned back toward the enemy flight line, strafing what was left of still-intact enemy airplanes. By the time they were done, all that was left of the Cult squadron were shattered, twisted, and smoking hulks of blackened scrap metal.

The A-7s immediately exited the target area, catching up with the Viggens that had streaked off seconds before. The mission had been a huge success, but it was apparent that both Viggens were hurting badly. Each had vital electronic functions knocked out, Viggen One's landing gear had fallen open and couldn't be cranked up, and Viggen Two was handling poorly due to damage to its left wing.

The pair of Strikefighters quickly rallied around the battered Swedish fighters, and as one the four planes turned east, starting the treacherous flight back to the *Fitzgerald*.

In all, the air strike had taken less than ninety seconds.

Activity aboard the USS *Fitzgerald* was approaching sheer pandemonium.

The two Tornados had already "landed hard"—logbook terminology for "crashed." Both had their landing gear and control surfaces chewed up; both ended up sliding in on their underbellies and catching the last arrestor wire after skidding almost halfway down the deck.

Viggen Two had returned about ten minutes later. Its right-side ailerons were completely shot away, and the pilot reported he was getting a negative light on his airbrake assembly. Its pilot somehow floated the beat-up Swedish fighter in, losing part of his wing but snapping his brakes into working condition with the first bounce on the carrier deck. He too connected with the fourth and last arrestor wire.

Viggen One bounced in for a fairly normal landing, its right-side gear bending but holding as the pilot caught the three wire. The Strikefighters held off on recovery, making way for the shot-up oddballs, the Yugo and the Marut.

Neither could slow down enough for a normal approach, so they were forced to lower the airspeed gradually by circling the carrier with the gear down, slowing their jet engines until they were barely airborne. Still, both came in hard and nearly out of control—their tailplanes were totally useless or so full of holes that they made no difference whatsoever as they hit the deck. The Marut hit the one wire so hard coming in, it snapped it. The Yugo sliced off three feet of its right wing by smashing into the island itself. Both pilots escaped with just cuts and bruises.

The flight deck was now awash in hot, slick oil, firefighting foam, and smoky jet fuel. Only by the professionalism of the crew and the superb skill of the pilots was order somehow maintained in the face of the chaos.

Damage control reports continued to be sent to the bridge. "The Ball," a series of vertical lights used to alert incoming pilots as to whether they are too low or high on an approach, had been hit by part of Viggen Two's left wing when it snapped off a plane as it slammed onto the deck. It could not be repaired. Elevator Number Two was jammed midway down its shaft from hot oil that had leaked down and shorted out its electrical power. It was now covered in Purple-K flame retardant foam and likely unrepairable.

There were at least six fires barely under control topside, and two more in the hangar deck that had just started in the heavily-damaged planes that had been brought below. The regular firefighting crews were stretched to the far edges of their abilities; now everyone on board who could be spared was battling the fires.

When the first A-7 finally came in, it skidded on the foam and oil, crashing through the netlike safety barrier strung beyond the four wire, stopping just inches from going over the side. With the pilot trapped inside the cockpit, the airplane teetered precariously on the lip of the carrier.

Without prompting, the USS *Cohen* was immediately alongside, several of its bravest crew members crawling out on its main loading crane and rescuing the dazed, grateful pilot. Then they attached a steel cable around the nose landing gear of the airplane, and thus stabilized, the deck crew on the *Fitz* was able to winch the Strikefighter back onto the deck.

It was now 0755.

115

Yaz was in the bridge, impatiently awaiting the arrival of the Fiat G.91 and the A-4E Skyhawk. In many ways it was those two airplanes that had faced the most difficult mission of them all.

Their assignment was to go directly to the center of the port city of Yokohama and destroy the main telephone switching station, a place which routed every phone call made on the main Japanese island of Honshu. In one sense, the switching station was a "soft target": it could be taken out with one or two direct hits.

But in reality, it was the hardest target any of them took on.

Besides being defended by the heaviest concentration of antiaircraft defenses than all the other targets combined, it was also situated between a civilian hospital and a prisoner-of-war camp. This particular strike called for absolute precision under the most difficult of circumstances. Jones knew it when he designated the mission; the pilots who were to fly this mission knew it when they accepted.

But the risks involved had remained unspoken.

Yaz and his entire bridge crew scanned the horizon. The two Yokohama planes were long overdue, way, *way* past their bingo points. Everyone was just about to give up hope when they noticed a single tiny speck in the distance, heading toward the carrier.

Radar confirmed the sighting, Yaz, relieved that at least one of the planes was returning, was remorseful of the loss of the other. Then the "speck" got bigger. Finally it was close enough for everyone to make out clearly what was coming on home.

The crew was simply astounded.

There was only six feet left of the right wing of the Fiat. The Skyhawk, precisely matching airspeed, altitude and attitude, was flying alongside and slightly ahead of his partner, his left wing almost touching the stump that remained of the Fiat's right wing, thereby providing what aerodynamic experts would call "false lift." (The airflow created by the Skyhawk's wing allowed the Fiat's busted wing to pass through much diminished air resistance, thereby not requiring it a lot of wing area to stay airborne.)

Yaz could only speculate the daring that the two pilots must have displayed in the attempt and the success of achieving this tenuous position. He knew quite well that when a jet loses a wing, it's no longer a flying machine, it's a rocket spinning wildly out of control. He also knew that they had only one chance of making it back onto the carrier.

Together the two planes flew, straight and true and right for the landing deck. Radio chatter confirmed the situation, and the bridge requested that the Skyhawk bring the Fiat in to the point of landing, and then break away, letting the Fiat try to come in by itself. It was the safest and most logical way to handle this most unsafe and illogical situation.

But then the Skyhawk pilot feigned radio breakdown. Everyone on the bridge knew it was an old trick that pilots often used to get what they wanted. It was dangerous, but no one dared call this brave pilot on it. Instead, they held their breaths . . .

The planes remaining on deck — the A-7s and the Yugo — were hurriedly pushed, by hand, by every available sailor and pilot that could be mustered, to the remaining working elevators, and deposited in a heap in the hangar deck. Seawater mixed with detergent solvent was pumped up through the firehoses and sprayed across the landing deck in an attempt to rid it of the hundreds of gallons of JP-8 jet fuel, hydraulic oil, and grease that had spilled or poured from the injured birds that had landed earlier. Last, a fresh layer of foam was spread out across the deck to prevent any fires from breaking out, and a double layer of steel netting was loosely stretched across the far end of the landing area.

All this was accomplished in a matter of two minutes, and everyone was standing by just as the two stricken airplanes made their last approach, demonstrating the tightest of precision flying possible.

Slowly, they both eased in, just above stall speed. The two pilots were bringing them on down so incredibly smoothly, that it looked like they *were* literally attached to each other.

With what was left of their landing gear they both touched down at once. Both planes' tail hooks snared the two wire at the same time, and instead of the pilots pushing to full power, they both immediately killed their engines. The two planes smashed into the safety barrier, stopped dead in their tracks with a screech of smoke and sparks, and then fell in against each other.

Within seconds, the firecrews had the pilots out and both planes covered in even more foam. From the bridge, Yaz saw the pilot of the Fiat and the pilot of the Skyhawk look up toward him.

They gave Yaz the "Thumbs Up." Mission accomplished.

Yaz returned the gesture with a salute for a job well done.

Then he checked the time. It was 0800. The only ones left out there were the two Alphas. And Hunter.

Thirteen

Both French Alpha Jet E trainers were struggling under the weight of the six bombs under their wings.

Their mission had been a long and arduous one so far. They'd been loitering just outside the estimated radar range of the Cult coastal defense units, flying at wavetop level for nearly ninety minutes. Down in the luggish air near the surface of the ocean, their jet engines were forced to work harder, churning up the heavy air and turning it into jet power. As a result, they were both burning up fuel at a dangerous rate.

Yet it was part of the plan that their journey was the longest of all the TF Squadron. The Alphas couldn't hit their targets until 0815 — when they could be reasonably sure that the other strike craft had completed their missions.

It was now 0810.

Flying just 500 feet above the Alphas, Hawk Hunter did one last check of his flights systems. Everything looked okay. He waited while another five minutes slowly ticked off the clock. Finally it was 0815.

"Showtime," Hunter thought.

He wagged his wings, the prearranged signal for the Alphas to follow his lead. As three, they climbed to 750 feet and broke in over the coastline. They had exactly three minutes to get to their target: the military stronghold of Tokyo itself.

Several klicks in, Hunter raced forward of the Alphas. He quickly judged the wind currents over the city, which they were approaching from the south.

"Winds are steady at about twenty knots," he radioed back to the Alphas, all need of radio silence now gone. "Looks like it's from the southwest."

The Alpha pilots quickly adjusted their approach to come in with the wind. Then they dropped back down low and went their separate ways.

Within a half minute, Alpha One had a visual make on its target: one hundred and fifty fuel storage tanks that prestrike intelligence said contained more than ten million gallons of gasoline, diesel fuel, oil, and kerosene. In other words, enough petroleum products to keep the industrial base of the Asian Mercenary Cult running for six months.

The Alpha came in over the fuel depot on a slow, lazy loop, a scattering of puny AA fire the only resistance rising up from the woefully defended target. He passed over the first two rows of tanks, waiting until he was over the third array to begin dropping the cluster bombs. They came off his racks quickly. In just ten seconds, he had dumped all six of his CBUs in a straight line across the middle of the 300-acre fuel storage site.

The resulting explosions ruptured eight tanks at dead center, their skins perforated by the thousands of small bomblets. Suddenly fuel was cascading out of the tanks, overflowing their safety moats and creating one torrent of volatile liquid so voluminous, it actually snuffed the few small fires started by the explosions. Within seconds, this river, consisting of thousands of gallons of a mixture of gasoline, fuel oil, diesel fuel, and kerosene, was raging through the complex, washing over every loading pipe and valve, and all pumping equipment, and in turn, puncturing other tanks.

Completely empty of ordnance, and, ironically, low on fuel himself, the pilot of Alpha One swept over the target one last time. The tidal wave of fuel he caused had already broken out of the tank farm's perimeter and was now flooding into the main sewer system whose branches reached throughout the entire city of Tokyo.

The pilot took a deep gulp of oxygen in celebration — dumping what were normally antipersonnel weapons in the middle of the storage tank facility had proved to be a good gamble — so far. He put his stubby little plane on a course due east and booted it, hoping the *Fitz* was where it should be.

His job was done.

At about the same time, Alpha Two was approaching its target: the natural gas refinery five and a half miles to the west of the fuel storage farm.

Dodging light AA fire, the pilot was able to bring the trainer right in and drop his payload of BLU-27 napalm bombs directly on the largest storage tank.

Within a millisecond, there was a white-hot flash of ignition that made the entire facility burst into one tremendous fireball.

Suddenly, it was like the sun had crashed into the

earth.

The pilot of Alpha Two was astonished by the size of the explosion he'd just created — fueled by the oxygen and natural gas that it sucked into itself, the fireball rose higher and higher into the sky, almost too fast for him to get out of its way. He had to act quickly. He immediately went into a steep vertical climb, barely keeping ahead of the blossoming explosion.

At 15,000 feet, the tip of the fireball briefly engulfed the tiny jet, scorching the entire plane from tail to nose, and burning off nearly every square inch of paint.

With all the skill he could muster, the pilot of Alpha Two finally was able to exit this holocaust, only to find that almost every electrical connection inside his cockpit had shorted out. None of his panel indicators were working, his radio was blown, and every needle on every gauge had dropped to zero.

Kicking in his thankfully-spared emergency systems, he turned east and began the long limp home.

Beside destroying the natural gas facility, the huge conflagration also served to ignite the millions of gallons of fuel coursing through the city's sewer system. Suddenly there were geysers of flame spewing up out of maintenance ducts, drainage pipes, and manhole covers.

The sudden injection of heat served to whip up the early morning breeze. The flames began feeding on themselves and on the heavily polluted air above the city. These were all the conditions needed to create a classic and frightening fire storm. Within minutes, more than a third of the buildings in the center of the city had burst into flames.

And descending directly into this manmade Hell was Hunter's jumpjet.

Hunter had to do two things and do them fast.

The first was to locate "The Castle of Three Turrets," occupied by the infamous Hashi Pushi.

To this end, he flew directly to the center of burning Tokyo, to the Chiydoda-Ku, the part of the city that had once housed the Imperial Palace. Once again, Jones's prestrike intelligence had been right. In the middle of the forested park rose the three turrets of the fortress that contained his quarry.

Surrounded by a wide moat fed from an underground aqueduct, the place looked impregnable. But Hunter would have to worry about getting inside later. For now he had to accomplish his second task: finding a safe place to put down in the Harrier.

Almost half the city below him was in flames, and the updraft of the heat currents was making it increasingly difficult to control the jumpjet. But time was of the essence, for the longer it took him, the harder it would be to land. Suddenly he saw the perfect spot — a patch of icy white in the middle of the towering flames about a klick from the palace. He checked his moving map display. The potential landing spot turned out to be smack-dab in the middle of the former Asashi City Zoo.

Hunter guided the Harrier directly over the patch of cool white blue — it was the climate-controlled area that housed the polar bears — and brought the airplane right on top of the manmade iceberg that sat in the middle of the swim tank. It would be perfect protection from the fire that was spreading throughout the entire area.

He quickly smeared fire-retardant grease over his exposed hands and face. Then, looping a double bandolier of ammo over his shoulder, he slapped a clip of 5.56mm tracer rounds into his laser-sighted M-16, popped open the canopy, and climbed out.

Trouble hit as soon as his feet hit the ice. Hunter turned and found himself face to face with an enormous polar bear. He froze absolutely still.

Hunter had no time to waste. He didn't want to shoot the beast, so he did the next best thing. He pointed his rifle in the air and fired off three rounds. The bear beat a hasty retreat.

Hunter quickly waded through the surrounding water, climbed the wrought-iron fence, and got out of the tank. Before him was yet another scene from a nightmare. The fire had already destroyed half the sprawling zoo, and now the surviving animals were running loose. Hunter found himself dodging lions, antelope, and sabre-tooth boars. Many of the animals were tearing each other apart, panicked into madness by the approaching wall of flame. Others were wildly smashing into walls, buildings, and even plate glass windows, more often than not killing themselves in the process.

Hunter grimly made his way through the carnage and headed toward the center of the city.

The heat was unbearable. The temperature of the air had long since passed 150 degrees, and now every building he saw that was made of wood was beginning to combust into flames. Some people were literally exploding, too. He saw several groups of terrified soldiers apparently bivouacked on the zoo grounds, running from the flames only to have their uniforms ignite, and in some cases, even their skin. It made for a horrible sight, but as the city had long ago been emptied of civilians, Hunter knew all casualties from the firestorm would be suffered exclusively by the Cult military.

Hunter had to be careful and stay off the main roads that led directly to the castle, knowing they'd be heavily used by the military. To this end, he ducked down the first side street that he came across after leaving the zoo.

It was almost totally ablaze. He had to run down the middle of the cluttered alley, dodging dozens of burning timbers that were crashing down all around him. Still more soldiers had died horrible deaths here, some of them the victims of their own exploding ammunition. Leaping over several dangerously sparking electrical wires, he finally made it to the end of the street, turned right, and dived into the doorway of the first building that was not yet on fire.

He had to catch his breath, but it was difficult. The fire, growing in intensity with each passing second, was sucking up all the oxygen. Hunter knew he had to keep going.

Three steps back out into the street, he was suddenly blown flat on his face by a tremendous explosion. The building that he had just left burst into a million pieces, accompanied by a tremendous roar which sounded like thousands of gunshots going off all at once.

Hunter rolled to the curb and was behind a red-hot steel telephone pole, M-16 at the ready. When he looked over his sights, he saw what was making the noises: firecrackers. He had temporarily taken shelter in the doorway of a fireworks factory. But he had no time to admire the irony of the moment. Taking a series of short, quick breaths, he started out again, racing at breakneck speed down the street.

Turning another corner, he literally ran into a patrol of Cult military police. They were wildly drunk on *sake,* and were carrying armfuls of stolen items. Hunter couldn't believe it. How greedy could these people be? Even as the city was burning down around them, they were on a wild looting spree.

One soldier, who only had one hand full, spotted Hunter, raised his AK-47, and squeezed the trigger.

But nothing happened. His gun had jammed, possibly due to the hellish temperature. Or maybe it had not been cleaned properly. A full burst of his tracer rounds stitched across the looter's chest and an instant later he fell to the ground, his dying hands still groping not for his gun, but for the stuff he'd stolen. He also began crying for help. But instead of aiding him, his comrades tore the stolen goods from his hands and then resumed running full-speed down the street.

Hunter sprinted down another side street. As he reached the far corner, he felt a rumble under his feet and began to run even faster. As he reached the end of the block, he dived head first into a shallow ditch just as the entire cobblestoned street lifted off the ground from the detonation of an underground gas main. Hundreds of blocks of concrete began to rain down around him. Yet he was off again, dodging and twisting, and barely escaping being crushed by the rain of these deadly projectiles.

The heat was becoming stifling now as he tried to stay a block or two ahead of the firestorm. But even the flame-reflective weaving in his flight suit could not handle the extreme temperature. The air was filled with the popping sounds of automobile tires bursting. Off in the distance he heard more controlled explosions, indicating desperate attempts by the Cult engineers to create firebreaks. But he knew that the situation was pathetically beyond their control by this time.

He moved over to a wider, shorter street, a place where, judging from the X-rated murals on the sides of buildings, an open sex market had apparently once flourished. Everywhere he looked, the paint on these garish portraits was beginning to smolder and peel. Trees were bursting into flames. Even the steel street signs were starting to melt. Even worse, the road itself was buckling from the heat.

He saw a small stream nearby suddenly disappear, instantly turning to scalding-hot steam. He saw more wild animals. He saw more soldiers simply explode into flames. He could hear a symphony of human screams. Huge explosions. Gunfire. The ear-splitting crackling of the approaching fire. Above it all the haunting wails of hundreds of sirens rose up into the sky, which was now black with smoke and completely blocked out the bright early-morning sun. It was as if the entire city had been shoveled into Hell itself.

Hunter just kept on running; he was almost to his destination. But making his way past the roaring fires that blazed on either side of him, he began to slowly sink into the softened blacktop. Each step became more difficult than the last, and finally he became completely stuck in the hot, gooey tar, the flames beginning to close in on him.

Now what? he asked himself.

Suddenly, the ground below him collapsed, and he

felt himself falling into the darkness, right into a giant water conduit. Clutching his M-16 to his chest, he was sucked feet first and carried through this pipe of surging hot water for what seemed to be forever. He thought his lungs were about to burst when he shot up into the air from the force of the raging water.

He couldn't believe his good fortune: he'd splashed back down into the moat that surrounded the castle of Hashi Pushi.

Yet he quickly realized he'd been thrown into another nightmare. Hundreds of soldiers had abandoned their posts and fled the burning castle for the safety of the water in the moat. But all these cowards had either drowned from the crush of the panic or from the machine guns that fired down on them from the parapets above. Now the moat was choked with their bloated dead bodies.

Hunter slowly floated to the base of the castle wall, where he climbed out and scrambled up to a small oak door that looked like it hadn't been opened in a hundred years. He expertly cracked the lock with his K-bar knife, and with the barrel of his M-16, slowly pushed the door open.

"I wonder if anyone's home?" he whispered to himself.

Fourteen

Hashi Pushi felt his right temple and found it was ice-cold. Things seemed to be getting dark. He checked his pulse and found it had slowed considerably.

"Soon," he whispered glumly to himself. "Very soon now."

Before him stood the seven top officers of his Home Island Air Defense Command. They were babbling something, but he wasn't really paying much attention.

"May I repeat, sir," the top air defense officer was saying. "We are under attack from the air. More reports are flooding in every minute. The situation is getting desperate. Can't you hear the commotion outside? That's the enemy burning down the city. They might even be using nuclear warheads on us!"

Hashi Pushi looked down from his throne at the seven gaudily-uniformed officers, tears forming in his eyes once again.

"The Blood Pool never lies," he said, more to himself than to any of them. "It is not lying now."

The seven Cult officers had a right to be concerned — and confused. It was clear that some kind of an attack was on. But just exactly what was happening, they didn't know. All the Cult's major airbases were still intact, as well as their weapons factories and ammo dumps—yet all of the country's major communications centers had been destroyed by the enemy aircraft. And a good portion of Tokyo was in flames.

Now the officers in charge of his airborne defense were before the deranged leader, begging for his orders to take off and catch the attacking aircraft.

They told him that no fewer than twelve squadrons of their air defense fighters were available to be scrambled to counter the enemy aerial attack. They were equipped with what constituted the Cult's most formidable air force, more than 100 super-modified Dassault Etendard fighters. They promised their Supreme Commander that every enemy pilot would be shot down and his body eaten—alive, if necessary—by scores of Hashi Pushi's most rabid civilian followers.

"Why was I made a turtle?" Hashi Pushi was asking himself, grim and rhetorical, staring at his unwashed, bumpy fingernails. "Why not a tiger? Or a polar bear?"

Totally mystified, and now on the verge of panic, the second-highest-ranking officer present stepped forward to plead the case.

"Sir, surely you can hear the explosions. You can see the flames. We must launch our airplanes now to stop this."

But Hashi Pushi did not give the order for them to take off. Instead, he summoned the woman in charge of his harem and, to the bafflement of his air defense officers, told her, "Bring me the woman with Cherry Blossom hair."

It was the second violinist of the Hi-Si Orchestra who saw him first.

The musician was halfway through the 391st rendition of "The Firebird." He and his colleagues had been playing in front of Hashi Pushi for so long, their fingers were bleeding. They had listened in on the bizarre conversation between Hashi Pushi and his air defense officers, since departed. They'd also heard another group of officers beg the Cult leader to order something called "the Fire Bats" into action — but Pushi had ignored them as well. Now they could hear the explosions outside getting closer by the minute. They could smell the smoke from the fires. They knew that some kind of disaster was approaching the palace — and fast.

Yet they continued to play on.

The violinist had just finished a *doreesimo* when he looked up and saw a tall man in a dirty black suit and a black helmet standing in the concealed doorway not twenty feet from Hashi Pushi's throne. On the floor directly behind this man lay three very still bodies; the musician recognized them as members of Hashi Pushi's personal guard.

The violinist looked back toward Hashi Pushi. Sitting on the overweight leader's bulging lap was the young girl brought to him about ten minutes before. Even from this distance and through bleary, tired eyes the violinist saw that the young girl was hauntingly beautiful, of delicate skin and lithe body, and possessing the most enchanting long red hair.

Hashi Pushi had already removed her kimono and his dirty robe and was now apparently attempting to have sex with her. The musician couldn't imagine a more embarrassing scene: the clumsy, intoxicated behemoth trying to enter the tentative, terrified, apparently-drugged young girl. Yet, after much squirming and grunting, it appeared that Hashi Pushi had successfully penetrated her, if only momentarily.

That's when the man in the black suit and helmet coolly walked into the hall. The conductor of the Hi-Si saw him now too, yet he continued to direct his musicians through the worn-out piece of music, providing a bizarre soundtrack for what was about to happen.

Two guards immediately appeared off to his right, but the man in the helmet dispatched them with a lightning-quick burst from his machine-gun. Two more guards appeared on the balcony right above him, but the man in the helmet quickly spun around, riddled them with the strange phosphorous bullets, and turned back again, all in the blink of an eye.

Hashi Pushi had finally taken notice by now. He unceremoniously dropped the unclothed young girl from his lap. Her skin was soaked in sweat, a small amount of blood, and other bodily fluids. She immediately crawled away, over the bodies of two guards and out a side door. The immense Cult leader seemed completely paralyzed now; suddenly his world was crashing down upon his gold-encrusted throne. The cream of his personal guard lay dead or dying all around him. He was unable to summon more help. The tremendous roar of explosions and panic was pouring in from outside.

His eyes went wide as the man in the black suit approached him with calm yet determined steps.

"Yushi-ma shmo shee-mashi!" Hashi Pushi bellowed. Loosely translated, it meant: "I was a turtle! Why?"

It was as if Hashi Pushi expected the man in black to have an answer. Instead, the man did something very strange. He reached into his belt, came up with a pistol, and threw it onto Hashi Pushi's ample lap.

"Kushi-ma Doshima," the man called to him in broken yet understandable Japanese. "You have the first shot."

The man then lowered his rifle and braced himself, to all minds waiting for Hashi Pushi to pick up the gun, aim it, and actually shoot at him.

But Hashi Pushi fooled them all.

The Cult leader did study the gun for a moment, and then turned to the man in black and smiled.

"Yakishi, muri-san do-ki-yimo," he said, his voice morbidly calm. "You have finally arrived. I thank you."

Then Hashi Pushi put the gun to his own cold temple and blew his brains out.

Part Two

The Great Wall

Fifteen

Aboard the USS Fitzgerald,
16 hours later

It was a night of celebration.

The carrier's large mid-deck hangar had been converted into a huge party room and was now packed with hundreds of crew members from all four ships of the Task Force. There was plenty of food, booze, and music. Backslapping and congratulatory handshakes abounded. The intoxicated chatter ranged from newly-elaborated war stories, to good-natured dirty jokes, to plans for when they all got home. In all, it was the relaxed, triumphant atmosphere that went with a job well done.

Operation Long Bomb was a complete success — of that there was no dispute. Hashi Pushi was dead, killed not by Hunter, but by his own hand. And with the head thus cut off the murderous snake, the huge mercenary army he commanded inside Japan would soon be in total disarray. Even more, the destruction of the Home Island's immense communications network would at the very least cause havoc among the rest of Hashi Pushi's far-flung legions.

Best of all, everyone from the TF Squadron had made it back from the airstrike alive and well.

So it seemed then that a celebration of sorts was definitely in order for everyone involved.

Everyone except Hunter.

He sat alone on the aft signal officer's platform deck, the metal extension which hung out over the side near the very end of the ship. High in the west, a bright and full hunter's moon lit up the sea and sky almost like daylight. The strains of music and conversation barely reached him from the ship's party below. But occasionally he would very clearly hear a spontaneous cheer of joy and relief. Sometimes those cheering would invoke his name.

But the music he heard was not coming from the party. Rather it was coming from inside his head. The mournful strains of the orchestra that had been playing when he had entered Hashi Pushi's throne room were still echoing in his ears. And he didn't know why.

He took a deep breath of night air and let it out slowly. Something was bothering him, something he couldn't quite put a finger on.

What was it?

Everything that could have been done was done, he told himself. Their mission had been a complete success. No loose ends, no cards unplayed. Hashi Pushi was dead, and it had been done in such a way that Hunter would be able to sleep peacefully again. The Cult was bereft of their long-range communications.

And though the *Fitz's* tiny air squadron was battered almost beyond recognition, all of the pilots had made it back in one piece.

Yet something wasn't ringing true, and *this* was what Hunter could feel. Deep in his inner psyche, a small vibration was telling him: *It is not yet over.*

"Hey, Hawk, my man . . ."

Hunter looked up to see Toomey weaving across the rolling flight deck toward him, a freshly-opened bottle of *sake* in his hand.

"What the hell are you doing out here, buddy? Everyone's looking for you."

He sat down next to Hunter and offered him the bottle. When Hunter declined, Toomey instantly went sober.

"What's eating you, pal? Shouldn't you be celebrating more than anyone else?"

Hunter just shrugged. "I'm not sure."

Toomey rolled his eyes and took another swig of the rice wine.

"I've seen this before," he half-laughed. "You think it went *too* easy. Is that it? Hey, Hawk — we kicked their butts. They know it. You know it. And soon *everyone* will know it. For once it was quick and easy. And I, for one, am damned glad it's over."

"But maybe it's *not* over," Hunter half-muttered.

Toomey was speechless for a moment, just long enough for Hunter to stand up and brush himself off.

"Where's Yaz?"

Toomey was up and standing beside him now. "Last I saw him, he was up in the CIC, writing out the detailed 'mission-accomplished' report to send back to the general. And when word gets out about this in D.C., *then* there'll be a party so big, I wish . . ."

But Hunter wasn't listening. He was sprinting back down the flight deck, heading for the carrier's island.

"Hey, Hawk, where the hell you going?" Toomey called after him.

Hunter never broke stride. "I've got to stop Yaz from sending that message," came the hurried reply.

Fifteen minutes later, Yaz and JT were on the bridge, nervously filling their inebriated bodies with thick black coffee.

Below them, Hunter's F-16XL was rising up from the hangar deck on elevator two. A skeleton flight deck crew was arming the Sidewinders and Sparrows under the 'XL's wing. An even smaller crew was filling the high-powered array of recon cameras in the airplane's nose with fresh videotape and film.

Yaz took a weary sip of the hot java.

"Jonesie isn't going to like this," he told Toomey. "We're already three hours late sending him the Mission Detail burst. He must be chewing on a whiskey bottle by this time."

"Better to have him wait than to send back a false message," Toomey replied. "Besides, he knows what it's like when Hawk thinks he's on to something."

"That's just it," Yaz said, worriedly. "Why is he going up at this hour? What's he looking for?"

"This may sound crazy," Toomey said, "but he told me he honestly doesn't know. He says he feels that something is not right, but he couldn't tell me just what that is. Hey, it may be nothing, but you know how he is. He'll go nuts unless he can check it out."

The pair watched in silence now as the deck crew finished preflight on the exotic F-16XL. The stillness of the bridge was punctuated only by the repetition of the three electronic bleeps coming from the sweep of the radar screen and indicating the *New Jersey* and the two accompanying supply ships.

Finally the deck crew finished and scattered to their assigned positions. Clouds of white mist began rising up from the deck's catapult channel, the distinct whooshing sound telling them that steam pressure was quickly rising beneath the airplane.

Then, with a wave and a salute from Hunter, the futuristic fighter plane rocketed off the deck and into the night.

"Damn," Yaz muttered under his breath, watching the tail lights of the 'XL climb nearly straight up. "For his sake, I hope he finds something."

"For our sake," JT replied, "I hope he doesn't."

Hunter brought the F-16XL back to 80 percent of full power and leveled off at 20,000 feet.

Now what? he thought.

He wasn't quite sure where he was going; all he knew was that he didn't have much time.

Hunter also knew the choice of which direction to take would not be a logical one. The reason? This was not a logical mission. This whole thing was being flown on little more than a premonition. A feeling deep in the gut.

How do I get there?

To find out, he knew he would have to go blank, to suspend his intellectual faculties and tap into the deep psychic river that coursed through him. He would have to attempt to reach the state of mind that he thought of simply as *the feeling.*

This was his most precious gift, this mindset that could infallibly clue him in on what was about to happen in the future—either minutes or seconds before, or sometimes hours or even days. *The feeling.* Was there a better name for it? Was it some kind of super-ESP? Some kind of ultra-clairvoyance? Divine intervention? Predestination? Synchronicity?

Or was it all just incredible dumb luck?

He didn't know. He'd been studied, tested, poked at. Some of the behavioral scientists doing the poking tried to describe his extraordinary ESP talents as normal electrical/neurological impulses that were simply miscoded or misdirected. Purely a "chemical" reaction, they would say.

But Hunter knew that this, just like many other equally vague explanations, never even came close to reality. Misdirected neurological impulses be damned—whatever it was, it had saved his life and soul too many times for anything to be *misdirected* about it.

He'd experimented many times on his own, trying to tap deeper into this psychic pool in order to understand it better. For if he did, he believed, it would be possible for him to realize its full potential.

And now was the ideal time to try once again, to let the otherworldly current take him along to a destination that only it knew—and do it at close to the speed of sound.

He took a deep gulp of oxygen from his mask and patted the American flag he always kept folded in his breast pocket. Then, with a surge of both excitement and trepidation, he began shutting down the 'XL's flight systems. Off went his radio, the early warning radar, the CRT displays, the HUD, and all the other noncrucial avionic displays in his cockpit. He wanted nothing to distract him as he prepared himself for a descent into deep meditation.

Lightly holding the side stick controller as one would do with the disc of a ouija board, he took ten deep breaths, letting each one out with slow precision. Immediately he felt his pulse rate drop. His breathing continued to become deeper and clearer. A sudden calm came over him.

Then he closed his eyes.

Colors were suddenly floating past him, as if they were being holographically projected on the insides of his eyelids. Gradually they began to take shape, going from a blur to a sharp image. The first vision was of Dominique, as beautiful as ever, standing nearly naked on a deserted stretch of beautiful white sandy beach. The wind was flowing through her blond hair, the surf pounding all around her; she stood, her arms stretched out, wanting, aching to hold him.

At least she is alive . . .

Hunter suddenly felt the F-16XL lurch up. For a moment, he almost broke his concentration to follow his heart, as if putting the jet fighter into an interminable climb into the heavens would somehow bring him closer to her again. But he stopped himself just as quickly. That was not why he was here. Someday he would return to her. And then he would forever lose himself in her arms.

But that time is not now.

Eyes still closed, he concentrated once again on his breathing, taking long, slow gulps from his oxygen mask. He pushed his thoughts of Dominique away and forced himself deeper and deeper into the pure, Zenlike

143

state. More and more startling images began to float by: scenes from the battles that he'd fought. Faces of the enemies he'd defeated. The faces of his friends that had been lost: Bull . . . the pilot named Elvis . . . his old friend Fitz . . .

With each of these images, the 'XL beneath him would twist and turn in different directions, guided now not so much by electrons, wing flaps, and computers, but by his own psychic vibrations.

Hunter knew that this part of *the feeling* would pass; he'd learned long ago that he must first exorcise his past before he could see into the future. And no matter what pain it caused, he knew he must ride it out, taking himself further and further toward his goal.

Minutes went by. Events were flashing before him much faster now: the bizarre death of Hashi Pushi, the air strike against Japan, the victory celebration, his gloomy conversation with JT.

The closer his self-imaging got to the present, the more rapidly the pictures in his mind's eye flew by, and conversely, the more erratic the flight of his F-16 became.

Suddenly, he "saw" a great burst of blinding white light. He imagined his brain was about to explode into a million incredibly thin laser beams, each point streaking out in a separate direction. But in the next sensation he felt these points of light suddenly reverse direction and begin racing backward, toward him, toward the center of his brain.

Then everything was calm again. A greater spiritual peace descended upon him. In the distance, he could "hear" a rhythmic pounding of machines. The mechanical racket got louder and louder as more ghostly images began to gently float before him. A laughing old woman with long white hair. Her corncob pipe. Human skulls on posts. Empty uniforms. Smoke in the air. Airplanes of a vague and indeterminable design.

Last, he saw three lightning bolts: the first two flashed out in the center of a rainstorm. The third appeared in the midst of a beautifully clear day.

What the hell does all this mean?

Try as he might, Hunter just couldn't make sense of any of the visions. What was his inner being trying to tell him? The predestined images seemed to be both soothing *and* frightening to him, a sensation he'd never experienced before.

It was only then that he realized the F-16XL was finally flying a true and stable course, his light, almost-disembodied touch on the right-side control stick making slight adjustments in altitude and speed. He was tempted to open his eyes and do a quick check of his crucial instruments — but in an instant he knew he didn't need to. He could *feel* that he was now on a true course with his destination.

A moment later, a surge of adrenaline raced through him. This was what he was waiting for, a reaction he'd felt before. Many times. It gave him his strength for whatever lay ahead, both mentally and physically. It was a wake-up call from the cosmos.

I'm ready . . .

Now it was time for him to open his eyes.

The sun was just coming up over the far eastern horizon.

Using this early light, he scanned the ocean below

and spotted a large island thirty miles away to the southwest. Flipping back on all his avionics, he commanded his computer to run up built-in memory navigation charts that matched the sea below and then asked it to ID the island.

The answer came back a few seconds later: *Okinawa*.

Sixteen

Aboard the USS Fitzgerald

Yaz sat on the bridge, staring out over the vast gray expanse of the Pacific Ocean.

It was now dawn, and the day had begun dreary and overcast. A half mile off to starboard, the two supply ships were keeping an even pace with the huge aircraft carrier, their bows plowing steadily through the increasingly-choppy seas. Far off to port, the outline of the USS *New Jersey* was barely visible. Typically, Wolf had the great ship on a course as isolated from the rest of the Task Force as tactically possible.

Far off to the northeast, he saw the beginnings of a storm system forming. A thin, dark line of angry clouds stretched almost across the horizon, the billowing winds making them look like a huge tidal wave heading toward the four ships in eerie slow motion.

"Not even the damn weather will cooperate," Yaz thought gloomily.

The Task Force was steaming due east, back toward United America. But per Yaz's latest orders, they were moving at a miserly pace of five knots, barely one-quarter as fast as its normal cruising speed. He knew this did not sit well with his crews. They were all understandably in a hurry to return home in one piece. Any delay could only mean trouble.

Yet there was only one reason why Yaz had given the order to cut back on the Task Force's speed: Hawk Hunter was still out there somewhere. And he would soon be overdue.

As he continued to stare at the storm clouds to the north, Yaz slumped further down into the captain's chair. His shoulders were feeling especially heavy now. He had not heard a word from Hunter since his sudden and unscheduled departure several hours before. All attempts to raise him on the radio proved futile, and there was no indication of the 'XL anywhere on the long-range radar screens. It was as if pilot and plane had simply vanished.

It was quickly becoming a question of time and numbers. The Task Force had to keep moving simply to keep up its defenses against attack, and it didn't have the fuel to waste to go in any other direction except toward friendlier waters. Yet Yaz knew that if he maintained his current speed and course, Hunter would be out of fuel range of the carrier in little more than an hour. Then Yaz would have to balance the concerns for his close friend Hawk Hunter against the safety of the hundreds of men onboard the ships of the Task Force.

He knew it wasn't going to be a pleasant decision.

Wearily he began to massage his temples — besides the situation with Hunter, there was another troubling factor weighing heavily on his mind.

This one was a mystery. Even though Hashi Pushi

was dead and the vast Asian Mercenary Cult's homeland communications network beheaded, the Task Force's radio net had failed to pick up any signals that would indicate a reaction by the enemy on any scale. The attack on Japan was already a day old. Surely the commanders of the overseas Cult troops would have learned the bad news from the Home Islands by this time. Such a disastrous turn of events should have lit up what was left of the Cult's communications network hours ago. But there had been absolutely no loose radio traffic from the enemy whatsoever. No coded messages, no distress calls, not even a panicky Mayday message from what was left of devastated Tokyo. If the Cult's command structure was distressed over their leader's death, they were keeping it a mighty tight secret.

And that just didn't make sense.

What was also making Yaz more than a little nervous was his promise to Hunter about not making contact with their commander-in-chief, General David Jones. Yaz did not like keeping his boss in the dark almost as much as he was sure General Jones did not like being cut off from receiving a full report of the Task Force's successful mission. In fact, at this point, Yaz knew that his actions almost bordered on insubordination. Yet he'd made a promise to Hunter, and he would stick by it — at least for now.

He shifted uneasily in his captain's chair. Suddenly it seemed way too big for him.

And now, more trouble was on its way.

At that moment, the weather officer hastily came on the bridge.

"I've just got the latest condition update, sir," the

young ensign told Yaz with a quick salute. "I thought you'd better look at it right away."

Yaz sat up straight in his chair.

"Okay, let's have it," he said firmly.

The young officer took a deep breath. "Sir, we've had a substantial rise in the barometer over the last hour. It's been combined with a dramatic temperature flux. Wind speed has picked up ten knots in the last five minutes alone and is continuing to rise. There is a large high pressure area moving in from the north, and . . ."

Yaz held up his hand, interrupting the man.

"Please translate, ensign," he said.

"In a nutshell, sir — if the weather conditions to our northeast continue to develop as they have, we might have a typhoon condition."

Yaz was stunned. He looked back out to the northeast: the approaching storm clouds appeared even angrier than last time. "My God, are you saying that's a *typhoon* out there?"

The ensign already had a sea chart pulled out.

"It's an eighty-five-percent possibility, sir," he began. "It's one hundred percent that we will run into increasingly rough weather very soon. Much worse than on the trip out. If the typhoon develops, it will be at its peak right in this area, at our present position. The good news is that it won't be here for another three to five hours. Six, tops. So if we were to increase our speed to twenty knots, we should be safely out of the way of the worst of it. We'll have substantial rain and wind, and the sea will be high. But we won't take the full punch."

Yaz's head was now pounding like a steam piston. His main problem had just been compounded. To speed up now would certainly ensure that Hunter

150

would never make it back to the ship. Yet not to increase speed would surely endanger the lives of the crews of the Task Force.

Yet Yaz surprised himself by making a quick decision.

"Pass the weather advisory to the rest of the ships," he told the ensign calmly. "And inform them they'd better batten down the hatches. We will be maintaining our present course and speed until further orders."

Seventeen

Okinawa was one of the last in the chain of Japanese mainland islands.

Relatively small, it was thin and crooked and surrounded by many other smaller islands. At the moment, its center seemed to be wrapped in a thick fog.

Hunter had been circling at 70,000 feet twenty miles north of the island for the last two hours. The high orbit not only kept him off any radar screens, it also allowed him to conserve fuel while waiting for dawn to come. He'd done a lot of thinking in that time—but he'd yet to come up with an answer to the most important question: Why had his mysterious instincts compelled him to come to this place?

He just didn't know. But now, with the eastern horizon brightening, so, too, came the light he needed to do a proper recon of the island. Maybe then he would learn why *the feeling* had brought him here.

He did a quick check of his flight systems and nose cameras. Everything came back green. He checked his weapons; everything was prearmed and ready. He took a deep breath of pure oxygen and felt the smaller resultant rush in his bloodstream.

"Time to get to work," he thought soberly.

With that, he booted his afterburner up to full military power and put the 'XL into a screaming dive. Down he went, his futuristic airplane almost blurring from view as its velocity increased in vast geometric proportions. Only when the jet was 200 feet above the water's surface did the frightening supersonic plunge end. At that split second, Hunter pulled up on the side-stick controller and evenly leveled off to an altitude of exactly fifty-five feet. It was a maneuver so violent, it would have blacked out the best of fighter pilots. For Hunter, it had barely caused him to blink.

Now down low, under any known radar levels, he lined his tail up with the ball of the rising sun and headed west, toward the mist-enshrouded island.

Yet no sooner had he turned toward the island than his inner psyche began buzzing.

Something was wrong.

He suddenly detected small splashes in the water around and ahead of his airplane. At first, he thought it might be hostile fire from the coast now just five miles away. But he saw no smoke or any other activity coming from the island that would indicate hostile fire. Still the small splashes continued. He scanned the control panel once more, looking for any hint to explain this odd phenomenon.

That's when a glint of a metallic reflection high above him caught his eye. Twisting around to see behind him, Hunter was uncharacteristically stunned.

"Jesus, what the hell is that?"

In an instant he had pulled back hard on the stick

153

and booted in his afterburner. A second later, he was screaming straight up at full military power.

It took him just two seconds to appraise the situation. Right above him, at about 1500 feet, there was a pack of airborne unfriendlies. All of them were diving toward him, guns blazing in his direction. Yet it was no longer a mystery that his threat-warning radar had failed to alert him: these aircraft were incapable of shooting any kind of sophisticated weapons that would be picked up on the device. In fact, he knew that aircraft like these hadn't seen combat since the days of World War Two. And that in itself was astonishing. The enemy airplanes were Mitsubishi A6Ms, the airplane once called the "Zero."

As he streaked up toward them, Hunter took another two seconds to wonder why his ESP warning system failed to alert him to the flying museum pieces until the very last moment. Had he been dealing with enemy jets so long that he hadn't needed to tune in with anything built to fly before 1945?

He didn't know.

Maybe I'm still in the dream . . . he thought.

But now he had a more immediate concern. The ancient airplanes had initiated hostile action against him. He had to answer it in turn. With a flick of his finger he armed his nose cannons. An instant later, the climbing F-16's snout erupted in a fusillade of vicious fire.

Panicking now, the mysterious green-gray Zeros scattered. Diving, climbing, twisting, turning, they began moving completely independently of each other, abandoning any pretense of group battle tactic.

Within seconds it was every man for himself. That suited Hunter just fine.

His first salvo ripped through the brushed aluminum underbellies of two Zeros. Before the pilots could appreciate how Hunter had come up underneath them so fast, their planes exploded into balls of shredded flaming metal. A third Zero was unlucky enough to pass in front of Hunter's crosshairs; he never knew what hit him. Hunter's cannons sliced through the old propeller-driven airplane like a welder's torch, cutting it in two.

Hunter quickly pulled level a thousand feet above the sudden action and surveyed the situation. There were four Zeros remaining and they were weakly attempting to regroup. He couldn't allow it.

He put the XL into a shallow dive, streaking right through the middle of their hastily reassembled formation. Two more Zeros were dispatched by Sidewinders. Fired nearly simultaneously, their heat-seeking nose-cones were barely able to key in on enough engine warmth to make the kill. Once hit, though, the Zeros simply disintegrated, their near-microscopic remains leaving thousands of smoking trails behind as they fluttered toward the surface of the sea below.

Five down, two to go, he told himself. *This might be too easy.*

He was right. The two remaining Zeros suddenly split up. One streaked northward, the other to the southwest. Hunter had no choice but to go after the Zero closest to him, the one heading away from Okinawa.

155

The piston-driven engine of the Zero was hardly a match for Hunter's turbofan, and he was up on the Zero's tail in no time. He was amazed to see the outstanding condition of the Zero. Obviously this was not a reconditioned aircraft—rather, it appeared to be brand new. This twist only added to the mystery surrounding the sudden appearance of the fabled World War Two airplanes.

Hunter was now merely 500 feet behind the aircraft, in perfect position for a cannon shot. But he did not fire—a vibration deep within his psyche told him that destroying the airplane and killing the pilot would not help his true mission here. What he needed was information.

Throttling back, he rapidly decreased his speed to match that of the fleeing Zero. Then he pulled right up alongside the legendary warplane. Something was telling him that he needed to get a good look at this pilot and to see just who was attacking him.

The pilot of the Zero was dressed in an authentic leather flight suit, with headgear to match. Glancing over at Hunter, he suddenly broke into a wide smile. Hunter didn't smile back. But he was not prepared for what happened next.

Calmly, the Zero pilot drew a pistol from his side holster and placed the barrel against his temple. Never losing his eerie grin, he squeezed the trigger and sent a slug crashing through his skull.

Instantly the inside of the Zero's cockpit was splattered with blood. Hunter watched in utter astonishment as the airplane nosed forward and went into a flat, winding spin. It finally struck the water and disintegrated in a ball of smoke and flame.

Hunter took a long, deep breath. A distinctly unnerving chill went through him. The psychic warning had been correct. Witnessing the suicide of the Zero pilot had certainly given him a quick, grisly lesson on who he was dealing with.

Now he quickly turned his attention to the last Zero. Within seconds, his incredible vision located the airplane just as it was making landfall at Okinawa. At that moment, his bingo warning light snapped on: he was now critically low on fuel. Yet his inner vibes were telling him that locating the mysterious Zeros' base was suddenly very important. And following the last Zero was his only hope of doing that.

Swinging the 'XL around to the west, he once again hid himself in the direct rays of the rising sun.

Then, still shaken by the sudden, violently self-inflicted death of the smiling Zero pilot, he grimly increased the F-16's speed and headed straight for the heart of Okinawa.

Lieutenant Fatungi was still shaking.

Never before had he made the treacherous landing directly into the mouth of the cave on the first attempt. There always had been, at the very least, one fly-by to make sure that the landing crew had properly drawn back the enormous camouflage netting that covered the cave opening, as well as check the area's unpredictable air currents and poor visibility. But this time he did not have the luxury of checking anything.

There was simply no time. If the strange-looking jet had caught him out in the open, he would have died.

Thus, Lieutenant Fatungi's brief radio message to the secret base moments before had been clear: "You must open the netting immediately and you must close it immediately behind me."

As it turned out, the landing crew had performed flawlessly. No sooner had Fatungi flown his Zero through the cavernous 200-foot-wide opening than the 55-man crew had the netting closed. Just seconds later, the pursuing jet roared right over the covered opening. The landing crew watched with amusement for the next two minutes as the seemingly-confused enemy pilot searched the smoke-obscured valley floor below them, vainly looking for an airfield that was right under his nose.

When the strange jet finally went away, Lieutenant Fatungi breathed a long sigh of relief. At last he was certain that making such a hasty landing had been the correct tactical decision.

Rather than fighting to the last man in what was most surely a one-sided battle, Fatungi had made the decision to return to the secret mountainside base and make a full report, hoping that the information he would supply on the strange jet would please his superiors. Now, as he climbed down the built-in steps of his prop fighter, he was met by his commanding officer. Half-expecting a compliment on his superb landing, Fatungi was stunned when the officer slapped him hard across the face with his pair of leather dress gloves.

"You have disgraced us all!" the officer screamed at

him, before turning on his heels and casually strolling away. As he passed by his personal guard, two of the soldiers came forward and took Fatungi into custody.

Relieving him of his personal sidearm and short symbolic *samurai* sword, the two soldiers began marching Fatungi toward the lower passageway that led deeper into the cave, their razor-sharp bayonets prodding him along. As Fatungi shuffled past the fellow members of his flying squadron, not one of them would look him in the eye. These pilots were the men with whom he had spent the last five years of his life, training together in the most rigorous conditions. They had shared among them their most personal secrets, their food, their *sake*. Now each one turned away from him, disgraced by the dishonor he had placed upon them and their unit.

Oddly it was only then that Lieutenant Fatungi knew without any doubt that he had made the *wrong* decision. In the world of the Asian Mercenary Cult, misguided honor *was* more important than solid battlefield intelligence.

As the guards marched Fatungi deeper and deeper down the twisting and turning passageways, the disgraced pilot had to summon what little strength he had left to keep from vomiting out of sheer terror. No one brought to the lower compartments of the secret mountain base ever returned alive. Fatungi was certain that this too would be his fate.

After twenty minutes, they finally reached the end of what Fatungi supposed was the base's deepest passageway. Before them were two massive oak doors, each with obscured numbers carved into them. Fa-

159

tungi's breeches were soaked with urine by this time, so great was his terror. He was sure he had only seconds to live.

But then he got a surprise. After knocking twice, the two guards quickly left, leaving Fatungi alone. Oddly, he could smell something cooking on the other side of the massive doors.

Then he heard a woman's voice call out: "Come in, please."

Totally confused, Fatungi opened the oak doors and was astonished to find not a vast death chamber but a spare, well-lit, elaborately-appointed apartment. A young woman in a sheer silk dressing gown was standing in the middle of the room, smiling and bowing to him.

She was beautiful. Small, with delicate features, she had the most amazing long red hair.

Fatungi was suddenly very embarrassed about his soiled pants.

"Please don't worry about that," she reassured him. "I understand it happens to everyone. Please take off your clothes. I have just arrived here myself, but I think I have something over here you can wear."

The woman walked over to a small closet and retrieved a man's red silk dressing gown. Walking back toward Fatungi, she stopped briefly in front of a small shrine. In the center of this flower-laden altar was a tiny photograph of someone Fatungi could not make out.

The woman bowed twice and then stared for a long time at the photograph, seemingly caught by the stare of the eyes of its subject.

Meanwhile, Fatungi had quickly stripped off his clothes and was now standing totally naked. Though he was still baffled by the sudden turn of events, his appreciation of the woman's beauty, hinted at through her sheer silken dressing grown, was becoming more and more apparent.

The woman knelt briefly, then rose from the altar and turned toward Fatungi. This time there was a faraway look in her eyes.

"I hope you don't mind the smell," she said, motioning toward a small portable stove. "I'm cooking a small meal. Will you join me in dinner? Do you like liver?"

Fatungi was terribly confused now. Dinner? Liver? But he was smart enough to say yes.

Or so he thought.

The woman smiled, beckoning the naked pilot toward her. With that, she pulled a long, razor-sharp carving knife from her gown and plunged it deep into Fatungi, just above his pubic bone. Lifting it up through his stomach, and then all the way up to his ribcage, she had expertly gutted him before he even realized what was happening.

"Bon appetit," she hissed in his ear.

Eighteen

Washington, D.C.

The young officer hesitated once before knocking twice on the door simply marked "Commander."

"Come on in," came the casual reply.

The officer went in and found General Jones behind his desk as usual, buried in paperwork.

"Got a very unusual message from Task Force, sir," the officer said. "It's been decoded, checked, and double-checked. It's legit. It's got to be . . ."

Jones looked up over the piles of documents, his well-chewed unlit pipe in his teeth. "Well, what's it say?"

The young officer bit his lip for a second.

"It says they've stopped," he told Jones.

Jones's glasses nearly fell off his face. "They've stopped? Stopped for what?"

The officer passed the yellow cable paper to the commander in chief.

It read: "URGENT . . . REQUEST THAT ALL MEMBERS OF THE TASK FORCE COME TO AN

IMMEDIATE STOP. ALL CAPTAINS TO MEET ON USS *FITZGERALD* IN THIRTY MINUTES."

General David Jones dropped the intercepted radio message on the desk and then looked up at the officer.

"What the hell is going on out there?" he asked.

The small boat was being violently tossed in the swelling fifteen-foot seas.

Wolf stood in the prow of the launch, his black cape snapping behind him, sea spray soaking his mask. Off in the distance, he could make out the launches of the two accompanying supply ships, the USS *Cohen* and the USS *Tennyson*, making headway through the rough water toward the *Fitzgerald*.

The choppy seas and the howling wind made the trip to the aircraft carrier a twenty-minute affair. Finally arriving, Wolf alighted onto the carrier's bow access ramp, where two of the *Fitzgerald*'s staff officers were waiting for him. They escorted him through the various decks and up to a small conference room located next to the carrier's Combat Information Center.

The captains of the *Cohen* and *Tennyson* were already present when Wolf walked in, as were Yaz, Toomey, and Ben Wa. The weariness of the past mission and the critical nature of the present situation were apparent on all their faces. Wolf knew they wondered if the same was true with him. Was his face as worried and lined with concern as theirs? But he was also confident that none of them had a clue as to what was going on behind his mask. And no one would dare ask. That was the whole point of his strange garb.

Wolf took a seat and politely refused a cup of coffee. That's when Yaz stood up, a prepared set of notes in hand.

"Gentlemen," he began, "I appreciate your efforts in coming aboard on such a short notice and under these conditions. However, I felt that this matter was so grave we had to handle it face-to-face. In light of the impending storm, I will be brief.

"As you know, Hunter left on a reconnaissance flight last night. He has not returned. He hasn't responded to any radio signals, and he has not been spotted on any of our long-range radar screens.

"I've kept the Task Force almost at a dead crawl for the past few hours, and finally ordered it to stop approximately one hour ago. I gave these orders simply hoping that Hunter would catch up with us — but that hasn't happened. Frankly, gentlemen, I fear the worst."

No one stirred. Although everyone in the room was aware of the situation, it was still grim to hear it presented in such a sobering way.

"As commander of this Task Force," Yaz continued, "my obligations are clear. My orders call for the speediest, safest return of our men and these ships to friendly waters. But . . ."

Suddenly Yaz's voice began to crack. Still he pressed on.

"But . . . I am also Hawk's friend. I know what he'd do if it were me still out there."

Yaz cleared his throat; his voice was close to breaking completely. "The USS *Fitzgerald* will remain at these coordinates for another two hours. That will be ninety minutes past Hunter's fuel range. If the current climatic conditions persist, that will also put us directly in the path of the approaching typhoon.

"I fully understand the obligations you men have to your ships and crew. Therefore, I am ordering you to continue on course, at full speed."

At that moment, Wolf stood up.

"Captain," he said in a deep Norse accent, "I refuse."

Yaz stared at the imposing costumed figure for a moment. "There's not really a question to this," he told him. "The safety of your crew is . . ."

"My crew agrees with me," Wolf interrupted. "They know, as I do, that should Hunter make it back to the vicinity of our present position and have to ditch, it is very unlikely that you could retrieve him. On the other hand, we have many launches and other lifesaving means. It would increase Hunter's chances of survival dramatically."

Before Yaz could say another word, the captains of the *Cohen* and *Tennyson* also stood.

"We will wait, too," the top officer of the *Tennyson* said, speaking for the both of them. "Everyone aboard our ships owes something to Hunter somewhere along the line. There's no way we're going to leave when there's still a chance he'll make it back."

Yaz felt as if the lump in his throat had swelled to the size of a basketball.

"As you wish, gentlemen," was just about all he could say. "And thank you . . ."

At that moment, the carrier did a deep roll, a fair indication that the storm outside was growing even worse.

"You'd best be getting back to your ships," Yaz told them.

At that moment, there was a quick rap at the door and a midshipman hastily stepped inside. He walked quickly over to Yaz.

"Excuse me, sir," he said, his voice slightly betraying a tone of hope. "You're needed on the bridge. Radar reports something is heading this way."

Nineteen

Hunter was out of gas.

His fuel gauge had blinked empty about twenty minutes before; the 'XLs on-board emergency flight-maintain systems had been clicking off one by one ever since.

He wasn't so much flying now as gliding. Shortly after his quick recon of Okinawa, he'd climbed to a eye-watering 82,000 feet, beyond what would normally be considered safe operating parameters for the F-16XL. This forty-five-second ascent had burned up about two-thirds of his remaining fuel, but he knew it was a necessary expenditure of what was his most vital resource. He was so far away from the *Fitzgerald* his only hope was to get as high as possible as quickly as possible. After that the only question would be whether the wind currents and his piloting ability were enough to get him at least close to the Task Force.

He knew it was a long shot at best—one of the longest he'd ever faced. Piloting a shot-up airplane was a snap compared to trying to coax one home on an empty fuel tank. After all, there was only so far you could go.

Finding the carrier was not a problem. In fact, he knew exactly where the *Fitzgerald* was. Before snapping off, his radar had picked up the carrier and the three other Task Force ships right where he'd hoped they'd be: at his absolute bingo point. The fact that they had waited for him caused a proud ringing in his heart, and to his lips came the line from an old, sad sweet song.

"You did not desert me, my brothers in arms," he thought.

But though in many ways they were endangering their lives just to save his, even under the best of circumstances, reaching the carrier was not even his biggest problem. Setting down in one piece would be. He was flying completely unpowered—one shot at a landing was all he would have. There'd be no opportunity to bolt, fly around, and try again. If he was off by one fraction of a degree, he'd wind up bouncing the 'XL off the deck. Then he'd have to do a split-second eject and his beloved plane would end up lying on the ocean floor. And maybe him along with it.

Still, it wasn't all doom and gloom. After all, there was that typhoon brewing below him.

Hunter had been wrestling the sidestick with both hands for the past ten minutes. Every warning buzzer and light was going off on his display. But then he finally began to feel the tug of the typhoon's swirling winds. Now came the biggest part of his dangerous, yet simple plan. With nothing but momentum and glide power, he had little choice but to get sucked up into the maelstrom, using the ferocity of its winds to propel him forward and downward and, hopefully, toward the Task Force's current position.

He entered the vortex and was now flying blind — his visibility was absolute zero. The black clouds around him made it seem like night, and the torrents of rain only added to the unnerving descent into darkness. Buffeted by severe gusts of wind, the 'XL was rattling from every bolt and screw as it spiraled downward into the angry 100-mile-wide swirl.

Hunter was too busy fighting the controls to be more than passingly concerned about his situation. Yet he couldn't help but notice that the angry swirl of the typhoon looked exactly like a black hole, sucking up everything in sight and hurling it into the abyss. This made him think of a graduate thesis a friend had written back in his school days at MIT; it had advanced the notion that at the seemingly-bottomless end of an authentic black hole lay Hell itself.

I wonder if he was right, he thought.

Down he plummeted, almost straight down, losing altitude at a rate of a thousand feet every few seconds. He was falling so fast into the darkness he felt almost weightless. The plane was almost totally out of power. His cockpit displays were all but extinguished. His altimeter clicked off at 38,000 feet; his airspeed indicator died at 35,000. And still, he could see nothing below him but thick, black, swirling clouds.

By 28,000 feet he was down to one last auxilliary generator which was producing just enough electricity to keep the control stick operating and little else. Oddly, the twin cameras in his nose clicked on at 24,500, their self-contained microprocessors ordering them to run off the last of their film and video and then shut down completely.

Hunter smiled ruefully at this last bit of electrical glitch theater. Not many pilots were lucky enough to have what could be their final plunge caught by the movie cameras.

When he passed through 19,000 feet, only the cameras, his radar, and what was left of the control stick functions were working. He stripped off his oxygen mask; no matter what happened, there was enough air inside the cockpit for the last few seconds of this flight.

Besides, what he needed now wasn't air; it was light.

It was readily apparent as he passed down through 15,000 feet that he would need more than a little luck to pull off this stunt. The blurred and fading images of the carrier on his lookdown radar weren't so good—they showed the large target riding about ten miles south from the wall of the storm, but the exact location was far from precise. Yet the same black clouds that were enveloping him were also blanketing the carrier in almost total darkness. In order to eye it in, Hunter needed at least a momentary glimpse of the flattop; only then could he put the near-lifeless 'XL on its proper glide path.

Suddenly, there was a tremendous crack of lightning, the mother of all thunderbolts. It lit up the sky with an intensity brighter than the brightest daylight. The initial flash nearly blinded the Wingman — but he recovered quickly, and for a couple of seconds he was able to see the carrier quite clearly. It was practically below him, maybe a mile or two to the east.

He had only enough time to make one last adjustment with the stick, altering his direction by just a few degrees. He was now lined up with the flight deck center line. The carrier was lit up to the maximum, as were the three ships around it. Brightest of all was the amber light on the bow of the *Fitzgerald,* the so-called Meatball. It looked good to Hunter, not too high and not too low — but it was much too late to be delicate about this. He was coming down toward the deck too hard and too fast for him to use the Meatball to any effect.

He took a deep breath and patted his breast pocket.

At least it will be interesting, he thought ruefully.

Five seconds later, the F-16XL hit the *Fitz's* deck at approximately 175 miles per hour. Just as it touched down, the carrier pitched forward, its prow dropping thirty feet between two big rollers. Hunter's tail hook missed the first, second, and then third arresting wires. He had to decide in less than a split second whether to put his nose down to catch the fourth and last arresting wire, or hope that the ship came back up to catch him. If he timed it wrong, he would slam into the rising deck, or worse, miss entirely and go off into the sea. Hunter decided

171

to gamble—he pushed down on the stick and literally slammed on the brakes.

His tail hook caught the fourth wire and he was yanked to a halt within 350 feet. It was all over in less than two seconds.

A flight deck crew member instinctively signaled Hunter to cut power and Hunter just smiled. "What power?" he yelled back.

Dozens of deckhands appeared on the rolling, windswept deck and with sheer manpower steered the 'XL to the flight elevator. Hunter rode it down to the hangar deck. Waiting there for him were Yaz, JT, and Ben. Despite their brave faces, Hunter could not help but see the evident relief in their eyes.

"Welcome back, Major Hunter," Yaz told him, finally breaking into a wide grin. "I hope you aren't planning to make this sort of thing a habit. . . ."

Twenty

Okinawa

The woman with the cherry blossom hair had spent the last few hours lying on the floor of her subterranean living chamber, sensuously licking the blood off the long-bladed carving knife.

Now she finally gathered herself up to her knees and lit a candle from one of the dozens already burning around the photograph of Hashi Pushi. Then she dutifully placed the gleaming, clean knife back on the shrine, took two steps back, closed her eyes, and bowed.

"You have done well, my child," a voice whispered from behind her left ear. *"I am very proud of you."*

The woman bowed even lower.

"We must now join together again."

She felt her face flush.

"Lie back, my dear. Reveal yourself . . ."

Following the eerie whispered commands, the woman slowly lay back, her silk gown bunching up around her waist.

"Lift up your knees, my darling . . ."

She obeyed and felt her eyes go up into her head.

A rhythmic low roar now filled her ears, like that of the ocean surf washing up on a beach. Suddenly it seemed as if the water was upon her, crashing on top of her. Soaking her. *Cleansing* her.

Though her eyes were shut tight, she imagined she saw herself lying on a deserted beach. A bright sun was rising before her; it slowly began to burn her flesh. Inside her, the woman felt a welling-up of emotions, emotions impossible to describe, ones that shook her very being.

The surf began to sound louder and louder now, pounding her harder onto the beach. The waves were frothing and swirling around her, each wave receding and then returning upon itself, each growing bigger and louder and more powerful than the last. The heat of the sun was becoming both intolerable and pleasurable. The frequency of the waves suddenly increased and she felt the sun roast her flesh. She knew there could be no turning back now. Faster and faster, harder and harder, hotter and hotter, she felt it all until she could stand it no more . . .

Then she felt her body suddenly stiffen — as if a lightning bolt went through her. And then the beach and the waves and the sun were gone. Now she saw only the two eyes, the two beautiful, mystifying, captivating eyes drawing nearer to her. Did they belong to Hashi Pushi? She couldn't tell. She began to lose consciousness once again, hearing only the strange voice saying *"We are one . . ."*

Then it was over.

She opened her eyes to find herself once again lying on the floor.

She lay prone for several minutes as the last of the strange experience drained out of her. Slowly, reality began to creep back in. Her head began to hurt, her body began to ache. She looked around the large living chamber and through bleary eyes began to recognize certain things: a painting, the vase of flowers, the simple bed and stove. The shrine.

"It's so cold in here," she thought, wrapping her arms around her waist. That's when she realized that her hands and gown were covered with a sticky red substance.

Then she turned and saw the lifeless body of Lieutenant Fatungi on the floor next to her.

"What is happening to me?" she screamed.

Her cry brought three guards immediately into her chamber. She stared at them for a long time, and they back at her. Gradually, they too began to look familiar to her.

"Please," she whispered in horror, pointing at the naked, gutted body. "Please get it out of here."

The guards obediently dragged the corpse out of her quarters, closing the heavy oak doors behind them.

Hysterical now with fear and confusion, the woman took a sheet off her bed, got down on her hands and knees, and used it to scrub every last trace of blood off the floor. Then she retreated to her bed and pulled the remaining silk sheets over her trembling body.

I remember when my name was Mizumi . . . she thought. Then she softly cried herself to sleep.

Twenty-one

Aboard the Fitzgerald

"The one good thing about that long flight home," Hawk Hunter was saying, "is that I had plenty of time to think about what I saw. And I'm afraid it's all going to be very bad news for us."

He was speaking to a small audience of six men gathered around the large table in the conference room next to the *Fitzgerald's* CIC. Yaz was sitting at the far end, drinking coffee nonstop. To his left sat Toomey and Ben Wa, to his right Wolf and the captains of the *Tennyson* and the *Cohen*. Everyone looked decidedly concerned—even Wolf, despite his imposing comic-book-style mask.

"First of all," Hunter said, slipping the videotape of his flight into the room's VCR unit, "when I finally got where I was going, I met up with some very interesting characters."

He hit the VCR's PLAY button. Within seconds the six men were riveted to the screen as Hunter's bizarre dogfight off of cloud-enshrouded Okinawa played out. There was no need for Hunter to narrate the sequence; it was plain as day that he was in air-to-air combat with World War Two vintage fighters, and that they were no match for his F-16XL.

Hunter froze the tape just after the Zero pilot shot himself. His audience was astonished, to say the least.

Ben Wa was the first to speak. "Are those really *Zeros?*" he asked. "Who the hell would be flying those relics these days? And why?"

"I don't know," Hunter replied. "But keep watching."

Hunter started the tape again, picking up with his pursuit of the last Zero and culminating with one long, extremely high pass he made over the mist-covered island.

"Where the hell did the Zero go?" the captain of the *Cohen* asked. "Even with all that fog, it looked like he just vanished into thin air."

"Close," Hunter said. "But I believe that just after he got down below the clouds he flew into an airfield hidden in the side of a mountain down there called Shuri."

"Sounds pretty elaborate," the captain of the *Tennyson* said.

Hunter smiled grimly. "We don't know the half of it," he said.

He quickly fast-forwarded the tape to a spot where the entire island was in view. Then he froze

177

the frame and punched up the infrared enhancement system on the console.

Suddenly the entire island was lit up in a deep shade of red. Again, each man was astonished. The intensity of the red colors could mean only one thing: there was a tremendous amount of heat being thrown off by the island's surface.

"My God," Yaz said. "What could possibly cause all that heat under those clouds?"

"There's only one possible explanation," Hunter said. "There has to be some kind of activity going on *inside* that mountain, as well as *under* the ground all around the island, something that is so intense, it allows this much heat to reach the surface."

"But what could it be?" Toomey asked. "A volcano?"

"We're not that lucky, I'm afraid," Hunter said gloomily. "Look at the pattern of those heat lines. They're not exactly random."

It was true. On closer examination it was apparent that the intensity of heat was actually centered in places: at both ends of the island, as well as in the fog-shrouded mountain valley where the Zero had disappeared. Ringing each heat center was a series of extremely bright red shapes that looked like small funnels.

"There has to be some kind of industrial activity going on underground all over the island," Hunter said. "And those aren't clouds or mist we're looking at. It's smoke, or more accurately, smog. Super-pollution. And it's being vented at all those funnel points which show up as the brightest red. They are, in fact, smokestacks."

A leaden silence descended on the small room.

"I'd say someone's building something on a grand scale inside and underneath that island," Hunter said in grim conclusion. "With all that heat and all that pollution, it can't be anything else."

"But building what?" Yaz asked.

"That's what we've got to find out," Hunter told them, turning back to the frozen heat frame of the island. "Whatever's going on, it obviously linked to those Zeros. The one that got away didn't disappear or crash. Let's look at that big mountain. It looks like it's got an old castle on top of it. Notice this dull hot spot on its side. I think that's the entrance to a hidden airstrip. They could cover it, but they couldn't prevent the heat from leaking out."

Again, those gathered were speechless.

"Whatever the hell is going on, I think we have to assume it has to do with what is left of Hashi Pushi's boys," Hunter said, measuring each word carefully. "And if that's the case, then I don't think we can really call our recent mission a success until we find out."

"How can that be done?" Wolf asked, speaking for the first time.

Hunter let out a long, troubled breath.

"It's simple, really," he said. "Even though it's

179

the last thing in the world that I want to do, I've got to go back there."

Two hours later, Hunter was strapping into the Harrier.

The conditions outside were improving as the center of the storm moved off to the south. Still the seas were very high and the winds were blowing at gale force. It was not exactly ideal flying weather.

But it would have to do. Hunter was in a hurry. He had barely taken the time to shower and jump into a fresh flight suit. He was still eating a sandwich as he was climbing into the jumpjet. The reason for all the rush was simple. Theoretically, the sooner he left for Okinawa, the sooner he would return to the *Fitzgerald*. Then, again in theory, the Task Force could continue on its way home.

But now, as Hunter began clicking on his cockpit displays, his instincts were telling him it wasn't going to be that easy.

The takeoff itself promised to be an adventure. The crosswinds on the flight deck were far too dangerous for any kind of normal launch, horizontal *or* vertical. So he had to improvise. His plan was to taxi out to the elevator platform and have it brought up about halfway to the deck level. Then he would do a close-to-true vertical ascent, using the leeward side of the carrier to protect him, if only momentarily, for the first crucial seconds of liftoff.

After he cleared the ship, however, it would be him against the storm-tossed elements.

As soon as all his critical systems came back green, he began the procedure to fire up the airplane's powerplant. The four-man service crew stepped back, covering their faces as the slowly accelerating turbine began to churn out twin clouds of jet exhaust.

Suddenly Hunter was aware of a fifth person waving at him from below the cockpit. It was Ben.

With a hand signal from Hunter, the service crew chief wheeled an access ladder up to the side of the Harrier and Ben climbed up. Hunter cut his engine back to standby, lowering the engine's volume enough so he could talk with his friend.

"Just dug some old information on Okinawa out of our computer," he said. "It's not too pretty."

"I don't expect it is," Hunter told him. "Let's hear it."

"Apparently even the people living around here think it's an extremely dangerous place to be these days," Ben said, reciting from computer printout. "Many people fled there after the Big War, and even before Hashi Pushi came to power. Businessmen. Bankers. Stockbrokers. Crazy men. They stole everyone's money and had to run. But some didn't get very far. They say they live in the jungles on Okinawa now. They say they've turned wild by now.

There are even a few reports of cannibalism, none confirmed."

Hunter stared at him for a moment, and then smiled grimly. Businessmen? *Cannibals?*

"I also hear it's a bad place to breathe these days," he said to Ben.

Ben had to grin back. "Can it get any crazier?"

Hunter shook his head. "Don't ask . . ."

They shook hands and Ben was quickly down the access ladder.

Suddenly Hunter felt the elevator moving upward. By the time it had raised to half level, he had eased the Harrier's throttle up almost to full power. The wind and rain were soon on him again. He felt the aircraft beneath him begin to strain. Then the elevator stopped. He took a deep breath, patted his chest once, and then let her go.

The Harrier exploded into the air, its engine blasting out on maximum downward thrust. No sooner was he past the carrier's deck when he was hit with a gust of wind that spun him around nearly a full 360 degrees. Vectoring the jet's thrust to reverse, Hunter pulled back on the stick and quickly elevated the nose of the jet up to 80 degrees, almost straight up. Then, just as quickly, he booted the vector thrust to full forward. The Harrier hung there for a long second, battered by the dying winds, drenched in the still-driving rain.

Then, slowly, it rose up into the blackened

clouds, back into the storm that had nearly killed him and at the same time saved his life.

Yaz was alone.

Everyone else had left the conference room an hour before—the various ship commanders back to their vessels, Toomey and Ben to check on the condition of their battered air squadron.

He was rewatching the tape of Hunter's flight over Okinawa, playing over and over the infrared image of the smoke-enshrouded island. The more he studied it, the more it looked like one big factory, belching heat and pollution, under the cover of natural flora.

We're not going home anytime soon, he thought gloomily.

After watching the Okinawa tape more than a dozen times, he was prepared to shut down the TV system when the tail end of the tape came onto the screen. This segment depicted Hunter's harrowing dive down through the typhoon, ending with the tremendous crack of thunder, which had also damaged the carrier's main antenna.

Yaz was fascinated by the footage—right up until the very end. But then, just before the lightning bolt closed down the cameras for good, he was suddenly overwhelmed with the feeling that something wasn't right about the video. He played it over again and felt the same mysterious sensation, this time almost to the point of nausea.

"What the hell is going on?" he wondered, his head aching, his stomach doing flips.

He played the tape a third time, now slowing it down to a crawl just as the lightning bolt made its appearance. It was actually painful to watch, but in the middle of the storm and the rain and the clouds, he thought he saw a flash of what was making him queasy.

Or did he?

Terrified, he quickly shut down the system.

"I don't believe it," he said, doubling over and doing all he could to prevent himself from vomiting. *"I can't believe it . . ."*

Twenty-two

Okinawa

Sergeant Dimitri Karbochev checked his Rolex watch. If it was working properly, then it was just about high noon.

"Two hours left," he thought, adjusting the regulator on the small oxygen tank slung over his shoulder. "Just enough to get to the Great Wall and back."

He pushed on, carefully moving down the winding path which led into the mountain valley, his NightScope-equipped Kalishnikov rifle up and ready. At many places the pathway was tangled with dead and dying underbrush, some so thick he had to hack his way through with his machete. He had to constantly remind himself not to overdo it — the more he worked, the more oxygen he would use. The more oxygen he used, the shorter this one-man recon mission would be.

Once he got down below the thickest smog line, he was forced to use his high-powered search lantern to see his way. Even so, the pollution was so dense in some places he could barely see his hands working in front of him. The path down into the valley was also littered with bones, some seemingly new and even recently gnawed. Others were old and in a state of rapid decay.

"Nothing lives down here," he thought, sidestepping the carcass of what might have been a dog. "Not for long, anyway."

The further he walked deeper into the smog-filled valley, the more evident the decay in his surroundings became. When the smog was so thick it could hide a noonday sun, anything that grew did so in a high state of malformation. Yet he did see signs of living, breathing civilization down here. Tiny plastic yellow rings were scattered about. About the size of a thimble, they were, he knew, safety washers for oxygen tanks used by the soldiers who patrolled this valley. Whenever a new oxygen tank was used, the yellow safety ring was snapped off. It was typical that the soldiers simply discarded them — and why not? What difference did dozens of plastic rings lying about make in a place which had long ago become an environmental nightmare?

But Karbochev knew it was also very stupid for the enemy to so carelessly discard their waste, something that the original inhabitants of the island never dared to do. By closely following the trail of yellow plastic rings, a good recon man could easily determine the direction of an enemy force. By counting the number of discarded styrofoam food containers a recon man could determine the size and strength of the enemy unit. By counting the number of discarded throwaway canteens, he could tell just how thirsty the unit was, a good indication of how long they'd been in the field.

But tracking a small enemy patrol was not on Karbochev's mind this dirty day. His was a strategic mission.

He walked for another half hour before reaching the Great Wall. Though its name conjured up visions of the great ancient stone structure in northern China, this wall was not made of bricks. Rather, it was made of weapon emplacements.

It stretched for nearly forty-four miles around the perimeter of the island, running up and down hills, through small valleys, and along the top ridge of two small mountains. The guns themselves — 155mm howitzers, mostly — were aligned in neat, interconnected rows of concrete bunkers, three guns to a site. Each gun barrel had freedom of movement of about 100 degrees, meaning all three guns in any given bunker could lay down an incredibly wide interlocking field of fire, whether it be in close range, or out into the sea.

In front of each bunker was another line of weaponry: either an antipersonnel rocket launching site, a heavy-mortar revampment, or, in some of

187

the higher areas, a fearsome weapon which could send a stream of napalm-fueled fire a distance of a mile or more. A third line, consisting mostly of .50-caliber machine gun nests, ran in front of it all, and indeed, there were more of these emplacements than anything else.

When this firepower was factored out over the many miles of the Great Wall, it was clear that anyone attempting an amphibious landing on Okinawa's smoky coastline would be decimated before they hit the beach.

Karbochev had surreptitiously visited the Great Wall several times before; his job was nothing less than to get an actual count of the number of massive pillboxes. This was considered military intelligence of the highest by his superiors, but frankly, he never could see the point of it. They did not have the resources to attack the island, or take out the hundreds of howitzers, never mind defeat the enemy that lived underground. Still his officers sent him, and others like him, on these long, uncomfortable covert journeys to gather information, to count guns, as if hoping that someday, by some miracle, the intelligence would be put to good use and the enemy would finally be taken to the sword.

But Karbochev knew that day was a long way off.

He completed his recon of the southern tier of the gun line in under thirty minutes. As always, he found concealment to be easy. All enemy troops manning the gun sites were equipped with oxygen gear bulkier than his own. Being weighed down by such equipment did not allow them to do anything but the task at hand. Without any sharp eyes about, Karbochev needed only a large bush or perhaps a good-sized crevice in which to hide while he completed his mission.

When he added up his totals, they were astounding. He had counted ninety-nine 155-mm guns, three hundred and ten .50-caliber machine gun emplacements, fifty-three long-range flamethrower pillboxes, fifty-one rocket launching sites, and forty-eight heavy mortar revampments. He also counted more than three dozen ammo-delivery cars being driven along the small railroad track that ran the length of the great wall. And this represented barely two miles of the steel curtain.

"My grandchildren will be too old to fight this battle," he thought grimly, sealing away the gun numbers in his small hand-held computer. "And so will *their* grandchildren."

He checked his oxygen supply and found he had about forty minutes left. This would give him just enough time to backtrack to the entrance path from which he had come, and head for higher ground.

Only then he knew would he be able to take off his mask and breathe normally again.

It was not an hour later when Karbochev heard the frightening mechanical scream.

He immediately dived into some bushes, his AK-47 up and ready. Within seconds the scream turned into the roar of a jet engine. Then, to his astonishment, he saw the dark outline of an airplane descending through the polluted mist.

Karbochev immediately recognized the airplane as a jumpjet. Years before, he had become quite familiar with the Yak-38, another VTOL aircraft. But who would be landing such a technologically advanced airplane as this on the woebegotten island?

He stayed hidden until the airplane floated to a touchdown. But suddenly there was a rustling in the bushes near the landing site. In less than five seconds, a score of island natives had rushed out of the brush and surrounded the strange airplane.

The pilot emerged from the cockpit to find himself looking down the barrels of a couple of dozen AK-47s, RPGs, bolt-action Springfields, and even a blowgun or two. The pilot diplomatically put his hands up and climbed out of the airplane. The natives closed in on him, and then, speaking in some undecipherable language, the native who seemed to be in charge ordered the pilot to come with them.

Karbochev followed them for the next five miles as they trekked through the jungle, following trails that only the pilot's abductors could read. They broke through the heavy smog line and Karbochev was finally able to remove his oxygen mask. Beyond the haze above him, he could almost see the sky turning a smutty blue.

Throughout the march, the natives would suddenly burst into laughter that shattered the silence of the jungle, a laugh so hideous that it caused hundreds of birds in the treetops to lift into the air, adding their screeching and cawing to the great horrid symphony. This would go on for several minutes and then the jungle would be silent once again.

Karbochev reached the edge of the village about ten minutes after the natives and the pilot did. Hiding once again in the underbrush, he saw the pilot brought to the center of the settlement where the largest hut was located.

From this hut an ancient white woman emerged. Her pudgy face was framed by long, flowing gray-white hair. The woman walked forward and began talking to the pilot. Only then did the pilot take off his helmet and did Karbochev get a good look at his face.

He was instantly astounded. He thought he actually recognized the man.

Can it be? he wondered almost aloud. *Can that really be the famous pilot they speak of?*

There was no way he could tell—at least, not now. He had to get back to his pickup point or he would lose his ride back to his base.

Taking a quick set of notes on what he'd seen inside the native village, Karbochev melted back into the woods.

Aboard the battleship New Jersey

It was so dark inside the cabin, even the light from the single flickering candle seemed like no light at all.

Wolf put his hands to his eyes, squeezing them through his mask. It was a useless exercise — nothing could stop the flow of tears running down his face.

Why was it always this way? he wondered. By what curse had he been condemned to live a life of such brooding and despair?

He knew part of the answer lay in his longing for home.

The closer the Task Force had gotten to Japan to carry out the raid, the deeper Wolf had plunged into depression. He knew each mile spent going toward the target area meant he was that much farther from his home in the country once called Norway. Yet as soon as the United American ships had started on the return journey home and the distance between him and his homeland had begun to shrink, the heavy weight on his mind began to ease. The inner clouds of darkness that swirled in his soul dispersed before the wind. He was almost cheerful at one carefully guarded point.

But now, everything had changed. Now he was not sure which way the wind would blow.

The storm outside, however, had begun to calm down. The heavy seas which had rocked the massive battleship were now settling down. The rain and wind had subsided. The return of normal conditions allowed the gloomy captain of the battleship to get some much-needed sleep.

Wiping his face and eyes with a well-soaked kerchief, Wolf stripped off his all-black, Zorro-like caped uniform. Then he blew out the candle, plunging his cabin into near-total darkness. Only then did he remove his mask.

Stretching out in his oversized bed, he tried to push his troubles to the recesses of his mind, begging for the deep sleep that soon overcame him.

But it was not to be a sleep of sweet dreams . . .

He was alone aboard an ancient Viking ship. Its forty unmanned oars were rowing at double speed, and each powerful stroke made the fiery-tongued dragon atop the prow seem to leap into the air. Faster and faster he could feel the ship slice through the night fog that enveloped it, barely missing rocky shoals that seemed to be all around him. Where was he going? Where had he been? Would he ever find out?

Suddenly a powerful gust of wind came up and stripped his cape and mask away. An instant later the night and fog were gone, too. What he saw next startled him deeply—it was a highly disturbing image even for a Scandinavian's nightmare.

He was in the middle of a red sea, one which contained hundreds of identical enormous slate-gray battleships. They were all steaming out of the southwest, flowing past him, heading to the north. As each ship passed, its crew would jettison scores of shrouded bodies that seemed to float down from the sky like cherry blossoms in the spring.

Soon Wolf's vessel was coursing through a sea of wrapped corpses, so many that they hindered his ghost ship's progress. But the unmanned oars continued to propel the Viking ship, and Wolf continued on and on and on, cutting through the sea of bodies and smashing over the wake of each battleship that passed by.

That's when he looked up to the bow of one battleship passing dangerously to port and saw a ghost of an image of himself beckoning down to him.

Seconds later, he awoke with a scream.

Twenty-three

Okinawa

"How much cuff do you want?"

Hunter shrugged somewhat uncomfortably. "You're asking the wrong person. What's everyone clse have?"

The man fitting him for the pants of the dark yellow uniform shook his head in mock disgust.

"My old partner should be having you for a customer," he said, despite a mouthful of pins. "Then I would have nothing but good memories of the thief."

The man was a tailor—or more specifically, a wardrobe coordinator. He was fitting Hunter for a field uniform made to replicate exactly that of an Asian Mercenary Cult sergeant. It certainly *looked* authentic—right down to the intentionally-frayed collar and sun-bleached insignia.

He had learned several truths in the last few hours. The people inhabiting the small village were hardly natives. They were, in fact, a movie crew, survivors of a plane crash on the island shortly before Hashi Pushi's armies had begun their well-coordinated rampage of the South Pacific two years before. Not so much trapped as having no place to go and no way to get there, the movie people established the camp high in the Okinawa mountains hoping that someday the area would revert back to its formerly-anarchic ways and allow them to resume their filming.

The village itself was a testimony to what a gang of bored, talented people could do with a lot of free time on their hands. It contained twenty-five "huts" in all, though, as Hunter had seen, they were hardly the ramshackle shelters they appeared to be. Instead they were all fairly well-appointed cabins, cleverly disguised by the movie crew's special effects people to look like typically rundown South Pacific jungle dwellings. Several of these places were actually burned out and abandoned, or, more accurately, built to *look* that way, giving the village the intended dangerous and desperate appearance.

Even odder than the inhabitants was the elderly woman who had greeted him on his arrival. She was not part of the movie crew; rather, she'd been living on various islands in the area for nearly seven decades, mostly among the small and civilization-shy authentic native tribes.

She had recognized Hunter as soon as he arrived, but she still questioned him extensively about his intentions. She was very sharp, and it took Hunter some time to convince her that he was simply on a recon of the island, with the intention of reporting back to a small expeditionary force waiting further out to sea.

Once he had won her over, her demeanor changed 180 degrees. She became a very friendly, extremely intelligent earth-mother granny type. Her language was sometimes as salty as a sailor's, and she had a corncob pipe to match. Every time she exhaled, Hunter detected the sweet smell of marijuana.

She would not give him her name, but it was quite clear that the movie people counted on her to show them the correct means for survival in the jungle. She was their resident sage—an unlikely diva, playing the part of their adventure's *grande dame*. They accorded her much respect, which she seemed almost uncomfortable accepting.

Now that they were friends, she arranged to have Hunter accompany one of the village's routine missions against the brutal occupying force that lived underground on the island, the same people who had been befouling its air and water and plant life since arriving two years before.

"I've heard of Hashi Pushi," the old woman told Hunter when he returned from his uniform fitting. "His raiding parties first came here about three years ago. They were like Vikings: raping, pillaging, murdering, taking anything they could carry. It was evident that they just looked at this place as a stopover point, a rest stop in their conquests to the south. Then, about a year and a half ago, a large landing party arrived and stayed. They blasted out the hollows of the mountain and built whatever the hell they've got underground. The air began to stink in a few months, then it gradually got worse. The water went bad pretty quickly, too, and their foraging parties killed all the game and bird life.

"I hate them. This was a very peaceful place to live before they got here—one of very few left in this world, I suspect. It had everything: good crop growing, fresh water, and plenty of fishing. The weather is always great, too. That's why the movie people were coming here in the first place. They were filming a jungle-romance-type movie and needed a lot of sun and natural backgrounds."

As they talked, the notion gradually dawned on Hunter that this woman looked vaguely familiar, or at least, her features did. The slightly puffed cheeks, the curly brown hair, the freckled face— she resembled a throwback to a model on a 1930s magazine cover.

Suddenly, Hunter realized exactly who she looked like.

It was as if the woman read his mind. "I know what you are thinking," she said. "And the answer is yes, she was my mother. My father was the man she was flying with—her navigator—the day she was lost so many years ago."

Hunter was astonished. After all these years, he'd tripped over the answer to one of the greatest aviation mysteries of all time.

He could ask only one question: why wasn't her famous mother ever found?

The woman's answer was equally surprising: "She didn't want them to find her," she told Hunter matter-of-factly. "Oh, I'm sure she did at first, but they never looked where she was. She and the navigator were on a deserted island for years, all through the war and the years beyond. I was their love child, and I think that after I was born, she just felt she could never return home to face her husband. My father died when I was very young and she and I were all alone—for many years."

"There must be more to it than that," Hunter prodded her. "She was a very famous woman in her day. She must have known that half the world was looking for her."

The woman paused for a moment, then went on. "There *is* more. You see, when she first crashed, she and my father almost died from exposure and, I'm not embarrassed to say, it left both of them half out of their minds. They weren't sure sometimes exactly who they were. So they just fell into the island ways. They were friendly with various native groups, and after a while, no one even bothered to ask them anymore where the hell they'd come from . . ."

She cast her tired, sad eyes skyward.

"But ultimately," she added wistfully, "I believe she found peace out here. I don't think she ever enjoyed all the hoopla. She loved living the simple life—away from the spotlight. She died so long ago, I can't even remember what year it was."

"And you decided to stay because she did?" Hunter asked.

"Yes," she said, her eyes becoming watery. "I'm very much her daughter. I know more about these islands than many of the natives do. And look at me. Never did I think I would live this long. It comes from good eating, and a lot of exercise."

"Have you ever been in an airplane?" Hunter asked.

His question stunned her slightly. She shook her head no, tears now forming in the corners of her eyes. "Never had the chance to," she said.

Their conversation was interrupted by a group of men walking by the hut toward the village main gate. Two men were carrying silver platters, each holding a half dozen of what looked like recently-severed human heads.

"Were you afraid you'd end up like them?" she asked Hunter with a laugh.

Hunter nodded. He'd landed in that particular spot ten miles away just on a hunch, a flash he'd gotten from his inner self. But when he saw the "natives" surround him, he wondered for a moment if his ESP had at last failed him. Only upon entering the village and finding out the "real story" did he relax.

Now he studied the skulls as the men walked by. They seemed real, gruesomely pulpy and covered with real-looking blood. But he could tell there was something wrong with them.

"They're fakes," the old woman finally told him. "There are more than a few special effects people here. They spend the day perfecting those things. They compete on who can make the most realistic human head."

"They do good work," Hunter noted. "But what's the point?"

She shrugged, and relit her pipe. "Part of the security plan," she said. "They stick them on spikes and then plant them up on the hill outside the main gate. It's a remarkably effective way of keeping the Cult soldiers out of this territory. You'll know what I mean when you hear the screaming later on."

"Screaming?" he asked. "Real screaming?"

"Tape-recorded, prefabricated screams," she told him. "Sounds like someone's getting fileted. They blast them out of here several hours a night. One of the music directors has a battery-operated synthesizer. He's adapted it to do amazing things. He can actually produce a wide variety of screams. Screams from torture. Screams from gunshots. Screams of delight."

"Also part of the security plan?"

"Another very effective part," she replied. "They set out to create the impression that a pack of bloodthirsty head-hunting boogeymen live up here and they've done a hell of a job keeping the Cult soldiers away. I probably wouldn't be alive today if it wasn't for them."

"If they're all so smart, how come they're still out here?" Hunter asked. "I don't imagine it's impossible to avoid the Cult patrols. They could have at least made it to one of the smaller uninhabited islands nearby. Wait for friendly faces over there."

She laughed again. "Oh, I think they could have left a long time ago. I think they just don't *want* to leave. They're still filming their godforsaken movie. They still do miniature work on it every day. They think it's their duty to carry on. As if they're starring in their own movie. It's like they won't leave until a rescue team from Hollywood arrives and takes them out of here in grand fashion. Then they'll have their proper shoot-'em-up ending."

"That's show biz," Hunter observed.

A young woman appeared from the hut next door and began applying yellow-brown make-up to Hunter's face and hands. Then the wardrobe man appeared and told Hunter to climb into his uniform, its alterations now complete.

Hunter did so and was simply amazed at the workmanship. The wardrobe guy had done a great job; the uniform fit like a glove.

The make-up person finished applying the last of the color under his eyes, then helped him on with his gas mask. It, too, fit perfectly.

His three supporting cast members arrived, the men he would accompany down into the smog-filled valley. Two were armed with AK-47s, and the third was lugging a small movie camera. They gave

Hunter his authentic-looking wide-brimmed Cult helmet. The make-up person tucked his overly long hair up inside the steel pot and then brushed out the last of his Caucasian-colored neck area.

"You look ready, Champ," one of the ersatz Cult soldiers told him. "But do you *feel* ready?"

Hunter shrugged. "Sure," he replied. "I've always wanted to be in the movies."

He quickly reloaded his M-16 with a fresh clip of tracer shells and checked its NightScope. Then, just as he was turning to go, the woman lightly touched his arm. "Just one more thing, Mr. Hunter," she asked, her voice a whisper. "Will you promise me something?"

"Anything," Hunter told her.

She smiled sadly. "If you make it back to America, will you be sure to tell someone that I'm out here?"

Hunter politely shook her hand and bowed slightly.

"I promise," he said.

With that, he and the three "natives" walked out of the village gate and quickly disappeared into the blackness of the jungle.

Twenty-four

It didn't take long for Hunter to gain admiration for his guides.

They moved so expertly through the bush, Hunter was glad they were on his side. Without them, he would have spent hours trying to find his way. They were also heavily armed, with both rifles and fierce-looking blowguns. Yet they were amazingly relaxed.

They called themselves the Extras, after the original roles they'd been hired to play in the film. Since coming to the island, they had excelled in learning the ways of the treacherous, polluted jungle. They now served as the eyes and ears of the beautiful people living back up in the village.

The plan was for Hunter and the Extras to backtrack to the Harrier and secure it and then move down into the valley of smog itself. Hunter told the guides that he wanted to get as close as possible to an entrance to the underground facility. What he didn't tell them was that he really wanted to get inside the place and do a quick covert reconnoiter.

After reaching the Harrier and finding it untouched, they hid the jumpjet under a cover of leaves and branches and then pressed on. About halfway down the mountain, they turned off the trail and cut over a ridge. Then they dropped down into a small ravine and chopped their way through a mile or so of elephant grass. After crossing a small river, they picked up another trail that headed further down from the mountain to the smog-enshrouded valley.

About a half mile from the smog line, the lead Extra suggested they stop for a blow before descending into the polluted fog. Leaving the trail, they sat in the cover of a large overhanging tree, their weapons up and ready for any possibility.

The lead Extra produced a small satchel that was tied to his waist, took out a handful of small green leaves, and then passed the pouch around to the other two. Each man popped the leaves into his mouth and began to chew. In only a few moments, all three were grinning. At that point the lead Extra offered the pouch to Hunter.

"Let me guess," Hunter said. "Coca leaves, as in coke?"

The lead Extra seemed offended. "Coke? As in cocaine?"

"Isn't that what it is?" Hunter asked.

The lead Extra shook his head slowly. "Where

you been, baby? Coke was out years ago. This stuff is a vitamin plant. Gives you the energy to run around in all that smog."

Hunter was mortified. He had just assumed the Hollywood types would be . . .

"So, you want some?"

Ever the diplomat, Hunter grabbed three leaves and started chewing, hoping to make up for having offended his hosts.

The lead Extra started laughing once Hunter had reduced the leaves to mouth mulch.

"Got him," he yelled to the others, who were now giggling. They were obviously coconspirators in the prank.

After another minute or so, they packed up, lowered their gas masks, and began moving down the trail again. While the three others were still occasionally chuckling, Hunter felt no different than before.

Whatever the leaves were, they had absolutely no effect on him.

A mile away, deep under the smog cloud, eight men were making their way up the main trail in single file.

The first four in line were unarmed and bound at the wrists. Barely clothed, these men hadn't eaten a morsel of food in days. Their bodies were covered with welts, cuts, and bruises, and their

206

noses were bleeding from lack of a proper breathing apparatus. Though they were once men of substantial esteem — all were former stockbrokers on the Tokyo Exchange — they were now simply slaves.

Behind them were four Cult soldiers. Besides wearing a standard-issue gas mask, each soldier also carried a shovel as well as an AK-47. To the trained eye, the mix of equipment gave away their mission. These weren't simply prison guards. They were executioners, about to eliminate the quartet of "native" slave laborers who were no longer of use to them.

This sad parade left the main trail and turned a sharp corner which revealed a clearing bordered on three sides by a deep pit. Hundreds of shell casings were scattered about the clearing; off to one side was a large metal barrel containing powdered lime.

Knowing what was about to happen, and forlornly resigned to their fate, the weary prisoners took their positions at the edge of the pit. Each soldier then took one shovelful of the lime and threw it onto the prisoners' heads and chests, then took another to cover their torsos and legs.

Then the soldiers picked up their rifles again, marched off twenty paces, and lined up in a row. While the prisoners awaited their death in silent terror, a good-natured argument broke out among the Cult soldiers as to who would get to fire first. When this was decided by the Cult version of bucking-up, the losing soldiers taunted the winner to shoot his prisoner in the groin instead of the heart, as had been mandated by the Cult's Rules of Executing Undesirables in an effort to save bullets.

After much laughing and poking, the first executioner agreed to shoot the man in his abdomen. As his friends moved a few paces in back of him, the designated shooter turned his attention toward the first prisoner and then took careful aim.

His comrades laughingly began a countdown, shouting through their gas masks: "Four . . . three . . . two . . . one . . ."

But when they got to zero, the man with his rifle raised didn't pull the trigger. Instead he just stood there for a moment, seemingly paralyzed. His friends looked at him blankly. What was wrong with him? He seemed to be gasping for breath. Was something wrong with his mask?

After a few long seconds, the man turned back toward them to reveal a long, steel-stemmed dart shot directly into his left eye socket, the wound bleeding so profusely it was filling up his gas mask's goggles and snout.

The man finally let out a long, painful, muffled scream and toppled over, his throat already stiffening from acute curare poisoning. After ten excruciating seconds, his stomach and windpipe seized on him, causing him to throw up and choke to death on his own vomit.

His comrades instantly raised their weapons, but it was way too late. Each man received his own blow dart filled with curare: two to the eyes, the third, appropriately enough, in his groin. In less than twenty seconds the four-man execution squad was dead.

Only then did Hunter and the three Extras emerge from the underbrush.

Even before the lime-covered prisoners realized that their lives had been saved, Hunter and the Extras had dragged the soldiers' bodies over to the edge of the pit and kicked them in. For the first time Hunter saw the pit was filled with the skeletons and rotting corpses of less fortunate prisoners.

"They throw lime on them so the animals won't eat the bodies," one of the Extras explained. "If they did, then the Cult couldn't eat the animals."

Hunter took one look at the lime barrel and then back down at the four Cult bodies.

"I don't think we should do them the favor," he said, disgusted. "Those guys deserve to be someone's dinner."

The Cult guards at the main gate to the Okinawa Underground Manufacturing Facility never knew what hit them.

In their last few moments of life, however, they had beheld a strange scene. The firing squad patrol that had been dispatched to eliminate four no-longer-productive slave laborers just thirty minutes before had come marching back down the trail, its four prisoners still alive, covered with lime, and, inexplicably, wearing gas masks.

The gate guards couldn't fathom what had happened. The frequent executions usually went off without the slightest complication.

Two of the four gate guards walked out to meet the returning patrol, their weapons lowered and uncocked, the faces behind their gas masks etched with curiosity. Neither man got to say a word. Each quickly received a large knife in the throat, ensuring that he died without a scream. Before their two remaining comrades knew what was happening, they were cut down by a hail of bullets from a silencer-equipped 9mm pistol.

Leaving the bodies and their weapons in the care of the liberated prisoners, Hunter and the Extras boldly moved on. Once they were inside the perimeter of the facility's large main entrance, it was easy to mix in with the hundreds of similarly clad gas-masked Cult soldiers, all of whom were either moving in or out of the facility's entrance cave mouth, not speaking, not looking up, like hundreds of mindless drone ants.

It was that easy. Hunter and his companions simply walked in through the main entrance and down the large crowded man-made tunnel that ran straight into the mountain's side. They walked along this passageway for nearly ten minutes, until they were literally on the other side of the mountain. It was here that they saw the secret airstrip that Hunter had theorized the last Zero had escaped into. He couldn't help but admire the scale of the work done by the Cult soldiers. The airstrip was large enough to handle dozens if not hundreds of airplanes, yet with the covering over its huge entranceway, it was practically invisible from the outside.

They followed the sound of rhythmic pounding coming from the other end of the gradually sloping tunnel. Whatever the Cult was manufacturing here, the work was obviously being done deep in the bowels of the mountain.

It took another twenty minutes of walking down the crowded descending passageway before they saw the greenish reflection of halogen lights up ahead. Hunter tapped his breast pocket twice for good luck. He was about to accomplish the major part of this recon mission—to ascertain exactly *what* the Cult was building deep inside the vast underground chambers.

Whatever was ahead of them, it certainly sounded impressive; the constant mechanical pounding was almost ear-splitting by this time.

Still, Hunter was not quite prepared for what he saw.

For as they rounded the last bend in the tunnel they found themselves on a crowded metal walkway which looked out on the biggest aircraft hangar that Hunter had ever seen, underground or otherwise.

All four of them were simply astonished.

As far as they could see, thousands of air-planes—almost all of them Zeros—were parked wing-to-wing, all with either torpedoes or block-buster bombs strapped under their wings.

Hunter swallowed hard.

"Holy canoli," he muttered under his breath.

The lead Extra and his men were similarly amazed. Though they'd been on the island for al-most two years, they'd never dreamed the under-ground facility which had been slowly killing off the island was so vast or elaborate.

And this was just the first level.

The chief Extra cocked his head to his left and Hunter turned to look. A large freight elevator had opened up and six more Zeros were pushed out on the floor. As that one closed and dropped down for more, another elevator next to it opened and six more planes were pulled out, like clock-work.

Hunter and his comrades boldly walked over to the elevator and stepped inside. The "hangar rats," dressed in immaculate white smocks and pants, and wearing a fancier style of gas mask, paid little attention to these "killers" who were bumming a ride.

The elevator descended all the way to the lowest

floor, the rhythmic pounding that Hunter and the Extras had first heard as they'd entered the facility growing ever louder and louder. The elevator stopped and the doors lifted open. Now the pounding was breaking the decibel barrier. Hunter stepped out and again was simply astounded by what he saw.

Before them lay a complete state-of-the-art aircraft factory, one that featured hundreds of computers, robots, and VDT screens, yet totally manned by native slaves, all of them either chained to their stations or shackled as they moved around the heaviest sections of aircraft from place to place. Hunter saw that anytime one of these slave laborers faltered, he was pulled off the line and consigned to a trio of soldiers dressed exactly like him, who put him in a holding pen. Then another healthier slave was in turn assigned to that position, knowing full well the fate if he failed to produce for these masters.

"This is sick," Hunter whispered.

He'd seen enough. Signaling to the lead Extra, the three of them walked over to what was the holding pen for depleted slaves. They silently took charge of the latest ten unfortunates consigned to death and prodded them into the freight elevator. As they rode up to the main level, the elevator stopped at three different floors, each revealing a separate factory: one for torpedoes and blockbuster aerial bombs; another for the sole manufac-

213

ture of small arms, heavy machine guns and their ammunition; and a third which appeared to be dedicated to the manufacture of uniforms. It was evident that this was in fact the busiest; racks upon racks of fatigues, boots, helmets, and webbing were being turned out by the minute.

Hunter was almost numb by this time. He felt like he was walking through a nightmare, a reprise of the heavy state of mind he carried leading up to his special targeting mission. The vast underground industrial sprawl was even more frightening, simply because it presented such a concrete example of just how strong the Cult was—even without Hashi Pushi. There was no way Jones or any of them could have imagined something like this. It defied imagination. What chilled him most was that the facility was so large, he was sure it had been set up for more than just keeping the Cult's occupying armies supplied. The place had obviously been built by people who had much bigger and grander expansionist ideas in mind.

The last of whatever exhilaration remained from the successful airstrike on Japan drained out of him at that moment. His hunch on the carrier had been sadly correct. The battle against the Cult was far from over.

They were out of the main gate and back up into the jungle within forty-five minutes, setting their "prisoners" free along the way. Then, after a hurried farewell and a promise to meet again, the

Extras proceeded back up the mountain out of the smogged-in valley while Hunter rushed back through the bush to his Harrier's hiding place.

He had much to tell them back at the Task Force.

Twenty-five

Aboard the Fitzgerald

The young ensign poured out two cups of thick, black coffee and delivered one to the captain.

If there was one person on the bridge who looked like he needed some caffeine, it was the carrier's extremely harried-looking commander.

"Sugar, sir?"

Ben Wa turned toward the ensign and shook his head no.

"Why start now?" he asked, accepting the enormous cup of joe.

Ben had been many things in his life: stunt pilot, a member of the Thunderbirds, mercenary fighter jockey. But never in his wildest dreams did he ever think that he'd be commanding a major fighting vessel like the *Fitzgerald*.

But here he was, sitting in the captain's chair, pumping down the coffee, and counting the new gray hairs on his head. A lot of people were counting on him. The fifteen hundred men on the *Fitz,* the thousand or so other men aboard the *New Jersey,* the *Tennyson,* and the *Cohen.* The millions of people back in America.

"Things are in tough shape when they have to put an Air Force guy in charge of a carrier," he said for the hundredth time. "No wonder Yaz is in such bad shape."

The bridge door opened, and JT came in like a gust of wind. He helped himself to the coffeepot and then slumped into the seat next to Ben.

"What's the latest situation?" Ben asked him.

"Fucked up on all points," JT replied.

Ben just shook his head. "Okay, let's have it."

JT took a small notebook from his pocket. "Item one: we are low on all kinds of fuel. Same with the other three ships. Item two: we are low on food. Same with the other three ships. Item three: we are low on fresh water. Same with the others.

"Item four: there's no word from Hawk. Nothing on the radio. Nothing on the long-range stuff.

"Item five: we've been so lucky no Cult ships or planes have seen us sitting out here that it's just a matter of time before our luck runs out. If that happens, we can throw up about four of those very banged-up jets and start praying. If they can't stop whatever's coming at us—like submarines, for instance—and Wolf's guns can't do it, then we will be the deadest ducks in military history."

"And Item seven . . . ?" Ben asked.

217

JT paused, then slumped further into his seat.

"Item seven is that Yaz is not doing so good. I was just down to see him in sick bay. I'm not a doctor, but he looks pretty bad to me."

Of all the strangeness that was swirling around the Task Force, the sudden illness of Yaz seemed the most baffling. He'd been found shortly after Hunter took off, sitting in the conference room, watching the tape of Hunter's harrowing return through the typhoon. He was as stiff as a board when they found him, barely breathing and with a pulse down near the low fifties. The carrier's two doctors agreed that he had suffered some kind of seizure—they used the phrase "trauma shock"—but just what kind still remained a mystery. The closest guess was a form of shell shock, the kind soldiers got after hours or days in heavy battle. This is what had the doctors puzzled. Yaz had certainly been under enormous stress helming the *Fitzgerald,* and it possibly made him a candidate for battle fatigue syndrome. But shell shock? It didn't make sense.

With Yaz out of the picture, the only logical choice as to who would take over running the ship was Ben, who had been serving as Yaz's Executive Officer. Not a minute went by now that Ben didn't think he'd wind up like his friend.

"The docs are doing everything they can for him," JT went on. "Got him on fluids and intravenous feeding. And he's still breathing on his

218

own. But I'll tell you, brother, I've seen dead guys in better shape."

"And those sawbones got no idea how or why it happened?" Ben asked.

JT just shook his head. "They said the only way to find out is to ask him, and to do that they've got to get him conscious."

They sat in silence for a long moment, suddenly realizing that their worried discussion had taken place within earshot of the eighteen crew members and officers standing on the bridge.

Ben leaned in closer to JT and lowered his voice to a conspiratorial whisper. "Okay, first thing we do is put the whole Task Force on some kind of rationing program. Essentials are to be used only for must-do stuff. All routine crap should cease immediately. No one's going to care if we all have a fresh coat of paint when we're sinking.

"Number Two: we've got to get as many airplanes working as possible. We shouldn't worry about what to strap on them, or whether every little cockpit gizmo comes back green. If it can fly and shoot and drop ordnance, then it should be combat ready.

"Number Three: we send a message to Wolf, tell him to get his ship tucked in here with us. We'll have to count on him for close-in protection. It's not going to do us any good if he's cruising way the hell out there."

JT was writing it all down in his notebook.

"You're the Task Force commander, Ben; I think you should contact him directly. And you should do it before something else goes wrong."

But as it turned out, JT had spoken too late. Bad news walked in the door in the form of a message from the *New Jersey,* carried by one of the carrier's communications officers.

"Just in from Wolf's Executive Officer," the man told Ben, handing him the cable. "He's requesting an immediate reply."

Ben took the message, read it and then handed it to JT. "It just got worse . . ."

JT read the message and then read it again, making sure he got it right.

" 'Wolf is missing?' "

Twenty-six

Okinawa

Major General Nauga Zuzu was sweating so profusely his uniform jacket was almost soaked through.

He had reason to worry. He was the production manager for the vast underground industrial miracle beneath Okinawa, and as such, was responsible for everything that went on inside the strange subterranean world as well as above it. His position was one which gained him little praise when things went right and much criticism when things went wrong.

It was the first day after a full moon. In the past, this was the day the great Hashi Pushi himself would actually leave the safety of his palace and visit Okinawa to learn from Zuzu the factory output figures, production projections, estimated usage of raw materials, and slave labor depletion figures—subjects in which the Great Leader had unlimited interest and knowledge. During this review session, Zuzu would also be obligated to discuss overall strategy, defensive battle tactics, troop estimates, and general supply allocations for the island's vast but almost secret garrison, though Zuzu felt Hashi Pushi never understood nor cared to understand the military half of his mission.

Although there was always an air of unpredictability whenever Zuzu made his monthly report to Hashi Pushi, the Great Leader would always impart a sense of fairness. Like any good CEO, Hashi Pushi would reward Zuzu if the numbers were good and chastise him if the numbers were bad. Then, after a short lecture on the Cult's destiny in the world, the Great Leader would board his special transport plane and fly back to Tokyo, and not return for exactly another month.

All in all, it had been extremely nerve-wracking anytime the big boss was on the island; Zuzu's ever-increasing number of gray hairs served to prove this.

But never did he think that he would actually long for those days. But he did, now that the woman was in charge.

Just who this strange woman was, Zuzu didn't know. She'd suddenly appeared several days before, announcing that she was Hashi Pushi's hand-picked successor. Though it seemed to be a fantastic claim, there was no doubt that Hashi Pushi had indeed sent her. The Great Leader himself had cabled Zuzu a few days before, and in a rambling, disjointed message, informed him that a young girl would soon succeed him as head of the Asian Mercenary Cult. After that, all communications with Tokyo had mysteriously ceased.

The woman fit Hashi Pushi's description exactly—right down to her bright red hair—and she had dominated practically every aspect of the Okinawa Manufacturing Facility since her arrival. She seemed to enjoy terrorizing just about all who had come in contact with her. Bad service, bad food, a bad mood were enough to send her into a blind rage. Anyone unlucky enough to be in her presence during these fits more often than not paid with his life.

Any hopes that the woman would not require him to report his "full moon" figures were dashed an hour before. That's when Zuzu got the word to report, unarmed and alone, to the woman's underground living chamber. He hastily reviewed his meticulously prepared information; the numbers he had to report to her were good. The problem was, they weren't great. And that was the reason Zuzu was now bathed in flop sweat. Because the woman had already established the fact that she disliked getting even the smallest amount of bad news, he feared what was about to happen to him when she heard his numbers weren't through-the-roof terrific.

The long walk down to her chamber seemed to take forever. In the background was the perpetual *thump-thump-thump* of the underground facility's machinery working as always at a nonstop pace. Zuzu wondered if he would ever see the vast underground factory again.

Finally he reached the end of the long, deep tunnel. Pausing before the door to her place, he took a deep breath and then knocked twice.

She opened the door a second later.

Zuzu had seen her up close only once before and now he was struck by just how young she was.

"You are late," she said in an odd, lilting voice, one that suggested she wasn't entirely in control of her faculties.

Zuzu bowed deeply and attempted to babble an apology.

"Please, none of that," she said, her sinisterly subdued voice cutting him off. "Time is of the essence. Please begin."

Zuzu took another deep breath; he'd spent the entire night before memorizing the report. Now he would have to repeat it verbatim.

He began slowly, moving carefully from point to point, boasting of the accomplishments that his men and machines had squeezed out of the thousands of slave laborers who toiled deep within the bowels of the island, and passing quickly over the small tidbits of bad news.

"In less than three weeks," he said, getting to the heart of the matter, "we will have manufactured, fueled, and armed a total of two thousand, five hundred A6M Zeros—this number, as you know, was our Great Leader's goal.

"I might add that Hashi Pushi's masterful plan of manufacturing the planes of the 1940s continues to be brilliant. The marriage of these simple designs to our super-efficient technology has enabled us to mass-produce on a scale that would have been unthinkable if we had only undertaken the production of jet fighters."

As Zuzu was giving his report, he was aware that the woman was slowly circling him. She was now halfway around the room and directly in back of Zuzu. This made him even more nervous.

"I am also pleased to note," he continued, hoping his voice would not betray his concern, "that our experimental division has reported success in remanufacturing an Me 262 jet fighter, a Luftwaffe design. We call it a *Sukki*—we would be honored to give it to you as our gift."

The woman was now standing directly behind him.

"Gifts do not impress me," she whispered from behind his left ear. "I am concerned only with progress. You say *all* our airplanes will be ready in three weeks?"

"That is correct," Zuzu answered. "We are currently working at all-out capacity."

At that moment he felt something small and cold against the skin of the soft spot behind his left ear.

The woman firmly gripped the pearl bead at the end of an eight-inch hatpin that she had taken from a fold in her gown, a hatpin whose point was what Major General Zuzu now felt.

"Three weeks is too long," she whispered in his

ear, "*Two* weeks is too long. What is the problem? Why are there delays? Are your workers lazy?"

Before Zuzu could answer, she calmly forced the hatpin about an inch deep into the base of his skull, thoughtfully wiggling the end as she did so.

"Two centimeters more and I will pierce your brain," she continued whispering to him. "An additional inch further and you'll be brain damaged for life. Two inches and you will die. Can you understand all this?"

Zuzu was twitching almost uncontrollably by this time, his underpants instantly becoming soiled. The pain at the base of his skull was unbearable, yet he dared not move. He tried to speak, but all he could manage was a series of high-pitched squawking sounds. The woman thought this was funny. She began to laugh, a deep, throaty masculine laugh that made Zuzu tremble even more.

"Shall I put you out of your misery, Major General?" she asked Zuzu in a hushed toned more suitable for lovers about to co-mingle.

Zuzu managed to shake his head no.

"Then I ask you again," she said, still whispering. "How soon will you be ready?"

"We . . . can be . . . ready in . . . forty-eight hours," Zuzu managed to gasp, his mouth quickly filling with blood. "Even sooner on your orders."

The woman withdrew the bloody pin, licked it clean, and then smiled.

"Forty-eight hours will be fine," she cooed.

Twenty-seven

Over the Pacific

JT Toomey was at the wheel of the creaking airplane. Beside him, serving as co-pilot and navigator, was a Free Canadian officer named Kenny Hodge.

Their airplane was ancient by any measurement. It was officially called an ASR Mk 1 "Seagull." The ASR was for air-sea-rescue—in other words, it was a seaplane. Its single engine was placed atop the wing, which was elevated six feet above the long thin boatlike fuselage on a heavy-duty pylon. The wing itself was thin and flappy, with a stabilizing float strut at each end. The tailplane rose up at a 45-degree angle, with tailfins that looked like Mickey Mouse ears.

Over all, the airplane was the ugliest contraption Toomey had ever laid eyes on.

Just where it came from, he had no idea. It was found stored away in the bottom of the *Fitzgerald*, significantly in crates marked "ballast." The crew of the *Fitz* had put it together just prior to the mission, but had never test-flown it because of higher priorities. Now it was up to Toomey and Hodge not only to give the plane its first test flight in almost five decades, but also to perform a very important mission with it.

That mission was to find Wolf.

The last anyone had seen of the mysterious ship captain, he was lowering himself in one of the *New Jersey*'s high-speed recon boats. He left no word as to where he was going, or why, or whether he was ever coming back. He simply wrote a message to his executive officer, telling him in effect to carry on. Then he disappeared into the wide-open Pacific.

Though this had happened around 1900 hours, the xenophobic *New Jersey* officers waited more than three hours before contacting the *Fitzgerald*. Only then, when Wolf did not return, did they inform the Task Force command with a request to launch a search plane.

With the strike jets on board the *Fitz* in such sorry shape, the old Seagull was the only aircraft that could do the job. It could stay airborne for nearly seven hours on relatively little fuel and thus could cover large sections of ocean. The only trouble was that no one was certain the Seagull was put together correctly. In the rush to commence the search, there hadn't been time to make sure every screw was tightened and every wire properly attached.

Launching the fifty-year-old seaplane also became an iffy situation. Having no wheels or surface landing gear, the service crew had little choice but to lower the thing off the side-flight elevator, and then hold it steady while Toomey and Hodge clamored down the auxiliary walkway and climbed into it. Takeoff had been tricky in the still-turbulent seas, but once they were airborne, the Seagull behaved as well as could be expected.

Now Toomey was bored out of his mind.

They'd been flying for four hours over the dark expanse of the Pacific Ocean and had seen not a single sign of Wolf.

"How far could he have gone?" Hodge asked Toomey about once every half hour.

As with most things, it came down to numbers. The boat Wolf had taken boasted a top speed of 34 knots and a high fuel capacity. He'd been missing almost five hours before they got word on the *Fitzgerald* and organized the search. Toomey and Hodge had been looking for him for another four hours. That meant he should be within a three-hundred-mile radius or so.

The trick was, which direction?

"This is fucking ridiculous," Toomey kept saying over and over again, almost like a mantra. "This guy's so weird, he probably doesn't *want* to be found."

Though Toomey respected Wolf's military prowess, and appreciated his skills as a military commander, he had always given the costumed Scandinavian a wide berth. People like Toomey just didn't take to people like Wolf; they were, in fact, exact opposites. In his opinion, the dark, brooding, eccentric Norseman—the man Toomey had once dubbed "Mister Shitty Day"—had an attitude problem. What was the point of living if every day you felt you had to make it one long drag? The Socket Philosophy was that life was what happens between episodes of booze, broads, and laughs. Why not enjoy it? Will it really make any difference in the end?

Then there was the whole thing with Wolf's costume: all black, the Batman cape and the Zorro-type mask. Many times Toomey had asked Hunter why Wolf wore the weird threads; each time Hunter told him that he honestly didn't know.

"This guy must've read too many comic books growing up," Toomey muttered to Hodge, as they switched over to the next search grid. "Someone once told me those Scandinavian comic books are *really* bad. Really fucked up."

"You're right," Hodge replied. "I hear they are *very* fucked up. Or is that their movies?"

They were getting near to the end of their fuel range. Another half hour and they would have to turn it around and head back to the Task Force.

They settled on one last grid, sweeping south by

230

southwest for ten minutes, then north by north-west for another ten, and then ten minutes to the northeast. But both pilots knew if they didn't spot evidence of Wolf in that time, the chances that the strange man would ever be found dropped dramatically.

Hodge saw it first.

It was the outer ring of an enormous glow off the southwestern horizon, so bright it could have mimicked a sunrise.

Toomey put the Seagull into a steep climb to get a better visual angle on the light. From 20,000 feet the glow looked like the brightest of auroras, enough to turn night into day. It was so intense, Toomey imagined he could feel its heat coming right through the cockpit window.

"Somebody is definitely cranking out a lot of juice over there," he said. "We've got to at least get a better look."

He put the Seagull into a steep bank and then dived, almost straight down until he was barely a hundred feet above the water. Then he leveled off, gradually decreasing altitude until he was barely twenty-five feet above the surface, and headed for the bright, eerie glow.

Then he had a sudden thought

"Do we have any weapons on board?" he asked Hodge.

231

The co-pilot stared back at him. It was the first time the subject had crossed their minds.

"Damn, I don't know," Hodge finally said.

Toomey took another look at the fast-approaching glow. It was getting brighter and looking more ominous by the second. He thumbed Hodge to the back of the airplane. "You better check."

It took about a minute for Hodge to go through every supply compartment inside the old plane, a time in which the Seagull had drawn within six miles of the glow. He had just about given up when he looked in the airplane's first-aid compartment and found an M-16 with four clips of ammo.

He reported the find to Toomey, who told him to bring the gun forward. But he had a funny feeling it wasn't going to be anywhere near enough.

They were about two miles out when they discovered the source of the intense illumination. The glow was being thrown off by hundreds of giant movie-set arc lights that had been installed all over a chain of small islands, turning a square-mile area into something the equivalent of a night ballgame.

And what they lit was mind-boggling.

Shipyards, at least two or three of them, were on each of the five islands that made up the chain.

Row upon row of dry docks ringed these islands, obviously churning out vessels in an

232

around-the-clock operation. Dozens of ships already built were assembled in the islands' large mutual harbor. There must have been four or five dozen of them.

But the most frightening thing was the kind of vessel being built here.

"Christ," Toomey swore, "they're all *battleships*."

It was true. Not only had they stumbled onto the largest shipbuilding facility imaginable, it was also one that seemed devoted to turning out enormous battlewagons.

And neither man had any doubt that the gigantic ships were being built by the Asian Mercenary Cult.

They flashed by the five islands at top speed and about a mile and a half out. Banking back to the north, Toomey got down even lower and closed to within a quarter mile of the islands. He was hoping that the blinding glare of the enormous lights would actually shield him from unfriendly eyes.

As they shot past again, they both noticed that something didn't appear right within the harbor. It took them a few moments to figure out just what that was.

"They're all moving," Toomey finally said. "They're moving like crazy."

It was true. Many of the battleships in the harbor were actually under way and moving. But what was weird was that they weren't moving in any precise pattern, as one would expect capital ships to do. Instead, they seemed to be moving very haphazardly, almost as if . . .

"As if they're being attacked," Toomey said.

"Attacked? Those monsters?" Hodge exclaimed. "Who would be attacking *them?*"

Unlike his good friend Hunter, Toomey did not believe in ESP, clairvoyance, synchronicity, or any other kind of cosmic junk. Yet now, something deep inside his gut was telling him to investigate closely the strange activity of the battleships, even though doing so would mean risking both their lives, either to hostile fire or dwindling fuel.

"Get that gun ready," he told Hodge, who was strapping in even tighter to his seat. "We might need it."

Toomey knew the only way they could do this and get out alive was quick and low — and with maximum surprise. He put the Seagull down to barely ten feet off the surface of the bay and gunned the gangling bird's engine. As it was still an hour before dawn, he had no sun in front of which to hide.

He chose the next best thing.

Exploding out of the glare of a long bank of lights, the Seagull was suddenly sweeping through the weaving battleships, getting so close to some that the pilots could see the astonished faces of the crew members as they flashed by.

Most of the battleships were moving in the center of the islands' mutual bay, and that's where Toomey was headed. They began seeing muzzle flashes coming from the islands themselves, and instantly Toomey had the Seagull twisting and turning around dozens of tracer trails and small cannon explosions. At the same time, he was trying to take in as much visual information about the place as possible.

Suddenly Hodge was grabbing him on the arm. "Look! Over there . . . *Jesuzz* . . ."

Toomey saw it seconds later. In the middle of the frantically moving battleships, there was a tiny but speedy motorboat weaving crazily around the harbor. Incredibly, some of the battleships were maneuvering in order to get out of its way, while others were trying to get a proper angle and distance from which they could fire on it.

But this was not the most astounding aspect of this bizarre confrontation.

"God damn, is that him?" Toomey yelled as they roared right over the top of the motorboat. "*Is that Wolf? . . .*"

It *was* Wolf. He was standing behind the motorboat's controls, cape whipping behind him, frantically steering with one hand and madly firing a machine-gun of some kind with the other. It was classic ants versus elephants. The ships were too big to get a bead on the motorboat, yet Wolf was firing on them with a puny MG.

"He's gone fucking nuts," Toomey yelled, "He's

235

totally flipped out."

They both knew this was a knifefight the ant would eventually lose. Because once just one gun on one ship got a fix on the motorboat, it would blow it and Wolf to pieces.

That's why they had to go back and try to save him.

Toomey put the Seagull into a gut-wrenching, rivet-popping turn. Soon they were screaming back into the water-tossed fray. Toomey knew he had about enough time to overfly the motorboat once, then set the Seagull down as close to it as possible. If Wolf didn't make a move to climb on damn quick, he would simply gun the engine and get the hell out of there, leaving the insane Viking to his fate.

"Get that gun up, Hodgie!" Toomey yelled as they went into the final turn for landing. "Fire at anything!"

Hodge already had the M-16 up and out the open side vent. He began firing wildly, filling the Seagull cockpit with smoke and cordite. Toomey killed the engine and slammed the old seaplane onto the water's surface. Wolf's motorboat was coming at a slight angle and at full throttle, leaping into the air as it crossed behind one battleship's substantial wake.

But there was another battleship coming right down the middle of the bay, intersecting the distance that separated the Seagull from Wolf. Many

236

of this ship's deck guns were suddenly coming to life. Instantly Toomey knew he would not have a chance to slow down and stop completely for Wolf.

"Hodgie, get back by the big door," Toomey screamed to the co-pilot. "Drag this clown in if you have to."

With that, Toomey gunned the Seagull's engine, banked so hard to the left that the wing touched the top of the water, and flung the seaplane right around the bow of the approaching battleship. Then he slammed the controls back down, bouncing the seaplane off the choppy surface. Wolf's boat was now just a hundred yards in front of them and coming straight on. Yanking the throttle back to half power, Toomey looked behind him and saw Hodge bracing himself at the open door.

"Ready, Hodge?"

Hodge didn't have time to answer. They were suddenly right on Wolf's boat. With much derring-do, the young co-pilot reached out and violently collared the wild masked man, grabbing hold of his cape and yanking it. Wolf was pulled right up out of his seat and halfway into the bay door.

That was enough for Toomey. He gunned the seaplane's engine and yanked the controls back to his ribcage. The air around them was filled with all kinds of tracer fire now as the seaplane desperately struggled for altitude and speed. All the while Wolf was still hanging out the door, madly firing his weapon down at the battleships, even as Hodge was trying with all his strength to haul him in.

"This guy is nuts!" Toomey screamed over the immense racket. *"Fucking nuts!"*

Finally getting some speed and height behind him, he twisted the Seagull around in the tightest turn it could handle without ripping apart. And then, when he saw that Wolf was finally inside and safe, he ran the old seaplane out of there as fast as its wings could take them.

Twenty-eight

Aboard the USS Fitzgerald

The door to the infirmary opened slowly and Ben Wa quietly stepped in.

It was dark inside, the only light coming from the gaggle of equipment set up around the room's only occupied bed. The bed was covered with an oxygen tent, and was lousy with tubes and wires running inside the plastic sheet. Many more strings of sensors and connecting wires were strung out above.

Underneath it all lay Yaz.

Ben had visited his friend several times already that day, but now it was obvious that things were getting worse. The comatose officer was wheezing with each breath, and his face had turned even paler. There seemed to be a larger tube sticking into his mouth now, and he had IV lines in both arms and even one in his leg.

Never realizing it would be this bad, Ben quickly turned away from the bed; just seeing Yaz in such a condition felt like a punch in the gut.

He retreated from the room to find the ship's two doctors just on their way in.

"He's getting worse, isn't he?"

The doctors looked at each other and then nodded grimly.

"His condition is deteriorating," one finally said.

Ben just shook his head. "And you still have no idea what's wrong?"

"If I had to put a label on it, I'd say it resembled the worst case of shell shock on record," one doctor said. "Whether it's the result of an accumulation of combat-related stress or whether something triggered it, there's just no way to determine."

Ben bit his lip. He knew both doctors, and both were excellent. He trusted them, knowing they would not pull any punches.

"Is there anything any of us can do?" he asked them.

Again they shook their heads.

"Nothing," one replied.

Over the Pacific

JT Toomey checked his fuel gauge again and grimaced.

They were already halfway through their reserve fuel, and still had more than a hundred miles to go to reach the Task Force.

Even though he'd be able to set the Seagull down on the ocean, the last thing he wanted was to wind up in the extremely vulnerable position of floating out in the middle of the Pacific with no fuel, little firepower, and no way of getting where they had to be.

Unless we paddle, he thought glumly.

Hodge was in the rear compartment, throwing out anything nonessential to lighten the load and thus help stretch the airplane's fuel. Already their auxiliary radio and power pack were gone, as were the spare toolboxes, several jumpseats, and the extra strut assembly. The effort was helping, but not by much.

"I can think of about another 180 pounds we can get rid of," Toomey grumbled under his breath.

He was referring to Wolf. At the moment, Toomey would have liked nothing better than to bounce the caped comic book character right out of the aircraft—the weight displacement would probably be just enough for him and Hodge to make it back to the Task Force.

The mysterious ship captain had said not a word—not even a thank-you—since they hauled him aboard and pulled his ass out of one very big fire. Instead, he had crawled up to the very end of the compartment and was now sitting there, head in hands.

Hodge climbed forward again, carrying Wolf's weapon with him.

"It's an old Browning BAR," Hodge said, inspecting the large gun and its lengthy ammo belt. "These things get hot—it's a wonder he could even fire it. His hands must be burned to a crisp."

"Guys like him don't even feel that stuff," Toomey replied. "They really don't feel anything."

"Well, he'd better include us in his will or something," Hodge said, strapping back in. "Because if it wasn't for us, he'd still be . . ."

Suddenly, Hodge couldn't finish the sentence. Toomey looked over at him and saw the young man was simply pointing straight up through the canopy, his mouth open but silent in utter astonishment.

Toomey looked up and felt his own jaw drop.

"Jesuzz, we're dead now," was all he could say.

Directly above them, cruising at around ten thousand feet, was a formation of airplanes so huge it actually blotted out the early morning light.

"God damn, what the hell are they?" Hodge finally managed to spit out.

Toomey already knew the answer. They were Zeros.

Although it would all but deplete their fuel, Toomey put the Seagull into a dive, putting as much distance as possible between him and the swarm of Zeros. By the time he got the seaplane to just barely five hundred feet, the main body of the formation was passing right overhead.

"There must be five hundred of them," Hodge

242

said, not yet over the initial shock of spotting the aerial armada.

"Are you kidding?" Toomey replied. "There's at least a *thousand* of them. I know Hawk ran into a handful of them the other day—but who could build *this* many of these fucking things?"

"Same people who built all those battleships," Hodge replied.

The Seagull was bucking and creaking as they plowed through the thick, turbulent air just above the sea. Their only chance was to stay as low as possible and hope that they weren't spotted.

But as it turned out, they already had been seen.

Suddenly Toomey looked up to find Wolf towering over him.

"Give me my weapon," he was saying, in his icy Scandinavian accent. "We are about to be attacked."

In the next moment, all hell broke loose.

The first thing Toomey remembered was that the canopy glass suddenly shattered away. The next thing he knew, he had a lapfull of glass and the wind was blowing straight into his eyes. A second later, a distinctly green-colored Zero flashed right off their nose, its cannons still blazing away. Another Zero was right behind it. Its barrage caught the Seagull on top of the left wing and strut, absolutely perforating it. Normally the wing would have contained some fuel, but the aircraft was so low on gas, no fire was able to break out.

A third Zero was now bearing down on them at eleven o'clock. Toomey looked down at his hands and for the first time realized they were covered with blood. At the last moment, Hodge yanked the steering column to the left, probably saving their lives as another barrage of cannon shells raced by, just missing them.

Toomey put his hands to his face and saw that he was suffering from many small cuts as opposed to one large gash. But his relief was only momentary. Another stream of cannon shells ripped through the cockpit a second later—the third Zero was following them down, its guns blazing.

Despite the murderous fusillade and the steep dive, Wolf had managed to stay on his feet and was even firing his BAR out of the broken canopy at the attacking Zero.

Even amid the blood, bullets, and confusion, Toomey was able to yell out to Hodge, "I told you—he's *fucking nuts!*"

Hodge wasn't paying that much attention, however. He was trying with all his might to pull the steering column back up before they smashed right into the water, now just a hundred feet below. With much pain, Toomey grabbed onto his own column yoke and together they were able to level out the seaplane at the very last moment.

But now they could see more Zeros breaking off from the swarm and diving on them like blood-thirsty bees, ganging up on the all but helpless critically wounded Seagull.

Toomey had been in tight situations before, but this was the worst. He turned and looked at Hodge, who gave him a kind of shrug that said, "Well, this is it."

A second later, two more sprays of flaming 20mm shells slammed into the airplane, causing it to shudder down to every bolt and nut. The right wing was now aflame. The engine was sputtering. And three Zeros were coming at them dead on.

Good-bye cruel world, Toomey whispered as the trio of Zeros opened up all at once. Then he tightened his chest and began to close his eyes, waiting for the fatal blow.

That's when he saw the Harrier.

As the survivors of the battle would later tell it, the Harrier jumpjet had suddenly appeared from nowhere.

One moment, the airspace just above the deep blue ocean was filled with a dozen angry Zeros mercilessly pursuing the stricken seaplane, and the next, two, then three, *then four* of those Zeros were going down in flames, trailing a stream of smoke and debris in their wake.

One second the Harrier was no more than ten feet off the tail of a Zero, blasting it to Kingdom Come with its cannon pod guns; another second and it had screeched to a hover and was letting loose a pair of Sidewinders. Rocketing forward again, it maneuvered two fleeing Zeros in such a way that they collided, exploding in a ball of sud-denly-fused flaming metal.

Within ten seconds, everything was peaceful again inside the Seagull. It was filled with holes, and smoking in more than a dozen places, but miraculously, it was still airborne.

Toomey and Hodge could barely recover from the shock of what had just happened. It seemed so unreal that they were still alive. They watched in shock and awe as the Harrier, having disposed of the attacking Zeros, was now in a screaming climb, heading right for the heart of the huge formation of airplanes, its cannons firing all the way up.

"He is valiant!" Wolf was screaming in Toomey's ear, as he watched the jumpjet ascend into the thick enemy swarm. *"He is truly a great warrior . . ."*

But now neither Toomey nor Hodge was paying attention. They were too busy trying to control the airplane. For not only were they on fire, smoking and full of holes, they were now completely out of gas and going down.

"Hang on!" Toomey yelled above the racket of the smashed and shattered cockpit. "This is going to be rough . . ."

Twenty-nine

Ben Wa and the captains of the USS *Cohen* and the USS *Tennyson* were gathered on the bridge of the *Fitzgerald,* scanning the southern horizon with high-powered binoculars.

What they were looking for almost defied a rational explanation—at first, anyway.

The radar men on the *Fitz* had picked up an over-the-horizon indication about twenty minutes before. It showed an unidentified object moving very slowly toward them, traveling barely twenty-five feet above the water. Though it was moving too slow to be an antiship missile, Ben scrambled two of the battered strike planes to intercept it. Their pilots had just radioed back to say that whatever it was, it didn't pose a hazard to the Task Force.

Just the opposite, in fact.

The ship captains saw it about a minute later. For the first time in a long time, a smile came to their faces.

What they saw was the Harrier, ass-end first,

247

moving toward them in a near-hover, a long line trailing from its extended front landing gear. At the end of this heavy line was the Seagull, filled with holes and smoking, but somehow still afloat and being towed by the Harrier. Toomey, Hodge, and the rescued Wolf were all visible sitting inside the blasted-out cockpit.

"Talk about backing in," Ben said, relieved as they all were that four very important members of the Task Force had returned relatively intact.

It took about ten minutes before the carrier could slow down enough to meet the strange pairing. Hunter circled above while Toomey, Hodge, and Wolf climbed out of the smoking hulk of a seaplane and up onto the carrier's aft access walkway.

No sooner were they safe than the Seagull's right tail strut broke, causing the seaplane to capsize. It went wing over, quickly filled with water, and disappeared beneath the waves.

Toomey stopped climbing up the walkway long enough to watch the seaplane go down.

"See you, old buddy," he thought.

Three hours later, six men were sitting around the CIC conference room table. They were barely talking, and their faces were somber and showing extreme concern. It had not been a pleasant discussion.

It was the captain of the *Tennyson* who finally broke the tense silence.

"Well, I guess we've got a very big problem here," he said, understating the immense gravity of the situation.

"We've got *two* very big problems," Toomey said. "I just don't know which one is worse, a place that can build dozens of battleships or a place that can manufacture thousands of Zeros."

The meeting had begun two hours earlier with Hunter's chilling report on the underground fortress/aircraft factory on Okinawa. This was followed by Toomey's equally-stunning recounting of finding the massive shipworks, a report which was verified and elaborated in spots by the extremely sober Wolf.

"Shocking" was not the word for all the bad news—"back-breaking" would have been a better term. Or "disheartening." Because no one in attendance, nor anyone involved in planning the Japan raid, had ever dreamed the Cult possessed the brains, brawn, and know-how to create two such military-industrial complexes, both of which were clearly the largest of their kind in the world at the present time.

"Big ships. A lot of airplanes. Both problems are equally bad," Ben said. "The question is, what can we do about either of them?"

"How can we do *anything?*" Toomey asked. "We're low on everything except toilet paper and bullets. We've got a bunch of shot-up old airplanes that can barely fly. And these crews didn't exactly sign on for any extracurricular activities."

"We don't have to worry about the crews," Ben said. "It's organizing any kind of resupply effort that's almost impossible. If we start chattering all over the airwaves trying to get a lot of reinforcements out here, we'll give away both our position *and* our intentions damn quick. Sure, Jones might be able to rapid-deploy some people and material out to us, but by the time they get ample numbers here—enough people and stuff to handle just what we are contemplating here—we might all be at the bottom of the ocean."

Wolf sat up straight in his chair and cleared his throat. "I believe there is also a larger question here—that is, how is it possible that the Cult is able to continue operations like these after we've eliminated Hashi Pushi and his entire communications network? After all, wasn't that our objective? To cut off the head of the snake, so the rest of it would die?"

"Although it was against our intelligence profiles of him, he must have somehow delegated authority to someone," Ben replied. "But who? Who could possibly pick up the stick from someone like Hashi Pushi, who ruled almost totally on personality alone? I can't imagine *two* people possessing such despicable yet undeniably charismatic power. And if two, then why not three? Or four? Or a hundred such personalities? Who knows where they could be coming from? It's a frightening thought."

"That's precisely why it must be defeated

250

quickly," Wolf declared. "We must attack now. We must hurt them—*now*. To let these things go on, this shipbuilding, these airplanes—it would surely be suicide for us. Such military might will be projecting around the world within months."

Another silence enveloped the room. Suddenly all eyes were on Hunter. He'd been silent for almost an hour.

He looked up, pulled his baseball cap up over his brow, and then stared back down at the table.

"I agree with Wolf," he began slowly. "Although we are out here on a shoestring, we've got no choice but to attack them now, somehow, some way. To return to America and mount another, even larger effort than this, and then come *all* the way back out here—it would take too much time. And we know we can't adapt any more planes for carrier launch in a short time—at least, not enough to make a difference. Plus we don't know what the Cult troops on the West Coast would do.

"No, it's up to us. Sure, we're running out of everything, but we are here, now. The only real decision is where to hit first. And I believe it's got to be Okinawa. Especially if those planes are being built for what I think they are. Attacking the shipyards runs a close second, priority-wise."

"But you're talking about two very tall orders, Hawk," the captain of the *Cohen* said. "I mean, we'll be behind you one thousand percent. But to launch attacks on such a well-defended, well-entrenched enemy, against such overwhelming odds?

We'll be risking every man in the Task Force."

"I realize that," Hunter replied soberly. "But being on the wrong side of the odds is nothing new to us. With the exception of the Second Circle War, we haven't had an advantage in men or weapons once. So what's different now? We've just got to use our heads."

He looked up to see five very concerned faces looking back at him.

"Besides, maybe there's a way that we don't have to risk anything," he added.

"Well, I hope *you* have a plan, my friend," JT told him. "I can't close my eyes without seeing either a sky full of Zeros or a sea full of battleships."

"Not yet, I don't," Hunter admitted. "But I do know this: it's time to call General Jones."

At last, everyone in the room could agree on something.

Thirty

Two days later

For the first time in what seemed like a long time, the morning dawned bright and clear over the Task Force.

By first light, just about every member of the *Fitz*'s crew had gathered on the flight deck of the carrier. On the *Cohen* and the *Tennyson,* too, the decks were crowded with crewmen, some drinking their morning coffee, others enjoying their first cigarette of the day.

Even the decks of the huge battleship *New Jersey* were alive with men, though almost all were in the middle of their daily hour of rigorous exercises.

But it was neither good weather nor physical fitness which brought so many men out into the morning. Rather they were all looking to the East.

Suddenly a cry went up, first from the deck of the *Fitzgerald,* and then from the *Cohen* and *Ten-*

nyson. There were even shouts from the normally staid *New Jersey* crew.

Everyone seemed to be saying the same thing, "Here they come!"

A minute later, an all-black C-130 cargo plane roared overhead at an incredible speed, its four powerful engines shaking the air around it, causing just about everything on the ships to rattle.

The C-130 banked high and up to the right and began a long turn around the Task Force. Right behind it, flying even lower and louder, if that was possible, was a Free Canadian gray-blue KC-135 aerial tanker. Behind it was an escort flight consisting of two long-range A-7F Strikefighters, and two GR.1 Tornados, recently reclaimed from the Fourth Reich Air Corps. Each of the four fighters had huge fuel tanks attached to their wings as well as a bevy of air-to-air weapons.

The small aerial armada had left Vancouver in Free Canada some ten hours before. By making no fewer than seven air refueling rendezvous points, the six airplanes had flown the entire journey out to the Task Force nonstop. As if that wasn't arduous enough, the six airplanes had to make practically the entire flight at the truly scary altitude of two hundred feet—this to prevent enemy radar detection. Even the tricky in-flight refuelings were done at this ass-dunking altitude, maneuvers perilous beyond description. At that speed, at that height, if the slightest thing went wrong, in less than a second, tanker and tankees

254

would have impacted on hard ocean surface and gone up in a ball of flame.

The reason why the six airplanes had made such a perilous journey was evident as the C-130 came back around. Slowing to about 85 knots, with the aid of lowered landing gear, the big workhorse of an airplane began methodically disgorging paratroops. They were jumping out the back, their small, special-issue chutes immediately unfurling and carrying them quickly to the water below. There were forty-three of them in all, and all were carrying heavy supply packs. No sooner would they hit the water than they were being picked up by service boats from the *Cohen*, the *Tennyson*, and the *New Jersey*. Some of the paratroops even managed to land on these boats directly.

Within two minutes, all of the jumpers were safe and out of the water.

Hunter and Ben had watched the precision operation from the deck with the rest of the crew and now they marveled as the C-130 formed up with the KC-135 and began yet another aerial refueling at two hundred feet. It took about two minutes as the two planes made a wide circle around the Task Force, the long hose from the rear of the KC-135 feeding into a receptacle in the nose of the C-130. Once the C-130's tanks had been topped off, they broke off, and then each fighter refueled in turn.

Once the last Strikefighter was filled, the entire group formed up again and roared over the Task Force, each airplane wagging its wings. Then they all headed east, the fighters in the lead, disappearing over the horizon in less than 30 seconds.

In all, the operation took less than five minutes.

"Jonesie came through again," Hunter said to Ben as the last of the exhaust trails from the airplanes faded into the rising sun. "I hope he's able to keep it up."

Indeed, the general had delivered. The air-drop force was made up of troopers from two separate units, probably two of the most specialized combat teams in the world. One, consisting of twenty-two members, were from the Jacks-Are-Wild crew. Nicknamed JAWs, the highly-trained, highly-motivated commando crew had originated from a pre-Big War police force out of Johnstown (now "Jack Town"), New York. With Hunter as their guide, it was these crack troops who, at the end of a titanic battle several months before, captured the Fourth Reich's *Amerikafuehrer* headquarters in occupied Football City, effectively ending the short but brutal Nazi rule in America.

The second group of twenty-one soldiers were part of another highly-specialized unit: the 104th Engineering Battalion of the former New Jersey National Guard. Basically Special Forces' combat engineers, the 104th had a sterling history of which many regular service units would have been envious. In 1945, it was members of the 104th who captured the strategic high ground of Shuri Castle on Okinawa, basically heralding the beginning of the end of Japanese resistance on the island, and thus, the ground war in the Pacific.

It was more than fitting, then, that they should have a hand in what was looming as the second battle for the infamous island.

Hunter and Ben headed back up the *Fitz*'s CIC—they had much work to do. Hunter was readying a situation briefing for the officers of the two paratroop groups plus the principals from the Task Force. They would all play an important role in the strategy he'd spent the last 24 hours cooking up. Appropriately enough, he was jokingly calling it "Operation Wing and a Prayer."

Hunter and Ben were attending to some last-minute details when the intercom in the conference room squawked to life.

It was JT calling down from the bridge.

"Hey, guys," he yelled, "check your flight deck monitor." Then he signed off.

Hunter snapped the nearby TV monitor to ON just in time to see the live televised image of an airplane lining up for a landing on the *Fitz*. Although it was still several miles out, Hunter recognized the aircraft type right away. It was a rare bird called an RF-4X "Super Phantom."

And there was only one guy in the world who flew that kind of airplane. An old friend of them all.

Hunter turned back to Ben, who was grinning from ear to ear.

"I knew he wouldn't miss this party," he said.

"I just hope he brought us some decent booze,"

Hunter replied, smiling as well.

Five minutes later, a rugged yet stately middle-aged man walked into the CIC. He was holding his flight suit and helmet in one hand, two bottles of Scotch in the other.

He looked at Hunter, Ben, and Toomey, and then shook his head in mock disgust.

"Don't you guys ever take a vacation?" he asked.

His real name was Captain TJ O'Malley—but he was known to all as "Captain Crunch," or to JT as "Crunchman." He had once run a fighter-bomber-for-hire service called the Ace Wrecking Company along with a partner named Elvis. But the business was dissolved after Elvis was lost on a recon mission west of Hawaii prior to the AMC's West Coast invasion almost a year before. It was a loss they all felt, as Elvis, just like Crunch, had partaken in every major United American campaign since the end of the Big War.

Crunch was now doing a solo act. Beside providing general fighter bomber duties, he also flew the best armed recon in the business.

He was also a great guy to have around when things got hairy. Crunch was the type of guy who, no matter how dire a situation was, made it a little less so whenever he arrived. He was one of Hunter's closest friends, a person the Wingman considered an extremely wise man. He also owed Crunch a debt of everlasting gratitude, for it was he who'd saved Hunter's F-16XL from certain destruction during the dark days of the Second Axis invasion of America.

Hunter greeted his friend warmly, then examined the two bottles of Scotch.

" 'Old Black Boot'?" Hunter said, reading the label. "Where the hell did you get this stuff?"

"Same place I buy my ammo," Crunch said, beaming. "That stuff is 151 proof. I can run the jet on it."

They found a bunch of coffee mugs and Hunter poured each man a thick shot.

They raised their cups. "To Fitz," Hunter said.

"To Fitz . . ." the others replied in unison.

It took the next twenty minutes for Hunter to explain the situation to Crunch. The raid on Japan. The discovery of the Okinawa underground factory and the enormous shipyards.

Because security had been so tight on the Task Force's mission, Crunch was hearing most of it for the first time. He shook his head and whistled in amazement throughout.

"These Pacific cruises can be murder," Crunch told them. "You guys should really have read the small print."

Hunter poured out another round.

"What bothers me is that I don't think we've uncovered all our problems yet," Hunter said, after they all downed the second shot of gutty but tasty booze.

Crunch lit up a huge cigar. "How so?"

Hunter shook his head worriedly. "It comes down to this: the Cult seems to do everything in threes. When I was in Hashi Pushi's palace, everything looked like it was in triplicate. Three houses. Three towers. Three entrances. Three guards at every station. Three AA guns at every site.

"We've uncovered a huge air potential, and a huge shipbuilding facility. What does that leave?"

"An army," Crunch replied. "If he's got planes and boats, then he's got to have men somewhere. Probably a lot of them."

"Exactly," Hunter replied gloomily. "The question is where. Their pattern is to find some remote island or chain of islands and set up shop. There's a lot of islands in this part of the world, as everyone found out back in 1941."

Crunch blew out a long stream of cigar smoke.

"Well, that's what I'm here for," he said with a grin.

"Got some stashes in this part of the world, have you?" Hunter asked, pouring out a third round.

Crunch was smiling broadly. "I got stashes *everywhere*," he said, referring to hidden caches of fuel, ammo, and other flight necessities that a man in his position needed for long-range work. "And believe or not, I got friends in this part of the world. The Cult ain't on every single island in this pond."

"Not yet, they ain't," JT said.

Crunch relit his cigar. "I can do a three-thousand-square mile search in three days—four tops. Fuel me up here, and I'll be back in seventy-two hours. Just point me in the right direction."

A fourth shot was disposed of over a discussion of additional logistics and flight plans.

"You're right, Crunch," Hunter said after downing the shot and grimacing. "This stuff *does* get ugly with age."

"Just like jet fuel," JT said.

The CIC conference room was packed.

Sitting around the table were the principals of the Task Force: Ben, JT, Hunter, Wolf, and the captains of the *Cohen* and *Tennyson,* the command officer of JAWs, a man named Jim Cook, the ranking officer of the 104th Engineering Battalion, a man named Frank Geraci, and Crunch.

Gathered around the periphery were all the members of JAWs and the 104th, all of the carrier's pilots, officers of the flight deck crew, and the staffs of the supply ships. In all, it was more than seventy-five people, shoehorned into a room built to hold forty at most.

They were three hours and twelve pots of black coffee into the briefing. It had begun with Hunter's narration of his first Okinawa recon flight video, then the details of his clandestine visit into the underground airplane factory. Toomey's report of his discovery of the shipyards and the harrowing rescue of Wolf followed, a tale which elicited a spontaneous round of applause at its conclusion.

A lively two-hour discussion of the Big Picture followed, with just about everyone in the room — officers and non-coms alike — adding their own two cents. There were no arguments, really, just debate on the threat itself, and on just how dangerous their opponent could be.

One thing everyone in attendance *did* agree on: even though Hashi Pushi was dead, the Asian Mercenary Cult was, for whatever reason, still thriving and apparently going forward with a fevered passion that bordered on the mind-boggling. The recent discoveries were so big, in fact, that a deep chill inside Hunter was telling him that something even more sinister than Hashi Pushi's legacy or successor might be at work.

But either way, it had to be stopped. Or at least an attempt had to be made.

Now it was just a question of priorities.

"Those airplanes inside that mountain are like bees in a hive," Hunter said. "Some are obviously already on the loose. Once they *all* get out, we'll never be able to get every one of them — or even most of them. So I think we all agree that we've got to attack Okinawa first?"

Everyone nodded.

"Okay. Then let's talk about what we have to do the job."

Ben stood up, a long sheet of computer readouts in hand.

"First of all," he began, "all our airplanes are either operational or will be within six hours. I hasten to add that each one is hurting in its own way—and several are suffering from more than one ailment. Many are at the end of the operating parameters. But our air service crews have become miracle workers. All aircraft can be relied on—but again for only a short, quick engagement.

"Second, one thing we *do* have is weapons. We've got plenty of Sidewinders, Sparrows, and 'smart' bombs. Also a healthy supply of 500-lb. Mk82 general-purpose bombs, some Wasp air-to-surface minimissiles, a bunch of Penguin Mk3 antiship missiles, and several tons of 20mm ammo.

"Conclusion: our air arm is being held together with wires and strings, but it's as ready as it will ever be."

At that point, the captains of the *Cohen* and the *Tennyson* did a thorough job of bringing everyone up to date on the supply situation. There was a borderline amount of essentials like fuel and food. They were hoping for another long-range resupply effort from America after the Okinawa operation was complete. But each made it clear that the holds of their ships were closing in on empty.

Next came the subject of combat support. This was Wolf's department. The masked and caped figure stood, cleared his throat, and began a short speech.

"I'm sure you are well aware of our ship's 16-

inch Mark Two naval guns," he began, his voice heavy with dead earnestness. "There are, of course, nine in all, arrayed in three triple turrets. Each of these guns is capable of hurling a one-ton-high explosive shell a distance of more than twenty miles.

"We have a dozen semiautomatic five-inch guns which can serve as both shore attack weapons or in an antiaircraft mode. Our four Mk15 Phalanx Gatling guns—one port, one starboard, one fore and one aft—are each capable of firing one hundred rounds per second. We have adapted them for long-range firing. In addition, we have the ability to launch Tomahawk cruise missiles and Harpoon antiship missiles.

"All this," he concluded, "including the lives of myself and my men, are, of course, once again at your disposal."

The JAWs commander, Captain Jim Cook, was next.

"We're packing our fire suppression gear," he reported. "Each of the guys will be carrying two major weapons: his rifle, and anything from a grenade launcher, to a small mortar, to an antitank gun, to a flamethrower. We've drilled extensively in attacking what we call 'natural hardened positions'—caves, cliffs, and such, natural terrain where an enemy can dig in. I've got to admit, we're pretty good at it."

Major Geraci of the 104th now had the floor. "As a complement to the JAWs, we brought our blockbusting equipment. We work in teams of eight. Each team can clear a man-made obstacle — pillboxes, tank berms, barbed-wire barriers — in about a minute. When this is accomplished, the next team comes up and moves up to the next barrier, and so on. The objective is to leapfrog our way up and seize the objective faster than the time it takes the enemy to figure out what's happening. After all, that's a specialty of ours."

Throughout these reports, Hunter just sat back and drank it all in. He was proud of these men — and damned proud to be part of their common cause. The past success of the United American Armed Forces were not based entirely on weaponry, or skill or expertise, really. No, the rock-solid core of their success was that these men were Americans. *True* Americans. Their lives were simply dedicated to preserving the self-evident truths spelled out in the Constitution and the Declaration of Independence, and they had little time or patience with anyone who sought to muddy those waters. They knew these near-holy writs said all men are created equal — and that was that. No arguments. Everyone has a right to privacy — and that was that. Everyone has the right to be religious or not, everyone is entitled to a fair trial, everyone can go out and make as much or as little money as he wants. These were simple things to understand, for they are rooted in common sense and humanity.

Defending them was the hard part.

In the end, Hunter knew that these were smart men. They would no sooner fall for "patriotic" malarkey from right-wing conservatives who were actually closet racists as they would from left-wing Let-the-People-Rule-pretenders who were actually totalitarian wannabes.

And they believed in these ideals so deeply, he knew it was practically impossible for them not to give their all in this constant battle with both sides. This engagement would be no different, even though it was evident to all that they were a small, battered force, thousands of miles from home, with their butts hanging way, way out.

And if they did taste defeat, then they would have all died in a noble cause.

The discussion had come right around the table and now it was back to him. Everyone knew he had a plan. They were very eager to hear it.

"Okay, then," the Wingman said. "This is how I think we should do it."

In a darkened room two decks below the CIC, there was a flicker of life.

Yaz's eyes opened.

He couldn't move. He couldn't speak. But he *was* awake.

The long nightmare was still dancing in his brain. Rodents. Were they rats? Or mice? There were thousands upon thousands of them, all chanting in what sounded like squeaky, twisted English.

What were they saying? What were they doing?

They were throwing themselves off the White Cliffs of Dover, the tall sheets of chalk that circled around above him. Or was it La Jolla? They were landing on him, biting him. Gnawing on his bones, sinking their tiny pointed teeth into his flesh. They would not let go! No matter how hard he tried to shake them off, they held on with their bloody little mouths.

He closed his eyes and saw millions of the rodent bodies washing up on the beaches of California. Santa Monica. Malibu. Pomona. That's when he got a look at them close up for the first time.

That's when he realized they were lemmings.

He was covered in blood—or was it sweat? There were knives sticking in his arms and legs—or were they needles? And someone was trying to slowly choke him. Or was that a breathing tube? Did he really need air? Was he underwater?

He tried to talk out loud, but couldn't. He tried to focus his eyes, but saw only plastic—plastic sheets that were smothering him. Or were they protecting him?

Then the *real* nightmare came back to him. He is sitting in the CIC conference room. He is watching the videotape of Hunter's descent into the typhoon. There is a crack of lightning. And then . . .

He opened his mouth wider than the breathing tube and tried to scream. But nothing would come out.

"I've seen . . . his face," he wound up whispering to the empty room.

Thirty-one

It was midnight.

High above the slowly-cruising Task Force, a full moon was painting the sea with a pale orange glow.

The four ships were moving southwest at ten knots; each vessel was on complete radio silence, with all but essential lights doused.

This was why the service crew for Hunter's Harrier was working under the relatively-weak illumination of ordinary flashlights. They had brought the specially-adapted jumpjet up on the side elevator, its fuel tanks topped, its wings heavy with four Sidewinder missiles, its recon cameras full of fresh film and video. Hunter had helped the crew get the airplane flight-ready. Now he was sitting in the rather spacious AV-8F cockpit, bringing up his avionics and snapping his flight controls on line.

He had a dual mission tonight, both halves of equal and critical value.

Although he had related to those gathered in the CIC conference room his thoughts on how best to

269

do the shoestring Okinawa operation, if his hand was held to the fire, he would have been hard pressed to call it "a plan." It was more a notion. A theory. But like all theories, it had to be tested. That's why he was preparing to launch on such an eerily quiet and still night.

But once again, Fate would momentarily intervene.

He was about halfway into his engine preflight checklist when he saw the launch officer walking briskly across the dark deck, giving Hunter the "cut" signal.

What the hell is this, he thought, putting his startup procedure on hold.

Hunter popped the canopy and the officer was up the access ladder in a matter of seconds.

"Captain Wa wants you to hold up, Major," the officer told him. "He says it's urgent."

Hunter sat there for a moment, wondering what could possibly be so important that Ben would want him to delay his mission.

The officer seemed to sense this. "It's Captain Yastrewski, sir," he quickly added. "Something's happening down in sick bay."

Not a minute later, Hunter was coming through the door of Yaz's intensive care unit.

The room was dark, just as it had been the several times Hunter had come to sit beside his coma-

270

tose friend in the past few days. But this time there was a crowd of people inside.

It took him a few moments to realize that Ben and JT were standing over in the corner, purposely hidden in the shadows. Two doctors were hovering over Yaz's bed, the flaps of his plastic oxygen tent having been tied back with tape. One was leaning right over Yaz's body, his ear pressed to Yaz's lips.

"What the hell is going on?" Hunter whispered over to Ben and JT.

"Ask the Bones brothers," JT said, pointing to the doctors.

Hunter walked over to the bed and did just that.

"We're not sure what has happened," one of the doctors told him in a hushed voice. "But in some small way, he may be coming out of it."

Hunter felt a surge of positive energy go through him. Yaz was a tough guy, someone who'd gone through a lot in the past two years. He was also a very close friend. The hopeful news, although small, lifted Hunter's spirits a notch.

But soon enough, his good feeling dissolved into one of bafflement. He could see Yaz's lips moving—but was he really trying to say something?

The doctor leaning over the bed finally straightened up and shook his head.

"This is the damnedest thing," he said. "Believe it or not, people are usually conversational when they come out of comas. But all he keeps saying is the same word, over and over."

"Well—what the hell is it, doc?"

The doctor shook his head.

"It's weak and barely audible," he said. "But it seems to me that he keeps saying something like: 'Victory . . .' "

Ten minutes later, Hunter was back in the Harrier, waiting as the thrust from his VTOL engine built up to takeoff power.

As if he didn't have a hatful of things to worry and wonder about, now he had another. Previously the doctors admitted they had no idea why Yaz had gone into shock; now they were admitting they had no idea why he would come out of it just to repeat the same word over and over again.

Victory? The word itself was a strange choice. Was it the ranting of a man whose brain activity was admittedly out of whack?

Or was Yaz somehow trying to tell them something?

Hunter just didn't know.

He saw the go-light flick on, courtesy of the deck crew chief. It was time to launch.

With these thoughts in his head and a tap to the breast pocket, Hunter popped the Harrier's brakes. In less than a half second, the strange airplane was rolling down the deck, using a short takeoff roll to conserve fuel.

It rose slowly, banking to right as it did so. Then, once it was clear of the carrier, it accelerated quickly and disappeared into the night.

Thirty-two

Okinawa

The knock at her private chamber door shattered the last peaceful dream the woman once named Mizumi would ever have.

She rose from her bed and lightly powdered her small, naked body. There was another knock which she completely ignored. She began her teakettle and slowly climbed into her cherry-red blossom gown.

For the first time in a long time, she actually felt good. Strong. *Powerful.* These were new and strange sensations.

She was finally coming to understand what was happening to her—it was easier once she realized that there was nothing she could do to stop it. So why not surrender to it?

It was simple, really. It all came down to the fact that she, as Mizumi, had no destiny—not anymore.

Rather, it was the destiny of another that she had been selected to fulfill.

She poured her tea and knelt down on the bamboo mat next to her tiny stove. Numbers suddenly filled her head; where did they come from? Airplanes. Production in the underground airplane factory had tripled in the past forty-eight hours. Slaves. Her minions redoubled their efforts to put more slaves on the assembly lines of the great machines. They were even using Chinese and Koreans in key spots now—something unheard of before.

Now, on this evening, she knew they were truly ready. Within the week she would unleash a firestorm of conquest on the rest of the Greater East Asian Pacific, and eventually beyond. All of the vital resources Nippon needed to fulfill its destiny would soon be theirs again. Anyone of a lower race who was not enslaved would soon be dead. It was as elementary as that.

There was another knock.

"My Lady, the ceremony is about to begin . . ." a nervous voice from the other side called out. "We must go very soon . . ."

Gathering her gown around her, she finally went to the door and opened it. Two officers of the Imperial Guards sent to escort her to the main hall were waiting outside.

"Which one of you was doing all the knocking?" she asked.

"It was I," one of the officers nervously answered.

"It was too loud." Turning to the other officer, she simply said, "Shoot him."

The other soldier immediately raised his sidearm, put it against his comrade's throat, and squeezed the trigger, just as the hapless officer croaked out the words "I'm sorry."

"I'm sorry, too," the woman said as she stepped over the lifeless, and practically headless, body.

Petrified to the point of numbness, the remaining officer led her along the long stone passageway and into the center of the mountain. The route was lined with soldiers of her Imperial Guard; each one snapped to attention as soon as she passed.

Finally she reached her destination, the access doorway to the largest chamber in the subterranean complex, Underground Hangar Number One.

"Open it," she hissed at the three soldiers manning the doorway.

They immediately did so, and the woman once known as Mizumi, and now the Supreme Warlord of the Asian Mercenary Cult, stepped out onto a balcony that overlooked the vast Hangar Number One.

Three thousand pilots, each with a face made red by the hundreds of torches used to light the gigantic cavern for this special ritual, leapt to their feet and began to shout for her over and over again. The screams fell into a chant that grew louder and louder as the pilots were swept up into a blood-lust frenzy. Their short symbolic samurai swords were now drawn, and with each thundering call of *Aja!* thousands of these swords would stab through the air toward her. She smiled, and the pilots screamed even louder.

With a slight raising of her hand, each pilot's rabid cheering immediately ceased. The chamber instantly fell into silence.

Then she spoke, and as she did so, she knew that the simple native girl that she once was would be lost forever.

"My warriors!"

The pilots again screamed her name in delirious joy.

She raised both hands to quiet them once again.

"My warriors," she began, "you are already gods without earthly desires. I am proud of you!"

On cue, silk that covered the hundred long tables that ran through the hangar were lifted off to reveal thousands of individual *hachimakis,* the sacred white headcloths of samurai warriors of old. Each of these *hachimakis* was folded to emphasize the infamous insignia of the Cult: three red dots forming a triangle within a larger circle.

To the rhythmic beating of a hundred drums, every pilot stepped forward, bowed, and took a *hachimaki.* Each one also took a small black-and-white photograph of Aja to be worn next to his heart. In turn, each left a tiny black lacquered box containing his nail clippings and a lock of his hair. When this ritual was completed, the drums ceased.

"You have been given a beautiful and wondrous opportunity to die," she began again. "You shall fall like the sensuous blossoms from a radiant cherry tree. It is the way of the warrior."

With that, each of the pilots solemnly tied his *hachimaki* around his forehead and then stood at attention.

"May your death," she commanded, "be as sudden and clean as the shattering of crystal. You are all heroes."

Rigid in attention, these pilots, to a man, could feel tears well up. While many bravely fought it, soon almost all of the three thousand faces were stained by tears.

The woman clapped her hands twice and all six doors of the giant freight elevators opened, one precisely after another. The first elevator revealed a sumptuous feast, cooked to perfection. There were roast pigs, venison, pheasant, quail, duck, caviar, fruits, vegetables, and every imaginable dessert. The second elevator contained gallons upon gallons of liquor: whiskey, wine, *sake,* and beer. The third contained nearly a quarter ton of drugs; China White heroin, Lebanese hash oil, amphetamines, cocaine.

But it was the last three elevators that made the pilots' mouths water. Over a thousand naked female slaves, ranging from teenagers on up, stood tranquilized into submission, all ready to be ravaged by the hungry "gods" who stared wild-eyed at them.

For a moment it seemed to her that time had stood still. She could no longer hear the pilots' screams of adulation. She could only see the thousand slave girls, shivering in anticipation of their 3-to-1 fate. By tradition they were all Korean.

Wasn't she, not so long ago, just like one of them? she thought. *Innocent? Sheltered? Protected?*

Impossible, she quickly decided, pushing the thought out of her mind. That must have been just a dream. She willed herself to have absolutely no emotion toward the slave girls. She knew who she was. She was Aja—Supreme Leader of the Asian Mercenary Cult.

It was foolish to have thought anything else.

Once again she clapped her hands twice. Once again the huge chamber fell silent.

"Let the seven days of the 'Celebration of Death' begin," Aja ordered, "and then, my heroes, you will fly away like sparrows, and await me in the Greater Place."

With that, she turned and left the balcony to the screams of lust and joy below.

Little did she know that sixty-five thousand feet above her, a bird of prey was watching.

* * *

279

Even from this height, the island of Okinawa looked like a smudge of soot in the midst of an emerald-green sea.

Hunter buttoned the top of his flight suit; it might have been his imagination, but flying at this height, he found the Harrier's cockpit rather chilly. He was already more than 15,000 feet above the recommended ceiling for the jumpjet, but he was sure the airplane could take it.

He reached a coordinate he'd previously determined was the exact center of the long, thin crooked finger of an island. At that point, he put the jumpjet into a hover and threw all his camera pods' lenses to open.

Now, putting the Harrier into a slow 360-degree spin, Hunter studied the main screen on his cockpit panel.

It was showing an enhanced infrared image of the smog-clogged island. Just like his first quick sweep over the place, this IF image showed the enormous heatwave emanating from the underground aircraft factory, and specifically rising out of the massive opening to the hidden airstrip located halfway up the mountain. Also easy to spot were the dozen or so vent shafts, the pipes which brought all the dirty air to the surface of the island.

But now Hunter was looking for what he was certain would be far more subtle sources of heat,

280

those indicating any smaller entrances to the other-worldly underground factory. He found a few, most about the size of a typical road tunnel, wide and high enough to accommodate a truck, but that was it.

He was heartened by what he *didn't* find. Except for the huge maw that served as the entrance to the hidden airstrip, no other opening was large enough to accommodate aircraft.

He turned his attention back to the airstrip opening. It was located about halfway up the northeastern side of the 1500-foot Shuri Mountain. Just above it was an artificial cliff overhang that jutted some fifty-five feet out from the side of the mountain and served to anchor the Cult's elaborate camouflage net. Above that was another series of smaller cliffs leading all the way to the summit where the remains of Shuri Castle had long ago crumbled.

Once again, Hunter was encouraged by what he didn't find. There were no indications of heat at the top of the mountain itself, meaning the Cult had little or no presence on the peak. Even better, there were few defensive weapons arrayed on the mountain itself, the Cult choosing — and rightly — to concentrate its ribbons of massive gun emplacements on the lowest line (or "first line") of what would be considered the high ground. Indeed, the highest indications he could see of any weapons activity was at about the same elevation as the airstrip opening, and most of these were on the opposite side of the mountain.

He was now batting two-for-two.

His third objective, however, would most likely prove to be the toughest pitch. He switched off his main IF detector and then snapped on a jerry-rigged detection device of his own concoction. He'd nicknamed it the Juice Machine. What it did was locate surges in electricity, based not on heat sourcing, but on tiny electromagnetic measurements.

With this device he was concentrating on the miles of Cult gun emplacements ringing the smoggy island. Every gun down there had one thing in common: some kind of power supply. By activating the Juice Machine, Hunter was provided with an enhanced image of the powerline network stringing the guns together. The readout picture of the thousands of separate yet interwoven power lines looked like nothing less than a massive coil of spaghetti strands.

This information would take more processing, but on first glance Hunter was encouraged by what he saw. By studying the routes of the power line trunks, he would be able to determine not just the weapon type, but also its range, and most important, the limits of its fields of fire.

He stored as many as fifty separate images of the Juicer's readout into his main flight computer, and then finally took the Harrier out of its nosebleed-high altitude hover.

So far, so good, he thought, putting the jumpjet into a steep power dive.

Now for part two.

Sergeant Andrei Kartoonov was in the middle of a late tea break when he heard the noise.

He was taking a rest beneath the decaying limbs of a Pacific cypress tree, his camouflage uniform, his carefully painted face, and the dark night rendering him all but invisible to anyone more than a foot away. Starting out at midnight, he'd been on the trail toward the Great Wall for two hours now, and like his superior, Lieutenant Karbochev, who also frequently came this way, he had stopped slightly above the thick smog line to take a blow and prepare to descend into the polluted atmosphere of the valley below.

The noise had started as a high-pitched whine, and seemed so far off in the distance, he'd just assumed it was coming from the aircraft factory deep in the bowels of the mountain.

But the noise gradually got louder, and it was soon evident that it was drawing nearer to him. Carefully repackaging his mess kit, he slipped the safety off his AK-47 and waited. His field of view included a large, irregularly-shaped plateau of sorts which the trail skirted off to the right as well as a grove of red banana trees off to his left. He activated his rifle's IF scope and scanned the tree grove. He immediately got heat readings on six individuals who were hiding in the high brush at the base of the trees.

At that moment, the high-pitched whine grew into a loud, throaty roar. He searched the dark sky and was startled to see a speck of smoke and flame hurtling almost directly at him.

What was this? A comet? A meteorite?

It took Kartoonov a few moments to realize the object was actually a jumpjet, coming in for a high-speed vertical landing.

He crouched down further into his hiding spot and watched the VTOL airplane drop like a rock; it was going so fast, he was convinced it was going to crash. Only when the strange airplane got to a hundred feet above ground did its pilot gun his engines, in effect slamming on the brakes. Suddenly its speed was decreasing faster than its altitude, and by the time it was twenty-five feet above the ground, it was almost into a hover. It finally touched down without the slightest bounce, and with a great deal less noise than if it had made a typical jumpjet vertical descent.

He wasn't surprised to see the six individuals who'd been hiding in the tall grass come out to meet the airplane. Obviously he was watching a predetermined rendezvous.

But what was its purpose? Were these people allied with, or fighting against the Cult? His superior, Lieutenant Karbochev, had filed a report several days before, indicating he'd seen a jumpjet during his last reconnoiter of the Great Wall, and had witnessed its pilot being "captured" by some locals.

Obviously, Kartoonov was now watching a replay of that incident. Except this time, it appeared as if the pilot and the people on the ground were working together.

Using his rifle scope on simple magnification, Kartoonov was able to zoom in on the jumpjet's canopy just as it popped open. The pilot quickly unstrapped himself, crawled out of the cockpit, and jumped to the ground, where he was met by handshakes from the six men, who were attired in extremely well-tailored black camouflage uniforms.

The group of seven men then began a very intense discussion. The men in black were gesturing wildly, their orgy of finger-pointing seemingly indicating things far off in the highlands. The pilot, on the other hand, was pointing to various gadgets under his airplane's wing, and then every once in a while, to something far out at sea. Despite all the animation, though, Kartoonov didn't have the faintest idea what the mysterious figures were talking about.

So, like any good intelligence agent, he took out a pencil and some paper and began to take notes. He indicated the time, weather, and amount of covering at his location. He described as best he

285

could each of the seven individuals, who were now sitting on the ground and exchanging what looked like photographs. He even made a rough drawing of the jumpjet.

About ten minutes into the discussion, one of the men in the black uniforms retrieved a knapsack from the high grass nearby. After working over this sack for a minute or so, he placed it at the far end of the landing area and then rejoined the main group. A few seconds later the knapsack exploded in a great ball of flame. Yet there was no noise. Kartoonov was at first startled and then completely bewildered.

What was this? he wondered. *How can there be such an explosion with no noise?*

He'd seen enough. He quietly but hastily packed his gear and slipped deeper into the dense overgrowth. There was now a change in plans. He would not be going down to the Great Wall this trip. Instead, he would begin the long journey back to his faraway base immediately.

He had to tell his officers what he'd just seen.

Thirty-three

Okinawa, one hour before dawn

Not many of the 20,000 Cult soldiers manning the Great Wall saw the RPV fly over. And those who did weren't sure exactly what it was.

Barely six feet long, with a thin wing and a whining propeller, the RPV looked and sounded like nothing more than an elaborate model airplane, a child's hobby toy.

But the RPV was not a toy. For many of the Cult soldiers who saw it, it was nothing less than the remotely-controlled eyes of their own impending deaths, staring down at them.

The RPV (for Remote-Control Vehicle) was a robot version of an old-fashioned spotter plane, and the crew of the *New Jersey* had been using it for years. Launched from one of the battleship's scout boats and remotely controlled by its crew, the RPV contained video cameras that could send back live pictures of enemy positions. The gunners on the huge battleship would view the broadcast and divine from it such critical things as target size, location, precise range, even weather factors — everything needed for the most accurate and therefore most deadly shot.

The *New Jersey* had nine big guns in all, arranged in three turrets of three each. The guns were massive — 16-inch cannons capable of firing an explosive-packed projectile the weight of an old Volkswagen Beetle a distance of twenty-four miles. Whatever this warhead hit was usually vaporized, leaving behind a crater sometimes several hundred feet across. If all nine of the battlewagon's guns fired at once — which could be done, even though the recoil was almost enough to actually move the dreadnought sideways — the post-barrage landscape of the target area would look like it had been hit by a small nuclear bomb.

Combining the eyes of the RPV with the massive firepower of the 16-inch guns created a weapons system that could near-perfectly deliver, and in a rather cold and calculating way, a frightening amount of death and destruction.

Yet, it was all in a day's work for the crew of the *New Jersey*.

The battleship was cruising due north, eighteen miles east of Okinawa. It had been on this station all night, launching and retrieving the RPV three times in an effort to gather as much battlefield intelligence as possible. What the RPV's cameras showed the gun crews was that the ribbons of weapons ringing the island were as frighteningly interconnected as Hunter's high-altitude recon had indicated.

But the video also told them something else: that though the guns were manned and ready, there was no special activity going on—no ammo cars rushing about, no double-manning of the myriad of gun positions.

In other words, the Cult had no idea what was coming.

It was exactly four A.M. when the *New Jersey*'s gun crews got the order to fire.

Coming in from over the horizon, each shell found its mark on a bunker, a pillbox, or a fortified cave that made up some part of the Great Wall of interconnecting shore defenses. Cruising back and forth, and firing three times a minute for nearly an hour, the *New Jersey* and its great guns raked the Okinawan coastline, turning sections of the Great Wall's concrete, steel, and stone redoubts into desolate moonscapes filled with craters twenty feet deep. Many of the smoking holes were filled with bodies, most of them twisted and burned in the most horrible fashion. Though extremely valuable from a tactical point of view, the poststrike RPV footage was not easy to watch, simply because *whenever* the *New Jersey* went into action, the overall result usually resembled a slaughter, as opposed to a battle.

It was death at its most methodical.

Watching the massive show of destruction through high-powered NightScope binoculars from the bridge of the USS *Fitzgerald* was Ben Wa.

Men will go mad from the concussion alone, he thought, staring in awe as the huge naval shells roared almost right over the carrier and impacted up and down the island's coastline. *And madness can be worse than death.*

He checked the time; it was close to 0500. He'd been watching the bombardment for nearly an hour now. He checked his position: the *Fitz* was now just three miles off the east coast of Okinawa, cruising very slowly toward the south, and exactly where it was supposed to be. He crossed his fingers. So far, everything was going as planned.

At exactly 0505, three luminous shells streaked over the carrier and slammed onto the very peak of Shuri Mountain. This was the signal from Wolf. The *New Jersey's* pre-invasion barrage was over, and with it, phase one of the plan.

It was now time for phase two to begin.

Ben turned his binoculars toward the *Tennyson* and the *Cohen,* both cruising on a course parallel to that of the *Fitz.*

He could see troops of the CLF—the Combined Landing Force—waiting along the gangways of the *Tennyson*. The small force was made up of the JAWs team, the 104th Combat Engineers, and fifty additional troopers culled from the crews of the four ships of the Task Force. On the sounds of a single pipe whistle, these men went scrambling over the side of the *Tennyson,* down the newly-woven webbed nets, and into the *New Jersey's* fast patrol boats that were tethered alongside. As each one became full, the pilots kicked in the motors and turned them toward the beach.

All boats were away by 0515.

Hunter had launched in the F-16XL shortly after the CLF boats began heading for the beach.

Climbing to 20,000 feet, he was able to take in the entire Okinawa operations area, an ideal situation prior to commencement of action.

As he put the F-16 into a long, looping elliptical orbit over the smoky island, he played over and over in his mind the elements of the invasion plan.

There was always a major risk involved in any military operation—combat was, in the end, about little more than killing or being killed. Good planning meant that everything had been done to keep your casualties at a minimum while inflicting maximum casualties on your opponent, all while trying to achieve an objective. Good planning then involved the proper juggling of the known factors.

But Hunter knew there were some things that could not be planned for. *There were always the unknown factors* — the monsters out there waiting to bite back. A soldier's most dangerous enemy many times was the host of intangibles of combat.

These Jokers in the deck always made their appearance, usually at the most critical junction of the operation. Some commanders thought the trick was to deal with them when they arose, but this was faulty thinking. Hunter strived to at least identify them before they struck.

The most probable Jokers in this deck were the Zeros in the vast formation he'd encountered while rescuing the Seagull seaplane. There were at least a thousand of them at the time, and they had to be somewhere.

The question was, where?

Hunter doubted the Zeros flew in and out of Shuri Mountain on a regular basis. Their sheer numbers, and the resulting air traffic control needed to handle them, was nowhere in evidence on Okinawa. However, the immediate area around the smog-filled island was dotted with smaller islands, many dozens of which could support airstrips. A real nightmare would be if there *were* dozens of Cult airstrips spread out on these nearby islands, or even back on the big Home Islands themselves. Destroying so many bases would be next to impossible for the limited resources of the Task Force.

But Hunter was not worried about this multiple-bases scenario. He didn't think this was the case at all, and for a simple reason: it was just not in the style of the Cult to build a whole bunch of little bases. They did things big—big invasion army, big airplane factory, big shipyard. That's why Hunter believed that there was one big airstrip somewhere, probably close by, probably little more than a single runway, some fuel tanks—and a parking area for a thousand airplanes. A very temporary haven for recently-built Zeros before they were deployed to God-knows-where.

Common sense also told him that these airplanes had to be found. Doing so would prove to be the most dangerous, and, in the end, the most fatal part of the Okinawa Operation.

It was 0525.

Hunter turned back over the southern tip of Okinawa and headed northeast again.

In the past five minutes his radio had come alive with static and voices crackling all over the

UHF band. Calls between the ships of the Task Force added up to about a quarter of this cacophony, calls between the ships and the landing parties probably added another 25 percent. The rest of the calls were fake—recordings made prior to the operation's jumpoff and presently being piped onto the frequency via a long-playing tape recorder onboard the *Tennyson*. (The entire VHF band was filled with fake messages.) It was a simple yet effective psy-ops plan. The idea was to make the Cultists think the American strike force was larger than just four ships.

False radio was just one of the many deceptions that Hunter had factored into the overall plan. Unlike many military men, he believed absolutely in the value of psychological operations, especially in such an uneven engagement. Good planning was necessary, of course, but when the bullets really started flying, plans sometimes went awry. Confusion resulted—in fact, more often than not, confusion *was* the overriding factor in combat, for both sides. When this happened, it was usually the least confused of the two opponents who prevailed.

There was a difference between confusion and surprise. Surprise was especially helpful for the attacking force, more so if the defenders were completely unaware of what was about to hit them, as was the case for the United Americans in attacking Okinawa. Indeed, all indications were that the Cult didn't know they were coming, a big plus in favor of the Task Force.

But the element of surprise was only a temporary phenomenon. Eventually, the Cult *would* figure out what was going on, and then they would activate their own defense plans, probably fairly quickly.

This is where confusion came in—it was like prolonging the surprise. And the art of spreading confusion was, in fact, found in the science of psy-ops. Filling the airwaves with faked calls was just one part of the plan.

In the midst of the organized confusion on the radio, Hunter was able to key in on one of the legitimate frequencies.

"TF-One reports go-code Green," he heard someone say. "That's Green at Two-Delta-Seven."

He took a deep breath from his oxygen mask—it was the signal he'd been waiting for.

Putting the F-16XL into a steep bank, he rocketed down to just 2500 feet. The boats of the CLF were now just 500 yards off the beachhead—some very critical moments were coming up. Would the landing go off as they had planned?

He got his answer just an instant later.

With the roar so loud he could hear it 2500 feet above him, a large section of the Cult's great wall of weapons opened up all at once. Suddenly there were explosions going off everywhere. The early morning sky was awash in tracer fire. The perpetual smog bank on the eastern side of the island was suddenly lit up with flames and rocket contrails, so many guns were firing at once.

Hunter banked to the right, getting a better view of the landing parties. They were just reaching the beach now, the fast *New Jersey* patrol boats skimming in, seemingly right on top of the waves. By the time the first CLF troopers came clamoring out of the boats and into the shallow water, there were hundreds of explosions going on all around and above them. As they scrambled up onto the beach, the enemy fire all around them was escalating by frightening proportions. From this altitude, it appeared as if the CLF soldiers were walking in Hell itself, a fiery trap from which no one could escape.

Yet Hunter tapped the flag in his pocket and whistled with great relief.

So far, so good, he thought.

The CLF troopers hit the beach at 0530.

Above them on either side, in fact, all around them, enemy shells were exploding, mortars were going off, and tracer fire was as thick as the smoke. The combined firepower of the Cult's interlocking guns a half mile inland made for a very noisy, spectacular display.

Yet not one man among the CLF had been killed or wounded in the landing—in fact, not a one suffered so much as a scratch. Despite the awesome enemy fire, the hundred or so soldiers were protected, unhittable. *Invulnerable.* They had moved off the scout boats and up onto the beach in a hasty but orderly fashion, making sure that all of their valuable equipment was accounted for and carried ashore. Now they were flooding into the jungle itself, leaving the maelstrom of enemy fire to batter away at empty stretches of beach.

The first critical minutes of the small invasion had been painless for one reason: Hunter had found the G-spot.

No one was really sure who had come up with that name, but in the end, it did become rather appropriate. Sweet Spot would have done nicely, too, for what Hunter had found was the one section of Okinawa's beach where the massive combined firepower of the Great Wall *did not* interlock. Finding this magic piece of real estate had been the whole purpose of his high-altitude scan with the Juice Machine; indeed, it was the cornerstone of the whole invasion plan.

As it turned out, finding the G-spot had actually been fairly easy. A close examination of the Juice Machine's power-surge scan footage revealed a handful of areas on the island's coastline where gun placement on the Great Wall was low. This was not unexpected—no matter how in-depth the defense, few commanders have the luxury of spreading all guns evenly throughout an entire line. The rugged, constantly-changing terrain of Okinawa made this especially true.

The trick was to find the softest of the soft spots, and then further define it down to a narrow corridor of complete safety, that is, the place where not one of the enemy's thousands of interlocking guns could reach.

(It didn't take a military tactics expert to figure out that such a corridor of complete safety could exist. Common sense said that the deeper an enemy's defense the less likely there would be any holes. However, by the same reasoning, if there *was* a hole, then it might be absolutely safe to move through it, simply because you were reasonably certain the enemy didn't know about it. If he had, he would have smothered it long ago.)

Hunter found the G-spot just south of a place called Nin. It was a small nub of land which formed the top of a tiny bay about mid-point on the eastern end of the island. The beach here was very narrow; there was not even twenty-five yards of loose sand before the jungle began. The section of the Great Wall which ran just a half mile inland was not exactly thick with guns; the terrain was dense jungle, pocketed with deep volcanic crevices, and many high protecting cliffs—the natural defenses used by the Japanese

Imperial Army during the last bloody battle of 1945. Through a series of triangulations, Hunter had determined that one 200-foot wide section of the beach at Nin was just beyond the range of most of the nearby guns and just under the range of the others. And because of the reverse curving nature of the beach, the northern side was protected by cliffs from long-range guns to the south, and the southern side was protected by the same cliffs from the long-range guns in the north.

This was the G-spot.

For added insurance, the barrage by the *New Jersey* had subtly concentrated on the immediate area around Nin. Careful not to reveal the landing spot, the *New Jersey's* gun crews had spread out their fire as the battleship moved back and forth off the coast for one hellish hour. However, anytime Nin was within range, they fired an extra barrage per gun before continuing on their way.

So the CLF landing had been a noisy but casualty-free cakewalk. Once the troops moved into the jungle, the only sign they found of the enemy were scattered fragments of clothing and bone, the few discernible leftovers of the *New Jersey's* bombardments in the area.

They headed inland, through the lush tropical jungle, moving quickly in single file until they were well to the rear of the wall of enemy guns.

When they reached a small river called the Si, the force began splitting up. The JAWs teams, under command of Captain Cook, took the fifty extra Task Force troopers and crossed the shallow river. They were heading to a point one mile west, where they would divide once more and then move toward their assigned targets.

The 104th, its soldiers loaded down with weapons and combat engineering gear, would follow the Si River for two-and-three-quarters miles, until it brought them to the base of Shuri Mountain itself.

Thirty-four

It was 0600.

With a great burst of power and steam, the Tornado GR.1 roared down the deck of the *Fitzgerald* and screamed into the air. The A-4 attack bomber was right behind it, launching almost simultaneously from the carrier's side catapult. Next came the pair of Viggens, one Strikefighter, and the Yugo.

Once all six airplanes were airborne, they formed up over the carrier and then turned toward the island of Okinawa. Although the CLF troopers were deep into the jungle by now, the Cult was still firing weapons along the entire eastern length of the Great Wall of guns. The smoke from these firings, mixed with its own perpetual smog, enveloped the island in a strange, thicker-than-usual morning haze, not the best of conditions for airstrikes.

But the flight of six jets pressed on, their wings literally sagging from the weight of overloaded bombs. The poor visibility would be challenging, if not daunting. While the entire Okinawa land-sea-air operation was based on pinpoint timing, the men watching the clock most closely were the *Fitz*'s pilots. They had to accomplish their missions not only accurately, but also very quickly, for several reasons: fuel consumption was a factor, but also security of the Task Force itself. For every airplane in action over Okinawa meant there was one less airplane to defend the United American ships from any Cult aerial counterattack.

So time was of the essence for the six pilots.

Once they were within two miles of Okinawa, they broke off into pairs. The Viggens immediately went down to 500 feet, and began a long, slow turn toward the northern tip of the island. The Strikefighter and the Yugo went down to a similar breathtaking altitude, steering toward the midsection of the battered, smoky battlefield.

The Tornado and the Skyhawk turned south, toward Shuri Mountain itself.

Hunter was streaking back from his last pass over the southernmost tip of the island when he made rendezvous with these two strike craft.

Below them, the situation was intensifying. Just about all the mid-range guns along the Great Wall were still going off, even though their shells were falling far short of the ships in the Task Force, cruising out of range six miles offshore. IF readings as well as intercepted Cult radio traffic told of furious activity within Shuri Mountain itself. Though they had been taken by surprise, the Cult defense and command systems were coming to life. The legitimate Task Force radio traffic from the ground told them that both landing parties were moving toward their objectives and meeting absolutely no resistance.

Hunter knew this would soon change.

He tucked into a triad formation with the A-4 and the Tornado, established a cleared radio link, and then went into a loose orbit at 4000 feet. The Tornado's pilot, a British Canadian named Tandy, activated his ultra-advanced terrain targeting gear and began sweeping the area around the eastern end of Shuri Mountain. Sure enough, within twenty seconds he'd identified a column of troop trucks exiting what had previously been a hidden passageway at the southern base of the mountain.

He radioed the information over to Hunter and the A-4 pilot, who quickly broke off from the formation. Hunter put the F-16XL into a low dive, pulling up at 300 feet about six miles north of the emerging troop column. Throttling down to a 210-mph crawl, he activated the target designator in the nose of his airplane, painting the lead truck of the convoy with laser-light. At four miles out, he was locked on solid to the target.

That's when the A-4 came screaming right over the top of him at 400 knots. The pilot released a laser-guided Mk84 GP bomb and then rocketed away off to the right. The bomb deployed its tail control fins and in two seconds locked onto Hunter's target laser beam. Holding the XL as steady as possible in the bumpy, smoggy air, Hunter guided the smart bomb in toward the target.

The missile slammed into the radiator of the lead truck, its 500-pound warhead exploding somewhere behind the driver's compartment. The truck was blown backward into the truck behind it, and, fused together, they slammed into the next five trucks in a row. Flaming debris and shrapnel shot out in all directions, further destroying and heavily damaging the next six trucks, and igniting a large fire in the surrounding forest.

Hunter twisted the 'XL over and was quickly passing over the target from the south. The combined explosions had created a massive crater some thirty feet across, instantly rendering the road impassable. Already he could see those trucks that had survived the strike were hastily backing up and returning to the hidden mountain passageway.

"Target destroyed," he said coolly into his microphone.

In all the pinpoint airstrike had taken thirty-two seconds. More than two hundred Cult soldiers and a total of ten vehicles were incinerated.

He put the 'XL into a steep climb and rejoined the Skyhawk and the Tornado in the 4000-foot orbit. Already Tandy's target system was beeping again.

"We've got some mechanized movement on the west side, at Two-Two-Henry-Victor," he called over to Hunter. "Probably tanks, with some APCs. I'd say half dozen to a dozen vehicles."

Hunter punched in the target's coordinates and the F-16XL whooshed off to the next trouble spot. He was over the enemy column in ten seconds. Looking down from 4000 feet, he could see it snaking its way down a mountain road toward a bridge which spanned one of the island's many ravine-like crevices.

"We've got nine tanks and two APCs," he told the A-4 and Tornado pilots. "The bridge is a two-lane concrete. Support structure is obscured."

"We can go right in on top," the A-4 pilot radioed over. "I got a PAVEWAY on a 500-pounder that might collapse the bridge."

"We can't get them all," Tandy reported, following the progress of the tank column via his TV screen target system. "Half will be over before we have time to frame it. Thirty seconds and they'll all be over."

Hunter considered the situation. Hitting both the bridge and the tank column was the most economical thing to do, given their limited resources. But how could he slow up the enemy convoy in its attempt to dash over the span before they could deliver the PAVEWAY laser bomb?

He had the solution in a quarter of a second. Flipping the 'XL over, he was soon screaming down toward the bridge. The first tank in the column had just reached the northern end of the bridge, but now, spotting the three prowling jets, it had shifted into high gear and in a burst of smoky exhaust began rumbling across, the other eight vehicles close behind.

Hunter brought the 'XL down to the tree-scraping height of seventy-five feet, and in one motion illuminated his laser target designator and opened up with his nose cannons. His first line of tracer shells impacted all over the lead tank just as it had reached the other side of the short span. Its driver, either hit or startled, predictably slammed on the brakes, causing the second-in-line tank to slam into his rear, and setting up a chain reaction that ran right through the column.

Three seconds later, the A-4 screeched overhead

again, and unleashed the 500-pound PAVEWAY-equipped bomb. The bomb quickly deployed its steering mechanism and followed Hunter's laser-beam-generated path to the target. The missile slammed into the bridge just behind the lead tank and exploded as it was passing through the roadway, taking tanks two and three with it.

The bridge teetered for what seemed like a very long time, long enough for Hunter to punch the 'XL into afterburner. As he was streaking directly over the bridge it began to go down, slowly at first, but then gaining deadly momentum as the combined weight of the trapped tanks aided in its fall. By the time he did a tight turn and passed over the target again, there was nothing left. Tanks, soldiers, and bridge were all gone, disappearing into the flame and jungle below.

"Second target scratched," he reported.

Reports from the other two Task Force flights were coming in now.

The Viggens had destroyed a small, hidden port facility located on the north end of the island near a place called Huda, and then set aflame a vast fuel storage yard located on a small island off the western coast called Togi Shima. They were now attacking a column of troops moving down from the north with their cannons.

Using a HARM antiradiation missile, the Strikefighter and the Yugo had scored a major hit by finding and setting fire to what had to be the island's major power station, a huge camouflaged facility located in a dug-out crevice area, about two miles south of Shuri. As soon as this report came over, radio traffic inside Shuri dropped by fifty percent, a sure sign that the underground facility had lost a substantial amount of its electrical power. The aerial odd couple were presently strafing the facility.

Hunter checked the time. It was now 0620. They were keeping pretty much to their timetable, despite the high levels of smog and smoke obscuring important targets.

Things were going so well, Hunter dreaded implementing the next phase: signaling the entire strike force that it was time to return to the *Fitzgerald*. But it had to be done. The airstrikes, while certainly beneficial, were actually a little bit of window dressing. Their ferocity and accuracy had apparently convinced the Cult that they were being attacked in force from the air from all sides. Indeed, this was the intent.

But each airplane was using up precious fuel, and that was the lifeblood of the Task Force. So the plan called for the first strike to return to the carrier after barely twenty minutes of operation.

Only Hunter would remain over the island.

The woman named Aja opened the massive door to her underground chamber on the first knock.

Two men — a major general of her Imperial Guard and a young ensign pilot — walked in. Both were trembling, and with good reason. The entire mountain was shaking — not with the usual sounds of its underground machinery, but with the crash and rumble of explosions impacting all around it. The lights inside the chamber were flickering, the result of power outages and short circuiting that were now running rampant through the huge manufacturing facility.

Yet the major fear of the two men was the woman herself. She looked very serene in light of what was happening . . . *too* serene. Plus she had asked for both of them — the high officer and the lowly pilot — specifically by name. For what reason, they did not know.

She turned to the major general first.

"What is the present situation?" she asked him calmly.

"We are still under attack," the senior officer replied shakily, the mountain suddenly rumbling again as if to underscore his point. "However, our troops are deploying to counter the enemy."

"Are these United Americans who are bombing us?"

"We believe they are," the officer replied quickly.

"But where did they come from?"

"We believe they have connived to gather approximately twenty ships within the area," the officer answered, again with some zip. "Possibly more. It appears to be some kind of last-ditch effort."

"Could it be the same people who bombed our homeland?"

The officer froze. He had no idea that the Home Islands had been bombed.

"I can't say . . ." he stuttered for a reply. "I wasn't made aware of trouble back in . . ."

She held up her hand to interrupt him.

"Has there been an amphibious landing?"

The officer was recovering slowly. "We have no indications of a major landing, no," he finally answered.

"Have any helicopter troops been spotted? Is it likely we will be invaded from the air?"

The officer froze again. He had no quick answer to this one. In all the confusion, he'd neglected to consider this very frightening possibility.

"With these people," he said slowly, "anything is possible, apparently."

"How many of our airplanes are in flying condition?"

"Eighty percent!" the general replied, almost in a shout, the volume of his voice belying his terrified state.

The woman smiled at him. "And how many can be launched from our cave airstrip?"

"If all the elevators are working, four can launch simultaneously every ten seconds," he replied nervously. "Most of the entire workable fleet can be away in three hours. I believe they are waiting for your order to escape to safety, my lady."

She laughed in his face. "You don't really believe we have three hours, do you?" she asked him.

The woman then reached down, picked up the phone from her nightstand, and shouted three words into the receiver. Though the words were actually in code, the two men knew she had just given the go-word for the Zeros still within the underground facility to take off.

She added that the airplane known as the Sukki be brought up to the airstrip and prepared for launch. Then she calmly hung up the phone and turned to the trembling young ensign.

"What is your name again?" she asked him.

"Ensign Soho, my lady . . ."

"Can you fly the Sukki jet, Soho?"

He nervously nodded his head yes. "I am the only one here who can," he replied.

"Then take off your pants," she commanded him.

Both men became very confused.

"My pants?"

She nodded very serenely. "Yes, hurry," she said.

The young pilot quickly complied, his face equal shades of flushed embarrassment and ghost-white pallor.

The woman immediately went to her knees and began performing fellatio on the man. He became aroused. Then, letting her gown drop, she guided the young man to her bed and ordered him to insert himself. He did, and after fifteen seconds of furious pumping, the bewildered man climaxed.

She then ordered him to get dressed again.

"Have you ever heard of the *Fire Bats?*" she asked him. "Do you know what they are?"

The young ensign nodded, still confused as he put his pants back on. Every member of the Cult knew of the ultrasophisticated submarines which had their nuclear-tipped missiles pointing at the West Coast of America. That they were under Cult control was considered a major achievement, an example of the Cult's projection and power. It was a point hammered home by the Cult's high command on the lower ranks continuously.

"Do you then know where Island Facility Number Two is, Soho?"

"I do," the ensign replied, out of breath, but finally dressed again.

"You must go there," she said, her voice suddenly returning to its former girlish squeak. "You must go in the Sukki."

The young pilot was stunned. "Alone, my lady?"

"Yes, alone . . ." she replied, her face all of a sudden going very pale. "Believe me, you will know what to do when you get there. But you must hurry . . ."

But the young ensign didn't move, he seemed frozen to the spot. At this point, the major general stepped forward again.

"For what purpose is this, my lady?" he demanded, a little too heartily. "Surely there are more important officers who should be evacuated."

She never replied. Instead, she reached under her gown and pulled out her razor-sharp shortsword. In one swift motion, she reached out and slashed the startled major general's throat. He let out a blood-chilling cry and slumped to

313

his knees, not quite believing what had just happened to him.

The young pilot was aghast. He immediately vomited into his hands.

She turned to him, her face now again that of a young girl.

"My name was once Mizumi," she said, tears welling up in her eyes.

With that she plunged the knife into her own stomach and ripped it sideways. She, too, let out a chilling scream and then crumpled to her knees. She looked up at the ensign, her face instantly stiffening, her mouth going up in a nightmarish death grin. Then she fell over, dead.

Nearly gagging with fright, his uniform covered with vomit and blood, the young ensign finally got his feet moving. He ran out of the chamber and up the dark passageway, his eyes teary and wild at what he'd just seen.

"If they will not let me get into the Sukki," he thought madly. "I will kill them!"

Back in the chamber, the major general was gasping for his last breaths. He was bleeding profusely, the severed major artery in his neck spraying out his blood in a horrible rush of pressure.

With the last of his strength, he crawled over to the nearest wall, and using his own blood as paint, appeared to scrawl in English the word "Victory."

But he was dead before he was able to write the last letter.

It was the Free Canadian pilot named Kenny Hodge who saw them first.

He'd just arrived over Okinawa, leading the *Fitzgerald*'s second-wave airstrike in his small Alpha Jet. He had already been in radio contact with Hunter, who was presently orbiting 50,000 feet above the island, taking more IF and Juice readings. He'd also spoken with the commanders of both the 104th and the JAWs team. The situation on the ground was close to ideal: both groups were advancing toward their objectives with virtually no resistance. The hours of planning seemed to be paying off: thanks to the *New Jersey*'s guns, the first wave of selective airstrikes and the surprise painless insertion of the CLF landing parties, the Task Force had yet to suffer a single casualty.

But now a new twist was about to be added.

Hodge had just roared over the beach when his targeting warning system began blinking. There was an indication of unidentified airplanes on the northwest side of Shuri Mountain.

He booted his tiny jet's powerful engine up to

max and was soon closing in on the mountain, which even from a height of 2500 feet seemed to be entirely socked in with smog and smoke. He passed down through the polluted mist, his radar virtually burning with targets. Lowering his speed to 150 knots, he was soon within close visual range of the mountain itself.

That's when he saw them.

They *did* look for all the world like bees leaving the hive. Streams of propeller airplanes — he was sure they were Zeros — were pouring out of the side of the mountain, sometimes as many as four abreast. Hodge was astounded.

He activated his lip mike. "Flight commander, this is Alpha One . . ."

"Alpha One, this is Flight Commander," came Hunter's acknowledgment. "What've you got?"

Hodge didn't quite know how to say it. "Can you get down here quick, Flight?" Hodge said finally. "You've got to see this for yourself . . ."

Aboard the Fitzgerald

Not a minute later, JT's helmet speaker crackled to life.

"Delta Green Flight, this is Flight Commander."

"This is Delta Green. Go ahead, Hawk."

316

"Activate Plan Beta Two. Your heading is seven-five-zero south; four-four-six west. You'll get a lot of indications once airborne. Call when you need any help."

JT signed off and took a deep gulp from his oxygen mask. He'd been sitting on the deck of the *Fitz*, in Tornado Two, for almost a half hour waiting for this particular call and antsy to get into the action.

Finally, it was time to go.

The plane was surrounded with steam, its specially-adapted undercarriage attached to the *Fitzgerald*'s side catapult. JT immediately gave a signal to the *Fitz*'s launch officer, who sprang into action. Soon, there was a gang of yellow-jacketed deck crewmen swarming around JT's aircraft, making last-minute checks before launch.

He did a quick check of his cockpit essentials and found his engines were properly warmed, his flight systems up and green. He checked his weapons computer and found everything in order, so too with his fuel systems.

He gave the launch officer a thumbs-up, which was returned with a sharp salute. Then JT braced himself, lowered his head slightly, and took another deep breath. An instant later the Tornado was violently jerked forward in a rush of steam and pure engine power.

Two seconds later he was airborne.

He quickly brought the powerful Tornado up to 3000 feet and then turned toward Okinawa. He'd been held in reserve for this special mission, and now that it was happening, he wondered exactly what the result would be. Even a hipster like him worried about the future.

He looked to his right just as he was passing over the beach and saw Hunter coming up right beside him. JT flashed him a smart-ass peace sign. Below them, half the island of Okinawa seemed to be engulfed in flames.

"I'm fashionably late again, Hawk," he radioed over to the F-16XL.

"I'll remember that for the memoirs," Hunter replied.

Then they got down to business. Flying through the sludge that passed for air around Shuri Mountain, they could see the Zeros still leaving at a rate of about forty a minute.

"About eighty or so have already flown the coop," Hunter told him. "So far they're all heading south-southwest."

JT acquired the radar indications of the prop planes on his radar system, locking in the rather faint radar blips.

"Eighty should be enough," JT told Hunter. "There are only so many places they can go."

"Let's hope so," Hunter replied.

With that they broke off. Hunter immediately

swooped in and delivered a Rockeye cluster bomb directly on the lip of the cave's opening. The explosion shredded two Zeros that were just exiting the mouth of the cave, knocking one of them back into the hidden facility.

He roared back over the target and then launched a Maverick missile, guiding it right into the mouth of the enormous cave. The fire and damage resulting from both bomb hits immediately brought a halt to the Cult's launching efforts. Now only smoke was pouring out of the cave opening.

But Hunter knew this was only temporary. He had long ago determined that because of its location and sheer size, it would have taken many, many airstrikes and many, many smart bombs to close the cave opening completely, and because of its position, there was no way that even the *New Jersey's* 16-inch guns could have done the job. So while his two air-launched weapons had halted the flow of Zeros for now, he knew that the Cult would be able to clear the damage and begin launching again within thirty minutes. He hoped that was all the time he needed.

They had let the 80-odd Zeros go for one simple reason: they wanted to find out just where the Cult airplanes were deploying to. Most important was determining how many places they could escape to. By letting only a dozen or so go before temporarily sealing the cave mouth, there was a chance they would fly to just one of what could be a nightmarish number of bases.

By letting a good-sized number like 80 planes get out, the potential risk was balanced by the fact that they would probably deploy to many bases if given the option.

And it was JT's job to find the Jokers in the deck.

Even as Hunter was launching his weapons at the cave opening, JT had already caught up with the last of the fleeing Zeros and was now tailing them from 60,000 feet, well above the eyes of the Zero pilots or any rudimentary radar gear they might employ. He was especially relieved that the Tornado was flying so well. He and Hunter had worked through the night stripping the ballsy airplane of all unnecessary weight and adapting it with extra-long-range fuel tanks, additions that were not always so pilot-friendly once in flight.

They had also worked for some time on the high-tech jet's weapons-carrying system. For in JT's mission, he not only had to be able to fly for a long time, but also deliver a whammy of a punch once he got there.

It was not an enviable assignment.

* * *

Lieutenant Colonel Frank Geraci checked the time and then checked his map.

It was 0645. The sun was finally up, its morning rays distorted by the dense pollution all around him and his men. Every once in a while, one of the Task Force jets would roar over, either zooming in on a target or just pulling up from attacking one. Off in the distance, they could also hear the deep rumbling of the Great Wall weapons still firing, their gunners blindly firing out to sea, apparently convinced that a larger landing force was on its way.

The 104th Engineering Battalion/Combat of the New Jersey National Guard had returned to Okinawa. They had moved down from the beach at Nin intact and without firing a shot. Now they were huddled in a small ravine, about a hundred yards south of the Si River. Though it was difficult to see through the smoke and smog, the terrain ahead of them appeared to rise dramatically, and this was good news. Because according to Geraci's map, they had reached their objective, the base of Shuri Mountain.

He called the other officers together. They had the forty-man unit broken down into five teams of eight combat engineers, each team identified by the last name of the officer in charge. Each team had enough firepower and expertise to break through an obstruction and hold it long enough for the next team to push through and take on the next obstruction. Then the third team would move up and break their obstruction and so on, all the way up until they reached the objective. To keep the movement somewhat self-perpetuating, each man started out with nearly three full packs of weight, mostly explosives. As each team moved up toward the objective, they would leave behind supplies for the last in-line team, who would use them when it became their turn again.

The team led by Captain Don Matus would go first. The target was a line of chain wire reinforced with concertina wire, an obstruction which ringed the base of the mountain and was close to twenty feet thick. Matus's men silently crept out of the ravine, the heavy packs further weighted down by long sections of stainless-steel pipe. Reaching the objective, they quickly constructed two sixty-foot lengths of the metal tubing, stuffing the first twenty feet with HE.

Crawling through the rubble and discarded industrial waste, they managed to slip the powder-packed ends of the piping under two sections of wire about ten feet apart. On the quick count, the fire team ignited the end of the tube via a long firing cord. There was a great burst of fire, debris, and smoke—when it cleared, they could see they'd blown almost a straight path through the razor-sharp wire.

Matus's team was quickly up and through the hole, a team led by Captain Roy Cerbasi close behind. Both teams were horrified as they got on the other side of the obstruction and found the rear layer of barbed wire draped with dozens of bodies, some little more than skeletons, stretching for as far as the eye could see. Now the mystery of just why the mountain was so fortified had been answered. It was obvious that these were slaves of the Cult who had somehow managed to get out of the mountain only to die clawing their way over the sharp and deadly barrier. In other words, the obstructions weren't to keep people out; they were to keep people in.

Even though the men of the 104th were all hardened combat vets, the sight was unnerving to them. It was a true vision of Hell. They pressed on.

Cerbasi's target was a long line of concrete mounds arranged in such a mazelike way, it was impossible to pass through them quickly. After first checking the area for mines, two of Cerbasi's men zigzagged up the first row of stanchions, planted two packs of explosives, and ran back and ignited them. After making sure they'd done sufficient damage, they signaled the next pair of men to move up. Then the next, and the next. Within ninety seconds, Cerbasi's barrier was breached.

On and on they went. A team led by Captain Ray Palma took out another line of concertina wire, this one wired for deadly electrical shock, which was luckily not working because of the island's nearly total power blackout. A team led by General Tom McCaffrey—a man who'd come out of retirement to take part in the operation—quickly bore a path through a vast field of dung-covered punji sticks.

By the time this target was breached, the 104th was nearly a third of the way up the mountain.

That's when the team led by Geraci himself took on Barrier Number Five.

That's when things began to go horribly wrong.

Major Keni Hachomachi couldn't believe what he was seeing.

From his position on the side of Shuri Mountain, it seemed as if the entire island of Okinawa was aflame. Explosions were rocketing up through the smoke and smog, their fireballs reaching 200 feet and higher. The noise was just deafening, enough to cause his ears to begin bleeding.

He had more immediate concerns, however. He was commander of the Shuri Mountain defense teams, a poorly-equipped yet good-sized unit whose job it was to deal with slave escapees and protect the defensive integrity of the mountain itself. In the haste and confusion of the early morning attack, he and his men had been delayed in deploying to the battle positions. Now he was looking down at the result of that dawdle. A heavily-armed unit of soldiers he assumed belonged to the United American Army was moving up toward his position with both speed and ferocity. Hachomachi had eighty men hidden in the immediate area, another eighty or so close by, many of them equipped with old rifles, and some with only sidearms.

But their lack of armament didn't matter: his soldiers were not trained to repulse invaders by shooting at them.

"Squad one up!" he yelled, prompting six terrified young troopers to scramble up to him.

He took each man's meager weapon and checked all knapsacks. Then he pointed down to the soldiers who had just blown through yet another wall of barbed wire, and were now merely fifty feet away and moving quickly up the ever-steepening cliff. Hachomachi barked his order. With only a moment or two of hesitation, the six men of squad one went over the top.

The Mountain Defense soldiers had been instructed to scream at the top of their lungs when attacking, but the half dozen men now running down the mountain at Geraci's team remained silent, or perhaps they were unable to scream. The first one tripped and fell about twenty feet away from the startled American soldiers, the pack on his back exploding in a ball of flame, smoke, blood, skin, and bone. The second Cult soldier was cut down by the combat engineers' combined fire about thirty feet away, his knapsack igniting and blowing the man's headless torso right into the Americans.

The third and fourth Cult soldiers made it to within twenty feet of Geraci's men before they, too, were shot down. Only one of the soldier's knapsacks exploded, the resulting conflagration turning his body to bloody cinders. The fifth soldier hurled himself onto the concertina wire itself, inexplicably blowing an even larger hole in it. The sixth man, after seeing his comrades die so quickly, and for no particular purpose, simply skidded to a halt and detonated his own explosive charge, raising his arms in triumph or pain as he was obliterated in a wash of fire.

The 104th were stunned. They were trained for combat, they had the ability to take on an armed enemy and defeat him. But this was not combat. This was mass suicide.

Geraci wisely had his men withdraw to the other side of the wall of concertina wire to protect them from the human bombs. The other teams had moved up to the position by this time, and now all forty-two men of the 104th were hunkered down and protecting themselves, waiting for the next attack.

The deadly beauty of the suicidal tactic was becoming all too obvious. The American commander correctly guessed that the Cult had more soldiers willing to kill themselves to throw at him than he did troopers who were trying to get up to the objective. What was worse, if the Cult *was* able to punch a hole in the barbed wire barrier—ironically, it was now the 104th's only means of protection—then they'd be able to throw themselves right onto the engineers' position itself. Surely such a close-in fight between bullets and bombs would result in heavy casualties for the 104th.

Geraci checked his watch. It was now 0710. On top of everything else, they were running way behind schedule. If the 104th didn't reach their objective in time, it could prove deadly for the rest of the operation.

Geraci quickly discussed the situation with the rest of his officers.

Together, they all decided there was only one thing to do.

* * *

Hunter was at 2500 feet when he got the call.

He'd just thrown another Maverick missile into the side cave entrance, the resulting explosion igniting a large section of the camouflage netting which hung out over the cliff above the opening itself. With this section of netting gone he had been able to get a good, unobstructed glimpse inside the cave itself — the Cult service crews were frantically running around inside, trying to clear the damage he'd caused and get the Zeros launching again.

Geraci's request for assistance had Hunter on station in less than a minute.

The 104th was in the midst of its second full-fledged suicide attack when he arrived. At least a dozen enemy soldiers had already thrown themselves onto the barbed wire barrier in an effort to blow another hole right through it, and they were now about halfway to their goal, with more human bombs on the way. The combat engineers were firing at the Cult soldiers when they could, but the continual human detonations made it all but impossible to hit anything. The situation was quickly becoming desperate. Should the barbed wire wall be breached, the forty plus men of the 104th would be in a very precarious position, unable to stem the flow of human bombs that would surely come.

Hunter knew he didn't have time to think about it. He was down to the deck in an instant, his nose cannons blazing. Two Cult soldiers ran right into the murderous fire, their explosives-laden knapsacks detonating before they could reach the ever-weakening wire barrier. He pulled up and out to the left, putting the 'XL into a lung-crunching turn and coming back onto the killing field from the east. Two more Cult soldiers had sacrificed themselves on the wire, and three more were on the way.

Hunter opened up once again, spraying the enemy soldiers with 20mm fire. There were three simultaneous explosions as the cannon shells found their marks, but the suicide troops had come within fifteen feet of the 104th's position before Hunter could cut them down. And now six more were running down the hill.

He put the 'XL into an even tighter gut-crushing turn, and opened up on the half dozen human bombs. He got five, but one got through, blowing away yet another section of the 104th's ever precarious protective barrier. And now, ten more were on their way down the hill.

The dangerous situation was escalating very quickly. The Cult seemed to have an unlimited number of suicide soldiers. Hunter was the only thing between the 104th and certain annihilation, yet he could only cut down the enemy troops for so long until his ammunition ran out. Then what?

He quickly screeched around and strafed the horrible battle zone again, exploding eight human bombs, but missing two. Their explosives detonated no more than ten feet from the 104th's position. Pulling up, he saw ten more human bombs were on the way.

He put the 'XL into the sharpest turn of its career, an afterburner-assisted eye-popper that pulled his face back into an involuntary grin. While opening up on the latest wave of human bombs, he managed to activate his radio.

"Task Force Command, this is Task Force One," he gasped, yanking the Super Falcon into yet another rivet-popping turn. "We need your assistance — *quick.*"

The 104th got the order to "get low" less than a minute later.

Most of the combat engineers were already taking cover in the many craters on their side of the barrier; for some, getting any lower to the ground would have been impossible.

They heard it coming, of course, the long shrill whistling sound getting closer by the second. The 'XL had just completed its eighth strafing run in no more than a minute and a half when it suddenly pulled up and accelerated out of the area extremely quickly. Geraci had just enough time to yell to his men once more when the whistling became almost deafening.

Three shells from the *New Jersey*'s 16-inch rear turret slammed into the side of Shuri Mountain a second later.

The resulting explosion and concussion was so intense, it gave many of the combat engineers nosebleeds. But they all survived. The enemy soldiers were not so lucky. When the fire and debris cleared, the members of the 104th looked up and saw there was nothing left of the Cult's positions except an enormous smoking crater.

Thirty-five

Captain Jim Cook and the rest of the JAWs team felt the rumbling of the *New Jersey's* shelling clear around the other side of the mountain.

Though there were hundreds of deafening explosions going on all around them, it was easy to pick an authentic one and the battleship's fusillade had literally shaken the earth.

"*That* sounded interesting," Cook said to one of his officers, a lieutenant named Sean Higgens. "*Very* lifelike."

Higgens smiled wryly. The joke was that all the explosions going on around them were *not* lifelike. All of them were, in fact, fake.

They were standing under a cliff the top of which held one of a half dozen or so emergency exits from the interior of Shuri Mountain. The Cult guards had already fled inside—they'd been spooked by the first series of fake explosions—closing and locking the huge, camouflaged door behind them.

The entranceway was one of two main targets for the JAWs team. The other was approximately a half mile away, at the western base of the mountain. The two entranceways had been determined to be those closest to the places inside the mountain factory where the slave laborers were kept. An important part of the overall Okinawa operation plan was the safe release of these unfortunates. It was the mission given the commandos of the JAWs team.

Unlike their comrades from the 104th, the JAWs team was presently operating on a part of the island where the guns of the *New Jersey* could not reach. The heavy jungle in the area on the western edge of Shuri even made air strikes difficult. This is why the JAWs team appreciated Hunter's efforts to arrange for some psy-ops to assist them.

The "explosions" were merely flashpots igniting, the deafening rumbling nothing more than recordings piped over dozens of speakers set up in the area. The deception was the work of the stranded movie crew, specifically the special effects people. The F/X crew had wired the target zone two nights earlier, placing the fake charges and speakers around the little-used entranceways. When the *New Jersey*'s guns first opened up on the eastern edge of the island, the F/X men began activating their charges, visually and audibly mimicking a heavy cannon barrage.

As soon as the JAWs team made it to their objectives, the F/X men activated the second series of fake explosions, hoping to discourage any Cult reinforcements from coming near the operation zone. So far the plan had worked.

Cook checked his watch. It was 0725. Time to get moving.

He gathered his officers around him. Along with Higgens were Warren Maas, Clancy Miller, and Mark Snyder, all veterans of the JAWs previous campaigns, including the capturing of the Fourth Reich's American headquarters in Football City. This plan called for Snyder and Miller to take twenty men around to the second entranceway while Higgens, Clancy, Cook, and the remaining JAWs troopers concentrated on the one above them.

The problem was that the slave laborers had no idea the rescue attempt was about to be made. There had been absolutely no contact with them, if indeed any were still alive inside the beleaguered mountain. Even their nationalities were, for the most part, unknown.

Snyder and Miller counted off their detachment and departed. Cook, Higgens, and Clancy waited for another five minutes and then began to move up toward the large bolted set of doors.

One minute and a charge of SEMTEX later, the doors were open. There were no Cult troops anywhere near the opening. In fact, all the JAWs men saw was a long, very dark tunnel which curved down away from them and smelled heavily of cordite.

Leaving a guard at the door, Cook, Clancy, Higgens, and a dozen commandos entered the tunnel, their only light in the pitch black from Cook's field flashlight set on dim. The deeper they went into the tunnel, the thicker the smell of smoke filling the air. Explosions deep underground could be heard, and also the whine of propeller engines, even though they were nearly on the opposite side of Shuri from the entrance to the hidden airstrip.

They moved quickly and quietly for about ten minutes before they saw a light at the far end of the tunnel, about 200 feet away. They could hear shouting and even screaming as they moved toward the light, guns raised. The scream of prop engines was even louder.

About twenty-five feet from the opening, the group stopped and only Cook and Clancy went forward. They crept up to the edge of the tunnel to find they were looking out on a vast brightly-lit cavern. Below them were several hundred people who had to be Cult slaves. All were women and girls, all were kneeling in long rows, barely clothed, many of them visibly trembling. At the far end of the cavern was a squad of black-uniformed Cult soldiers, many of them displaying long, shiny swords. An officer was standing ramrod straight in front of these soldiers, hastily reading something in Japanese from a document.

Cook and Clancy didn't need a translation to figure out what was about to happen. It was clear the soldiers were being given orders to slaughter the women.

The Cult soldiers turned as one and with the click of their boot heels raised their phalanx of swords above their heads. Many of the women in the first row of prostrate slaves began whimpering. Death was just seconds away.

In an instant, Cook and Clancy had their M-16s up and firing, not at the Cult soldiers, but at the rows of lights on the ceiling of the vast hall. Their combined fusillade KO'd most of the lights, and short-circuited the others. Within two seconds, the entire cavern was plunged into darkness.

The men of the JAWs team quickly flowed into the cavern, down the metal stairs to the floor of the hall below. They were yelling at the women to stay down, that they were being rescued, but many of the slaves were too frightened to move in the first place.

The JAWs men found themselves crawling over the frightened, screaming half-naked women, their NightScope-equipped guns picking off the Cult blackshirts one at a time. Some of the Cult soldiers chose to skewer themselves rather than face a bullet, but others fought ferociously. Hand-to-hand combat broke out all over, the JAWs troopers battling sword-wielding Cultists with rifle butts and small arms.

The fighting was sharp and bloody, but it was over in a matter of a minute — temporarily, at least. As the last of the surviving Cult blackshirts fled the chamber, the JAWs team rounded up the women and began hurrying them up the stairway toward the exit. Shots were now being fired at them from deeper inside the mountain, a sure sign that more Cult troops were on the way.

Two of the JAWs troopers ran ahead to the opening, making sure it was still secure. They made radio contact with the other JAWs team who had run into a similar execution ceremony, but with a much larger group of slaves, possibly as many as three thousand. They were now streaming out of their exit and fleeing into the jungle. There were also reports that other exits had been opened by the slaves themselves, further emptying the Cult's subterranean chamber of innocents.

By the time the Cook-Clancy-Higgens team reached the entranceway opening with 600-odd female slaves, the F/X team had already activated their last series of fake explosions.

Using the ersatz explosions as cover, the JAWs team slipped into the jungle too, shepherding their rescuees safely out of harm's way.

According to JT's map, he was looking at a place called Iko Shima.

It was an amazingly square island about 210

miles south of the southern tip of Okinawa.

Unlike that smoky place, Iko looked like a prime piece of pristine Pacific real estate. Clear air. Lots of beaches. A cooling mountain. Lush jungle growth. Everything seemed perfect and natural.

Everything except the huge Cult air base.

He'd tracked the Zeros for nearly an hour, staying high and far behind them to avoid detection. At 53 minutes into his flight, the huge formation of Zeros began breaking up and diving out of their 15,000-foot cruising level. Soon the eighty or so Zeros began orbiting the small postage stamp of an island. The place was probably six or seven square miles in all, and at least one-third of that was taken up by the vast triangular parking areas that had obviously been constructed for the newly-built Okinawa Zeros.

Just as predicted, the place had only three runways, each running parallel to the one edge of the huge triangle. There were three separate oil storage tank farms, one at each corner. There were even three separate control towers.

The bad news was that the place was ringed with hundreds of antiaircraft weapons — fixed SAM sites, mostly, many surrounded by AAA batteries and some smaller mobile missile units. JT felt his heart sink a notch. Their job would have been much easier if the Cult had neglected to provide for air defense for Iko as they had done com-

338

pletely on Okinawa.

He keyed his lip microphone and sent a coded message back to the air control center on the *Fitzgerald*.

"Delta Green Flight to Task Force Command . . . we've got stormy weather. Repeat . . . stormy weather."

Hunter was orbiting very high about thirty miles east of Iko Jima twenty minutes later.

He and JT had already worked out their strategy. They couldn't possibly hope to wipe out all of the Zeros on the island—the eighty from Okinawa had now joined approximately 400 or so on the ground. Their only chance was to damage the air base to such an extent that it would be inoperable.

JT's Tornado carried a weapon designed for just that: it was a weapons dispenser pod attached to the hotshot airplane's underbelly. Inside were packed 600 bomblets, each the size of a ping-pong ball. Though diminutive in size, each bomblet packed a wallop equal to several sticks of dynamite. They were also weighted in such a way as to blow downward on impact, driving themselves into a concrete runway and cratering it.

Hunter was carrying a different kind of anti-runway bomb. It was a French-built Super *Martielle*. Half-bomb, half-rocket, once launched, the weapon powered itself straight down, striking the concrete with enough force to drive into it at least six feet. At that point, the warhead would explode, leaving a crater that could be as large as twenty-five feet across.

The problem facing them was that they would have to attack the base and create substantial damage—all in one pass. To loiter over the target for very much longer than that would put both of them past their bingo point, as well as at the mercy of the vast arrays of AA weapons.

Hunter went in first. He selected the northernmost runway; several of the recently landed Okinawa Zeros were still parked on its end. He was down to fifty feet and screaming across the base before the Cult gunners had any idea what was going on. Just as on Okinawa, the defense system on the island, though elaborate, was slow to respond. This told Hunter something very important: obviously the hardware was there to do the job. Apparently the training and readiness for the troops manning the high-tech weapons was lacking.

He deposited the Super *Martielle* halfway down the 800-foot runway, its warhead boring into the concrete and exploding as advertised. Because traditionally the Zero A6M needed a longer than usual takeoff run, the midshot had rendered this airstrip unusable.

Hunter opened up with his nose cannons on his pullout, scoring a barrage of hits on the control station for the runway's oil storage facility. The air was filled with AAA fire by this time, but Hunter was able to twist the F-16XL straight up with enormous acceleration, causing all of the AA shells to fall short.

At the same time, JT was sneaking in from the west. His weapons pod crackling with flame and smoke, he neatly dispensed half his load of bomblets on the north-south airstrip, then banked to the right as only a Tornado could do at such a low level and dropped the rest on the west-south strip. He, too, had his nose cannon firing throughout the bomb run, strafing a control tower and a fuel truck parking area. Unlike Hunter, he stayed low, below the AA fire going off all around him, and exited the area to the southeast.

He and Hunter formed up about six miles off the island. They had one last duty to perform before scooting back to the Okinawa battle zone. Hunter had to take a recon photo image of the base for poststrike assessment.

But when he did and checked the results, he realized that although he and JT had indeed made all three runways unusable for at least several days, they had apparently arrived just minutes after a large force of Zeros had taken off. Hunter knew this by studying his infrared scan. Not only could the device detect objects giving off heat on the ground, but it was also able to detect "heat ponds"—pools of heat left behind by an aircraft which had warmed its engines on a certain spot and had now departed.

His IR scan showed at least 200 airplanes had been on the island as little as forty minutes before. He radioed the grim news over to JT even as they formed up again and headed eastward at full throttle.

Both pilots knew there was only one place the 200 Zeros were heading.

Thirty-six

For Lieutenant Kawishi Waki, this was to be his final day.

He was flying the lead airplane in the first wave of a formation containing more than 200 Zeros. Each wave contained twenty airplanes, and as they were now in the preattack formation, each wave was separated from the next by about ten miles.

The Zeros carried no weapons—no torpedoes were strapped under the fuselages, no machine-guns decorated their wings. Rather each was packed with nearly a ton of high explosives, most of it located in a compartment just behind and below the pilot's seat.

They were from Iko Jima. They had launched within an hour of receiving word that Okinawa was under attack. For many of the pilots, it would be their first test in combat. Nearly all of them were actually pilot-trainees, men hastily instructed in how to fly the Zeros out of Shuri and over to Iko.

In a short ceremony before they left, their commander exhorted them to do their duty. He also made it quite clear that each Zero was fueled with just enough octane for a one-way trip. There was no discussion. The pilots were ordered to thank their commander for sending them on this death mission, a long bow from the waist and a mumbling of words. Then they tied their *hachimakis* around their foreheads and each received a shot of *sake*.

They toasted in unison to the spirit of Aja, downed the rice wine, and climbed into their cockpits.

Then, one after another, they flew off Iko Jima and headed north and east.

Lead pilot Lieutenant Waki didn't even know the nationality of this enemy they'd been sent out to kill. Their commanding officer never bothered to tell them. All he knew was that he was but one cog in millions within the enormous industrial and military giant known as the Asian Mercenary Cult. And now someone had attacked them, someone trying to prevent advancement, to hinder production, to stop flow.

And Lieutenant Waki had been ordered to give his life to stop it.

Ben looked into the CIC's long-range radar screen and counted 200 airplanes in all.

They were coming out of the southwest, flying in ten waves of twenty each, and at the moment the closest wave was about thirty miles from the Task Force.

He immediately sent word to Wolf, who had already activated the *New Jersey's* massive anti-aircraft arrays. At the same time, the captains of the *Tennyson* and the *Cohen* were told to prepare for an aerial attack.

The eleven fighter jets lined up on the carrier's deck were ready for launch. One by one, they were catapulted off the *Fitzgerald,* each one quickly gaining altitude and heading for the on-coming enemy armada.

They met them head-on about two minutes later.

Hunter had briefed the *Fitz's* pilots on tactics to use when dealing with the slower-moving Cult planes. It proved to be time well spent. Attacking with superior speed and agility, the jets plowed through the first formation of unarmed enemy planes, nose cannons at full bore. With their unprotected explosives compartment needing only the slightest spark to erupt, the cheap, flimsy aluminum Zeros began exploding all over the sky.

Soon the air was filled with twisted, fiery chunks of steel, glass, and flesh, all falling into the calm waters of the Pacific below.

The eleven jets never let up—they continued to pounce on the Zeros, many of which were valiantly flying on. After three passes though, the Zero formation finally disintegrated. Now the jets were able to blast away at the individual enemy pilots breaking away from the pack.

Within two minutes, the *Fitzgerald's* pilots had expertly broken the enemy's first wave, destroying all twenty enemy planes.

But no sooner had they accomplished this than another wave of twenty Zeros came into view.

Once again the jets tore through the chevrons of enemy planes, mercilessly firing and scoring kills at will. Once again the Zeros began exploding and falling. Indeed, the biggest danger for the jet pilots was avoiding all of the flaming debris that had filled the sky. These twenty Zeros were dispatched in less than a minute.

But then another twenty arrived. And after that wave was dispersed, another appeared. And after that, there was another. And another. And another. On and on it went for nearly fifteen minutes, the jet pilots shooting the bomb-laden yet completely defenseless Zeros only to have twenty more appear.

It was a turkey shoot in all senses of the term, but it would not be a total victory for the United Americans. For although the jets continued to shoot down the Zeros, they were all running low on fuel and ammo.

And that had been the Cult's plan all along.

After twenty minutes of the aerial slaughter, Tornado One was forced to return to the *Fitz*. The Viggens were close behind, as were the Orao and the Fiat. The Alpha jets were able to stay for about twenty-five minutes, the Morat about a minute more. In the end it was the A-4 and the Strikefighters that lasted the longest, but even their larger fuel tanks began to run dry.

They managed to scatter the eighth wave of Zeros, but then were forced to return to the *Fitz*.

The antiaircraft crews on every ship were ready when the first line of surviving Zeros appeared high above the Task Force about ten minutes later.

The chevron of propeller planes quickly broke and one by one came screaming down at the four ships.

The gun crews opened up. Dozens of 40mm Bofors, two-pound Pom-Pom "Chicago Pianos," Phoenix Gatling guns, 5-inchers, and heavy machine-guns let loose at once.

The wall of fire put up by the ships—especially by the *New Jersey*—was frightening. So many explosive-packed Zeros were blowing up above the Task Force, it looked like a fireworks display.

But for *Cohen,* it wasn't enough.

Hit dozens of times on the way down, one kamikaze pilot was still able to steer his burning craft into the supply ship's main cargo hold. The airplane exploded on impact, blowing a gaping hole in the side of the ship just above the waterline. A few seconds later, a second Zero got through and impacted directly on the *Cohen*'s bow. Almost simultaneously a third explosives-packed kamikaze slammed into the ship's stack, continued down through two decks, and detonated into its main engine room.

Within seconds, huge secondary explosions began to rock the supply ship. She was quickly on fire in a dozen places—so many her crew had no chance to fight all of the spreading flames.

Twenty seconds later, another Zero plummeted into *Cohen,* glancing off the bridge and impacting into the center cargo hold. The resulting explosion literally lifted the ship out of the water and slammed it back down again. The ship went to a 60-degree list, allowing seawater to flood into its lower compartments. Smoke was pouring out of every hole in her, and the flames were so intense they actually melted large sections of the superstructure.

No one would ever know whether the order to abandon ship was ever given—some of the *Cohen*'s crew were already in the water around the dying ship, most of them had been blown overboard in the initial explosions. The *Tennyson* had valiantly moved up alongside its stricken sister, its crew sending streams of water on several of the fires. Others were trying to pluck the *Cohen*'s sailors from the sea even as the battle still raged around them.

But it was clear that the supply ship was mortally wounded. When the fifth Zero dropped out of the sky and exploded directly on the ship's aft cargo hold, it was the final blow. The ship's rear end literally disintegrated. The *Cohen* went down in less than five seconds.

Of the 338 men on board, only twenty-seven survived.

It was 0810 when the 104th finally made it to the top of Shuri Mountain.

Almost miraculously, they'd reached their objective virtually intact, suffering only two wounded.

Their triumph in reaching the 1500-foot summit was quickly dampened, however. For it was from this vantage point that they had watched the titanic air battle between the *Fitz*'s pilots and the waves of Zeros, and eventually, the sinking of the *Cohen*.

It was a grim reminder of what they had to do.

Most of the firing had stopped by this time. It was clear that the vast majority of the island was now without electrical power. For the most part, the Great Wall of guns had fallen silent. The enemy's will to resist had also been broken, or at least they were in need of a major regrouping. Any opposition the 104th met on the way up the second half of the mountain scattered as soon as they fired on it. Now, according to Task Force radio reports, there were no Cult troop movements in evidence anywhere on the island.

The 104th quickly set up their equipment and went about their task with workmanlike authority. They had carried nearly 800 pounds of XHE — for extra-high explosive — up the mountain with them, and now much of it was being placed by troopers in repelling equipment along the precarious overhangs which dominated the northwestern side of the mountain peak.

Below them was the valley of smog, now made extra thick by two hours of explosions both real and fake. Hidden in the polluted gloom directly underneath them was the enormous cave mouth that served as the opening for the hidden airstrip.

Their charges were all in place by 0830. Previous radio traffic between the 104th and the Task Force told them that the JAWs teams had determined that most if not all slaves were out of Shuri Mountain. Now came the report that the JAWs team had sealed all smaller entrances not previously blocked by the earlier airstrikes.

At 0835, the second-to-last barrage of fake F/X explosions went off, the idea being to keep any Cult soldiers in the jungle at bay until the JAWs team reached the beach at Nin again safely.

Then at 0840, Geraci got a call directly from Ben Wa on the *Fitzgerald*. Everything was go for the 104th to complete its mission. With one twist of a detonator handle, Geraci did just that, triggering the 800 pounds of XHE to explode out and downward, causing an enormous landslide down the northeastern face of the mountain.

It took five full minutes for the smoke and dust to clear, but when it did, there was no doubt that the 104th had completed its mission. The landslide had completely covered the entranceway to the hidden airstrip, sealing it forever.

The vast Shuri Mountain aircraft manufactur-

351

ing facility was now one enormous tomb.

Hunter and JT touched down on the *Fitzgerald* shortly after the 104th detonated their charges.

Their fuel tanks were so low, neither one would have had enough gas to make another go-around should their first approach to the carrier not be true. Both made perfect landings, however, quickly securing their airplanes and unstrapping from their cockpits.

They didn't have to be told the grim news about the *Cohen* — they had followed the battle via their radios on the dash back from Iko Jima. As it turned out, they had caught up with the last wave of the Iko strike force, knocking down six Zeros and scattering the others. Had it not been for that action, the kamikaze raid on the battered, depleted Task Force could have been much worse.

But there was no celebrating as they wearily climbed out of their airplanes. With the loss of the *Cohen* and a large part of her crew, even the reports of the successful completion of the Okinawa campaign did little to lift their spirits.

The grim reality of war had finally hit home.

They spent another full day in the waters off

352

Okinawa. Heavily-armed landing parties helped the 104th strip dozens of usable weapons from the now-silent Great Wall while others scoured the island for valuable fuel. A contingent from the F/X group joined in these efforts and then took up stations on the *Fitzgerald*.

The following morning, the three remaining ships of the battered Task Force sailed away, leaving countless thousands of Cult soldiers entombed in Shuri Mountain, and 311 Americans and the USS *Cohen* at the bottom of Okinawa Bay.

Part Three

At The End of The World

Thirty-seven

"Crunch" O'Malley's back was killing him.

"Maybe I'm getting too old for this," he muttered, trying to reposition himself in the tight pilot's seat. "Or maybe I should lay off the Scotch. Or the stogies."

He'd been flying for sixteen hours now and had at least another two to go before he reached the coordinate where he hoped the USS *Fitzgerald* would be. He'd last taken on fuel ninety minutes before, an expensive midair gas-up courtesy of a very high-priced mercenary refueling company flying out of what passed for New Guinea these days. It was his third such aerial pump-up since leaving a small, secret airstrip located on Aitku Atoll, one of the smaller Carolina Islands, just after midnight.

Now it was four in the afternoon and his back was getting stiffer.

It had not been a pleasant mission. Three and a half days of flying over the vast South Pacific made for looking at a lot of water and little else; the distances between islands or island chains was simply mind-numbing in some cases.

But when he *did* find a "live island"—one that was under control by the Cult—all the news was disturbing. In fact, his camera pods were filled with video showing island after island of Cult facilities: weapon assembly plants, staging areas, supply depots, ammo dumps, fuel farms, and above all, troop barracks. The Cult's domination of the area was so vast, Crunch couldn't imagine it being any different from the Imperial Japanese occupation of the area back in the 1940s.

But actually, there *was* one big difference, and in fact, this was the most disturbing aspect of Crunch's long, long flight. For although he'd reconnoitered upwards of 200 separate Cult military and support facilities, they all had one thing in common.

They were all empty.

He had had a hard time believing it at first—the Cult sites were elaborate in the extreme, frightening examples of the Asians' military industrial power, yet they were all abandoned. It was only after he'd done several unopposed low—level runs that it began to sink in. The wishful thinking was that the Cult had simply dissolved, perhaps after finally hearing about the Tokyo Raid and the death of Hashi Pushi—but this was definitely not the case. No, the hundreds of thousands of soldiers who had been staging at these island sites had not disappeared, nor had their units disintegrated. Rather, they had obviously deployed to other areas.

This was the disturbing news Crunch was bearing for Hunter and the rest of the Task Force. All the evidence of Cult power was there, spread throughout the South Pacific like a plague. But that power had moved on.

The question was, where?

It was ninety minutes later when Crunch overflew the chain of five small islands where the Cult had built its enormous battleship manufacturing yards.

Just like the rest of the Cult's military installations, this one was absolutely deserted. There were no soldiers, no workers, not a smokestack puffing or a light burning or an AA site manned.

Nor were their any battleships.

He buzzed the necklace of islands, grimly fascinated that such an example of pure military might could be so utterly empty. It looked like a scene from a 1960s end-of-the-world movie.

But unlike the other abandoned sites, this one bode not well at all for the Task Force. From the looks of things, there were anywhere from two to three dozen battleships roaming around out there. If just two or three located the shoe-string fleet of the United American Task Force, it would prove catastrophic.

That's why Crunch had to reach the *Fitzgerald* as quickly as he could.

Leaving the chain of islands behind, he swiftly climbed to 15,000 feet and headed east, toward the Task Force's prearranged coordinate.

That's when he saw it.

It was coming right at him—head on—a sickly pink airplane leaving a long trail of dirty gray smoke. Crunch instinctively banked away, preventing what would surely have been a fatal midair collision. Still, the strange airplane came so close to his nose, he'd almost clipped its tail-plane in his evasive dive.

As it screamed past, he got a brief but telling glimpse of the airplane itself.

Crunch was startled that he recognized the type right away—it was an Me-262 *Strumvogel*, or Stormbird, the Nazi-designed airplane that was the only combat jet to see regular action in World War Two, all of it at the end of the hos-tilities in Europe. As such, its fuselage was made primarily of wood and nonmetal layering. No wonder his radar hadn't picked up the air-craft.

"Son-of-a-bitch!" Crunch yelled into his mask. "An antique stealth!"

But a second later, he had other problems.

Deep into his evasive maneuver, the right-side engine on the RF-4X Super Phantom flamed out, stalled because of the radical banking. Crunch coolly but quickly stomped on his left rudder and punched the left aileron, twisting the venerable fighter-bomber in such a way that air-flow into the sputtering right engine became constant again.

He did this twice before the suffocating engine relit on the third attempt. He was able to get out of the dizzying spin and level out at a hair under 8500 feet.

The Me-262 was long gone by this time, disappearing into the huge cloud bank to the south.

Though safe, Crunch was in a mild state of shock. He was not surprised by much anymore. Ever since the Big War, the world had gone crazy; having the granddaddy of all combat jets nearly collide with him at 15,000 feet was just another example of the madness. And even seeing one which was painted in a hideous pink blossom color didn't phase him much.

But something about the lightning-quick encounter incident *had* shook him. It was the pilot himself. Their eyes met for what could have only been a tenth of a second—but it was surprising how much one could see in such a short amount of time. The Me-262's pilot was a young Oriental. He was wearing a red kerchief around his head instead of a helmet, and an old leather flight suit which also harkened back to old Imperial Japan.

But it was the pilot's face that sent a chill to Crunch's bones and back again.

For what Crunch saw was a look that, for lack of a better word, could be described only as totally evil.

It was weird, a sensation that baffled him at its depth of spookiness. He knew he'd never forget it . . .

Recovering to 20,000 feet, Crunch shook off the chill with a deep gulp of oxygen. His back no longer hurting him, he booted in his afterburner and felt the corresponding kick as the engines devoured raw fuel being dumped into their tails.

He had to get the Task Force with all haste.

The Next Day

The four-prop P-3 Orion antisub plane banked low over Punta Eugenia and then went into a sweeping orbit above the small island.

It was 0800. The P-3 had been airborne since leaving Vancouver around midnight. The long-range airplane was on a dangerously routine mission: to keep tabs on *Fire Bats* One, the Cult-controlled submarine which continuously

362

plied the waters off the southern coast of occupied California, its 18-megaton nuclear missile targeted at any one of the West Coast's population centers.

Sitting at the controls of the P-3 was Major Pietr Frost, the Free Canadian officer who served as his government's liaison with the United American cause. In the uncertain times following the Tokyo Raid, General Jones had asked Frost to oversee the crucial *Fire Bats* tracking operation personally. If the Cult made good on its threat to nuke a West Coast city and incinerate millions of innocent Americans, the chances were that Frost would be one of the first to see the missile go up.

The island of Punta Eugenia was located off of Baja, the virtually abandoned isthmus which provided the tail for California. A tiny, top secret United American coast-watcher base was located deep inside the desolate rocky atoll. In one of several such stations hidden along the West Coast, the fifteen-man crew kept track of *Fire Bats* One by monitoring radio signals, sonar waves, and the general commotion made by submarine operation with their ultrasensitive listening devices.

Normally, the base at Punta Eugenia would keep a running account of the *Fire Bats'* ever-changing underwater course, transmitting the information to the P-3 via a satellite uplink. The

363

Orion would then locate the *Fire Bats* and trail it from a safe altitude until the plane's fuel ran out, at which time another P-3 would take over. (A similar system was in place off the coast of northern California, where *Fire Bats* Two usually operated.)

The hound-dog procedure served as a rudimentary early warning system should the *Fire Bats* ever launch its nuclear weapon. If and when that happened, the P-3 was under orders to sink the sub immediately, a task it couldn't do before then for fear that such an action would provoke its sister vessel *Fire Bats* Two to launch its weapon.

But on this day, something was not routine.

This was because the Punta station had not been able to locate *Fire Bats* One for nearly eight hours. The P-3 had been searching for it all night, too, with no luck.

What is going on? Frost wondered over and over. If the equipment on Punta was operating properly—which was why the P-3 was orbiting over the island, to check the station's triangulation—then the lack of sub noise could mean only one of two things: either the *Fire Bats* was laying dead cold on the bottom somewhere, or it had left the area.

Either way, it would be a significant event.

The P-3 continued circling the small island for another ten minutes. Finally Frost's communica-

364

tions officer told him that all of the equipment at the top secret station had checked out. Losing track of the *Fire Bats,* then, was not a mechanical error.

Frost turned the big prop plane back north and began the low-level, radar-avoiding run back to its base at Vancouver. At the same time, he told his communications officer to establish a secure scramble line direct to United American headquarters in Washington.

General Jones had to be alerted at once.

Washington

It was 1115 when Jones got Frost's decoded message.

The general had been up since three A.M., poring over a bevy of strange reports coming in from the various spy posts monitoring Cult activity on the occupied West Coast.

The truth was, Frost's emergency message did not come as a complete surprise. In fact, the stack of fax lines and yellow-paper cable messages in front of Jones all reported some kind of puzzling event happening on the other side of the continent.

Just minutes before learning that *Fire Bats* One had disappeared, Jones had received a similar report from the people tracking *Fire Bats*

Two. It, too, had dropped off their listening screens, and either was on the bottom running extremely silently or had left its usual patrol area. What disturbed Jones the most was that either position might be a prelude to a launch by both enemy subs.

Or it might mean something else.

Another report had come in to him from a spy cell operating on the ground just outside of LA. The message came in quick and garbled, but decipherable. It said the Cult ground forces were on the move just about everywhere in and around the city. Another report from an agent located near Santa Monica told of huge Cult convoys tying up traffic on the nearby freeways. Similar reports had come in from San Diego all the way up to Frisco.

By noon, Jones had more than fifty separate reports, all stating that the Cult was mobilizing for something big.

But what?

He had to find out. Jones picked up his secure phone and punched in a code which transmitted directly to the UA's defense command center located on the other side of the Pentagon. With this simple action, the general was ordering all United American forces on full alert. A second quick call informed the Free Canadian government of the situation.

A third call was made to a private outfit out

of Texas called Sky-High Spies. So far, Jones had been monitoring the situation on the West Coast via secondhand information. He wanted to see for himself what the hell was going on in California.

Four hours later, a dark, sinister shape was rocketing over southern California at an altitude of nearly 100,000 feet.

It was an SR-71 Blackbird, the ultra high-speed, high-altitude spy plane which had been unceremoniously retired back in the late 1980s. Its two-man crew—they were brothers, Jeff and George Kephart—had located the airplane two years before, hidden away in a bunker outside Mexico City. How it got there, no one knew, but the brothers had promptly bought the magnificent airplane and spent much of the ensuing time secretly getting it back in flying condition, using rebuilding diagrams drawn up by Hawk Hunter himself.

They were just getting to flight trials when the Second Axis invaded America. Once the Fourth Reich was ejected from the eastern part of the country, the Kephart Brothers went back to work and got SR-71 up and flying. They'd been doing secret recon work for Jones and the United American Armed Forces ever since.

Once the SR-71 reached the proper coordinate,

Pilot Jeff told Brother George to get the cameras rolling. The SR-71 was so fast it could do 3000 mph, and its cameras were so powerful it could photograph the entire coastline of California in a mere twenty minutes.

Their run started directly over San Diego and lasted past Port Orford, in what used to be Oregon. Even though they were flying more than eighteen miles high—and thus way beyond detection by the Cult's barely adequate AA radar systems—they really didn't need the long-range lenses on their cameras to show them what was happening below.

Up and down the entire coastline, there were Cult troops massed on the beaches and at various staging points. From these locations, they and their equipment were being packed onto troopships. And those troopships were clearly setting sail.

It didn't take a military genius to figure out what was happening: the Cult was pulling out of California.

The question was, why?

As soon as their photo run was completed and the camera bays checked, Brother Jeff turned the big plane east and booted its massive ramjet engines up to top speed.

They and the precious photographic evidence would be in Washington in less than an hour.

* * *

Master Sergeant U Suk Bum was the highest-ranking noncommissioned officer in his unit.

But still he was not a happy man.

Although he had more than seventy men under his direct command, he knew that he would never be elevated to the better-paying Asian Mercenary officer corps simply because the Cult never promoted anyone who was not full-blooded Japanese beyond the rank of sergeant.

Bum was not Japanese; rather he was Korean — or Chinese, he really didn't know. The point was that he was not born Nipponese, and therefore would never be entitled to the full benefits of what was actually the misnamed *Asian* Mercenary Cult.

Bum's unit ran the supply line between downtown Los Angeles and the suburb of Azusa. As such, they were responsible for keeping the four divisions of Cult troops arrayed along the line supplied with bullets, bombs, water, and food. It had been an easy assignment during what was a tense but nevertheless leisurely occupation.

That was, until this morning.

Now his unit was being ordered to work harder than he thought possible. All four divisions along the Azusa Line were pulling out and heading for the LA docks. Bum's trucks and men were responsible for driving them there.

But even with fifty troop trucks operating at once, it would take Bum's unit dozens of trips and many, many backbreaking hours back and forth to move the 40,000-plus troops and their equipment. But the Cult High Command was demanding it be done by 0900 the next day or Bum and his men would face a firing squad. It was such an unreasonable mission, Bum had already been forced to break up an attempted mutiny of his ranks, shooting and killing two of his drivers who'd balked when he'd first given them their do-or-die orders.

Now it was close to midnight, and fully half of the four divisions had yet to mount up, never mind be driven the ninety-minute trip down to the docks. Bum was sitting in his broken-down staff car in a highway rest stop located on Route 395A, counting the number of his trucks that were passing by. Each one that was delayed or going slow meant he was one step closer to eating a bullet courtesy of his commanding officers. It was not a pleasant task.

At this moment his hate for the Japanese commanders reached its zenith. Though they claimed to be conquering the planet in the name of all Asians, Bum knew this was simply bullshit. In addition to being stingy and petty beyond all belief, his commanders were overtly racist toward the other non-Japanese Cult members, especially the certified Koreans. On the slightest whim, the officers would shoot any Korean who they believed was out of line, or, even worse, ship them back to one of the manufacturing facilities which dotted the South Pacific islands where nothing waited for them but a life of slave labor followed by a guarantee of a painful and terrifying death.

Bum sighed as the last of his trucks finally ambled by. There was no way they were going to make the 0900 deadline. And he had no doubt that his officers would make good on their threat to kill them all, starting at the top.

Bum got out of his car, lit a cigarette, then sat down on a nearby wall. Stretched before him was the panorama of Cult-occupied LA County. Despite the thick, omnipresent smog, it still looked like quite a prize, an uncomparable spoil of war for as far as the eye could see.

He drew heavily on his butt, contemplating the brightly-lit landscape. Too bad they were all leaving. He had actually come to like this place.

The next thing he knew, there was a gloved hand wrapped around his mouth and nose. He was yanked back off the wall and thrown into a high bramble bush. Two men were suddenly standing over him, dressed in black, wearing camouflaged ski masks and pointing laser-sighted M-16s at his heart.

371

Bum was instantly frozen with fear. Surely these were his executioners, sent by the Cult command to eliminate him.

Purely on instinct, he tried to roll away only to have one of the men kick him in the groin. After that he knew it was useless to struggle.

They dragged him down the embankment, across a dirty stream, and into a gully next to a water culvert. Finally they stopped at the end of the gully, throwing him against a concrete support adjacent to the culvert and kicking his legs out from under him. They searched him and, finding little, tied both hands behind his back.

Only then did they remove their masks. Bum couldn't believe it: they were both Caucasian.

"Do you speak English?" one of them asked him gruffly, his M-16 not an inch away from Bum's runny groin.

"Yes, I do," he breathed, still petrified.

"Then get this straight," the man ordered him, jabbing him with the snout of the M-16. "Answer my questions or you're singing falsetto. Understand?"

Bum did.

"Why are you guys pulling out?" the second man asked him.

"Orders from the top," Bum replied trembling.

The first man applied more snout pressure on Bum's crogies. "Don't be a wise-ass," he said. "He asked you *why* you're pulling out. Is it an evacuation before a nuke strike?"

Bum shook his head vigorously. He didn't know much, but he was sure that the reason for the sudden withdrawal was not related to an impending nuclear attack.

"We are being redeployed to a major battle zone," Bum told them, repeating what his commanding officer had told him.

"Redeployed?" the first man asked. It was the last thing he expected to hear.

Bum sensed right away that the men didn't believe him. He was right.

The man slipped the safety off his M-16. "You're lying."

Bum was terrified beyond words now. "No—please, listen to me," he pleaded. "If we were pulling out because they were going to nuke the place, do you really think it would be like this?"

He was referring to the traffic jam of troop trucks heading down into the valley on a number of nearby highways.

"You see? Everyone's in a hurry," Bum went on. "If they were going to drop a nuke, they would have given us orders to strip the entire countryside, and the time to do so. Believe me, I know them. They think they're coming back."

The two men still seemed unconvinced.

"And," Bum hastened to add, "they'd be raping anything that walked. Of that you can be sure . . ."

On this, the two men grudgingly had to agree.

"Okay, then," the second man said. "Tell us everything you know. Starting with where the hell you are deploying to."

Bum was only too happy to oblige. It took him fifteen minutes to spill his guts. Times, dates, locations. Estimated troop strength. The works. When he was done, his captors were both angry and impressed. He had no doubts that they believed him.

"You're one of the lucky ones," the first man told him, finally removing the snout of the M-16 from Bum's privates.

With that, they put their masks back on and took off down the culvert, leaving Bum still tied, but safe in the gulley.

Five minutes later, the Cult sergeant heard a slight mechanical sound off in the distance. Then, silhouetted in the full moon, he saw the shadows of two Cobra gunships rise into the sky and dash off at a low level to the east.

Thirty-eight

Two days later

The pilot named Soho had never known such luxury.

He was surrounded by sixteen young women, all dressed in little more than leis and grass skirts. His chair was expertly woven of silk and bamboo. The coconut cup in his right hand was filled to the brim with some alcoholic concoction; the massive pipe in his left hand was filled with hashish.

Before him stretched a view of scenic beauty found nowhere else on the planet. The dramatic cliffs, the gently swaying palm trees, the friendly green ocean.

To the Cult high command on Okinawa, it had been known as Greater East Asian Warriors' Association Military Manufacturing Facility Number Two, but soon after his arrival, Soho learned that the title was intentionally misleading. There was little military here, few "warriors," no smog, and certainly no manufacturing. Rather, this was tropical heaven on earth.

This was Fiji.

He had no idea what time it was, no idea what day it was. And he really didn't care. The traumatic events leading to his escape from Okinawa and his journey here were already slipping from his mind, oozing out of him like the greenish foam running out of the corners of his eyes, ears, and mouth.

The seven Cult high officers waiting off in a corner of the huge outdoor ballroom had been anxiously whispering since their arrival several hours before—but Soho had no idea what they were talking about. He had simply chosen not to speak with them at this time. Why would that make them uneasy? He'd given them their orders as soon as he'd arrived, and they'd assured him that they were being carried out at the moment.

So what was the problem? He was in paradise—there were as many girls for the taking as he could ever want. There was an abundance of drugs and liquor. And the food was outstanding.

He didn't want to waste time trying to figure out how to conquer the world.

Mounted on stilts on the edge of the cliff overhanging the beach nearby was the pink Sukki jet. It was now covered in flower petals and multicolored blossoms. Six smoking urns surrounded it, their firepots billowing cinnamon incense. There had to be more than five hundred candles arrayed around it in wonderfully haphazard fashion. Despite the wind, they were all burning quite brightly. Nearby was the island's native band, playing his favorite song on ukes and conch shells. He didn't know the name of it — it was, in fact, Stravinsky's "Firebird Suite" — but he certainly liked the tune, so much so, he'd ordered them to keep playing it, over and over again, day and night. So far, they had complied.

He took a refill on his coconut drink and had the hash pipe relit. The warm wind felt so delightful on his face, he reached to touch it. But in doing so, he found a surprise. His face felt uncharacteristically rough with stubble, or at least, his chin was.

Was it true? Was he really growing facial hair for the first time in his young life?

He drew out the razor-sharp knife from his belt and studied his skewed reflection on the gleaming blade.

It *was* true! There were definitely signs of hair growing through on his chin and upper lip. He was delighted. He'd sprouted a thin goatee over night.

He lowered the blade to find the seven Cult officers standing before him again. They were bowing, mumbling. *Groveling.*

"This is getting uncomfortable," Soho told them with his newfound haughty exasperation. "What is it that you want?"

"We ask only a minute of your time, sir," the eldest of the group pleaded. "It is extremely important."

He wiped the ooze from his mouth and face and slowly shook his head.

"One-half minute," he said, "and only if you promise not to disturb me for another forty-eight hours."

The seven officers exchanged worried looks, and then all seemed to shrug at the same time.

"One-half minute," the oldest officer agreed.

Soho pulled one of the lovelier girls around him closer to his thigh and took another long drag of the hash pipe.

"Well, you have twenty-eight seconds left," he informed the officer.

The man inched forward a little and bowed one more time. "We really only have one question, sir . . ."

"And it is?"

He crept forward just a few steps more.

"Well, sir," he began, his voice barely above a whisper. "Now that we're redeploying all our troops as you ordered, what shall we do next?"

Soho stopped drinking from his coconut in midsip.

"*I* told you to redeploy *what?*"

The officer looked genuinely startled. "Our occupation forces, sir," he answered shakily, "our entire army on the West Coast of America is being pulled out, redeployed. So are our troops in this part of the domain. We have emptied all the garrisons. On your orders, sir. Don't . . . don't you recall?"

Soho thought about it for a moment. Something about what the officer was saying sounded familiar, almost as if he'd been thinking about this very thing just moments before.

But it was gone now.

"Of course I remember," Soho lied. "Do you really think that . . ."

The officer was suddenly bowing like crazy. "I meant not to offend, sir," he was saying between grunts. "Please forgive my . . ."

Soho held up his hand and the man went suddenly still.

"You have eighteen seconds left," Soho said, happily sucking on the hash pipe again. "To finish your question, I mean . . ."

The officer, certain that he'd just avoided a quick death, coughed and started again. "Sir, our redeployed forces are simply awaiting your further orders."

Soho stopped a moment to think again.

"Just how many of our troops are we talking about?" he asked.

The officer bowed quickly, almost proudly. "Twenty-five divisions. Two hundred and ninety-two thousand combat soldiers. Several thousand support and supply groups. We are moving them day and night, on both aircraft and ships, from California as well as the islands on our Pacific rim. There has never been a military maneuver of this scale in the history of . . ."

"Have them solidify their present position," Soho suddenly heard himself say. "They must prepare immediately for an attack from the air as well as the sea."

The senior officer was stunned. "At their *present* position, sir?"

"That is what I said, isn't it?" Soho replied, really not quite sure himself.

"Yes, sir," the officer stumbled. "But our present position is little more than a staging area. Our port of redeployment. It's extremely crowded at the moment, and grows worse as more and more of our troops arrive. Surely you mean for us to *expand* our perimeters. To take the high ground, build our positions in depth, and . . ."

"No!" Soho suddenly screamed. He knew this would upset him. "I said solidify our *present* position. For an attack from the air and from the sea."

The six other officers were now gritting their teeth and staring at the ground. It was happening again.

The senior officer began to speak again, but Soho was done with him.

"You are dismissed," he said coolly.

The officer looked him square in the eye for a

380

moment, but quickly shrank away. "Yes, sir . . ."

The senior officer fell back into the ranks of his six comrades. They bowed as one and began to sadly troop away.

"Just one more thing," Soho called after them, freezing them in their steps.

"Yes, sir?" the senior officer asked.

Soho took another long drag of his hashish.

"Exactly where *is* our present position?"

All seven officers went pale at once.

"Right where you stated in your orders, sir," the senior officer gasped his answer. "The place they used to call Pearl Harbor."

Thirty-nine

Washington

General David Jones reached into his bottom desk drawer and came out with a bottle of no-name whiskey.

"I've been saving this for a special occasion," he told the other two men sitting in his small, cluttered Pentagon basement office. "This just isn't what I had in mind."

The two men nodded in grim agreement. They were still wearing their black camouflage uniforms, their faces were still covered in charcoal paint. They even had their laser-sighted M-16s by their sides. Neither had had the time to change since their lightning-quick trip from occupied California to Washington.

They were Jesse Tyler and Bobby Crockett, better known as the Cobra Brothers. It was they whom Jones had sent to enemy-held Los Angeles to get some hard intelligence on the ground. It was they who, after finding and interrogating a

Cult prisoner, flew directly to DC via a high-speed Texas Air Force C-2 aircraft.

And it was they who bore the mysterious news that the Cult was pulling out of the American mainland and redeploying to, of all places, Pearl Harbor.

"It makes no sense," Jones said, pouring three drinks into paper cups. "It wasn't like we were ready to attack them — or even start harassing them. They've got the numbers. In weapons. In transport. In pure manpower. And they've got the nukes. So why the hell are they pulling out?"

Crockett took a sip from his drink. "Maybe our original plan worked," he said, grimacing at the bad yet effective booze. "Maybe by knocking off Hashi Pushi — or causing him to do the job himself, I mean — the Cult is literally falling apart. The officers out in the field just figured that when the Holy Word stopped dribbling down from Tokyo, it was time to pack up and go home."

General Jones sipped his drink too. "I only wish that was the case, Bobby," he said gloomily. "But it doesn't add up. If the Cult *was* disintegrating, would their people on Okinawa have stuck around and fought like they did? And where did all those battleships the Task Force reported go?"

"And where the hell are those subs?" Jesse Tyler added.

Jones downed his drink and poured out three more.

"We've been looking for them around the clock," he confirmed, "and we haven't turned up so much as a bubble."

"That's scary," Crockett said. "They could be anywhere by this time."

"It's all these Cult troops in Hawaii we've got to concentrate on," Jones said, throwing a folder on the table. "Take a look at these . . ."

He spread a dozen or so high-altitude photos across the desk. They showed the tens of thousands of Cult troops massed in and around Pearl Harbor.

"Look at the fortifications these guys are building," he told the chopper pilots. "And all those AA and SAM sites. We've also heard they've shipped out any civilians left on Oahu to the other islands, but not before stealing all of their food and water."

"Sounds like the bastards plan on staying for a while," Tyler said. "And expecting a fight."

"That's just what Hawk said when I talked to him," Jones said. He went on to explain that he'd had a long conversation with the Wingman earlier in the day via a jimmy-rigged secure line set up in the *Fitz*'s CIC. The Task Force had been slowly limping eastward since the titanic battle on Okinawa. With the mysterious new developments on the West Coast, Jones had no choice but to order them to remain on combat alert and be ready for action—or as ready as they could possibly be.

"And what are his thoughts on this situation?" Tyler asked. "Does he have any ideas on what the hell we should do?"

"He certainly does," the general replied, pouring out three more stiff shots. "Drink up, boys. You'll need it after I tell you just *what* he has in mind . . ."

Seal Cove, Old State of Maine

Al Nolan, a.k.a. "Ironman," was having a bad day.

First of all, his right index finger hurt. He'd spent the last eight hours recording data on his hand-held electronic notepad, and all that button-pushing had strained a ligament or something.

Second, he'd been standing before the 160,000-gallon saltwater aquarium for most of that time, and the damp conditions were already beginning to give him a head cold.

But third, and most of all, he was bored.

The big tank was the centerpiece of the New American Aquatic Institute, an organization devoted solely to the study of mammal marine life.

In the tank were two dolphins, each about three years old.

By trade, Ironman was an accountant, a numbers cruncher, and one of the best. He took the job as head accountant at the Institute simply because of the research conducted with dolphins there. In a matter of months, he had put the organization back in the black and showed them how to stay financially solvent for many years to come—no easy task in light of the catastrophic upheavals suffered by America in recent times.

In gratitude, the Ironman was given complete run of the aquarium, for the Institute had also come to respect his self-taught knowledge of the intelligence potential of dolphins.

Nolan was now probably the most knowledgeable researcher on dolphin intelligence on the American continent. In fact, he knew *so* much about them that he felt no further study was needed—and this was the source of his boredom. He felt it was time to act on the knowledge he'd gathered. Time to use the dolphins' intelligence to solve one of the world's most intriguing mysteries.

But with the country and the globe still in a constant state of confusion, the priority for Nolan's grand search was very, very low, to say the least.

The dolphins in the tank began to cavort, possibly beginning a mating ritual. Al stepped closer to the eight-inch-thick tempered glass. He didn't want to miss a thing.

Just then, the radio-phone down the hall rang. Nolan, the only one around, was momentarily torn between getting the phone and continuing to watch the dolphins. Finally, he grudgingly tore himself away from the tank and answered it.

He would soon be very glad he did.

"Ironman? *Hey, Ironman?* Can you hear me?"

Nolan couldn't believe it. "Hey, Hawk—is that you?"

"Sure is. But I don't have much time to talk, and I've got to ask you a big favor, old friend . . ."

Fifteen minutes later, Nolan hung up the phone, completely overwhelmed by what he had heard. Suddenly he wasn't bored anymore.

Without hesitation he went to his quarters, threw together a suitcase of clothes, and grabbed a fresh box of Ticonderoga No. 2 pencils. Before he left, he lifted up a loose floorboard in his bedroom and took out a small steel box. In it was his most prized possession: his Rolodex of names from the old days, when he'd worked as the top logistics man for the U.S. Navy's most secret projects.

Once packed, he went back to the tank. The Institute assistants would have to care for the dolphins for the time being—but he needed one last look. He loved the animals so much, tears came to his eyes. It was no surprise that the Greeks believed dolphins were once human beings. The animals' intelligence, and especially their individual personalities, were indeed quite human-like.

And though he knew his scheme to use them to unravel one of history's most perplexing riddles would have to be put on hold for now, he was more confident than ever that it would indeed happen someday.

This was because in return for his unique services, Hawk Hunter had promised to help him do so.

Ten minutes later, Nolan was heading for a tiny nearby airstrip where an unmarked T-45A Goshawk Navy Trainer and pilot were waiting for him. It was ready to whisk him down to Andrews Air Force Base outside Washington, D.C.

Then it would be a quick trip to the underground command center of the Pentagon, where a simple room with several telephones awaited him.

From there, the Ironman would work his magic.

Forty

Panama

It was as if they'd come out of nowhere.

One moment the lust-sticky streets of Sin City were being plied with their usual disreputable patrons of pimps, hookers, drug dealers, and insurance salesmen.

In the next, they were filled with heavily-armed soldiers running from doorway to doorway, waving their weapons at anyone who dared to stop and question what was going on.

Edsel Xavier was the chief of the small security force employed by the criminal cartel which ran Sin City. It was his bad luck that all of his bosses were vacationing in the Kingdom of Brazil this day. Their absence made Xavier the acting mayor of the canalside hedonist heaven. It was a position he accepted with the utmost reluctance.

When the soldiers came for him, Xavier was

where he always was on early Monday mornings: playing cowgirls and cattle rustlers at the Happy Accident Motel, with his hired guests the Sin City triplets. The soldiers didn't knock before they kicked the door in. In a flash, Xavier went from sucking on STT Number Two's garishly-painted breasts to staring down the barrels of six very recently greased M-16s.

Two of the triplets fainted dead away at the sight of the black-camouflaged soldiers; the third wet her pants. Xavier tried vainly to escape by an open window, but was cuffed by two of the soldiers and thrown back onto the disheveled, modality-scattered bed. The women were revived and permitted to go. Xavier was allowed to put on his pants, boots, and undershirt, but his cowboy hat, spurs, and plastic bull horns were left behind.

Placed in the back of a HumVee, Xavier was driven at high speed to the Sin City's mid-sized airfield, two miles away. The two-runway airstrip was now servicing both a wide array of attack helicopters and large C-141 troop-laden cargo planes. A huge Chinook helicopter was parked at the far edge of the airstrip. Xavier was taken inside. The big chopper was outfitted inside as an aerial battle command center. At one end was a large desk jammed with computers, maps, and communications equipment. Behind this desk sat an enormous black man wearing a major general's uniform of the United American Armed Forces.

He politely but firmly explained to Xavier that the shock troops which had descended on Sin City were members of the elite 23rd Battalion of the Football City Special Forces Rangers. He was their provisional commander. His name was Major Catfish Johnson.

The conversation with Johnson was brief: he asked Xavier how many armed men he had under his command. Xavier replied the number was fifty-seven within Sin City's city limits. Johnson then made a fifteen-second speech telling Xavier that it was in his best interests to order his men to report to the airport immediately and surrender their weapons. Xavier didn't argue. A radio was provided and he quickly put out the word to his small security force.

His men came straggling in just as the troops massed at the airport were moving out, a long stream of M-1 Bradley Fighting Vehicles and standard APCs leading the way.

Xavier was handcuffed and put in the back of Johnson's HumVee. With the general himself behind the wheel, they tore off after the convoy heading toward the main locks of the canal three miles away.

Xavier's spirits sank lower as they roared back through the heart of Sin City. All major intersections in the city were now under control of the heavily-armed invaders. The small radio station was surrounded with APCs and Bradleys, as was the satellite TV uplink facility which had provided Sin City with a wealth of pornographic films and features over the years.

Hungover and drug-starved, Xavier was slipping into a state of shock. The scale and precision by which the American troops had captured the city was mind-boggling. Even worse, it appeared they were intending to stay for good.

"This party is kaput," Xavier kept mumbling over and over.

That he was not exactly correct would be his first big surprise of the day.

They screeched past the enormous hole in the ground which at one time had been the site of the tower used by the men operating the main lock control station of the stretch of the Panama Canal nearby and soon arrived outside the control station itself. Advance elements of United American troops had completely encircled the large, washed-brick facility by this time and the sky above the station was filled with circling helicopter gunships.

Xavier was taken out of the HumVee and marched up to the front gate of the facility. Inside he could see the confused faces of the station's guard force staring back out at him. These men were employed by a private mercenary guard force totally independent from the town's security units. These men were tougher, better-armed, and technically better motivated. In fact they were under contract from Sin City's ruling cartel to hold the station with their lives should the occasion arise.

Xavier was given a bullhorn by the officer in charge of the American troops encircling the building. He didn't need to be told what to do. He simply turned the thing on and told the men inside to give up.

After a short delay, a similarly-amplified voice replied that they were all hired to go down fighting. It added that their commander was at that moment trying to raise their main office located on the old island of Cuba for instructions, and most probably, reinforcements.

Xavier turned to Johnson and shrugged. The general, in turn, gave a signal to his communications man, who spoke three words into his radiophone. Within a few seconds, one of the circling Cobra gunships swooped down and laid a frightful barrage of 6.76 rockets on top of the main control house, vaporizing the large radio antenna there. A second Cobra delivered a second barrage to the station's small satellite dish. A third gunship riddled the small shack which housed the station's automatic telephone switching computer.

The firing lasted ten incredibly noisy seconds. By the time it was over, the control station and the men inside were cut off from the outside world. No sooner had the smoke cleared when the holed-up security troops were walking out with white flags above their heads.

Fifteen minutes later, the canal locks and the immediate area surrounding them were under the control of the Football City 23rd Battalion.

Xavier was brought up to the main control house and kept there under guard as American soldiers began working the control of the main locks, using eleborate operating manuals as their guides. Within minutes, Xavier saw a large gray-black cargo ship enter the small lake east of the canal and approach the locks. There was a similarly-sized ship behind it, and another one behind that.

The first ship was successfully guided into the main lock, raised up, and sent on its way to the Pacific. Xavier got a good look at the ship and saw that it was stocked to the decks with wooden crates and black-tarped containers. The second ship was similarly loaded, as was the third.

By the time the trio of cargo ships was processed, three more appeared. And then four more, and four more after that. Each one was stacked with what had to be tons of military supplies, all of it covered, all of it under the watchful eyes of heavily armed sailors.

Five hours later, Xavier had counted thirty-three ships having gone through the locks, their decks packed to capacity, all heading quickly to the Pacific, all of them flying the American flag.

He was still there twenty-four hours later. And the ships were still coming.

Vancouver, Free Canada

The airplane was spotted on Free Canadian air defense radar at ten minutes after midnight.

Two controllers stationed at Ladysmith on Vancouver Island tracked the aircraft as it passed within fifteen miles of the entrance to Vancouver Bay. They watched as it swept back and forth in an irregular search pattern, cameras in its nose cone undoubtedly snapping off hundreds of feet of infrared film. They were certain it was a long-range recon aircraft owned either by the Asian Mercenary Cult or someone in their employ.

Yet they did not pass an emergency report on to their commanders which would have triggered a scramble order to the nearest unit of Canadian jet interceptors. Rather they watched the airplane for the next ninety minutes as it went about a normal long-range photo reconnaissance mission undisturbed.

Its cameras had plenty to record: out from Vancouver Bay, through the Straits around Vancouver Island, and out into the cold North Pacific was a convoy of full-to-the-gunwales cargo ships that stretched for more than 150 miles. All of them packed with crates typical of military cargo. All of them heading toward the Hawaiian Islands.

Forty-one

Oahu, the next day

It was a very happy group of Cult officers gathered around the large war table.

There were seven of them in all, the top commanders of the Asian forces who until recently had brutally occupied both the West Coast of America and the scattered islands of the South Pacific rim. Two officers were in charge of all the Cult land forces. Two represented the Cult's naval arm. The remaining three were connected with the Cult air force.

Before them was a large composite photomap of the Pacific Ocean, highlighting the broad expanse of water between the American continent and the Hawaiian Islands. It was quite easy to comprehend the current situation. The map clearly showed a long stream of ships heading toward Hawaii from the Panama Canal Zone, and an even longer line heading down from Vancouver. Sailing in classic convoy fashion—spread out for antisubmarine defense—the lead ships of the twin convoys would be within 100 miles of Hawaii within 24 hours.

The officers had just heard a presentation from the officer in charge of aerial photo recon. His analysts had concluded that most of the vessels flowing out of Panama were cargo ships, and that most of those coming from Canada appeared to be carrying troops. There were more than 150 ships in all—some fairly modern military vessels, others little more than the no-frills, slapped together Liberty Ship-style cargo vessels popular in the post-Big War world.

By calculating their average displacement, cargo capacity, and range, the Cult's top intelligence analysts determined that ten divisions of American or allied troops—210,000 men—and 23 million tons of ammunition and supplies were on their way to attack the Cult forces deployed on Oahu and in and around Pearl Harbor.

"It is Providence," the top army officer declared. "The wisdom of our redeploying to this location is now very clear. We were unwise to doubt our new leader."

"We can redeem ourselves," said the air force commander. "It is the divine intervention we have been seeking."

"It is true," the naval commander added. "The

foolish, lazy Americans are falling right into our trap."

It was now three A.M.

Major Sisan Mushi was hot, hungry, and tired. He'd been shouting orders at his men for nearly eighteen straight hours, and his voice was beginning to crack. He couldn't really remember the last time he'd eaten anything—maybe it was the raw smelts he'd consumed with his morning tea two days ago. He'd taken a nap sometime after that, though it hadn't lasted too long, for the noise of the commotion going on around him was much too loud for any kind of restful repose. And he hadn't bathed in four days.

But work was progressing, though, and this is what made him happy.

He was in command of an 1800-man Cult construction regiment. At that moment, his men were putting the finishing touches on the second of two temporary airstrips they'd been building nonstop for the past seventy-two hours.

The irony that the site of these runways was close to what was once known as Hickam Field was lost on Mushi—he was not a student of history. A distant relative had flown a torpedo plane on December 7, 1941, but that's about as far as his interest went regarding the sneak attack on Pearl Harbor on that fateful day so long ago.

No—Mushi was a man of economics, a true mercenary. He was in it for the money. His orders were for his men to build the two simple crushed-gravel runways and do it in three days, and they were just about finished. That sixty-six of his men had died on this project—all from sheer exhaustion and hunger—didn't faze him one whit. The mission was nearly complete, and when it was, he'd be handsomely paid. Everything else—including exactly what the runways would be used for—was more or less irrelevant for him.

Next to his instant airstrips, another construction crew was pouring the last of the concrete needed for a massive SAM emplacement. The missile site already had seventeen SA-6 launchers in place, each with three missiles, and when the cement finally hardened, six more would be added, making a grand total of twenty-three launchers and sixty-nine missiles. And this emplacement was just one of a string of fifty-two SAM sites which stretched along the inner coast of Pearl Harbor.

Seeing these sites now, lit by strings of bulbs and searchlights that reminded him of Firecracker Day back in Japan, Mushi heaved a sigh of true pride—not in any patriotic sense, but just for the sheer accomplishment of building the AA-defense line in such a short amount of time.

The Cult High Command had determined that a United American attack was imminent and that it would come in two forms: aerial and naval. The three-day orgy of building defense systems to counter the coming attack was the result of this determination.

Just how the enemy was going to attack was easy to figure out. Coming first from the air and then from the sea was, after all, how the Americans had pulled the sneak attack on Okinawa not long ago, a battle now known all the way down to the lowest private in the Cult forces. The struggle of the Cult martyrs on Okinawa was, in fact, the motivating factor for the massive mission of fortifying Pearl Harbor for the impending assault — at least for those who were paid so little, the economic return was not their prime motivation.

But unlike their recent attacks on the Homeland and Okinawa, this impending American action would not be a sneak attack. Everyone on the Cult side not only knew it was coming, they knew *how* it was coming.

Mushi knew it was really pretty simple. When it came down to it, after all the flash and bullshit, the United Americans were extremely predictable, as well as lazy. First of all, everyone knew the United Americans were airplane-happy—their top command was made up almost entirely of pilots. What other way would they choose to open an attack than with an airstrike? The Cult High Command knew the United Americans had access to nearly six squadrons of high-tech airplanes, most of them captured from the Fourth Reich. They also knew that along with their Free Canadian allies, the Americans could garner an impressive air-refueling capability. It would not be beyond their capabilities and foolish daring to launch a large number of these aircraft from the recently deoccupied West Coast, refueling them several times along the way and having them attack the Cult at Pearl Harbor.

And what would their targets be? The Cult communications network, what else? After all, the United Americans were convinced that by killing the eyes and ears and mouth of their enemy, they'd make the whole beast collapse. Along with this line of reasoning, then, it wasn't too hard to imagine that the United Americans would attempt to seize an airfield or two in some fashion on which to land, refuel, and rearm these long-range aerial attackers.

Next, the Americans were probably planning to land a large body of troops—but not in a typical hit-the-beach style; even they were too smart for that. No, they would attempt a large insertion of men at one carefully selected point, hoping that the majority of them made it ashore, and then would be able to run rampant behind the defense lines. Again, this was how they'd done it on Okinawa. This is how they would try to do it here.

Mushi had fought in all the major campaigns of the Cult—this was by far the biggest. There were more than 320,000 Cult ground troops dug in all around the Waipio Peninsula which served as the lead-in for Pearl Harbor itself. Each Cult soldier was armed with a rifle, a sidearm, a sword, and a flare.

The swords and the flares weren't standard combat issue. They were to be used in the inevitable celebration.

Mushi's second-in-command rushed up to him, and in a dramatic fashion completely in keeping with the circumstances, announced boldly that the two temporary airstrips were finally completed. Mushi checked the time. It was now 0355. They had finished five minutes ahead of plan.

Mushi turned his attention now to the sky. Within a minute he heard a low, deep drone. He cocked his ear to the west and the noise became louder, stronger. He ordered his second in command to line up the surviving construction troops, telling them to light their flares. When

403

this was done two minutes later, the two airstrips were brightly lit to allow aircraft to land.

Exactly one minute later, the first explosive-laden Zero bounced in for a successful landing. A great cheer went up from the exhausted construction troops. Right on its tail, another Zero landed, then another. Then another.

They kept coming, one right after another, nonstop for more than three hours. The construction troops went hoarse cheering for each arriving airplane, their hands burned and scarred from holding dozens of magnesium flares through the night.

More than one thousand Zeros would land before the rising sun began to light up the misty horizon.

And when the morning fog finally dissipated, and the first rays of the new sun appeared thirty minutes later, the Cult troops on the Waipio Peninsula and Pearl Harbor itself saw that the southern horizon was dotted with United American ships.

Forty-two

Warrior-support class private Ogasawara Gunto was in trouble.

He was the driver of a truck which was laden with hot breakfasts for an entire section of the Cult AA-defense line located in and around the former USS *Arizona* memorial. He'd left the Cult's one and only supply depot—Food and Water Distribution Center Number One, located near Halihi Hai Point—an hour before, 250 styrofoam containers filled with baked fish, boiled cabbage leaves, and reheated raisin pudding steaming in the back of his insulated truck.

His 14-mile trip along New Route 5 had been uneventful. But once he began the last long climb up Buckle Hill, the truck's engine began acting up. It started with a slight backfire and then a long run of sputtering. One hundred feet from the peak of the hill, his overheat light blinked on. Fifty feet from the top, his oil light began flashing.

By the time he reached the summit, the truck

had ground to a halt. Without enough lubrication to keep its cylinders moving, the engine had simply seized up. Gunto couldn't get it to go forward or reverse, he couldn't even get it going fast enough to roll either way down the hill.

He was stuck then, atop Buckle, looking down on the entire array of Cult positions in and around Pearl Harbor and the Waipio Peninsula.

From this vantage point, he would witness one of the most stunning battles in military history.

The sun was just coming up, and as the morning mist cleared, he could see many ships out on the southern horizon, apparently anchored on the far reaches of Mamala Bay. Down below him and off to the left, he could see a vast armada of green-winged Zeros taking off and forming a wide, slow-moving spiral high above Ford Island. To his right, another, even larger swarm of Zeros was growing over the temporary air base on the tip of the Pearl City Peninsula. And back even further to the east, a third spiral of Zeros was building over the place they used to call Hickam.

As Gunto watched, his mouth open in amazement, the three aerial spirals began to break up and then come together again in rigid chevron formations. He counted two hundred waves in

406

all, each containing ten Zeros. Several flew right over his head, and he could clearly see their wings were heavy with bombs and other types of explosive canisters. Some even had torpedoes chained to the underbellies.

It was now 0710 hours. Suddenly all of the sirens in all of the Cult positions went off at once. Gunto most definitely heard a thunderous cheer arise as each of the nearly half-million Asian soldiers screamed full-throated allegiance to the Cult and the guiding spirit of Hashi Pushi, wherever he might be.

Then the sirens quieted down and the cheering stopped. At that moment the enormous formation of explosive-filled Zeros dramatically turned south toward the vast fleet of United American ships.

Gunto didn't know what to do. If he chose to follow proper orders, then he should make his way to the nearest Cult position and radio for help to fix his truck. But he knew he couldn't do that. Not now.

He had to stay and watch nothing less than destiny itself unfold.

The first wave of Zeros arrived over the enemy fleet after only two minutes of flying time. Suddenly, as if someone had flipped a switch, the entire American fleet was lit up with the flashes of antiaircraft fire. Like long orange fingers, the streaks of AA fire climbed into the morning sky toward the great waves of Zeros. The noise from this sudden combined fusillade was ear-splitting even for Gunto on Buckle Hill, ten miles away.

Then, in little more than a flash and a glint of sunlight, the Zeros began dropping one by one. Gunto saw the first kamikaze hit; it went up in a great flash of fire and smoke, impacting on the bow of a cargo ship no more than four miles offshore. The helpless vessel rose up out of the water, so violent was the impact, slamming back down and breaking in two. No sooner had this happened than two more Zeros slammed into it. There were two more loud booms, and then the ship was gone.

The Zeros swarmed down on the next in-line ship, wielding their way through the wall of AA gunfire. This ship, too, was hit in the front, then the rear, then in the center. It exploded at once — possibly it was carrying explosives — and was gone in a great rush of flame and steam, the delayed sounds of explosion reaching Gunto's position a few seconds later.

The cascade of suicidal Zeros continued. A third ship was hit by three kamikazes simultaneously; a fourth was struck by two planes directly on its port side, capsizing it immediately. A fifth sustained five direct hits before quickly sinking after the sixth.

On and on it went, the kamikazes diving into

the American ships, flashing through the wall of AA streaks, steering true to their targets with deadly, suicidal precision. The sounds of explosions were buffeting Gunto now, the very force of explosions and death were in the hot morning wind.

Gunto was cheering wildly at first. This, he was told by his commanders, was the ultimate revenge against the lazy and despised United Americans, the culmination of a trap set by the Cult by evacuating the West Coast and its South Pacific bases and drawing the Americans into a trap at Pearl Harbor. But as the aerial massacre continued for five minutes, then ten, then fifteen full minutes, Gunto felt the enthusiasm drain out of him. The very scale of the suicide attacks and the destruction they caused became numbing. The Zeros were crashing into the American ships with a precision that was as perverse as it was effective. Despite the huge wall of AA fire being thrown up by the Americans, it appeared as if just about every Zero was getting through and destroying its target.

It lasted more than twenty minutes.

By then the horizon was littered with burning, dying American ships. Many of them, like helpless, crippled fish, belching smoke and flames, either sinking, or spinning wildly out of control.

Gunto had ceased cheering long ago. Now all he could feel was the lump in his throat and a

weight on his chest. Even though he was a dedicated member of the Cult, the one-sidedness of
what he'd witnessed was sickening. As many as
two thousand Cult pilots would sacrifice themselves, it was true. But the destruction they
wrought was simply staggering. Gunto figured
that each enemy troopship contained at least a
thousand men, probably many more. Now, as he
studied the sinking and dying ships, he felt tears
form in his eyes as his calculations told him
that more than 200,000 United American soldiers were either dead or drowning.

This was not war, he thought. This was
wholesale slaughter and he could watch it no
more.

Tears streaming down his face simply as a
protest against man's wrenching inhumanity toward other men, he turned on his well-worn
heel and started walking back down Buckle Hill.

The Cult had only one helicopter unit on
Oahu, a three-ship squadron consisting of
ageless UH-1s Hueys and dedicated almost
exclusively to hit-and-run terror raids and be-
hind-the-lines reconnaissance.

Their unit name was the Flying Dragons, and
today their mission would be different.

Confident that the United Americans would
be wiped out by the relentless, suicidal kamikaze

attacks, the Cult High Command was actually concerned that no American ship would be left floating, and therefore there would be no prize of war with which to commemorate what was surely growing into the Cult's finest hour.

So the High Command had ordered the Flying Dragons to chopper into the midst of the battle, attack one of the American ships, seize it, and keep it afloat during the battle.

This way, the Cult would have their trophy.

The three helicopters left a small base on Ford Island ten minutes into the murderous kamikaze raid. Flying at wavetop level, they flew right into the heart of the battle, dodging pieces of exploding ships, and kamikazes alike, the smoke and flames so thick they could barely see the individual American ships, never mind their desperate and dying crews. It took another five minutes of this weaving and incredibly perilous flying before the commander of the Dragons was able to select an appropriate ship to seize.

He found one right in the middle of the fleet, a mid-sized cargo vessel whose only damage so far appeared to be to its rudder and communications tower. Flying in the lead Dragon, the commander directed his Hueys to the rear of the smoke-obscured ship, where its helicopter platform was still intact. The commander's Huey slammed down to a landing, the sixteen troops crowded inside bursting out, their weapons firing in all directions.

The two other Dragon choppers came right in after the first, their pilots firing small rocket barrages along either side, being careful not to actually hit the ship's superstructure and thereby damage the precious war trophy.

Within twenty seconds, all forty-eight of the Flying Dragons were down and running through the ship, wildly firing their weapons, and hurling flash grenades at a host of imaginary targets.

The scene was so wild, it took the commander of the boarding force a minute or so to figure out that something was very wrong on the ship.

Gunto's feet were killing him by the time he walked the last mile to his base.

He'd thought he'd been lucky when, shortly after reaching the bottom of Buckle Hill, he was able to catch a ride with another truck from Food and Water Facility Number One returning from its morning chow run. The two crewmembers had also watched the *kamikaze* attack on the American fleet, and they were ecstatic. They were absolutely convinced that this battle was the beginning of the Cult's eventual world domination. With the United Americans out of the way, there was nothing stopping the

Greater East Asian Warriors' Association from turning the planet into one big red Rising Sun meatball.

Still shaken from what he'd seen from the top of Buckle Hill, Gunto was actually coming around to their point of view when suddenly their truck broke down. The crewmen glanced under the hood and declared the truck was out of gas.

Gunto considered this a very bad omen.

He agreed to walk the final mile back to the food and water depot, leaving the pair of true believers with their broken-down truck and dreams of world conquest to wait for assistance.

The holes on Gunto's boots were breaking old blisters with new ones when he finally turned the corner of the last bend and saw the entrance to Food and Water Facility Number One before him. It was no surprise that the place was in an uproar as the Cult supply soldiers celebrated news of the kamikaze attack on the United American fleet.

The guards at the front gate were practically waltzing together, their weapons discarded, cups of *sake* in hand. Walking through the entranceway and into the large storage facility, Gunto saw dozens of small celebrations going on throughout the place. *Sake* and beer were flowing freely, and martial music was being pumped out at twice the normal volume over the loudspeaker system. All semblance of work had stopped at the place, which eventually would be a problem. As the one and only food and water supply depot on the island servicing the vast Cult army, remaining in operation twenty-four hours a day was essential. If not, some unit somewhere would either miss a food run or get one late, and then the whole distribution system would be out of whack.

But no one on hand seemed to be worried about that at the moment.

Gunto went to the motor pool, reported the demise of both his truck on Buckle Hill and the second truck a mile away, and then walked to his barracks. It was empty—the seventy-two other men he slept with were somewhere out on the grounds, undoubtedly getting drunk and celebrating.

With no commanders to give him orders, Gunto simply grabbed a bowl of rice from the chow hall and walked to the end of the facility, where a sea wall provided its eastern perimeter.

He sat there eating the starchy rice with his dirty fingers. The racket from the victory party behind him combined with the blaring, squeaky military music was enough to hurt his ears. Gunto couldn't really blame his comrades for celebrating. He would have been right there with them if he hadn't seen what he'd seen from Buckle Hill. As it was, he was suffering from the first pangs of conscience he'd ever experienced in his thirty-eight years. If this was how the Cult planned to conquer the world—by conducting not battles but deceptive wholesale slaughters—then they would have to do it without him. As soon as he was shipped back to Japan for leave, he planned to go AWOL.

He looked out to the ocean and wished that he was on a boat and sailing away—to anywhere, just away from this place.

That's when he saw them.

Two airplanes were coming in *very* low and leaving two dirty, smoking trails behind them. There were two more right behind them, and two more behind them. All flying low, all trailing smoke, all heading right toward him.

Gunto was standing now, his breakfast dropped in his rising terror. These weren't Cult aircraft, Gunto was sure of that. They were moving much too fast. And this meant only one thing.

He tried to shout a warning, but nothing would come out when he opened his mouth. The first two jets passed right over him a second later and Gunto studied them in the blink of an eye. They were of different types; one was smaller than the other. Oddly, both appeared to be in somewhat battered condition—Gunto could clearly see that their underwings had been reinforced with sheet metal and wire and they were both badly in need of a paint job.

And they had one other thing in common: they were both carrying so many bombs under their wings they were actually sagging from the weight.

The second pair of aircraft screamed over just as the first pair were dropping their bombs right in the center of Food and Water Facility Number One. They, too, looked battered, paint-chipped, and beaten; they, too, were carrying enough bombs to bend their wings.

A total of twelve airplanes roared over his head in less than thirty seconds, each one raggedly yet effectively delivering its payload and swooping up and away again. Gunto watched it all, with his mouth open in shock as the food and water facility was destroyed in a series of huge bomb blasts and smaller, yet no less destructive secondary explosions.

The billowing smoke became so thick, Gunto had to get down on his knees just to breathe. The smell of the smoke was incredibly acrid, like the worst kitchen fire in the world. This was the result of the huge fire now burning away enough food — fish, rice, and dried fruit, mostly — to feed the Cult forces on Oahu for two months.

As soon as the attacking jets had completed their bombing runs, each returned for one brief strafing run and then quickly turned and roared away. In his half-conscious state, Gunto couldn't help but feel that the pilots flying the battered jets were somehow in a great hurry, as if the airplanes themselves would break apart if they didn't get back to wherever they'd come from soon enough.

As the last of the jets departed over the horizon, he turned to look at what was left of the Cult's huge Food and Water Facility Number One. There wasn't much that wasn't burning — warehouses of food, barrels of cooking oil, the bodies of his comrades. As the heat from the flames singed his eyebrows and beard, he knew the place was devastated beyond all hope of repair.

He also felt that he might very well be the only survivor of the lightning-quick airstrike. And that would not bode well with his commanders, who, in catastrophic cases such as this, prized the heroic death of their soldiers over survival.

Gunto felt a strange feeling of peace come over him. If he was, in fact, the only one left, then what should he do to justify his survival? Should he try to find a working radio and call for help? Should he run to the next Cult position and summon aid? Or should he simply throw himself on his sword and be done with it?

No, he thought, his mind slowly losing its capacity for rational thinking. Surely soldiers at other Cult positions nearby would see the smoke from the devastated supply depot. And he'd long ago lost his taste for dying for the Cult's brutal, misguided cause.

What Gunto decided he should do then is put out the fires.

By himself.

With this in mind, he began to walk along the seawall, shielding himself from the flames, heading toward the massive water tank farm located a quarter mile from the burning storage facility. From there he would unfurl a fire hose all the way down to the nearest burning structure and he would play water on to it until help arrived.

Half-mad now, he was running up the small hill that housed the water farm, giggling at the thought that he might have to use all of the twenty million gallons of water in the storage tanks to put out what was left of the burning supply base. What the hell would his officers think of that? Would they reward him for using the only clean water supply on the island of Oahu to fight an overwhelming losing battle to the flames? Or would they execute him? Would it matter either way?

He never really got to answer his questions — a low, thunderous roar suddenly overwhelmed him. It was so loud, so hot, it knocked him to the ground and sent him sprawling down the hill and back down to the seawall.

Only then was he able to open his eyes and see what had caused the ungodly fire and screeching. He looked up to see another airplane — but this one was unlike any he'd ever seen before. It looked more like a spaceship than an airplane. It was painted red, white, and blue and was shaped like an arrowhead. Unlike the other attack jets, this one did not look like it was in need of repair. Quite the opposite. It looked like the most sophisticated thing that had ever taken to the air.

Gunto watched as the strange airplane roared overhead and turned up to the right. Six bombs fell from its delta-shaped wings, all six slamming into the cluster of water tanks at the top of the hill. They all blew up at once, the explosions sending huge geysers of water and steam into the air. In an instant, Gunto suddenly found a tidal wave of hot, steamy water rushing down the hill toward him.

He leaped back behind the seawall before he could even think about it. In seconds the torrent of water was rushing over his head, carrying sand, dirt, stones, and tree branches with it. He screamed at the top of his lungs in sheer terror, and closed his eyes to await his end.

But just as suddenly as it had started, the boiling hot torrent of water stopped. He couldn't believe it at first; when he dared to look up over the protective wall, he saw that the water had gone in all directions, like one great fountain, and had thus dissipated quickly. Ironically, much of it flooded into the burning food storage facility, extinguishing some of the still-rampaging flames.

Sucker-punched with his third shock of the day, Gunto was drooling heavily, his heart racing so fast, it felt as if it was about to explode.

Then the roar came back and he turned to see the strange delta-shaped jet bearing down on him. Shaking, he reached for his sidearm, withdrew it, and pointed it at the oncoming jet. In what he imagined was his last second of life, he could *feel* the pilot's eyes burning in on him, one trigger press away from blowing him to bits.

He closed his eyes. He heard the guns on the airplane open up. He took one last deep breath . . .

It was over in a split second. He heard the cannon shells whizzing by his ears. He felt the searing heat on both sides of his face, he could *smell* the stink of the expended cordite.

But amazingly, he was still breathing. He opened his eyes and saw that his body was still whole.

He was still alive.

Gunto looked at the ground in front of him

to see two burning tracks, one on either side of him. He couldn't believe it. The pilot had laced two perfect rows of deadly cannon shells on either side of him.

Gunto turned just in time to see the strange jet rocket over the horizon, always to wonder, but never to know why the pilot had chose to spare him.

Off Pearl Harbor

It took the commander of the Flying Dragons twenty minutes to pass the ceasefire order to his rampaging troops.

Once the roar of weapons fire died down, a strange silence descended on the ship, one that somehow seemed to quiet even the racket still going on around them.

The commander cried out for his men to bring any prisoners to him, but none were brought forward. He demanded his NCOs do a quick body count of enemy dead, but again, he'd received no quick reply. There *were* no enemy dead.

It was slowly sinking in exactly what was happening on the seized ship, and by logical projection, what was happening all around them. He rushed to the ship's bridge, where, horrified, his worst fear came true: the ship's controls were set and being run by a small microprocessor unit. So too was the ship's modest array of AA weapons. They were being fired by another microprocessor which was crudely attached to the top of the fire control system panel by strands of duct tape. A quick study of the microprocessor's sequencer told the commander that the AA guns were simply firing in a completely random pattern, providing the full effect that they were being fired by human fingers on their triggers.

Taped above the panel was a gaudy metal plaque. It was engraved in both English and Japanese, the lettering set off by imprints of two frolicking dolphins.

The plaque said: "Compliments of Ironman."

The Flying Dragons' commander bit his lip as he stared out of the ship's bridge at the *kamikaze* still raining down on the ships all around them. In the midst of the "battle" he realized he was the only one on the Cult side who knew what was really going on. It was simple, really.

The ship he had chosen to seize was empty.

All of the American ships were.

Forty-three

Aboard the USS Fitzgerald, *five days later*

JT Toomey walked onto the bridge of the *Fitzgerald* to find his friend Ben Wa sound asleep in the captain's chair.

He couldn't blame him — more than half the bridge crew was sleeping, either in their chairs or curled up on the floor of the bridge itself. Things had been so hectic in the past ten days, and the crew so overworked, that many had simply taken to sleeping in any spot where they could lie down.

The bridge navigation officer was awake, though, and a simple nod from him told JT that all was well in the running of the aircraft carrier for the moment.

"We're cruising at five knots," the officer told him. "At this speed and course, we should be at the supply ship rendezvous point within ten hours."

JT wearily thanked the man and then turned his

attention back to Ben, who was slowly but surely waking up.

"Sleeping on the watch is court martial material, old buddy," he told the reluctant captain of the huge aircraft carrier, handing him a cup of coffee and then pouring one for himself. "They could throw the book at you."

"Let them," Ben replied, wiping the sleep from his eyes. "Maybe then I could get some *real* sleep—in a prison bed."

Just about everyone onboard the three surviving ships of the Task Force was beyond exhaustion—yet for the first time in a long time, all of them were also in a relative state of peace. Their long mission was at last coming to an end. They were slowly making their way eastward, heading for a meeting with a supply ship dispatched from recently liberated San Diego. The ship was carrying food, fresh water, fuel, and other supplies the men on the *Fitz* as well as the USS *Tennyson* and the USS *New Jersey* had gone without for what had seemed like ages.

The day before, Ben had written a letter which would eventually be delivered to General Jones. In it he asked that each member of the Task Force, both living and dead, be awarded a special medal in appreciation for his courage above and beyond the call of duty. Their participation in the attack on Japan, in the unexpected action against Okinawa, and finally their pivotal role in the final battle at Pearl Harbor more than qualified them for such a citation.

The original six-day Operation Long Bomb had stretched into more than a month of nightmarish combat and hellish conditions. And through it all, the members of the Task Force had relied on intelligence, élan, and above all, innovative strategy in order to emerge victorious against overwhelming odds.

Their role in the Pearl Harbor action was the epitome of this All-American brains-versus-brawn credo.

It had been Hunter's idea to send the 150 empty ships to the Hawaiian coastline — vessels provided in an extremely short time by his friend Ironman and made to look "real" with advice from the F/X battalion, who'd joined the Task Force after the Okinawa campaign. The hardest part was retrieving the skeleton crews from the decoy ships before dawn broke over Oahu on that fateful morning almost a week ago. This was done with the help of the *New Jersey*'s speedy fleet of small patrol craft.

By appearing to fall for the Cult's bait to invade Hawaii, the UA had, in fact, not only tricked the Cult into expending their entire force of *kamikaze* Zeros, but had also isolated more than 300,000 of their best Asian mercenary troops on the island of Oahu. Those soldiers were now surrounded by *real* UA warships and trapped on the island, facing at the very least a life of isolation on the very territory they had so brutally conquered. Bereft of substantial food and water, and cut off from the rest of the world, the Asian mercenaries would have somehow to fend for themselves — or die trying. One thing was clear: there would be no humanitarian relief drops from the UA or anyone else.

It was a somewhat disturbing yet necessary way to remove the brainwashed rampaging Asian hordes from further enslaving the helpless peoples of the Pacific and Asia itself. Yet in the final analysis, the harsh sentence was actually more of the Cult's own doing than anything done by the United Americans. It was the Cult which had foolishly redeployed to Oahu in the first place. It was they who had emptied the island of its remaining citizens (now all safe on nearby Molokai and under the protection of the combined JAWs-New Jersey National Guard teams), and then stupidly stored all their stolen food and water in one place. And it was they who had foolishly left that crucial target virtually undefended in the false euphoria following what they thought was the destruction of the Americans' "invasion" fleet.

The Cult had also succeeded in blocking their one and only escape route: by sinking the 150 empty decoy ships — and sacrificing nearly two thousand pilots and planes in the process — the Asians had created a massive underwater reef of wreckage so extensive, it effectively sealed off the approaches to Pearl Harbor, which was the mooring site for all of the Cult's remaining transport ships. In fact, there were so many sunken ships in the inner part of Mamala Bay that it would take an army of professional salvage experts years, if not decades, to remove them all, a task not likely to begin anytime soon.

Even hopes of escape by air had been quickly dashed by the Cult themselves. They had little in the way of large aerial transport in the first place, and the pilots of the few large airplanes that did exist had been too fearful to take off after the battle, so rampant was the belief that UA jet fighters were nearby, waiting to pounce. In reality, no UA jet aircraft from the mainland had come anywhere near the Hawaiian battle area — per Hunter's plan, none was needed. The Cult's simple yet incorrect assumption that the UA would attack from the air was enough to divert the Cult's energies into building their vast SAM and AA defense around Pearl Harbor, a mammoth effort that turned out to be a complete waste of time.

Now, as JT sipped his coffee, he passed a set of photographs to Ben. They were high-altitude snaps taken on Oahu by the Kephart Brothers in their SR-71 Blackbird and just transmitted over the radiofax to the *Fitz*. Some clearly showed gangs of Cult soldiers aimlessly wandering the countryside, obviously foraging for food, for water, for shelter. Other photos showed dozens if not hundreds of bodies floating at the bottoms of Oahu's many cliffs, evidence of the mass suicides that were inevitably taking place on the island.

Ben was horrified at the photographic depiction of the wide-scale *hari-kari*.

"Those are all the cowards," he said, pointing to the clumps of dashed, floating, broken bodies. "The cowards and the lazy bastards who don't want to put the effort into living."

"Ironic, isn't it?" JT said. "They did the crime, but now they don't want to do the time. I say, the hell with them. Maybe in a few years we'll go and help those tough enough to survive. But it ain't going to be anytime soon."

Suddenly, one of the carrier's corpsmen ran onto the bridge. His face was furrowed with equal parts of confusion and relief.

"Sirs, come quickly," he shouted to JT and Ben, all pretense of military protocol gone. "Something's happening in sick bay . . ."

JT and Ben burst through the door of the sick bay less than a minute later.

Crunch was there, as were the ship's two doctors, and their small staffs.

They were all gathered around the bed in the center of the room. The gaggle of wires, tubes, and IV lines had been pushed away from it. The oxygen tent was also gone. And sitting up in the middle of the bed, wearing a wide but weary grin, and eating a bowl of ice cream, no less, was a very conscious Yaz.

Ben and JT were pleasantly astonished. "What the hell has happened?" Ben asked.

"He's back," Crunch said, smiling broadly himself. "I was sitting here with him. One minute he's still out like a light, the next he's sitting up and staring at me with that shit-eating grin . . ."

JT and Ben both reached over and enthusiastically patted Yaz on the back. The relief that their friend seemed to be recovered was overwhelming.

"Welcome back to the land of the living," JT told him. "Have a good nap?"

Ben turned to the doctors. "Is he as good as he looks?" he asked.

"Better," the first doctor replied. "All his vital signs are stable. Heart rate, pressure, breathing — all normal, or better than normal. The only problem is that he's hungry — but only soft food first."

"Means no booze," JT told Yaz.

"After the dream I've had," Yaz replied, never losing a bit of his smile, "I never have to drink again."

The second doctor was nodding in agreement. "He's told us what happened to him," he said. "And it's the most extreme case of hypnotic suggestion I've ever heard of. One for the books . . ."

" 'Hypnotic suggestion'?" JT asked, mystified. "How in hell . . .?"

Yaz suddenly did lose part of his grin. "It was

from the videotape of Hawk's first flight back from Okinawa," he said. "I was watching it in the CIC when this whole thing hit me. It was like a kick right in the fucking head. It took me a while to realize what had happened exactly—I'm not really sure I even know now, at this moment. But I saw a face somehow projected on the storm clouds—maybe by a laser beam or something. But it was definitely caught on Hawk's videotape. And then, when I realized just *whose* face it was, well, I guess I couldn't take it. I guess I just went under and . . ."

Both JT and Ben interrupted at the same time. "Whose face was it?"

Yaz began to answer when one of the doctors intervened.

"Not now," he said, almost sternly. "Maybe later, but not now. We've got to be careful. There's always the chance of a relapse. Just make sure no one views that videotape until we get back to the mainland and get it into a controlled situation . . ."

A tense silence was broken when Yaz scooped up another huge spoonful of the vanilla ice cream and began devouring it. He was halfway through when he suddenly stopped and looked around.

"Hey, wait a minute—where *is* Hawk?" he asked.

Those in attendance shot sudden nervous glances at each other.

"Can we tell him?" Ben asked the doctors.

"Going to have to do it sometime," one said. "We've already filled him in on the Okinawa and Pearl Harbor actions."

Ben leaned in a little closer to Yaz.

"Hawk took off in the jumpjet yesterday," he began slowly. "Said he had an appointment to keep, back on Okinawa. We haven't heard from him since. He's long overdue . . ."

Yaz was astounded. "He's overdue? *Again?*" he asked incredulously.

"We're searching for him now," JT replied somberly. "But, as you know, with each hour, it gets a little . . ."

Yaz suddenly held up his hand.

"Wait a minute," he said, closing his eyes and straining his face as if he were deep in thought. Suddenly he stopped moving completely, his eyes shut so tight, the lids were turning a shade of blue.

Then he smiled again. "You want to know something?" he said, "I can tell you *exactly* where he is . . ."

Forty-four

Washington, D.C.

General David Jones pulled a bottle of whiskey from his desk drawer and uncapped it.

Before him was a well-worn, unopened file. His hands shook slightly as he reached for a paper cup and prepared to pour himself a drink. He never thought he would ever have to review this particular file again, never thought he would ever even have to pull it from his secure safe again. For the information contained within had so much potential for bad news, it could effect not just the United American cause, but freedom-loving people around the entire globe.

He picked up the whiskey bottle and poured a stiff shot into the paper cup. It was early in the morning—he wasn't even sure of the time—but he'd been behind the desk for at least ten straight hours now. In that time, he'd been accessing the UA's central security computer files, going over the names and profiles of various criminals and terrorists the UA had come up against in recent times, trying to determine who, if any of them, was responsible for the recent carnage in the Pacific.

But nothing was adding up. Not yet, anyway.

The only thing Jones *was* sure of was that the whole episode in the Pacific was not what it appeared to be. He was, in fact, absolutely convinced they'd all been hoodwinked. Fooled. Played like a violin for someone's hidden agenda. After studying the results of the recent actions in Japan, Okinawa, and lastly, at Pearl Harbor, his conclusion was that the Asian Mercenary Cult, though brutal, though powerful beyond all expectation, was not what it had first seemed to be. It was, he now believed, little more than a front, a facade for something else. Something even more sinister.

And Jones knew that after his analysts studied everything that went on in the Pacific, and debriefed all the principals involved, they would conclude that what had begun as "Operation Long Bomb" had not been a conventional combat engagement at all. Rather it had been orchestrated to *look* that way. Its intention was never really for one side to battle the other to gain territory or power or prestige. It had been simply a vehicle to take lives, to destroy both sides, militarily and morale-wise.

Furthermore, he was certain now that the man they knew as Hashi Pushi, the man they had targeted in the first place as being the be-all and end-all of evil in the Pacific rim, was, in fact, a front man drawn into the weird drama by God-knows-what forces to simply play a part, and then, when his usefulness was drained, eliminated to make room for the next player, and so on. *This* was why the Cult didn't collapse after the airstrike on Japanese Home Islands. *This* was why they kept on fighting even after losing the massive facility on Okinawa. *This* was why the Cult pulled out of occupied California, against all standard military operating principles, and redeployed to Hawaii only to be used as sacrificial lambs.

And someone was behind it all. Someone with incredible power — both persuasive and military, psychological and physical.

It was a scary thesis. But Jones was convinced he was right.

He'd spent hours going over and over in his head who this villainous mastermind might be.

There was no shortage of suspects: there was Duke Devillian of the fascist Knights of the Burning Cross, the unbalanced white supremacist who had brought wanton slaughter and unbearable suffering to the America Southwest less than two years before; there were the surviving leaders of the so-called Canal Nazis, the fascists who had mined the Panama Canal with nuclear explosives not three years before. There were the surviving members of the Family, the Super-Mafia that had once ruled a large section of the American Midwest with a corrupt and iron fist. There were any one of a number of officers known as the Mid-Aks, the wacko murder-for-hire army that rampaged throughout the eastern part of America shortly after the Big War and the deceitful disarmament and fractionalization of the United States that followed. Even Elizabeth Sandlake, the beautiful but highly unstable villainess, who'd aided the men behind the Norse invasion of America not a year before, and who, more than anyone else, was responsible for the presence of the still-missing nuclear-armed *Fire Bats* submarines.

Anyone in this gallery of rogues could have been responsible for pulling the strings behind the tragic events which had unfolded recently in the Pacific, except for one thing: all of them were either dead, or incarcerated in a United American prison.

This was why Jones now had the last unopened computer file before him. It contained the profile of the only villain the Americans had fought since the Big War who had the sheer bombastic mesmerizing charisma to pull off such a titanic feat of evil. And though he was thought to be dead, Jones knew that if anyone had the power to expertly fake his own death, it was this particular individual.

For unlike the others, this person could actually affect men's minds, he could actually steal their souls. He was, in fact, the walking symbol of Evil itself.

And if he was somehow loose again, in whatever form, then the entire planet was in dire circumstances.

Jones raised the paper cup full of whiskey to his lips, thought briefly about his brave men in the Pacific, who had just scored yet another victory for freedom, and then downed the shot of powerful no-name booze.

Thus bolstered, he opened the file and found himself staring at a photograph of a thin-faced, hard-featured, absolutely sinister goateed man.

Instantly Jones felt a shot of revulsion rip through him.

As much as he wanted to, he couldn't take his eyes off the photograph of the bearded devilish figure.

"God help us all," he whispered.

Somewhere in the Pacific

Hunter didn't know whether he felt more foolish or embarrassed.

"Bonehead," he muttered to himself. "Dumb. Amateur. *Rookie.*"

He was trudging up the side of a steep hill, carrying two containers full of engine oil drained from the Harrier. He wasn't sure exactly where he was—his best guess was Lisianski Island, a barren spit of rock and vine-covered cliffs about seventy

436

miles southeast of famous Midway Island and a few hundred miles northwest of the larger Hawaiian Islands.

He had run out of gas. It was the first time it had ever happened to him, and this was why he was so mortified. He wasn't quite sure *how* it had happened — one moment he was breezing along, heading back to the Task Force's location, the next, his bingo light was flashing. He tried every trick in the book to limp along, but Lisianski was as far as he could get. His engine, in fact, cut out on him while he was still in his landing hover, dropping the jumpjet twenty-five feet and causing it to bounce almost half that high before finally coming down for good on the island's rocky upper beach.

With no radio and no locator beam, he had little choice but to climb to the high ground, light a signal fire, and wait. This was why he'd drained about ten gallons of lubricant from the airplane's engine. Once he reached the top of the island's tallest peak, he would start a smoky fire and then cool his heels until help arrived.

His only consolation was that he wasn't on a combat mission. Rather it had been a make-good trip. He'd returned to Okinawa, not to survey what was left of the Cult's Shuri Mountain facility, but to land back at the movie set village. Once there, he'd found the gray-haired woman who had been so helpful earlier in his Pacific adventure.

And with little prompting, he'd brought her on her first airplane ride ever.

They had soared high above the still-smoggy island of Okinawa, past the former, now devastated Cult base on Iko, and back again. Throughout the high-speed romp, the woman sitting in the backseat of the AV-8F gasped in amazement and roared with delight.

"My mother would never believe this!" she yelled on several occasions.

After thirty minutes or so, Hunter returned her to the movie-set village and promised to report their location to a Free Canadian relief convoy he knew would soon be passing through the area. Then he headed back for the Task Force, making it about halfway before inexplicably running out of fuel.

He finally reached the top of the island's tallest peak and within minutes got a black, smoky fire going.

It was about an hour past sunset now, and as he sat watching the full moon rise, he contemplated the wildness of the last few weeks: the original plan for Operation Long Bomb. His bizarre journey into the heart of burning Tokyo. His confrontation with Hashi Pushi. The near-infallible instinct that led him to discover the huge war-making facility on Okinawa. The battle for the smog-covered island itself. The loss of the USS *Cohen*. The final action at Pearl Harbor.

Through it all, he'd kept his long-standing goal in mind. Fighting for the freedom of America was his number one priority. But now, looking out over the vast Pacific Ocean, he felt new feelings slowly coming over him. The planet was changing—the recent battles so far away from the American mainland had convinced him of that. Now, he was sure that the battles of the future would not be fought exclusively on American soil.

Rather, he saw global conflicts ahead—and with this new feeling came an overwhelming sense of new urgency. He could no longer labor under the illusion that fighting for freedom always meant just fighting for America. Sure, the American continent was once again free of invaders and reunited. But there had to be millions of people around the world who were *not* free, and until they were all released from the shackles of tyranny and terrorism, then America could not really call itself free.

He took a deep breath and contemplated the rising moon. It looked so crisp and clear, its mountains, valleys, and craters so sharply focused, it was breathtaking. He leaned back and actually felt his shoulders start to relax. He knew he'd be found eventually. Until then, he told himself, several days on a tropical island might not be the worst thing in the world for him.

If only Dominique were here with him.

He threw some more oil on the huge, blazing

439

fire and then leaned back again and closed his eyes . . .

He would never know if he actually fell asleep or not.

When he next *thought* he'd opened his eyes, he found himself staring once again at the full moon. But it looked different now. It seemed larger. More brightly orange. *More sinister.*

He closed his eyes—or at least, he thought he did—and upon opening them once more, he found that the mountains, valleys, and craters on the moon had suddenly changed shape. Now their shadows were forming a frightening image, one of a devilish-looking man with eyes of hate, a thin, pale face, and a sharp goatee.

And the face was laughing at him.

Fiji, the next day

The man known as Soho was walking along a deserted beach about a mile and a half away from his palatial cliffside residence.

With him was a young girl, one he'd selected from the local population for her virginal beauty, her innocent Polynesian features, and especially, her long, lovely dark red hair.

"I have a story to tell you," Soho told the girl

440

after a long time of just walking along the beach in silence. "You must remember this story, for it will be important to you later on. Do you understand?"

The girl nodded shyly. "I guess so," she replied.

They stopped near a waterfall which was splashing into a tiny shimmering pool. Sitting on its edge, they let their feet dangle in the pure, warm water.

"Not long ago," Soho began, "there was a man who tried to show the world that he was a supreme being. He did this by gathering some trusted people around him. They were a small group at first. But quickly their numbers grew, for this man had the ability to attract and influence ordinary people, and convince them that they could do extraordinary things.

"Soon, the name of this man was on the lips of many, many people. Some walked for miles just to hear him speak. Others began to pray to him. They were the first to realize that this man had a vision for the world, one which all people would live by."

The girl was listening very intently, equally fascinated and confused.

"Where did this great man live?" she asked.

"He lived in an area of the world we once called the Middle East," Soho went on, as always, not really knowing where the words were coming from. "It's very hot there, very dry. There's lots of sand, like here, but not a lot of water. It's a desert.

"He lived there and spoke his beliefs there, for he was sure that this was where the human race began. He was trying to build a new way for men to live—but not everyone agreed with him. Many disliked him. Many tried to kill him. Soon many were waging battles against him, wars of struggle over men's souls.

"Soon, these battles went out of control. This great man knew that only by sacrificing himself could he really influence how others thought of him. And so, in that place called the Middle East, he was killed, murdered by those who disagreed with him."

"That's very sad," the young girl said.

Soho smiled and stroked his chin.

"It is," he agreed. "But this sadness didn't last long. Because this man was *so* great that not even death could prevent him from telling the world his ideas, his beliefs."

"But how could he do that?" she asked.

"By rising," Soho said. "By rising from the dead and walking among his followers once more."

"What did he look like?" the girl wanted to know.

Soho smiled. "He was tall. Very strong. He had long hair, and a short beard."

Suddenly the girl became quite animated. "You know, I think I have heard of this man," she said. "My grandmother told me about him when I was small. Was his name Jesus?"

Soho looked at the girl and laughed.

"Jesus?" he said, suddenly slipping his hand around her lower waist and fondling her upper leg. "No, my dear. His name was *Victor. . . ."*

ZEBRA'S HEADING WEST!

with GILES, LEGG, PARKINSON, LAKE, KAMMEN, and MANNING

THE SEVENTH CARRIER SERIES
By PETER ALBANO

THE SEVENTH CARRIER   (2056, $3.95/$5.50)
The original novel of this exciting, best-selling series. Imprisoned in a cave of ice since 1941, the great carrier *Yonaga* finally breaks free in 1983, her maddened crew of samurai determined to carry out their orders to destroy Pearl Harbor.

THE SECOND VOYAGE OF THE SEVENTH CARRIER   (2104, $3.95/$4.95)
The Red Chinese have launched a particle beam satellite system into space, knocking out every modern weapons system on earth. Not a jet or rocket can fly. Now the old carrier *Yonaga* is desperately needed because the Third World nations — with their armed forces made of old World War II ships and planes — have suddenly become superpowers. Terrorism runs rampant. Only the *Yonaga* can save America and the Free World.

RETURN OF THE SEVENTH CARRIER   (2093, $3.95/$4.95)
With the war technology of the former superpowers still crippled by Red China's orbital defense system, a terrorist beast runs rampant across the planet. Out armed and outnumbered, the target of crack saboteurs and fanatical assassins, only the *Yonaga* and its brave samurai crew stand between a Libyan madman and his fiendish goal of global domination.

QUEST OF THE SEVENTH CARRIER   (2599, $3.95/$4.95)
Power bases have shifted drastically. Now a Libyan madman has the upper hand, planning to crush his western enemies with an army of millions of Arab fanatics. Only *Yonaga* and her indomitable samurai crew can save the besieged free world from the devastating iron fist of the terrorist maniac. Bravely, the behemoth leads a rag tag armada of rusty World War II warships against impossible odds on a fiery sea of blood and death!

ATTACK OF THE SEVENTH CARRIER   (2842, $3.95/$4.95)
The Libyan madman has seized bases in the Marianas and Western Caroline Islands. The free world seems doomed. Desperately, *Yonaga's* air groups fight bloody air battles over Saipan and Tinian. An old World War II submarine, *USS Blackfin*, is added to *Yonaga's* ancient fleet and the enemy's impregnable bases are attacked with suicidal fury.

TRIAL OF THE SEVENTH CARRIER   (3213, $3.95/$4.95)
The enemies of freedom are on the verge of dominating the world with oil blackmail and the threat of poison gas attack. *Yonaga's* officers lay desperate plans to strike back. Leading a ragtag fleet of revamped destroyers and a single antique World War II submarine, the great carrier must charge into a sea of blood and death in what becomes the greatest trial of the Seventh Carrier.